Shadow Dance

By John Harrison

Published by C. E. R. Ellwood
under the House of Harrison imprint

ISBN-10: 1-947061-10-0
ISBN-13: 978-1-947061-10-1

Printed in the USA
Second trade paperback edition, September 2019
First trade paperback edition, 2007

This series is for those that love life…and all of its possibilities.

I also dedicate this book to my dad, Howard G. Harrison, for all of his support throughout both my life and his.

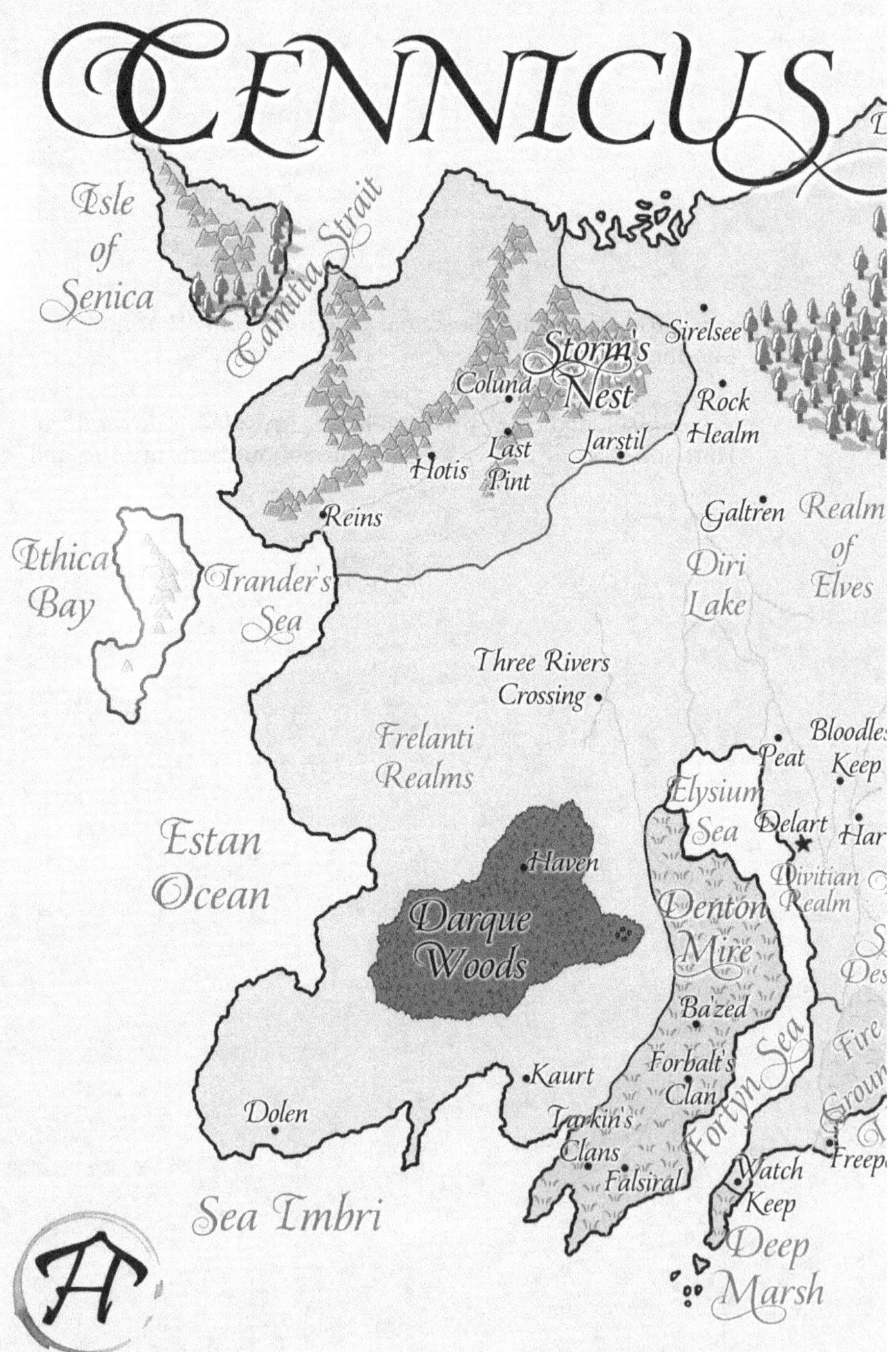

CENNICUS
Isle of Senica
Camutia Strait
Storm's Nest
Sirelsee
Coluna
Rock Healm
Jarstil
Last Pint
Hotis
Reins
Galtren
Realm of Elves
Diri Lake
Ithica Bay
Trander's Sea
Three Rivers Crossing
Frelanti Realms
Bloodles Keep
Peat
Elysium Sea
Delart
Har
Estan Ocean
Haven
Divitian Realm
Denton Mire
Darque Woods
Ba'zed
Fortyn Sea
Fire Groun
Forbalt's Clan
Kaurt
Tarkin's Clans
Dolen
Falsiral
Watch Keep
Freep
Sea Imbri
Deep Marsh

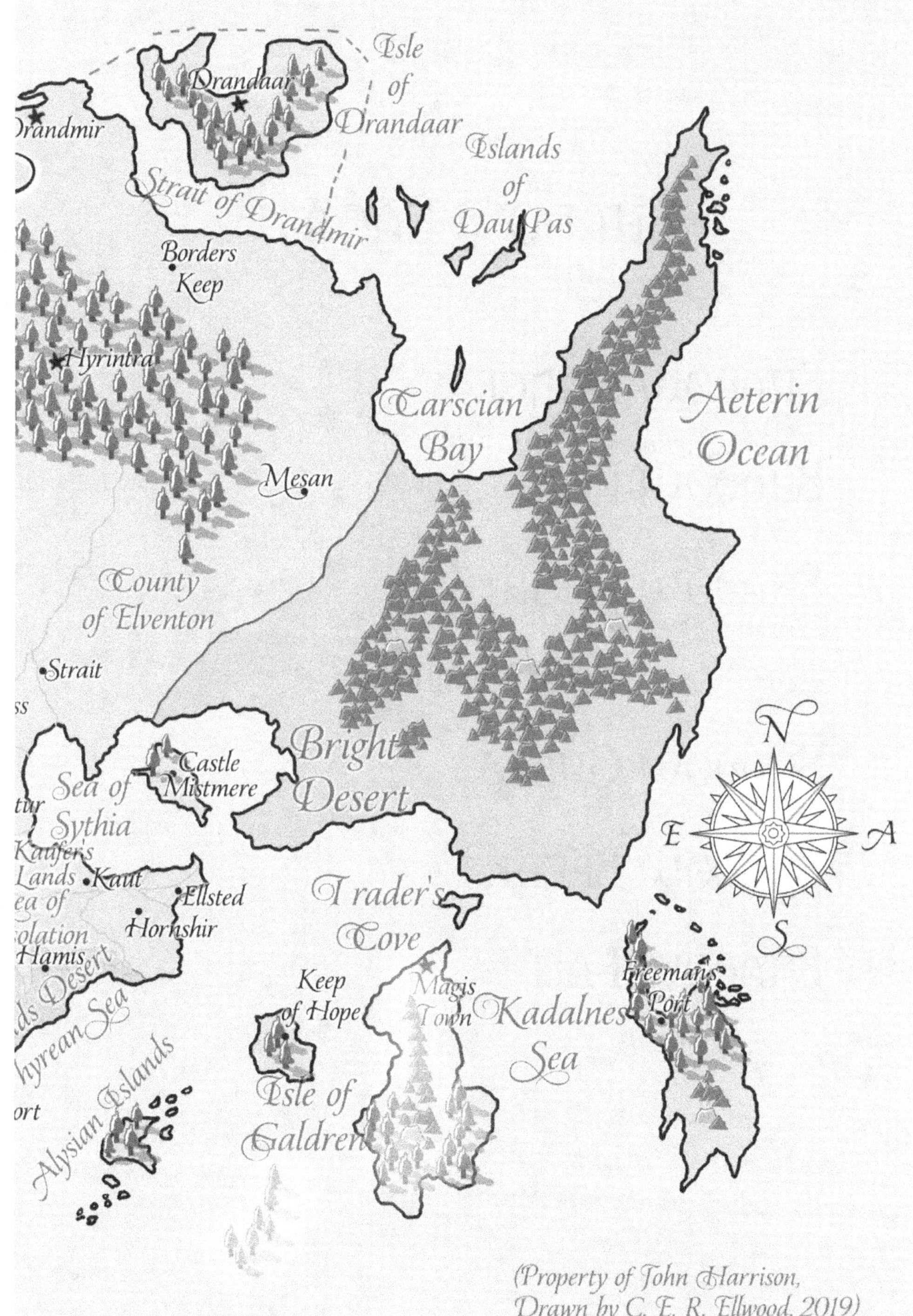

Isle of Drandaar
Drandaar
Drandmir
Strait of Drandmir
Borders Keep
Islands of Daul Pas
Hyrintra
Mesan
Carscian Bay
Aeterin Ocean
County of Elventon
Strait
Bright Desert
Castle Mistmere
Sea of Sythia
Kaufer's Lands
Kaut
Sea of Desolation
Hamis
Hamis Desert
Ellsted
Hornshir
Trader's Cove
Keep of Hope
Magis Town
Kadalnes Sea
Freemans Port
Thyrean Sea
Alysian Islands
Isle of Galdren
N
E
A
S

(Property of John Harrison,
Drawn by C. E. R. Ellwood, 2019)

Shadow Saga

Shadow Dance

Shadow Play

Shadow Flight

Forthcoming:

Shadow Guard

Shadow Break

Shadow Fall

PROLOGUE

One day I will be free!

Words spoken to the winds…meaningless.
Hopes and dreams uttered time and again…
…time out of mind.

Lost desires for an uncertain future lying in
antiquity.
Yet, these words are the very stories
That spark our imaginations…and our hearts.
Striking a chord deep within us, until our very
essence vibrates with its resonant stirrings.

Will they lead us to salvation?
Or deeper into the very darkness we seek to escape?

What shall come of them then?

Indeed…
What shall come of us all?

Chapter One:
Prelude

"The boy must stay here!" The edge in his voice was tangible as these words escaped Carness's lips. The constable glared across the darkened table at the inn's owner as he spat out these words. His wiry frame leaned on the table for added emphasis. Carness held Daffer's gaze with his golden brown eyes fiercely as he said each word to ensure his understanding.

"Why? I owe nothing to you or yours." Daffer's deep voice filled the hall with its reply.

All other conversations halted as Daffer all but rose from his seat. His broad shoulders and massive frame towered over most of those assembled at his table. Even seated he loomed like a brutish giant.

"You invaded my establishment, try to force me to aide you in this, to what end?" Daffer broke Carness's gaze quickly as he responded. "What is in it for me? Why would I want to open my home to my brother's brat?"

"We approached you because you are our family, Daffer." Cerona said from the shadows to the left of Carness. Her voice was calm and soothing as she attempted to ease the situation as much as she could.

Daffer's glare only deepened as his dull brown eyes bore through Cerona. "And the rest of you, you're all just here to witness this then?" Daffer's scowl deepened as he took all of the information in. Everyone present could tell that something did not add up to him, he just could not quite put his finger on what it was.

Before Daffer could object again, Kalta cut in. "The council members are here to look after the town's interest and to witness all that transpires here, including whether or not you accept my offer." His voice was terse and he wasted no time cutting to the point.

He knew his brother was going to be difficult to deal with. Kalta just wished he did not have to ask Daffer for anything, let alone this.

"What offer?" Daffer growled. He did not like what was happening, but he could not figure out why.

His glare turned from Cerona to her husband, Kalta. He hated the ease that settled around his younger brother's lean and fit frame like a cloak. The only thing they shared as brothers was their strong jawline and the way they both tied their long brown hair into a queue.

"The offer is simple. You provide food and lodging for our son while Cerona and I are in Hornshir." Sensing his brother's objection, Kalta continued hurriedly. "Don't worry, you will be paid. I plan on sending you money to pay for Namir's upkeep as part of our deal." Kalta paused as he waited for his brother to mentally digest the information he was given.

Everyone knew that Daffer was not the fastest when it came to making decisions and Kalta did not want to rush him in case he rejected the offer without really considering it.

"The other part of it is my council seat." The words were hard for Kalta to say.

He had fought so hard to have a nonelected seat on the council of their new town. The other founders of Ellsted had agreed that there should only be two nonelected seats, the head of the merchants and the healer.

It had taken weeks for them to agree that Kalta should fill the position as the head of merchants, now to lose it all for a trip he didn't want to take seemed almost too much to accept.

"You offer me something I don't covet, brother. Why would I want to take on this added responsibility and be stuck with your child?" Daffer retorted as he stood and paced the large room that he had turned into the main room of his inn, the Gathering Place.

Daffer was glad that he had ensured the room was well lit, yet shadowed at the same time. Daffer found that rooms with enough shadows allowed for customers to relax more and it lent itself better to some of the shadier sides of his business.

"Ellsted may still be small, Daffer, but it will grow. It will be the council that decides how this growth occurs and how it affects the town." Armani added from his seat.

Armani rose slowly as Daffer paced past him. Although his lean body was easily dwarfed by Daffer's large one, the newly elected mayor paced a few steps behind Daffer as he tried to reason with him.

"So what?" Daffer's response held an edge that warned his patience was wearing thin.

"So, as Ellsted grows its needs shall grow with it and bring you unwanted competition. Other inns will invariably open and you will lose business." Armani's long dark hair was already peppered with white and fell freely about his shoulders as he kept pace with the inn's owner. "In the short run it doesn't sound bad, but in the long term your inn could lose enough business and reputation that it will be forced to close." Armani replied still a few steps behind Daffer's hulking form.

"Besides, mine is a nonelected seat," Kalta added, "which means you could not only help shape where and when your rivals open, but you can't be voted out either."

A cold smile pulled at the corners of Daffer's lips as he turned to face the assembly. He slowly walked back to the table as he formed his thoughts carefully. Daffer only paused long enough to look at each person in turn.

After he made sure that everyone present knew he was in charge of this agreement, he continued as he took his seat, "And when you return… then what? Do I just step down as head merchant and you resume your title, or do I get to keep it as my own?"

"I would resume my title once I returned," Kalta said, not

breaking Daffer's gaze.

"Then your answer is no." Daffer responded with uncharacteristic speed and started to leave.

"If I said yes," Kalta stammered, "if I were to say yes, would you agree?" The importance of the trip to Hornshir bore heavily upon him and he hated to lose his title, but he knew it was worth the loss if Daffer would agree to help.

The air in the room filled with tension as the two brothers glared across the table from one another. The council members looked from one to another as they tried to discern who would relent first.

"My question still stands," Kalta asked after several moments had passed. His inquiry only seemed to add to the building tension.

"You don't leave me much choice, brother. Just don't forget that my acceptance of your position is only part of my payment," Daffer all but growled across the table. "Leave your bastard and go."

"DAFFER!" Cerona erupted to her feet as her voice filled the room. Her blonde hair cascaded off her shoulders and framed her seething face delicately. "Never refer to my son like that again!" Her fingers closed around the hilt of her dagger as she leaned into the table. Her sky blue eyes fiercely held Daffer in his place. Cerona's unspoken threat hung palpably between them.

Their eyes locked across the table as Daffer processed her intent. He glanced from Cerona to Kalta and then around the room to each of the council members and finally rested on Carness's taut and ready frame.

"You have my apologies," Daffer felt the eyes of the Ellsted's remaining elders upon him as he replied. "I spoke out of anger for the events of the day. Just don't forget to pay for his keep while he is in my care."

"We won't," Kalta replied to his brother quickly in an attempt to diffuse the situation. "We do appreciate your graciousness in this."

"What is so important in Hornshir that makes the two of

you reluctant to take your child with you?" Daffer inquired as he tried to pry more out of the two.

"That we cannot say," Kalta answered as he and his wife rose to leave. "We will be leaving in a few hours, so please make sure Namir's room is ready by then." Kalta exchanged glances with Daffer to ensure he understood, then left the Gathering Place closely followed by the rest of the council.

Daffer waited a few extra moments after the council left before he rose from the table and crossed the room to the fireplace. He slowly lowered himself into the new high-backed chair adjacent to it and worked through the details of the agreement.

'I know it's for the best, but I can't help the feeling that I am going to lose in this somehow.' His mind continued to race as he wrestled with his decision and the possible outcomes they brought with them. His wife's screams snapped him from his turbulent thoughts.

He leapt to his feet and practically flew to the stairs. As Daffer bound up the stairs he bellowed, "Get Saril NOW!" His concerns shifted from the problems Kalta faced to those of his pregnant wife, Lysanta.

The first thing Daffer noticed as he burst through his chamber door was how starkly pale Lysanta looked. Her long ebony hair was gnarled and matted by the sweat that beaded along her scalp. The oil lamps on either side of the bed bathed the room in a soft glow and starkly exposed her features.

The look of pain that etched itself across Lysanta's brow was almost too much for him. Although Daffer knew little about the arts of healing, he knew something was wrong with his wife.

Before he fully entered the room, he bellowed down the gaping stairwell, "Get the cook up here... and anyone else experienced in birthing!" Daffer's fear was as plain on his face as it was in his voice.

Kalta fingered the note Aras had sent him requesting his presence in Hornshir as he impatiently paced around Tipin's inner courtyard.

'What is taking them so long?' Kalta wondered. Try as he might, he was unable to shake the feeling that settled in his stomach like a stone. Inside Saril, Cerona and Allair made all the arrangements for Namir by plotting out the important skills he may need to learn should their journey take longer than expected.

The cool evening's breeze pulled at his leather jerkin as he paced between the well and the main house. Although night had fallen while they had been persuading Daffer, Tipin's courtyard was well lit by the stark white stones of the well and the surrounding wall.

"I hate the waiting," Kalta muttered as he made another lap around the well.

"As do I," Tipin answered unbidden. "Let me read the letter again," Tipin asked as he stretched his massive arm toward Kalta.

Tipin's long black hair was pulled into a queue in a way that revealed the silver streaks that seemed to capture the moon light and eerily redirect it onto his surroundings.

"It makes little sense," Kalta said as he reluctantly walked over to his old friend and handed him the already worry worn parchment. "It instructs us to meet him at the manor in Hornshir as fast as possible. He mentions the horses he sent us and urges us not to stop for any reason. He makes a point to inform us that only Cerona and I make this trek, and that we do not bring the child with us." Kalta shook his head unconsciously as he repeated the contents of the letter aloud from memory. "Aras knows we named the child Namir, why wouldn't he use his name? And why can't we have the pleasure of your company, Tipin?" Kalta's furrowed brow betrayed his confusion as much as the worry in his voice did. "You and Allair know just as much about Namir and his origins as we do. This summons doesn't make sense."

"I am as unsure as you, but Aras knows what he is doing, he always has." Tipin confided as he grasped his friend's shoulder.

Whether it was the unspoken truth of what Tipin said or the amount of trust Tipin displayed towards Aras that made Kalta feel as if Tipin knew more than he shared he did not know. Kalta only knew it unsettled him.

"If Aras hadn't served with us in the army defending Watch Keep and the queen's only escape route… and if his skills weren't so well honed, I'd be doubtful of his intentions." Kalta watched Tipin's reaction carefully as he tried to discern what he was not sharing. There was an odd sense of loss about Tipin when he spoke of Aras that Kalta had not noticed before.

"Aye, but Aras is all we have in this situation. Only Aras has the ability and connections to find out more about Namir's true lineage." Tipin responded, his steely grey eyes holding his friend's brown ones as if to instill strength in him.

"I'm not sure I want to know anymore." Kalta said more to himself than his friend. He glanced up and saw Tipin about to reply so he raised a hand to silence him. "It's just that Cerona and I have started to think of him as our own. It's hard to let that go. That's one of the reasons I wish you could come with us and why I wish I knew more about Aras," Kalta confided to Tipin. "Why does he need to be so surrounded in mystery?"

"I'm sure he has his reasons." The tone in Tipin's deep voice held a certainty that only added to Kalta's confusion.

"What do you know of him?" Kalta asked with the sound of concern deep in his voice, "aside from what you told me four years ago when you introduced us?"

"Nothing… " Tipin's response was cut short by the sounds of his door being pounded on and frantic screams issued from the other side of the white washed walls separating his courtyard from the rest of the city.

"YOU ARE SURE THEY WILL COME?" The voice was less than a whisper, yet clear to everyone present.

"They will be here; you can rest assured of that." Aras said as he lifted his goblet to take another drink. "I have known these two for far too long to not know this much." His reassuring tone did little to ease the looming oppression in the room. Aras sighed deeply as he pulled his still mostly blond hair into a queue before continuing, "I have sent word to them and I have been assured that they will be here as soon as they are able." Aras looked around the gathering and made sure to catch the eye of everyone present with his own grey ones.

Although the manor was not overly large, this room had been built to accommodate a large amount of people for meetings such as this. As he scanned the room, he was a little amazed at the diversity he saw. He let his grey eyes glide from his elven wife, Alequa, to her guard Jerine, then to the Divitian twins from Freeport that had vowed the service of their ship to his cause, then to Natlia, the maid that had already helped him hide a few of the items of power, and finally to the Devanagari shrouded in shadows.

"I have also sent them steeds so their journey here can be swift. The only thing I cannot guarantee is their safety once they leave the sanctity of their home."

Aras's stormy grey eyes darted around the room again to gauge the amount of faith he still commanded in his compatriots.

"I fear the ills that will befall them when they do leave," Jerine's voice was melodic, yet firm and managed to convey the sentiment felt by everyone in the room.

"I fear that as well, Jerine, and I hope that Patiun and Faesin will guard their steps until they arrive." Aras's words and tone were so reverent that everyone fell silent.

"AND IF THEY DON'T ARRIVE; WHAT THEN?" The shadow walker's voice shattered the silence completely as he asked his question.

The worry in his voice was a little alarming to everyone

present in the room. The shadow walker rarely let his presence be known amongst them in the past, now he seemed to be the most vocal.

"If they don't, we will just have to come up with another plan." The lilt in Alequa's voice soothed most of the nerves in the room and allowed some tension to dissipate.

"No, the plans have changed too much as it is," although Aras was getting on in years, the air of authority in his tenor voice still rang true. "If they do not show, for whatever reason, we shall proceed as planned. I will continue to track down as many of the Items of Power as I can and I will keep them safe until the time is right for their rediscovery." He slowly rose from his chair as he said this and turned to face the rest of his co-conspirators one at a time in order to read their expressions.

"If you fear their arrival, why don't you use your unique talents to go get them?"   The twins spoke almost as if they were one.

They turned to the shadow walker as each one completed the others' words almost unnoticeably. Their red hair moved in eerie unison as if the subtle breeze in the room affected both of them as if they were the same person.

"I SHALL."   His response was swift and left no doubt to those in the room of his intentions as his features faded into the shadows once again. Only the most astute amongst them felt the slight chill take hold in the room.

Daffer's fist was the first and last thing Saril saw as he entered Lysanta's room.   The unexpected darkness that accompanied the punch was welcomed as he felt his limp body slam into the wall a few paces away from where he once stood.

"Wake him up!" Daffer bellowed to the cook as he watched the healer's frail frame hit the wall with a loud thud.

"With what?" The shrill voice of the cook erupted over his shoulder. "We need everything we have here 'cept that pot on the fire!" Her glare only managed to make Daffer madder and she realized it too late.

"I don't care!" He bellowed as he spun to face her. "You're just lucky I need you awake or you'd end up like he is!"

"Sorry but, I've got me hands full over here trying to save your daughter!" She spat back at him angrily. "Why don't you make yourself useful and wake the sot up yourself?"

Daffer growled angrily as he yanked the scalding pot of used rags and water off the fire and splashed it directly across Saril's eyes.

"What the 'ell do you think you're doing?" The cook shrieked from behind Daffer. "We need him alive! I know precious little about birthing a child and what I do know I used up an hour ago!"

"I don't know!" Daffer yelled at the top of his lungs. Someone wake him up!"

The stable maid quickly let go of Lysanta's pallid hand and scurried over to Saril's writhing body. She quickly took some salve from her pouch and spread it across Saril's eyes and face as she lightly patted his cheeks gently with her other hand.

When she saw him start to rouse, she quickly whispered, "Do not open your eyes. You've been burned and the salve will seep in if you do."

Saril only nodded as he attempted to sit. "What's happening?"

"The mistress, lady Lysanta, is birthing her child, but something's wrong." The stable maid offered quietly.

"What?" Saril asked as he regained some of his senses. "What's wrong?"

"I don't know! But what I do know there is lots of blood and the baby is not moving!" This time it was the cook's shrill voice that responded to Saril's question.

"Fine, I will see what I can do." Saril said hastily, "but I am not sure if it will be enough given my current condition." He shot his comment in the direction he thought Daffer was in as he set about his work.

Kalta looked over at Cerona cautiously as he entered the room. "What happened and where did Saril rush off to?"

"The Gathering Place," Allair responded before Cerona had a chance to. "Evidentially there is an emergency that needed his attention."

"Should we go as well?" Kalta felt as if everything was slipping away and he hated it.

"No." Tipin replied unconsciously. "We need to get Namir and your things ready." Tipin put a hand on Kalta's shoulder reassuringly as he said this. "Besides, you can find out what happened when you come home."

"Always the task master." Cerona smiled at Tipin and Allair as she said this. "It is still alright if we just leave from here, right?" Her uncertainty barely masked the fear in her voice.

"Of course it is." Allair responded with a smile. "In fact Namir can stay with Nurn for the night." Her smile hid her concern for her sword sister elegantly.

"Good." Kalta responded. "Then we should leave. The horses Aras sent are tethered to the racks in the smithy."

Kalta and Cerona hugged Tipin and Allair one last time before they walked down the hall to Nurn's room. A smile creased all of their faces as they saw the three boys playing on the floor.

The three boys looked up as their parents entered the room. Kalta motioned to Namir and the boy dutifully rose to his feet and walked to his parents somberly. The look of disappointment on his face was almost too much for any of them to bear.

Cerona knelt down and scooped Namir up into her arms as she kissed him on the forehead, "We have to go… but you can stay here with Nurn for a while then you will stay with your uncle until we get back." She gazed into Namir's steel blue eyes as she said this hoping he would understand.

Kalta kissed Namir on the cheek as he took him from his

wife and added, "We love you Namir, know that always." A sinking feeling filled the pit of his stomach again. "We are going to Hornshir, so we won't be gone too long." Somehow, he felt like he was lying, he just did not know why.

Daffer brooded as he looked across the table at the mercenaries that glared back at him. "I need it to look like a robbery, nothing more."

"Fine." The brigand to his right responded nonchalantly. Her sultry voice made Daffer a little uncomfortable with its hidden innuendos. "Why do you want him dead?"

"That is none of your business." Daffer glared at her defiantly.

"But it is," the other one responded as she cleaned her unusually long claw-like nails with the tip of a throwing knife. Her words came out in more of a growl than actual speech. "Because if we don't know why; we won't work for you."

"Besides," the other mercenary cut in, "we are curious why the owner of the only inn in this town would need to have anyone killed." The mercenary's brown eyes played along Daffer's muscles as she coyly twirled a lock of her brown jasmine scented hair.

Daffer focused his attention on the gruffer of the two women to shake the awkwardness he felt as he responded. "Let's just say I need to assure the future for my establishment and my son." Daffer nodded toward his son, Jaconis, as he said this.

Daffer was sitting in his new favorite chair by the fire with Jaconis seated beside him and the table he had used to meet with his brother and the council separating the two women from them.

"So do we have a deal?"

"One more thing," the woman with the long fingernails purred from under the hood that shrouded her features. "Is there any penalty for killing anyone travelling with him?"

"No." Daffer's response was unusually cold. "I thought

that was a given when I said I want it to look like a robbery.”

“Good.” She said as she licked her lips and an unusually long fang. “We will take our money first and we will not be back.”

“Fine,” Daffer replied as he tossed a bag onto the table. “Now be gone!” As the two women in dark leather armor left, Daffer looked into his son’s jade green eyes. A pang of loss crept into his voice as he said, “I only do this for you. Now that your mother is dead, you are all that I have left… and all that I have will one day be yours. Do you understand me?” Daffer smiled when Jaconis nodded his head without hesitation. “Good. Say nothing of this meeting to anyone… ever.” These final words bore an edge to them Jaconis had never heard in his father’s voice before and it scared him.

“THEY ARE GONE!” All of the shadows in the room erupted with his voice at the same time.

“What do you mean they’re gone?” Aras was the first to recover from the stunning sound of the shadow walker’s voice.

“I MEAN THERE IS NO SIGN OF THEM… NOT IN THEIR HOUSE… NOT ON THE ROAD TO HORNSHIR… NOT EVEN WITHIN THIS CITY’S WALLS!” He seemed to materialize in the shadows as he entered the room in a huff.

His black hair streamed like the shadows themselves and played across his alabaster skin as he strode towards Aras. He stopped abruptly a few paces away from Aras and held out his left hand balled into a fist with a medallion dangling from it.

“THIS IS ALL I COULD FIND ALONG THE ROAD FROM THEIR TOWN.”

“Let me see that,” Aras replied as he reached for the dangling medallion.

With a quick twist of his wrist, the shadow walker concealed the medallion in his fist artfully. “YOU MAY NOT TOUCH IT.” The shadow walker leveled a dark glare at Aras. “IT’S ENCHANTED AND THOUGH YOU ARE UNIQUE AMONG YOUR

KIND, YOU WOULD STILL BE ENTHRALLED BY IT."

"At least tell me what the symbol on its face looks like." Aras felt somewhat foolhardy and slightly irate. He knew the Devanagari would have offered it to him if he believed it were safe instead of just holding it forth.

"IT'S A HAND CLEFT IN HALF BY A DAGGER." His tone was flat and somewhat more detached than normal.

"Is the tip of the dagger up or down?" Aras found his friend's detachment odd and it bothered him.

"UP. LIKE THE DAGGER IS AN EXTRA FINGER ON THE HAND."

Aras scrutinized the shadow walker as he described the symbol. Something was wrong; Aras just wished he knew what.

"It is as I feared. The Followers of Transcendence, the Dark Travelers of Lotevilar." Aras's face darkened as he thought about the implications.

The Dark Travelers make up the inner echelon of Lotevilar's faith here in Cennicus. Aras knew there were powerful forces aligned against him; he just was not prepared to find the queen of darkness and pain as the one spearheading the charge.

It made sense, however, when he thought about it. The increased sightings of her nassarid and only proved her interest in his actions. Aras looked over the shadow walker once more, as he thought about the ramifications of Lotevilar's involvement with the items of power. Aras's eyes widened as he finally saw the burn marks on the shadow walker's cloak.

"Douse the lights!" Aras's order was more barked than spoken as he threw himself at the nearest sconce and extinguished it.

Thankfully, the others in the room followed suit and in a matter of moments the room was enveloped in utter darkness. Complete silence engulfed them and the only sound anyone could hear was the sound of Aras fumbling for something in his desk.

After what seemed like a hours, the room was bathed in a

soft blue light emanating from a box Aras held as he walked back over to the Devanagari.

"Why didn't you say you were attacked?" Aras's voice betrayed his fury and concern as he spoke to his longtime friend.

"It wasn't important enough to mention." The shadow walker replied gruffly. "I've been attacked before… this is no different."

"But it is. It means the dark travelers know how to hurt you." Aras's worried look conveyed his emotions far better than his words could hope to. Unfortunately, his concern only managed to upset the shadow walker further.

"I will be more careful then." The soft blue light accentuated a slight hint of pain was engraved starkly on the shadow walker's face. "This is not the first time an enemy of mine has learned one of my kind's weaknesses and I doubt it will be the last."

Chapter Two:
Beginnings

To be completely free, compelled by none to do as they wished; that was his dream. Namir smirked as he thought of this fantasy. Unrealistic as it was, he felt the necessity to hope it could be achieved.

The cool spring breeze blew along the tall grasses of the glade and played through Namir's golden hair. In the distance, a wren chirped melodically. Times like these always brought him here, to sit and revel in nature's glories.

'Why can't Ellsted be this peaceful?' Namir sighed as he felt the cool breeze enter his lungs. He breathed deeply and savored its crispness. His gaze flitted from the pleasant mountainside onto Ellsted itself.

The sleepy little town lay nestled between its crops and the surrounding hills, lying precariously close to the river. Every year they wondered if the rains would swell the river too much and if it did who would become the unlucky ones claimed by it.

The light reflecting off the river glimmered along the dew covered thatched roofs of the outlying houses and caused various shadows to fall onto the cobblestones beneath them. These little glints of lights played and danced with the shadows that they created amidst barrels and sacks stored on the side of the lane.

Already people were rising and starting their chores.

Watching the town awaken was always a treat he savored. Namir grinned as he saw the stray dogs meander down the roads away from the more permanent building of Ellsted's center plaza. The morning's light played across the brownstone structures lazily as he watched.

'Soon the whole town will be either toiling in the fields or plying their trade in the vain hope of reward.' Namir thought to himself lightly.

'This peacefulness won't last; in a few days the rains will start again.' Namir mused wistfully. 'A few weeks more and Belanui's feast will pull the whole town into a bustle of cooking and dancing. With the fair being setup and travelers flocking in from all points of the shire, Ellsted will become a very busy place. Every year it's the same, with only one difference… fewer travelers.'

Namir had noticed the problem early last year and so had the town fathers. 'Hopefully I can live up to their expectations, Ellsted's continued wellbeing counts on it,' Namir thought bitterly to himself.

His thoughts drifted from Ellsted's concerns to those of his childhood. Before he knew it, he was reminiscing about the grand adventures he had created for his friends and the wonderfully exciting exploits that always seemed to get them into trouble.

It seemed to Namir as if just yesterday he was running his little menagerie, standing outside the blacksmith's trying to figure out a way into the pub unnoticed. Stealing barrels and flasks of ale and going down to the river to drink them; always avoiding his uncle and his uncle's friends at all costs.

Life seemed more exciting then, and there was always a new adventure just waiting to be pursued. A tear crept into Namir's steel blue eyes as he thought of these things.

The valley seemed to hold its breath as Namir stood slowly and stretched his wiry muscles and broad shoulders to keep them from cramping. Already he felt the morning's chill setting in as the dew seeped through his black canvas breeches.

Namir was not an overly tall lad, but he was well built and

pleasing to the eye. He brushed his golden blond hair from his eyes as he hunched forward feeling his overly taut back muscles loosen. His hair settled back into place obediently as he righted himself, falling down to the edge of his jaw on either side to silhouette his face perfectly. He smoothed his tawny colored tunic under his belt before he turned to take on last look over the town.

Then with a wistful sigh, Namir allowed his feet to carry him home. "One day I will be free," he muttered as he reached the trail at the bottom of the hill that meandered towards town.

"And one day I'll be king," came a mocking voice from over his right shoulder, "or at least the pub's owner. Besides… what would you do with freedom, eh Namir?" The person posed in a nasty nasal tone.

Namir stopped and slowly clenched and unclenched his fits as he replied without turning. "I would be free of you and yours at least. That is freedom enough for me, Jaconis." With this said, he renewed his trek back to his uncle's pub.

As Jaconis followed Namir home, he watched closely as Namir threaded his way through the growing throngs of townsfolk. 'Namir will not shirk his duties today if I have anything to say about it.' Jaconis thought to himself quickly as he ran his fingers through his well-oiled black curls. 'Hopefully the town fathers will decide to send me to Hornshir instead of Namir.'

He worked his dark thoughts around in his mind as he padded quietly behind Namir. "If only my father would support me in this," he muttered hopelessly, more to himself than to anyone nearby.

Jaconis knew that his father had eagerly anticipated any way to rid himself of Namir ever since he had been thrust upon them as a young child by the death of his parents. Now that Namir had come of age, Daffer grew even more restless.

'This fool's quest Namir dreamt up is the perfect way to accomplish my father's goals. The problem is,' Jaconis mused, 'it's not a fool's quest. Unfortunately, Namir is correct. Ellsted needs more supplies. It also needs renewed interest in our fair in order to survive the coming winter.'

Seeing Namir veer into the opening of a building broke Jaconis free from his thoughts and hurried his step. He did not wish to brave his father's wrath should Namir choose to forsake his chores again. As Jaconis surveyed the building, he realized that Namir had taken refuge in Tipin's Smithy.

The smithy was one of the older stone buildings just on the outside edge of the town's center. Its brownstone walls were almost black from years of soot that had been deposited by the bellows of the forge.

The opening to the main work area was sheltered under a low roof and consisted of a mixture of stout wooden beams and the dull tan ceramic clay shingles common to the area. There were no walls, just thickly hewn beams and what little boards that were needed in order to create shelving to house their wares.

Just inside the opening, a large man was working with something on the polishing wheel. His large muscular bronzed arms strained with his task and seemed oblivious to Namir slipping through the cramped area behind him, easily dodging the open coals of the main forge pit.

The man's exposed chest glistened with his exertion and his dark brown hair pulled back into a queue was soaked with sweat as well. As Jaconis saw the tattoos on the side of his head, he recognized him as Tipin's eldest son, Nurn.

To Nurn's right was a trough full of water. Immediately behind him was the large coal bed of the forge and the huge bellows laid to his left. The glittering fruits of the forge hung all around him, polished metal pots and pans were interspersed with horseshoes and a wide variety of cutlery. Rising up behind the work area was Tipin's house, built with the same sturdy construction techniques used in the forge's construction.

A low rising wall made from river rocks enclosed their private courtyard and helped to create some space from the other encroaching buildings of the town, not to mention the temporary tents of transients and gypsies pitched up against them.

Nurn looked up from the finishing wheel as Namir walked in and he saw the hungry look in Namir's eyes. Nurn immediately understood all too well what needed to be done.

He let the corded muscles of his right arms relax a little to let Namir pass. Although Nurn was Namir's elder by two years, there was nothing Nurn would not do for him. He proved this time and again throughout their childhood. No matter what it was Namir needed, Nurn did without hesitation.

Nurn was a quiet youth, big in frame and long in patience. He stood easily a span or two taller than Namir, who was tall for his age, and was doubly as wide in his shoulders as most grown men were.

Although Nurn had lived to see ten and nine rebirths of the sun, many believed him to be far older. Some attributed this to his silence, while others claimed that it was the way he wore his brown hair. Nurn kept his unruly brown hair long on top and pulled loosely into a queue that fell to his shoulders from the top of the back of his head. The rest was not only clean-shaven, but ornamented by the dark tattoos of his faith.

The most interesting thing about Nurn was not his great size and strength, but his beliefs. He swore his allegiance unto the Calanari gods and would not sway from them or their teachings no matter who railed against them.

Like Namir he was not from Ellsted, neither was he from the Three Rivers Shire. Instead, he was birthed in the sweltering heat of the Burning Lands, only to move to Ellsted shortly after his fourth year.

His skin, colored the hue of pale gold in the winter and a burnished bronze when tanned, indicated his Calanari descent in a way that his tattoos never could, yet his brown tufted hair and cold black eyes screamed of his Ellstedian heritage.

Nurn turned slightly away from the wheel and lifted the broad blade of the axe's head that he was polishing. He placed it into the trough momentarily as Namir moved deftly around him and darted into the shadows of the shop just as Jaconis entered.

Nurn briefly glanced at Jaconis's slight build before he hefted the axe head back up and onto the wheel again. Nurn pretended not to notice Jaconis enter the smithy. However as Jaconis was about to brush past him, Nurn let the axe slip from his grip and slam into Jaconis's right knee.

Jaconis collapsed to the flagstones of the shop hard enough to jar the wind from him, his dark blue woolen cloak bunched up enough to stop the back of his head from smacking the granite floor.

"Are you alright?" Nurn asked sardonically. "I am so sorry… I didn't see you come in." Nurn fought hard to keep a smile from spilling onto his lips as he crouched beside Jaconis.

"Lea… Leave m… me be!" Jaconis spat gasping for air. "I know you saw me enter!" His breath returned painfully as he struggled to rise.

Placing a hand passively on Jaconis's shoulder easily stopped him from his feeble attempts at movement. "I am sorry that you feel I meant you harm, young master." Nurn nodded mockingly. "What boon would come to my father's smithy had I acted purposefully against you?" He let his smile play across his lips, half hidden in the shadows of the shop.

"To your father's smithy none; to my cousin, your friend and companion, your actions could be a great boon indeed!" Jaconis roared as he attempted feebly to remove Nurn's massive hand from his shoulder.

Squeezing Jaconis's shoulder lightly Nurn felt the fibers of Jaconis's cloak press against whatever cloth Jaconis wore beneath it. Nurn could not restrain his smile as he continued. "You injure me to imply that I would harm you, isn't your father the owner of the only pub in Ellsted? Isn't he also one of this smithy's most notable patrons? If I intended to harm you, my father would lose money and services. This in turn would not only upset my father, but it could force him to demote me back to junior journeyman! Why would I risk my family's livelihood and my own for your cousin's gain?"

Nurn glowered deeply into Jaconis's pale green eyes. He

tried to let his smile turn into a frown as he shook his head mockingly, but instead it took on a maniacal quality.

Jaconis shrank from Nurn's icy stare and his bottomless black eyes. "I will tell my father of this," he hissed, "you can count on it."

"I think not." Nurn rumbled as he started to stand. Nurn hefted Jaconis to his feet by his left shoulder as he stood. "That is if you wish to ensure your continued health."

At this, he pressed his fingers into Jaconis's shoulder hard. Jaconis's shoulder gave too easily for Nurn's liking and he had to stop quickly in order to keep from dislodging it from its socket.

"If any word of this incident spreads past here I will not hesitate to clear my name and call you out." Nurn slowly rotated his hand clockwise, "Do you understand?"

Pain shot across Jaconis's comely face. He felt Nurn's grip harden and a fiery sensation ripped through him. Jaconis was unsure if it started in his shoulder or his knee, either way the pain made his head swim as he felt the burning sensation flow through his body and up to his head.

He heard Nurn clearly, yet felt completely unable respond. A new pain welled up in his chest from stifling his screams for so long. Nurn held him up a few moments longer, to allow the depth of the consequences to fully sink into Jaconis's thick skull.

"All you need to do is nod once. If you do I will release you." Nurn spoke slowly to add emphasis on the gravity of Jaconis's situation.

Nurn's voice echoed in Jaconis's ears. He felt the blood flow from his head as he struggled for consciousness. Limply he acquiesced and felt his head nod forward once and hang there useless.

Blackness closed in around the edges of his senses and brought with it a feeling of weightlessness and serenity that seeped through his very being. An eternity free of care and pain seemed to pass all too abruptly before he was ripped from it and thrust back into the waking world.

A sharp pain erupted in his head and strange noises buzzed loudly around him. Slowly everything refocused as a bright light burned through his eyes and etched the images of reality into his brain once more.

He saw a burly shirtless man kneeling over him and was instantly afraid. The man easily dwarfed him in size and stature. The giant's golden skin gleamed painfully to Jaconis's acute senses and his silver mane hung in a loose queue that cascaded off his left shoulder and hung down over Jaconis's chest as the man stooped over him. His clean-shaven face and temples jogged Jaconis's memory. After a few moments, the distinctive tattoos on the side of Tipin's head became clearly visible.

"He is coming to," Tipin declared. "This is a sore accident. You need to practice more care Nurn. Remember, you must always be aware of those around you, even if they are not where they belong." This last part was directed at Jaconis, his cool grey eyes held Jaconis's green ones in an intimidating stare.

Pain wracked Jaconis's body again as he attempted to sit up. He let his eyes slowly focus on everything around him as his hands wandered over his stomach and belt deftly assessing his belongs.

Jaconis was about to chide Nurn in front of Tipin for his actions when he felt Nurn's cold black eyes cut into him from over Tipin's shoulder. Instead, he slowly ran his right hand through his oiled curls again trying to decide on what to say.

After a few moments, he found enough courage to speak. His lean frame shook as each word passed his dry lips haltingly. "It was my fault," he eventually muttered hoarsely. "I thought I saw Namir in here so I thought to hurry in before he could run away again. I was evidentially mistaken," he added. "May I have some water please?" His parched throat ached as he uttered each syllable.

Laughing robustly Tipin motioned to a tawny haired youth standing silently in the smithy's entryway to fetch some water for Jaconis. It was not until Jaconis saw the boy's grey eyes that he recognized him as Nurn's younger brother, Halin.

"You shall have your water, boy. All you needed to do was ask." Still smiling Tipin turned to Nurn, "have you apologized to him yet?" His voice held a lethal edge that his smile masked perfectly.

Nurn lowered his head and slowly shook it. "No father, I have not." Nurn lied ruefully. "He passed out as soon as the axe blade knocked his feet out from under him."

"Well, there's nothing to be done about it now, then." Tipin remarked. "You have your chance, go to it. When you're finished I will be going through the work for today." His deep voice held a promise that made Nurn flinch.

"Yes father." Nurn's reply came acridly to his lips. He waited patiently for his father to leave. When he was certain that they were alone, again he turned his full attention to Jaconis. "I deeply regret my actions, young master." His voice, laced heavily with sarcasm, lashed into Jaconis and each word stung as they struck his ears. "Please take my apology with you when you leave."

Halin sped off through the house muttering darkly, his short cut tawny hair blew fiercely in the wind. 'Why didn't he have to get the water, wasn't it his fault. Shouldn't Nurn be getting it instead of me?' He stalked into their inner courtyard so lost in his thoughts he did not notice Namir sitting beside the well.

"Is he gone yet?" Namir inquired softly as Halin almost stepped into him.

Halin jumped, his already pale skin becoming more pallid as he looked at Namir's lean form in surprise. He was speechless. He found himself staring dumbly at Namir as the sunlight played through his fine golden hair. All his wits fled him. It was not until Namir reached out and shook him lightly, patiently repeating his question that Halin came to his senses.

"I... I... I'm s... sorry. What?" He stammered.

"Has Jaconis left the smithy?" Namir quickly reworded

his question, hoping that Halin would follow it easier.

"No… he has not." Halin stated, regaining more of his composure as he replied. The color slowly returned to his cheeks. "What happened?" Halin's tinny voice made him seem even younger than he was.

"I think I should ask you," Namir baited the youth, but instead of waiting for Halin's reply he launched into his own explanation. "Jaconis was shadowing me again." He waived an unconcerned hand to make light of the situation as he continued, "Deciding to evade him I ducked into the smithy and let Nurn handle Jaconis in his own austere manner." Namir could not hold back the tinge of pride from his voice as he thought of what Nurn may have done to Jaconis.

"Why do you never trust me to do this stuff?" Halin whined. "I could do a great job at something like that. I know I could." The pout that came to Halin's lips forced Namir's smile to broaden.

Namir slipping one arm around Halin's shoulders as he reassured him, "You are like the little brother I never had. Besides, Jaconis is easily twice your size and he is more skilled at evasion than you know." Looking into Halin's mist colored eyes he added. "When I get the town fathers' permission to go to Hornshir, I would like you to come with me. Maybe on the way Nurn and I can teach you a few things about fighting and stealth."

"I would love that!" Halin burst in energetically. "That would be great. I can see it now," Halin slipped from Namir's grip and easily leapt onto the edge of the well nimbly as he spread his arms wide. "The three of us bounding across the countryside, freeing damsels in distress and fighting rogues along the way. That would be a great adventure." Spinning quickly he grasped Namir's tunic tightly to keep from falling. "You will take me with you right? I mean… you weren't just saying that were you?"

Filled with mirth by the boy's antics, Namir laughed. "Yes… yes you will come with us. I promise. We need to have someone with us to make the journey seem shorter." Still smiling broadly he said as he regained his composure a little, "What did you come out here for anyway? Surely it wasn't only to jest with me and brighten my day."

Halin gaped as his original task rushed back to him. "No. I am supposed to be getting your cousin some water." He realized that Tipin might be upset at his delay.

Halin could just imagine his father's hulking form pacing the courtyard waiting for him, selecting the toughest chores a boy his age could do because of his tardiness. Halin could imagine Tipin's silver hair as it caught the morning's light to reflect it back onto his surroundings to fill the courtyard with an eerie dancing light. Halin shivered as he thought about Tipin's ire.

Watching Halin's face fill with regret, Namir eased the young boy's thoughts by placing his hand on Halin's shoulder and handing his own water skin to the boy. "Here take this to fill Jaconis' glass. He won't know the difference between water from the inn and water from your well. When he's gone, come back and tell me what happened in full. I have faith that you can get me all the information I seek from Nurn."

"What of my chores?" Halin lamented. "Certainly my father will assign me some for today. What should I do, forget about them?"

Shaking his head Namir countered, "Tipin knows what happened, I am sure of it. The thing to remember is that there is no love lost between Tipin and Daffer. Besides, he likes Jaconis less than we do. Simply tell him that you need to talk with me." Namir made sure to keep Halin there a moment longer by gripping his shoulder a little tighter as he added. "I have already told him that I would like Nurn and you to accompany me to Hornshir. Besides... "

"He knows?" Halin interjected before Namir could complete his thought. "You already told my father that you want me to go with you? Why didn't you tell me?" Halin sniveled. "And what do you mean 'Tipin knows what happened'?"

"Easy... calm down, Halin." Namir soothed the boy and

cursed himself mentally for forgetting that Halin had only witnessed ten and four rebirths of the sun. "It isn't bad that Tipin knows. When I asked Tipin about Nurn coming with me, your father suggested that I take you as well. I was going to tell you, it just slipped my mind." Namir allowed himself another grin as he continued, "Besides this way I get to hear you complain about it."

"I have to go." Halin whirled away from Namir abruptly freeing himself from Namir's grip and darted back towards his house. Fuming as he went, Halin muttered crossly, "I wish… just once… someone would consult me before agreeing on what I'm going to do." With that, he pulled down a cup and filled it for Jaconis before he discarded Namir's water skin and hurried into the smithy.

Halin slowly stepped into the room, his lean form gracefully darting out of the shadows that surrounded them and handed Jaconis a glass of water. Jaconis drained it and slowly rose as he found his footing carefully. Jaconis looked around the smithy again as he carefully resituated his clothing by straightening the creases and flattening the folds. Once this was all done he stalked away gloomily towards home without Namir.

This encounter was far from over… and Nurn knew it. Nurn squared his well-muscled shoulders, after he was sure Jaconis was well away from the smithy, and sought out Tipin for his share of the day's work.

Jaconis hurried home; his jade green eyes darted down every alley and crevasse as he tried in vain to catch a glimpse of Namir. He became more and more irritated as he went. The realization he would have to face his father's wrath for yet another failure sank in. Reflexively Jaconis twisted an oily lock of his pitch-black hair through the fingers of his right hand.

'If I tell my father I failed to find Namir he might lose faith in my ability to lead the expedition to Hornshir as well,'

Jaconis brooded gloomily.

His long legs seemed hobbled by the meandering gait he chose to make his way home with. The overall effect was that of churning anger and he more stalked his way down the street than anything else.

Jaconis was completely mystified with what he was going to say about Namir's absence to Daffer. No matter what he said, he knew his father would be angry. Slowly Jaconis worked his way through the brief conversation he had with Namir. He hoped to find some small piece of information that he could use to his advantage. After this proved useless, he went over his thoughts about Namir and inspiration struck him.

'I can use Namir's delinquency in my favor.' Jaconis's stride lengthened almost to a run as he started to plan exactly what he was going to say to Daffer.

Jaconis had just closed his hand on the cold brass knob and pushed the solid oak door of the Gathering Place open as he worked through the last few details of his scheme.

As he entered his father's inn, Jaconis was immediately assailed by both the warmth of the fire in the main hall and the wonderful aromas that wafted to him from the kitchen. It took every ounce of his will to resist the urges of his stomach to satiate it with a bite to eat before speaking with his father. The old chestnut boards creaked welcomingly under his feet as he hung his cloak on the wrought iron hook near the door.

He quickly surveyed the large expanse of the main hall to see if his father was by the fire as usual. He was. Jaconis's brow furrowed in anticipation as he scanned the rest of the room eagerly. Thankfully, it was deserted at this early hour.

'All of the serving wenches must be in the kitchen helping the cook with her chores,' he thought somewhat relieved. 'At least something is working in my favor.'

Jaconis strode briskly toward his father with a visible determination. He quickly glanced into the stairwell making sure it was vacant as he passed it to ensure their privacy.

Aves glared at Jaconis as he ran down the street and almost knocked her down. She had narrowly avoided him by stepping into the open doorway of Mistress Clara's clothier at the last minute. Aves swore an oath under her breath as she watched him vanish into the gathering crowds of the morning.

She knew from the way Jaconis's handsome face was clouded and twisted that he was up to something. Knowing Jaconis, it was probably a plot against Namir. His jade green eyes gleamed fiercely, which forced Aves to believe that he was bent upon some form of mischief or another. The fact that he was not skulking about in the shadows like usual and that he did not try to hide his movements only assured her of this.

Aves took a moment to gather her skirts carefully into her hands as she slowly filled her lungs in preparation of the run that awaited her. Aves's crimson hair caught in a light breeze as she turned her hazel eyes upon Jaconis's path. Aves could easily tell that he was heading home to the Gathering Place.

Following him unnoticed proved easily done, although she had to run like the wind to keep up with his long strides. While perusing his fleeing form, Aves realized Jaconis's haste bode ill for Namir.

'This discovery of mine just might be significant enough to win Namir's gratitude and possibly Nurn's as well.'

She let a hopeful sigh escape her lithe form as her feet nimbly led her towards the inn. A few moments later she saw Jaconis hurry through the door as she slowed her step.

Before her stood the third largest building in Ellsted and it was impressive. It stood four stories tall and, unlike any of the other buildings in town, there were no tents or carts leaned up against it.

The outside of the inn was made completely out of heavy beams of oak that created an artistic latticework towards its shingled roof. All of the outer walls were plastered and whitewashed to create an almost otherworldly effect. The Gathering Place was not just an inn located in Ellsted; it was the only inn and it had served as the original meeting hall for the town fathers.

Instead of entering the inn, from either the main door or the kitchen entrance, she turned her steps towards the front left corner. As she neared it, she hastily looked around and once she was sure no one witnessed her actions, she swiftly pried at the boards where they met the granite chimney. After a few brief moments of toil she managed to pry open a niche in the outer wall of the inn.

She squeezed lightly into the little area behind the pealed plaster into a very tight area almost no bigger than she was. Here she could easily see and hear everything that happened in the pub's main hall.

Aves quietly allowed air to seep into her lungs slowly forcing her ample bosom to heave against the confines of her narrow surroundings. She almost cursed as her stomach grumbled quietly at the smell of fresh baked bread that wafted to her from the inn's kitchen.

The heady scent brought back memories of the first time she had discovered this spot, although calling it a spot was almost ludicrous. It really was not much more than a crack in the outer wall of the pub. The boards forming the outer wall had buckled slightly from where a runaway cart collided against it.

The outer boards lay slightly awry after that and bowed away from those forming the pub's inner wall and although the main room on the other side became drafty, it proved to be a useful vent that allowed the aromas from the kitchen to draft out into the streets and gather people in to sample the food. It worked so well, in fact, that Daffer never even bothered repairing it, especially since it was hardly noticeable from outside.

Aves was certain that if Daffer had known Namir and her had used it as a rendezvous point from time to time, mainly as a place they could go to shirk their duties or to spy on the local townsfolk, he would've boarded it up long ago. Thus, it had become their little secret and they guarded it dearly.

Chapter Three:
Hunted

The old man ran down the tunnel blindly plunging into the darkness. The sounds of battle pursued him as he fled deeper into the endless labyrinth of caverns and tunnels. He could tell his pursuers were getting closer and he had run out of ideas. His once white shirt now hung from his frail form caked with filth and sweat. The gashes caused by his escape still felt fresh.

The sting of the open wounds caused him to wince as the slight breeze in the tunnels blew across it. He rounded a corner and, in his haste, collided with another wall. The force of his collision pushed all thoughts of his wounds from his mind.

Winded, he stopped and scrapped the gleaming blade of the sword along the floor of the tunnel causing just enough sparks to illuminate his surroundings. He allowed his eyes to dart from one tunnel to the next as he got his bearings.

'Which path should I choose,' he wondered as he vainly attempted to discern where each path might lead. The absolute darkness had closed in around him again and he recalled the first time he had been in these tunnels. Lost and alone, not like now.

The sounds of steel on stone compelled him back into action. He plunged wildly into the closest tunnel and stifled an exclamation as he collided with another wall unexpectedly. He winced as he pulled his arm away from the jagged wall and felt the sticky warmth of blood seep into his sleeve.

He took a few more moments to feel along the wall to determine which way the tunnel went, then threw himself along it as fast as he could. He felt his tunic and breeches catch and pull as the narrow walls clawed at him. Carefully he held his left arm extended in front of him in an attempt to navigate the narrow tunnel as deftly as possible.

At times, it seemed as if the winding tunnel was trying to hamper his movements. Its sharp corners and abrupt dead ends forced him to retrace his steps too often for his liking.

"He went this way!" The words were more barked than yelled and somehow motivated him to run faster. His pursuers sounded as if they were only a few yards behind him.

"He can't have gotten far, the blood is still fresh!" Another barked

The old man practically fell to his knees in fear as he felt another wall lurch forth from the darkness to block his way. He spun frantically around desperately searching for an opening to duck into, anything that would allow him to avoid detection. They were too close and he knew it.

"There he is!" The darkness before him started to get a red tinge to it.

He closed his eyes and prayed for mercy as he urgently swung the sword at the wall to his left. He felt the now familiar jolt as the sword bit through the stone. The shining blade caused the wall to crumble where it hit and revealed a gaping black hole.

Frantically he dove into its welcoming darkness as he heard his pursuers' bowstrings sing arrows towards him. He heard the arrows meant to take his life as they clattered against the wall he had stood against a few moments before.

He plummeted into the impossible blackness that engulfed him and fought against waves of nausea as he continued to fall. He grasped the sword tightly as he stretched out his limbs. He hoped to grab something to slow himself down.

His fear consumed him as his outstretched hand felt nothing by emptiness. He desperately spun himself around as he scrambled to touch something… anything to no avail. He hit the ground with bone breaking speed and his impact forced all of his fear, and breath, out of him. The darkness wavered and shifted about him as he tried to move.

He was unsure if it was the normal blackness of the cavern or if it was caused by his impact. He did not care which, he was safe for now and that was all that mattered.

"He went through here!" The guttural voice raved overhead somewhere in the darkness above him.

"Then go get him!" This new voice he recognized from his nightmares, Morcant. Although it hurt, he felt his body shudder involuntarily. Morcant's demand was shortly followed by several thuds as a few of his minions threw themselves through the opening and hit the ground lifeless.

"Aras, I know you're in there!" Morcant's deep growl rolled off the cavern walls.

The old man noticed the darkness above him light up from the unnatural red glow emanating from the nassarid's eyes.

"Did you really think your puny elven guards could keep you from me forever?" Morcant's evil raspy laugh peeled off the walls and completely surrounded him.

Aras ignored the pain that racked his body. He groped for the sword he had kept away from the foul beast looming above him in the darkness. Aras feebly pulled himself along the ground as he searched for it. His left arm was mostly unresponsive, as was his right leg.

'To many broken bones,' he thought hurriedly as his frantic search continued.

The familiar twang of bowstrings drifted down to Aras's ears as a new pain blossomed just behind his left shoulder. He stifled a shriek of pain. He could not afford to alert Morcant of his location. More arrows skittered around him as he slowly moved a little further continuing his desperate search.

"I will find you!" Morcant shouted again. "Loose more arrows! I want the floor of the cavern littered with nothing but arrows and blood before I descend to claim my prize!" Morcant's hybrid troops nodded as their doglike hands fired another volley into the cavern's depths.

The tent flap flew open as she strode in with a determined look on her face. Although her golden waist length hair was hastily pulled back into a ponytail, the look in her azure eyes only added to her deadly charm.

"Can't this wait?" The melodic voice bore his impatience heavily in its tone.

"No it cannot." The lilt in her voice, normally soothing, was more abrasive than anything he had ever heard.

"What is so important then, Alequa?" His patience was at an end. Ever since he had agreed to let this healer and her husband stay in their encampment, it had been one issue after another.

"Your guard says that you are not going to send anyone after them… is this true?"

"Aye, it is." He slowly leaned away from the troop reports he had been poring over for the last hours as he said this.

"Why won't you?" Her disgust was as evident as his lack of sleep.

"I have a few reasons. First, I have very limited resources. I explained this to you when you and your husband demanded sanctuary here." He rubbed his temples deliberately in an attempt to control his emotions. When he felt a modicum of restraint, he continued. "Second, he told me not to. Your husband asked me for some men. He specified that he only needed twelve men to escort him to where he needed to go. He also requested that I do nothing if he fails to contact me again." His crimson eyes bore through her azure ones as he stated her husband's request. So you see, hebasii Alequa, I cannot do more on this matter."

"No, Landolin, you mean you won't." She scowled at him as she watched the way his crimson hair fell about his shoulders. "No matter that he saved countless elven lives during the war, or that he is a decorated hero."

Each word stung as Landolin felt her contempt for him

deepen. "What would you have me do?"

"Help him." The way she stated it, everything seemed so simple.

"You would have me go against your husband's wishes?" He was aghast at her daring, yet moved by her sincerity.

"Aye," she looked at him over her shoulder as she turned to face the flap as if to leave. "After all, he told you to do nothing more if he failed to contact you. What of your soldiers, are you to ignore their reticence?"

Landolin stifled a laugh as she said this. 'I may have misread her,' he thought to himself as he watched her leave his tent.

Aras first saw the red glow from Morcant's eyes swirl and dance with the shadows along the length of the blade as he neared it. As his eyes adjusted to the unexpected light, he noticed the sword hilt laying at the base of the cavern's wall with its tip partially embedded in it.

He made his way to the sword slowly. He timed each volley so as not to be hit by any more arrows. The blade was almost in his grasp, as the room grew quiet. Aras slowly reached his hand toward the sword one more time and was pleasantly surprised to feel the sword's hilt slide into his hand.

"I am coming down Aras and I hope to find you waiting. I yearn to kill you in full resistance!" Morcant threatened as he glared into the darkness below.

"Patiun and Faesin guide my hand and protect me," Aras prayed as he pushed the sword deep into crack at the base of the wall.

He pushed as far as he could and hoped no one would see it until it was needed again. The now familiar tug pulled at his consciousness as the sword slid into place, completely hidden from view.

Aras rolled over and waited. Morcant would descend into the cavern soon and it would all be over. A strange calm passed over him as he let the darkness consume him.

Landolin held his breath as they crept toward the encampment. Although there were signs of life, nothing moved within it. He motioned for his men to surround the camp. He only hoped they were approaching the camp as cautiously as he was.

Landolin mentally went over the details of Aras's last report. According to it, Aras and his men used this place as a base of operations while Aras explored the nearby caves.

Landolin looked over the deserted camp again, something was wrong. His gut roiled with anticipation as his senses screamed danger. He waited silently for his men to make their way to the outer edge of the camp. He did not like this feeling, but there was nothing he could do about it.

He slowly drew a black arrow from the small quiver tied to his right thigh. After a few terse moments, he nocked the arrow and gauged the distance to the small bucket in the center of the camp. The sunlight gleamed off the sharp magnesium tip as he loosed it. He held his breath for a few moments as he waited for the arrow to hit its mark.

Suddenly the bucket exploded in flames as the arrow hit it. Landolin instantly sprang to his feet as he pulled a regular arrow from the quiver on his back. He was pleased to see his men react the same as he did. In a matter of moments, the camp was secured.

"Report," Landolin's voice was scarcely louder than a whisper, but it was easily heard throughout the encampment.

"There is a body in the tent at the far end of camp and another two in the tent to your right," his guard replied dutifully.

"Then the total count is six," another guard replied as he motioned to another three tents.

"Are all of them ours?" Landolin already knew the answer before he asked and grim resignation overshadowed any hope that he may have held.

"Aye," his guards replied in unison.

"What killed them?" Landolin asked as he moved to the first tent so he could see the body for himself.

"They were mauled." One of the guards replied coldly.

Landolin motioned to his guard to keep the tent secured as he entered the tent. The body was mangled and laid as if some creature casually tossed it aside. Whatever killed his men was not interested in them as food. "They were murdered in their sleep." Landolin said as he exited the tent.

"Where is the sentry?" Another guard asked in response.

"Which tent had two bodies?" Landolin asked as he studied the silent camp again.

"Over here," the guard that had reported initially replied as he made his way over to it swiftly.

Landolin carefully entered the tent his guard had indicated. He moved through the tent slowly, careful not to disturb anything. He scanned both blood soaked cots and scowled. "I found the sentry." Landolin said coolly. "We need to find Aras… now!"

"Ready the ropes," Morcant instructed to his animalistic minions. He felt a twinge of pride take hold as he saw them jump to his orders.

"The ropes are ready," the hyena-like beast spoke as he bowed deeply. The sound of awe in his voice was unmistakable and it irritated Morcant.

"Good." Morcant growled as he stalked away from the groveling creature. "It is a mistake to worship me." Contempt laced his every word. "Lotevilar is the only being you should worship!"

Before his minions could react, Morcant caught the pathetic creature by its throat and lifted it above him. "She is a jealous goddess and refuses to share Her place with anyone." Morcant stepped precariously close to the hole that Aras had dove through. "Do I make myself clear?"

He scanned his minions' faces to ensure they understood the gravity of his words. Once he was sure of their complete attention he carelessly released his grasp of the beast's throat and watched it plummet into the awaiting blackness.

The beast howled in fear as it fell and Morcant reveled in its cries as it plummeted towards his prey in the utter darkness. A satisfying thump resonated up to them as the beast's body was impaled on a stalagmite.

Morcant's tongue flicked across his wolf-like teeth as he faced his remaining minions, "now I want the rest of you to descend into that pit and make sure Aras is still alive."

The mouth of the cave was a few hundred yards away and the elves covered the distance in a matter of moments. They darted across the lush landscape as if they were shadows. Their senses tingled as they strained to detect any threat as they all but sprinted to the entrance.

Landolin motioned to his personal guard to stay alert as they entered the cavern. He would take no chances this time. Already six of his seasoned soldiers were found dead and there was no sign of what killed them.

The five of them fanned out as they allowed the darkness to envelop them, their keen elven eyes instantly dilated to allow greater visibility than normal. Each of them moved in unison along a deliberate course to hold their v-shaped formation as they explored the main opening.

It was paved and much cooler than what they had been used to. Landolin moved closer to one of the walls and noticed how smoothly the paving stones fit together to form the slope of the wall. He reached out, touched the smooth granite, and marveled at the artistry needed to carve a stone of this size. The last time he had witnessed construction like this was in the dwarven city of Rock Helm and even then, it had amazed him.

"Over here," the statement was more of a whisper carried on the breeze than it was spoken. Landolin turned and saw where the guard had pointed. "The passage branches off here. I think Aras and the others fled this way from their pursuers."

"Why do you say that?" Landolin replied as he made his

way over to his sentry silently.

"One of the creatures that pursued them died while trying to get at them." The elf replied matter-of-factly. He waited until Landolin was closer before he rolled the corpse onto its side.

Thickly matted hair covered the creatures exposed arms and chest. Its build lent itself more to that of an animal than it did a man of any kind. Landolin delicately traced the broken arrow shaft that had buried itself in the creature's throat. It was elven.

He looked at the helm that covered the beast's features and signaled to his men that he was going to remove it. "Let's see the face of our enemy, shall we?"

Landolin carefully reached down to touch the side of the rugged looking helmet. As he did so, his men set up a hasty defensive perimeter to ensure that there were no more unplanned surprises.

Landolin carefully unfastened the beast's chinstrap and slowly tugged the helmet off of the hyena-like face that lay beneath it. His closest guards gaped at the beast in awe and fear as a thin wisp of smoke appeared from the top of the furry forehead. Within moments, flames were visibly licking across the things features.

"What's happening?" Landolin shouted as he dropped the helmet and attempted to smother the flames with his gauntleted hands in vain.

The helmet hit the ground with a dull thud and rolled slowly towards the feet of the beast. As the helmet rolled across the floor, a trail of clear smoldering liquid followed in its wake. Almost instantly small plumes of flames sprung up along the flagstones where the trail of liquid had been.

The guard at the tail end noticed the trail of flames and sprang into action. He covered the distance between himself and Landolin in a few steady strides. He tucked his shoulder and braced himself as he hit Landolin's side with enough force to send both men sprawling across the floor.

He felt his full weight as it impacted the wall through his

right shoulder and screamed, "Get down!"

He heard the rest of the guards as they threw themselves to the ground in unison, almost as if planned. Thankfully, their training had taught them to react to any command shouted by their compatriots for just this reason.

The guard looked down at Landolin's face and instantly hated himself for causing the contorted look of rage that consumed it. He held his general tightly as he felt the shockwave hit them. The initial blast was followed closely by a second wave comprised mostly of blood and gore as the beast exploded.

"How did you know?" Landolin asked shakily after his guard released him.

"During the war, my family was killed by a nassarid hunting party." The soldier recounted emotionlessly. "When I was finally able to catch the first of them I ripped its helm off before killing it. It exploded into a ball of fire before I could cut its head off for the crimes it committed." He locked his gaze with Landolin as he continued, "When I saw the flames on the floor I had to act. It's odd that this one had flames first, but I'm glad for it."

Landolin looked at his soldier approvingly as he stated, "very well. We shall proceed with more caution. I want you in the lead with me. It seems you have more experience with these nassarid than I."

Landolin grasped his soldier's arm as he said this and turned to look over what was left of the creature.

'I wonder who Aras has angered to get a nassarid hunting party sent after him,' Landolin's thoughts raced as he looked over the grizzly remains.

Memories of his own encounter with a nassarid played before his mind's eye unbidden. 'If these nassarid are anything like Skara, then I fear for Aras and my men.' He thought as he quickly banished the memories.

Morcant watched as the last of his followers slipped into

the darkness and down the ropes. He could barely contain his excitement. 'Soon Aras, you will be mine.' Morcant thought anxiously as he looped his own rope through the metal ring his minions had fastened to the wall.

He stared at the ring absently as he tied his rope tightly to it. "They must be at the bottom already," Morcant muttered as he saw the ring fall slackly.

"No... they are not." The voice whispered from the darkness behind him. "They are dead." The finality in the tone sent chills down Morcant's spine.

Morcant spun to face the darkness as he crouched in anticipation of a blow that never arrived. "Who are you?" Morcant growled.

"You know who I am," The reply was almost instant and its tone held an air of menace that Morcant usually gave to others. "I am the reason your minions burst into flame when they are killed."

"Shadow walker," Morcant snarled.

"Yes, come into my realm... if you dare." The shadow walker's tone mocked Morcant as he stared into the darkness angrily.

"This doesn't concern you!" Morcant snarled at the darkness like the wolf he was.

"It does. I have one message for you. Leave Aras alone or face my wrath."

"I'm not afraid of you." Morcant lied.

"You are." The shadow walker all but laughed as he said this. "But that is of no matter. They come. You are too late."

"Who?" Morcant took a deep breath and filled his nose with all of the surrounding scents. "Damn you shadow walker!" Morcant exclaimed as he caught the scent of elven armor heading toward him. The shadow walker's laugh pursued Morcant as he deftly severed his rope and bolted down the corridor.

Aras lay silent and still in the darkness for hours trying to stifle the pain that wracked his body from his wounds. His head swam and he was certain that every passing moment would be his last. The scraping sound of metal against stone confirmed his worst fears and forced a chill down his spine painfully.

He was going to die; he just hoped it would be swift. More time slipped away as the sounds of steel shod boots hovered ever closer to his soon to be corpse. Aras closed his eyes and mouthed a prayer silently.

"You are safe, Aras," the voice was less than a whisper and seemed to emanate the darkness all around him.

"Who are you?" Aras asked as he peered into the darkness that surrounded him. The voice seemed hauntingly familiar to his pain wracked brain.

"He's over here!" The reply that echoed from a hallway somewhere to his left forced Aras into renewed silence.

"A friend... one that you helped in the past and now returns the favor," the voice replied again softer than it had been. "We are now even."

"What of Morcant and his troops?" Aras asked as the sounds of metal on stone erupted into the cavern in which he lay.

"Morcant fled and there is no sign of his nassarid." The melodic reply came from the mouth of the cavern to Aras' left causing him to start again.

"Who's there?" Aras's voice cracked as he tried to develop an air of authority and failed.

"Landolin, and as you know, the commander of the elven royal guard and general of the elven war contingent lent to Hornshir," the melodic voice replied succinctly. "Alequa summoned us to your aid, Aras. I am just glad we made it here before Morcant had a chance to finish you."

"As am I," Aras responded. "Any chance I can get a hand up, or are you and I all that are here?"

"Bring a torch and a few hands." Landolin ordered to his guard in response to Aras' subtle hint.

Elven arrows clattered past Morcant's ear as he darted down a side tunnel. His steel shod paws sprayed sparks as he slid across the flagstones and into a wall. Instinctively he pushed off and continued his mad flight through the cavernous tunnels.

Another volley of arrows clattered against the walls around him as he changed his path again and dove into the awaiting darkness of another tunnel. He cursed under his breath as he yanked a few arrows out of his cloak. Morcant frantically searched the cistern he was forced into for any means of escape.

'There's my exit,' he thought to himself as he threw himself at another wall and deftly scurried up it toward the faint glint of light emanating from the ceiling. Morcant had just barely gasped a handhold on the ceiling as the sounds of Landolin's guards forced him to freeze precariously.

An eternity seemed to pass as he waited for them to leave. Only the briefest whispered noises from their armor allowed him to realize that they had not left. He clung impossibly stuck halfway between the wall and the ceiling tenuously as the elven sentries searched below him.

The elves searched meticulously in complete silence only occasionally trading glances to relay their findings. Almost spontaneously, the elves left and continued their search further down the tunnel.

Morcant forced himself to wait a few more moments before he allowed himself to let down his guard enough to continue his ascent. He forced himself to focus only on getting out of the cavern, instead of allowing his mind to dwell on new plans to get Aras and his accursed sword.

Several hours passed as Morcant squeezed his way through the precarious cracks that promised freedom. After several agonizing hours, he finally clawed his way to the surface and took his first breath free from the dirt and stale air of the caverns.

"THINK YOU ARE SAFE? THINK AGAIN." The voice was a ragged whisper that seemed to fill the air around Morcant.

Morcant spun around and desperately searched his surroundings as he turned in place slowly. "Where are you shadow walker?" He growled as the question slipped passed his barred teeth.

A whispered laugh filled the air all around Morcant as he replied, "I AM EVERYWHERE."

"That isn't true and we both know it. Save your parlor tricks for the weak and show yourself!" Agitated, Morcant stopped circling as he scanned the open clearing all around him for some clue of the shadow walker's location.

With a deft flick of his wrist, the shadow walker cut the medallion free from Morcant's neck as he materialized behind him. "IS THIS PROOF ENOUGH?" He asked as he swiftly brought his dagger back around to Morcant's neck and nestled its tip against the beast's jugular.

"Aye," Morcant grunted.

"GOOD," the shadow walker replied, "NOW LISTEN CLOSELY. I DON'T WANT TO KILL, NOT YET, THAT IS UNLESS YOU FORCE MY HAND."

"What do you want then?" Morcant all but spat as he voiced his thoughts.

"LEAVE ARAS ALONE," the shadow walker stated bluntly. "IT WOULD ALSO BE WISE IF YOU LEFT THIS PLACE AND RETURN TO YOUR MISTRESS." He waited for Morcant to respond. "NOD ONCE IF YOU AGREE TO THESE TERMS."

"And if I don't," Morcant snarled.

"I KILL YOU NOW AND SEND MY REGRETS TO YOUR MISTRESS." He waited as Morcant contemplated his response. "WELL?" The impatience in his voice was unmistakable. Morcant obliged the shadow walker's raising impatience by nodding.

Alequa leaned forward and placed her hand on her husband's chest as she closed her eyes. To her dismay, nothing happened. A look of fear and confusion creased her lovely face.

Aras smiled up at her with a knowing smile as he took in her beautiful features. The light from the torches danced through her golden hair and forced him to remember the day he first laid eyes on her. She had seemed as much an angel to him then as she did now.

"My love," Aras sighed, "I am past even Tayant's skillful aid." A tear crept into the corner of his eye as he said this. "My end approaches faster than we thought. Have we summoned the boy?"

"But there may be something my order can do for you… " Alequa interrupted, but was immediately cut off by a cough that racked Aras's frail frame.

A sad look filled his grey eyes unbidden as he responded once he was able to, "We both know I won't survive the trip to your temple in Strait." The tenor of his voice echoed and resonated against the walls of the tunnel in a way that eased her fears. "Perhaps if Saril, or one of his students, were here it would be different. I fear I am past the confines and tenets of magic. My body can't take the stress of it any longer." More blood flecked his lips as he stated this. It was the finality in his voice that ended any further discussion about his fate.

"Let us at least get you back to our camp," Landolin interjected as he rejoined the couple. "Once we get you safe, we can see about finding where we are with the boy you spoke of." Landolin added trying to change the topic.

"Agreed," Aras and Alequa responded in unison. "But I have a favor to ask. Please send someone to my manor in Hornshir, I need to have a letter delivered to an old friend and there is an artifact in my study that will allow me to do that."

"I will do it," One of Landolin's guards responded. Her soft voice almost betrayed her emotions.

"Very well Haradine, but be quick." Landolin replied as

the motioned for his men to assist Aras in rising to feet again.

Aras watched as Haradine walked off and said a silent prayer for his daughter as she set out to do his bidding.

Chapter Four: Plots

The burly old man slouched in his favorite padded leather chair next to the large granite fireplace. His dirty brown hair, smattered with a little bit of grey that could have as easily been from soot as it could have been from age, was slicked back with oil and pulled into a long curly queue falling halfway down his back.

Although it was early, some strands of his thinning hair had managed to pull themselves free and fell across his face leaving greasy tracks past his dull brown eyes. His chiseled features were frozen in a look that spoke of a hard life and an undying rage. The air around Daffer smelled of stale ale and his clothes, though clean, were as wrinkled as if he had toiled all day in them. He stretched his meaty hands open and slowly curled them into ham-sized fists a few times, as his son approached him.

"What took you?" Daffer asked abruptly. His voice was gruff through years of misuse and had always reminded Jaconis of steel being dragged through gravel.

"You sent me to find Namir, father, and I found him," Jaconis answered dutifully.

"So why didn't you return sooner… and where is Namir if you found him?" Daffer's rage grew visibly as he grilled Jaconis. Daffer's haggard face reddened to a light scarlet and his muscles corded slightly.

"He eluded me, father." Jaconis mumbled

"He what?" Daffer raised himself to his feet and closed the distance between them in one fluid motion. They were so close that Jaconis could feel Daffer's hot ale-filled breath upon his face. Daffer's thinning grey brown hair matted to his scalp as sweat started to bead across his brow with this new exertion.

"I lost him." Jaconis admitted slowly as he stepped back a pace from Daffer trying to stay out of his powerful reach. "Please do not strike me again, father. I found him greeting the morning on his favorite hill just outside of town."

Daffer was irritated and Jaconis could feel it. If he could play his father's wrath right, Jaconis knew he could get Namir thrown into the cellar during the council meeting. Then the town fathers would be obliged to send him instead of Namir.

"I made him aware of my presence as soon as he came down and for some reason it upset him that I was there. Like usual, I set aside any ill will I have for him and told him all that you asked me to." To this Daffer snorted derisively. "Then, I followed him to the market where he gave me the slip."

"Did you think of checking Tipin's Smithy, or is that too much for my son to think of?" Daffer asked gruffly as he started to settle back into his brown leather chair.

"No father," Jaconis retorted and then shied away from Daffer even farther for good measure, "I checked there." His sarcasm escaped him for a moment before he could hold it in check and continued. "In fact, I went straight there as soon as I lost sight of him. I even thought that I saw him enter the smithy, so I followed." He ignored the look of surprise that dawned on Daffer's age worn face. "I was so intent on tracking him; I didn't notice Nurn handling an axe head. Somehow it managed to wrest itself free from his burly clutches and took my legs out from under me… " he was interrupted again, this time by his father's raucous laughter. The half wheeze, half cough sent shivers down Jaconis' spine.

"I am sorry, son… continue." Daffer bellowed hysterically, tears filling his dull brown eyes and running down his cheek as he collapsed deeper into his chair.

"When I regained myself," Jaconis continued a little disconcerted, "Tipin was above me demanding to know what had happened."

"Did the wretch come clean and tell Tipin of his treachery?" Daffer blurted out, once again interrupting Jaconis' well-planned speech.

"No father, he didn't." Jaconis continued. "Besides, I told Tipin that it was my fault."

"By Bela's ungarnered tit! Why would you do that?" Daffer cursed. He lunged from his chair near the hearth at Jaconis's chest and almost caught him.

Moving deftly out of his father's reach again, Jaconis said in soothing tones, "I was merely looking out for your trade agreements with Tipin. If I were to bring charges, whether false or otherwise, against Nurn, surely the Gathering Place would be hindered in providing our services. I dared not risk our welfare over someone as vile as Namir." Jaconis then added, as if by afterthought, "I hope I did well."

"Aye," Daffer conceded. His temper cooled slowly as he paced around the room and then stalked back to his favorite chair near the fire and sat down.

Jaconis allowed his father a few moments to calm himself before he continued, "After that I came straight home, though I looked for Namir the whole way." He hung his head in mock shame as he baited his father, "I admit to failing my task father, I do not ask for mercy. I just ask that you be fair in my punishment."

"I see," Daffer exuded at length. A grim and brooding mood settled upon his age toughened features.

Inwardly Jaconis grinned; things were proceeding almost as he had hoped. In his most swaying tone, he added. "I feel I must mention something else, father."

"Then mention it and be quick about it!" Daffer snapped his patience at an end.

"It's about Namir's plan to gather supplies and spread our interests in Hornshir." Jaconis started and then paused trying to gage his father's reaction to his words. "Please rethink your approval of letting him lead it. I believe his actions today only prove his inadequacy as a leader further and they show how undependable he really is." Jaconis pressed delicately realizing his father's mood was not quite right for this ploy.

"Oh? And who would you send to lead it then?" Daffer demanded as he locked Jaconis with a fiery glare.

"Myself. I would not forget my duties in this, unlike my cousin. Namir has proved repeatedly how undependable he is. I yearn for travel."

Jaconis realized almost too late that he was defeating himself by declaring his desires so boldly. He veered back to the main points of his argument as he tried to salvage some footing.

"This trip would allow me to build new alliances for our inn as well, father. Who better to spread the news of our upcoming fair and of our cook's many talents?" He waited on Daffer's response with baited breath.

"We will see." Daffer sat with his chin cradled in his hand; a scowl creased his forehead giving him the semblance of being in great pain.

Every time Daffer thought, he would sit grimacing and scowling, sometimes for hours on end. He literally had to force thoughts and concepts around in his head by sheer strength of will.

"The problem I have with this is," Daffer's thoughts still clouded his face as he voiced them, "that I would be deprived of your skills and services while you were away. Another reason I am against this is for your safety. While you are gone how am I to know if you still live?" He queried tenuously exploring his own thoughts on the matter fully.

"What if Namir plotted to kill you. Where would I be left then?" His brown eyes bored holes through Jaconis and into his very soul. "I'll tell you where, without a son and short a servant to boot." A look of disgust flitted across Daffer's face as he continued. "I would be forced to hire someone to perform both Namir's chores and your own. Now that is not acceptable to me."

His gravelly voice gained a harder edge to it the longer he spoke. "So we will see, Jaconis. We will see if any other options arise before the council finally decides on the matter. If I decide that you are to remain here, then here you will stay. Do you understand me, boy?" Daffer defied him to speak out against his decision.

Instead, Jaconis bowed his head and replied, "Aye father," as he left the room quietly. Jaconis ghosted into the kitchen and grabbed a handful of rolls as he made his way out to the stables to see to the animals and the rest of his chores.

'The town fathers are going to decide today if Namir's proposition was to be allowed,' He mused dourly. 'Hopefully my father isn't too stupid to see the logic that I have placed before him.' Jaconis immersed himself in his chores as completely as he could in order to quell his thoughts and emotions. All he could do now was to wait and see if his seeds of reason would ripen or not.

A light perspiration broke upon Aves's brow and matted her deep red hair against her scalp. She labored to breathe as silently as she could. She hoped she would not be noticed.

She was so intent on being unheard that she almost missed Jaconis's plot against Namir. She cursed her stupidity silently and paid extra attention to Jaconis's statements in order to commit them to memory as the conversation unfolded.

Her eyes widened when she heard the crux of Jaconis's argument and Daffer's reply to it. A cold chill ran down her spine as she recalled that the council was supposed to meet this evening about this very issue. Aves felt her stomach drop as she realized the plot's ramifications.

'If Jaconis succeeds, all that we have worked for will have been for naught.' Her thoughts buzzed through her mind rapidly.

Jaconis's hasty movement brought her attention once again to the activities in the room. He was closer to her than normal… almost as if he knew that she was there. She held her breath and willed her heart to be silent as she waited for Jaconis to move away from her position.

An eternity passed, it seemed as if she was the source of every noise in the world and it drove her crazy. Finally, Aves heard Daffer's breath deepen as slumber overtook him. When she looked through the cracked timbers in front of her again, Jaconis had left the great hall and was no longer visible. Still she waited. A familiar pit formed in her stomach, warning her of trouble.

Movement, ever so slight, she felt it more than heard it. Someone was outside of her alcove, waiting. The hovel steadily grew warmer as the boards around her soaked in the sun's rays. Her senses became more attuned to the steady creaking of the inn as she tried to probe her surroundings without moving. Nothing. She was sure of it.

She breathed a light sigh of relief as she felt the person leave. Aves waited a few more minutes before she emerged from the hiding place and made her way home. 'I have to stop his schemes.' Aves thought desperately.

Mist rose from her exposed flesh as she stepped out into the open air of the market. Her thin chemise clung to her like a second skin. Its white expanse darkened to a rosy sheen where it lay flush against her skin, pulled tightly across her body and revealed every curve of her supple and athletic build.

Her skirt, light and flowing, clung to her as she ran through the market. The light red hue of her skirt became translucent as it drank in her sweat and became more and more pliable.

Aves was a vision of ardor, wild and free, and her beauty forced those in her wake to stop working and stare as she passed. Only a fortunate few felt her glistening skin brush against theirs as she nimbly slipped through the throng of townsfolk milling about in the streets.

Laughter filled the air as Namir listened to all of the

information Halin had gathered. "See, it's just as I said. We are free to go to the council. Now go and put on your best garments," Namir advised mirthfully, "I don't want anyone doubting why I chose you to accompany me on this trip." He knew that Halin needed no instruction in his attire, but he saw no harm in giving it.

Halin, had somehow managed to look dejected and excited at the same time. He blushed at Namir's words and its rosy hue spilled from his face down onto his chest. "… I just wish someone would have consulted me when these plans were made. Not that I mind going, in fact I'm really looking forward to it. It's just polite to ask a person first."

"Don't fuss," Nurn admonished as he walked up to the pair. "Namir selected you because he knows that you'll be a great help. However, if you keep acting like this, you may get left behind." Although Nurn tried to conceal his smile, it crept out.

'One day my brother will outgrow this habit of constant complaint; at least I hope he does.'

Pulling on his best tunic Nurn asked Namir, "How do you plan on getting to the Council Hall? I know you want to avoid Jaconis and Daffer, which is why we have to buy you new clothes, but getting from the market to the council hall will prove challenging, even for you."

"Why, my dear Nurn, we'll fly of course," Namir retorted winking behind Halin's back so that only Nurn saw his meaning.

As he nearly dropped his dagger, Halin exclaimed, "How… ? How do you intend on doing that?" The look on his face mirrored his surprised tone.

Following Namir's glance to the roof of the smithy Nurn said, "Through nimbleness, skill and luck. Should any of those prove not to be enough then maybe a miracle or two will be needed." Nurn commented sincerely as he nodded his approval to Namir.

Confusion and bewilderment played across Halin's features for several long moments. Finally, after Namir could no longer keep a hold of his composure, he showed Halin the secret. He carefully pointed to the roof of Tipin's Smithy and the latticework of boards and ropes adjoining the other buildings.

Halin followed Namir's gesture with his eyes and saw that the Council Hall could be accessed easily by traveling along Ellsted's rooftops instead of its streets. Halin giggled as he realized Namir's cunning. Surely, Jaconis and Daffer would never expect them to travel this route.

"All I need now is for you to go and get me some more appropriate clothes, Halin." Namir stated as he turned to look at Halin squarely in the eyes.

This snapped Halin out of his thoughts and he asked, "why me? I mean, why do you want me to go into the marketplace?"

"Because neither Jaconis nor Daffer will be looking for you," Nurn replied. "Are you afraid that we would put you in danger my dear brother?"

"No, I guess not." Halin sighed deeply. 'One of these days I'll understand why they like to pick on me,' Halin thought briefly as he wandered out of the smithy and into the marketplace.

Halin decided to buy Namir garments made of the finest cloth, at least the finest he could afford. 'I need to get money from Namir before I go on another errand for him,' Halin reminded himself.

He concluded that Namir and Nurn sent him to the market to get Namir's clothing since he was a better judge of fashion than they were. Halin laughed to himself about Nurn's choice of clothing, a nice white tunic with a light red belt to hold the tunic down and to keep his brown pants up.

'Nurn's taste may be fine for going to the market in, but to the council? Never.' He mused. He decided that Namir needed to be dressed tastefully in order to gain the proper respect and approval he needed, something more like Halin's own clothing.

Halin prided himself on his sky blue silk tunic belted across by a golden sash holding his deep gray pants in place.

He was more proud of his vest, which matched his pants perfectly.

'Yes, Namir definitely needs something as extravagant as my own clothing, if not a touch better.' He thought. 'Plus, if I select anything of lesser quality, someone might get suspicious. Besides, knowing Jaconis, he will pay people to look for anything out of the ordinary.'

Deciding to play it safe, Halin meandered through the crowded shops in earnest. Finally deciding on a gray silk tunic with a silver sash accompanied by a black pair of pants, he chose to buy a pair of black boots with silver trim to match the pants and accent the sash. Feeling confident with his choices, Halin paid and left the shop making his way back to the smithy.

Halin had just barely left the shop when he heard the commotion. By time he turned, he saw the most wondrous sight he had ever seen. Halin's breath caught in his throat as he saw Aves running down the street towards him. The sight of her running and the way the light played along her exposed skin held Halin enraptured where he stood.

He was unable to move or even think as she drew closer. Halin knew she was going to run into him, but he felt too weak to move out of her way. It was as if his bones had turned to stone and his muscles into jelly, so Halin just stood there with his mouth dangling open as Aves bore down upon him.

In order to avoid him, Aves was forced to pull Halin close to her as she passed. He felt her body press against his and her hands clung to his vest desperately as she pulled him into her. His legs buckled as she exhaled across his ear and onto his neck.

It only lasted a heartbeat, but Halin felt his desire rise and was surprised by his body's reaction to her. Before Halin's muddled and youthful mind could react, Aves was gone and he was left standing wonton and confused.

Gaining the sanctity of her home Aves darted to her

chambers shedding off her damp clothes as she went.   She hurriedly pulled the chord near her door as she closed it, leaving the sweat soaked garments strewn across the hallway and down the stairs.   Her maid entered moments later with a pitcher full of hot water and another of cold anticipating Aves's needs.

"Good." Aves nodded at the sight of the water.   "Please hurry, I must speak with my father before he leaves for council."

Aves stepped into her silver bathtub as her maid, Hessa, poured cold water over her feet.   Once it was up to Aves's ankles, she added the hot water slowly.   Hessa mixed the remaining water together as Aves lowered herself into the tub.

"Is the temperature right?"   Hessa asked as her amber hair fell across her face.

Giggling Aves replied, "Yes.   It is perfect, as always.   I need to look presentable today, more so than usual.   Can you please fetch my salts and oils?"   Aves loved how Hessa seemed to know exactly what she needed.   "Oh… do you know if my father has left yet?"   She asked before Hessa could leave the room.

Hessa turned, stopping at the door, and answered, "Yes I will get them, milady.   As for your father, I don't know.   I will ask on my way to gather your bath supplies.   I am sorry for forgetting them."   As an afterthought Hessa added over her shoulder as she left the room, "I am also sorry that I did not have time to collect your clothing either."

"Hessa, it's alright.   I have told you this before," Aves shook her head as her maid bowed deeply.   "You are the only one I can talk to… I mean really talk to.   Please don't fuss about a few chores.   In fact, leave my clothes where they are." Seeing a shocked look cross Hessa's face she added, "I'll take the blame.   Just return with word of my father and with my bath supplies… oh… and my finest dress," Aves paused eyeing Hessa, "nay, my two finest.   I think we have similar builds, though you may have a little more muscle than me."

At the thought of dirtying Aves's dress, Hessa blushed and

commented, "I couldn't, milady. Look at me… I'm filthy from cleaning all morning. Besides it wouldn't be right… "

Interrupting her, Aves remarked. "Please do as I ask. We will worry about your cleanliness and what is right and wrong when you return." With that, Aves looked away from Hessa and waited until she left the room.

Seeing this signal, Hessa hurried off. She was bewildered. 'Why would Aves ask me to wear one of her dresses?' she puzzled. Deciding that she could not understand her mistress's purpose, she hurried to perform her task. She returned with news of Aves's father, the bath supplies, and Aves's dresses. Hessa entered the room and crossed it quickly. She had also brought more hot water just in case it was needed.

As Hessa entered, the room Aves saw the water pitcher and smiled at Hessa's foresight. Looking deeply into Hessa's hazel eyes, Aves motioned her to come nearer. Hessa dutifully obeyed and started to kneel at the side of the tub. As soon as she was within reach, Aves grabbed Hessa's chemise and pulled it off. Hessa stood shocked as Aves peeled the rest of her clothes from her slender body revealing her well-muscled and attractive figure.

"Grab the water and get in here." Aves giggling playfully, urging Hessa by tugging lightly on her arms. "It just won't do to have you filthy today," she said as a mischievous grin flitted across her beguiling features. Their conversation, like their bath, was a quick one.

Halin slowly made his way back to the smithy carrying Namir's clothing. When Namir saw him approach he was instantly worried. Halin walked like a condemned man being led to the hangman's noose. His back was slumped and he meandered across the street as if he were lost. Nurn reached him before Namir could even stand, practically flying to his side.

"Are you all right little brother?" Nurn's concern boomed across the courtyard.

Halin nodded listlessly. As Namir walked up to him, Halin held out the package he was carrying silently. This worried Namir even more. Before Namir could ask what was wrong, however, Nurn shook Halin gently.

"Are you all right? What's wrong?" Dread edged its way into Nurn's powerful voice as he looked at Halin's face hoping to read some ailment there.

With a deep sigh, Halin finally responded. "I'm fine Nurn. There is nothing wrong." Halin miserably failed both his halfhearted attempt to free himself from his brother's strong grasp and at convincing them that nothing was wrong.

"Then why are you so downcast and moving like you are unsure of your surroundings?" Worry still filled Nurn's dark eyes as he struggled against the desire to hold Halin close.

"I… I saw Aves." Halin shook slightly as if cold. The words came haltingly from his lips as if they were wrenched from his very soul.

"Is that all?" Namir laughed as the words tumbled out of his mouth.

"Yes… and… sh… she touched me. She actually touched me. She was a vision… an angel." Halin twitched again, "I felt her breath in my ear… and her breasts… " Another sigh escaped him as he quivered and fell against a wall, twisted ever so slightly so that his back hit the wall first for support. "I was truly in heaven, I'm sure of it."

"What, did she have her way with you in the market in front of everyone?" Namir jested.

Feeling his anger rise, Nurn blurted, "I am sure Halin meant no offense, Namir." Namir's sarcasm finally registered in Nurn's mind as he finished his sentence. Feeling abashed he turned to Halin scowling as he added, "Please hold your tongue about Aves in the future."

Confused, Halin agreed. His blush still coloring his cheeks a deep crimson. "Honestly Namir, I meant no ill." Halin clamored. "It's just that she looked so divine when I saw her. The way she flowed through the market and around me was astonishing. I know she was in a hurry to get somewhere, but I couldn't move… I couldn't do anything but notice her." Dropping to a knee in front of Namir he added, "please accept my apology if I offended you."

Still chuckling Namir attested, "You haven't offended me, and please let's end this discussion before it distracts us further from our tasks."   Directing his next comment more to Nurn than Halin he added slyly, "I'm sure that whatever transpired between you and Aves was innocent, but time is wasting and we should go."

"I still don't understand why you want me to go with you." Hessa confided as Aves braided her long amber locks.

Hessa fussed with the dress closest to her while they talked. The dress was beautiful. Hessa was never allowed to wear anything like this. It was a deep burgundy red, made of velvet with pearls sewn into it to attract attention to the most suggestive areas of a woman's figure. She longed to feel the velvety sensation of the skirts and dreaded it at the same time.

"What if I stumble… or trip… or destroy your dress somehow? Don't you care about such things?"

Giggling at Hessa's comments, Aves finished the braid and wound it around Hessa's head in the same pattern as her own.

"No. I'm not afraid of you destroying my dress, although that one is my favorite… and the most expensive one I have… " She let her voice trail off and smiled as Hessa's face paled.

Aves gently traced her hands down Hessa's cheeks and let them rest on her shoulders before pulling the worried girl into her arms to reassure her, "If I was worried about it, I wouldn't let you wear it. Now, we must get ready. I really do need to speak with my dad before the council meeting today. I'm sorry for taunting you… it's just so easy."

Reaching up, Hessa pulled Aves's arm down across her and turned. "Thank you for caring for me." A tear rolled down Hessa's face and pooled between them.

"Though I don't fully understand why you need me to

wear your dress or why you are treating me as if you were my maid. Please tell me the reason for this charade." Hessa pulled slightly away from Aves and twisted her body so they sat facing each other.

"I fear for our safety." Looking deeply into Hessa's luxurious hazel eyes, Aves felt almost as if she stared into a mirror. Especially since Hessa sat across from her and wore the same style of braids as she did. Aves could easily imagine they were sisters, if not twins, there were only a few visible differences between them… and those were slight. Just a few small things like the color of their hair and the slight difference between their skin tone and build.

"I would give my life for you." Hessa's voice fell from her lips like a soft rain. "I just need to know how."

"I am afraid… " a sigh escaped Aves's lips as she pressed on. "Jaconis is plotting against Namir and if he succeeds everything Namir and I have planned during these past few months will have been for nothing." Aves trembled as she thought about all that time spent wasted so easily.

Hessa pulled Aves into a hug to calm her fears as they spoke. "What can I do to stop this plot?"

"My sweet Hessa, I don't question your loyalty. I just fear for what I must ask you to do." Aves paused as she waited for Hessa to realize the importance of her words before she continued. "I need you to be me, or at least to be enough like me so that anyone looking for me might be fooled. Jaconis will try to divert me from talking to my father. I know how he thinks. He wants to discredit and dishonor Namir in front of the council. Namir is my friend, although I think that many people believe there is more between us than friendship. Our tasks, both his and mine, need to be accomplished. The problem is that Jaconis wants to prevent both of them out of spite. I can't let him do this slight to Namir and I won't!" Aves declared.

"Why is this so important? Why must Namir perform this duty?" Hessa interrupted, immediately thinking better of her words.

Aves smiled slightly and continued, "Because his main goal isn't to raise support for the fair or even to bring supplies back to Ellsted, it's to go home. This is his only chance to learn anything about his parents, a chance Daffer has tried to stop for ten years. Jaconis wants to further his father's schemes by forcing Namir to stay in Ellsted as a slave to the inn."

Hessa saw the pleading look in Aves's eyes as she interrupted. "I ask again, milady, how can I help?" Getting flustered she continued. "Do you want me to just wander around pretending to be you until someone tries to divert me? How will this help… what will you do while I'm masquerading as you?"

Shaking her head Aves explained, "What you'll do is wear my dress… that one," Aves pointed at the burgundy dress Hessa was eyeing while her hair was being braided, "and exit the house before I do. Then I will slip out after you leave. Once I feel it is safe, I will go to council hall as fast as I can along the safest route possible." She took a hold of Hessa's shoulders again, she continued. "I need you to draw away any and all of Jaconis's goons. I don't care how you do it, just do it safely."

Hessa nodded in agreement. She quickly donned the burgundy gown that lay draped over the nearest stool. Aves watched Hessa for a moment as she dressed then did the same, pulling on a deep blue dress speckled with glass beads and silver trim. She was amazed at how ravishing Hessa looked in the gown and wondered if Hessa knew it. 'Hessa may need all of her charms to lead away Jaconis's goons,' she thought despairingly as she dismissed the idea.

CHAPTER FIVE: PATTERNS

Hessa hurried through the streets, making her way to the Council Hall. She had already managed to out maneuver two of Jaconis's minions. She laughed as she darted down the lane, getting closer to her destination with every step. She could not believe how stupid Jaconis's goons were.

She giggled as she thought about the first one. Though he was nice to look at, he was simple. He started tailing her as she left Aves's house. Knowing all Aves needed her to do was to lead him away from the main road; she decided to try a hunch.

Hessa figured he would follow her no matter where she led him if he believed her to be Aves… and she was right. After Hessa lead him away from the main road, she turned down an alley and led him into it. She hurried through the back door of the bathhouse and hastily informed the serving girl of her situation.

She exited the main door of the bathhouse back into the main market place before the man following her had fully entered it. Unfortunately for her stalker, Hessa had arranged to have him detained and knowing her friend he would be facing some serious charges as well, that is if he made it out of the bathhouse.

The second one was not as easy. Bile rose into her throat as her ordeal came flooding back to her mind as she tried to stop the recollection. 'The bastard had actually dared to touch me!' Her thoughts were full of hatred and rage.

She remembered the wave of anticipation that raced through her as she exited the bathhouse. The exhilaration of the chase still lay fresh in her bosom. She had just stepped out into the market, a few yards from the bathhouse, when it happened. Hessa remembered cautiously looking for any of Jaconis's scum as she made her way through the stalls of goods and the hawking vendors.

The horror of being grabbed from behind and forced into a wall face first drove its way into her consciousness painfully. She felt the man's arms wrap around her tightly as he pressed himself against her back, pinning her against the wall of the alley helplessly. He breathed into her ear as he freed one of his grimy hands.

He scoffed as she begged him to let her go. She remembered him saying, "Now… now Aves, if I let you go 'e would skin me alive. Now be a dear and quit your squirmin'. I promise I won't hurt you if you cooperate. Not to a young lady like yourself. Now be a dear an' tell me where you are hidin' your coins!"

His gruff voice boasted of recent ale and smelled heavily of mutton. She felt his hand pat around her waist and move up toward her bosom. She bit back a scream as he squeezed her rump with his other hand.

She tried to shrink away from him somehow. Her thoughts flew through her head at a maddening speed when it happened. His grip abruptly went lax and he slid onto the ground with a dull thump.

She stood still. She leaned against the wall for support a little dazed and too afraid to turn. 'What if he is just trying to get me to turn around?'

She remembered thinking. Her fear of exposing that she was not Aves had been all but forgotten. The moments marched painfully by, each one taking longer and longer to pass. She could not stop herself from trembling. Hessa finally steeled herself and turned to face her tormentor. Unfortunately as she was about to turn, someone gently touched her shoulder.

Hessa screamed.

It took Hessa a few moments to realize that no one was restraining her. Her scream faded quickly amongst the fading crowds lining the street, none of which seemed to have heard her cry out. Hessa looked back to the rest of the ally and her eyes met a very grisly scene.

Her attacker lay there, sprawled on the ground with his skull split in half. Another man stood a few paces away in the shadows of the two buildings. When he noticed Hessa's attention, he nodded and fled deeper into the darkness of the alley. All she could see was his ebony hair and pale white skin before he sped off. She stood there and wondered who he was and why she could not remember ever seeing anyone like him before.

Hessa shook her head from side to side, as she settled the thoughts that spun through her head madly. She had to continue. If she quit now, Aves might fall victim to the next assault. Hessa looked about her quickly and saw the Council Hall looming ahead of her in the distance. Hessa slipped out of the alley just in time to see Aves run past her.

Aves stood and watched until Hessa was completely out of her sight before she left the sanctity of her father's door. She was delighted as she watched Hessa move deftly through the crowded streets, the sunlight danced along the velvety folds of her dress and played across the pearls that highlighted her figure.

'That must be what the dress looks like to others when I wear it.' She toyed mentally with the image of her in the dress instead of Hessa and tried to picture herself running instead of her maid.

Lost in reverie, Aves almost failed to see Hessa leading one of Jaconis's crew into an alley. She followed at a respectable pace to make sure Hessa was all right. Knowing that Hessa was resourceful, she was not overly concerned for her. Nonetheless, her pulse quickened when she stepped into the empty alleyway. She puzzled over this for a moment and decided to move along.

'No need to make Hessa's attempts as a decoy to be in vain.' She flitted through the streets, moving from one group of shadows to the next.

She knew her dress hindered her attempts at hiding with its glass beads catching the soft rays of light and tossing them about in rainbow patterns, but she tried to obscure her movements anyway.

If she could slip past even one of Jaconis's minions, it would be enough. Aves breathed a little easier when she saw how well her deep blue gown blended in with the dark environment of the bustling market place, save the beads and the silver circling her waist and bust.

Aves stopped halfway through the market. 'Something is wrong.' Whether it was fear for Hessa, whom she had secretly hoped to keep in sight or woman's intuition Aves could not tell.

Instead of lingering on the feeling, she found a particularly dark shadow and paused to catch her breath. So far, she had seen only one of Jaconis's minions and for some reason that concerned her. Aves could not shake the feeling that Hessa was in some kind of trouble.

Something brushed Aves's shoulder and she jumped. She bolted toward the Council Hall instead of waiting to see what it was. 'Did I linger too long?' Her thoughts moved lethargically through her head as her feet pounded against the flagstones, all hope of stealth cast were aside in her mad dash.

"Slow down before you get hurt." The voice called to her from a side street.

Aves panicked even more before she finally realized the voice was soft and familiar. 'Could Jaconis have a friend of mine helping him?' Her troubled thoughts churned slowly through her mind as if she were in a dream. Aves had almost passed the street the voice came from when she placed the voice as Hessa's. Aves stopped instantly and almost lost her footing.

Hessa's hand grabbed Aves's arm to steady her. She quickly escorted her into a dark alley where they could find some privacy. The shadows of late afternoon were dwindling fast and shifting to accommodate the early evening. Aves's desire to speak with her father steadily increased with each minute they spent trying to get to the Council Hall.

Panting Aves threw out her question between gulps of air. "Are you injured… Hessa?"

Still a little shaken she replied, "No, though you almost had to survive without me."

"Why?" Aves asked stunned. Aves peered into Hessa's hazel eyes as if she could see Hessa's meaning in them.

"I was attacked, milady." Hessa cast her eyes down at her feet. The soft burgundy leather of the thigh high boots she wore matched her dress perfectly.

"What do you mean 'attacked'? By who? What happened?" Aves's thoughts slipped away too fast to control.

'Hessa was attacked. Who would have done this? Was it because of my ploy? Was she injured?' Too many questions to be asked and it seemed she could only form them haphazardly. In all of her exploits with Namir, nothing like this had ever happened.

"One of Jaconis's hired men. At least I think he was. I'm pretty sure of it." Hessa stated. She sighed as she continued, slightly shuddering at the memory of it all. "I had just led Canges, one of Jaconis's compatriots into the community bath." She paused when she realized Aves did not know who Canges was. "He's the tall dark haired one that usually delivers Jaconis's or Daffer's messages to your father."

"The oafish one that seems to have very little control of his limbs?" Aves queried.

"The same," Hessa agreed. Hessa decided that Aves might not know the names of her acquaintances, so she described them to her as she went on. "As I said, I had just led him into the community bath and into Hasia's care. She's the meek girl I occasionally lunch with, the one with dull grayish brown hair and the eye that looks off in another direction when she is talking to you." Aves nodded her understanding and Hessa continued.

"She agreed to 'take care' of Canges, so I went out the front before he could catch up with me. As you know, the front of the bath opens directly into the market. However, I had no sooner left the bath before I was attacked." Hessa's fears were written plainly upon her face.

"What do you mean… attacked?" Aves interrupted abruptly, her concern drew enough lines across her smooth features to age her a little.

Hessa swallowing hard as she revealed, "I mean… h… he grabbed me… and thrust me into an alley and against a wall. He pressed one of his smelly calloused hands against my mouth with enough force that I could taste the salt and dirt covering it!" Hessa almost stopped, tears already building in her eyes.

Regaining herself quickly she continued, although Aves motioned for her not to. "With his other hand he pressed me against the wall harder and he… he whispered in my ear that he was going to kill me if I didn't obey him." She fought back tears when she saw the look of horror on Aves's face. "It was worse… he thought I was you… " Her tears gushed forth. She grabbed Aves and held her close.

"I am so sorry. I… I never meant… I never meant for you to get hurt." Aves fought her emotions to restrain the flow of tears as she held Hessa, waiting patiently for her to be able to speak.

"I… I swore I would give my life for you and I meant it." Peering deeply into Aves's hazel eyes, Hessa pulled away from her slowly.

"H… How did you get free? He… He didn't do anything to you… did he?" Aves blurted.

Although the troubling memories were still fresh in her mind, Hessa smiled wistfully at the memory of her escape. "No. He didn't do anything to me. He put something in my mouth and started to bind my hands as he put his weight on me to keep me against the wall and… " she quivered, revolted at the thought, "Thankfully the only flesh of mine that he touched was my shoulder, my mouth and my wrists. I'll probably need to bathe for a week just to remove his stench." A look of distaste crossed her face closely pursued by sorrow. "I am sorry for allowing him to get filth on your dress, milady."

"Nonsense!" Aves was enraged by the thought of a man attempting this against any woman, let alone Hessa. "Please tell me, how did you get free?"

Hessa nodded and went back to the story, "It all happened so fast. He pinned me to the wall, the whole time breathing his foul breath into my face. I remember feeling his filthy lips upon my ear and his repeated demand for my coins." Aves made a sour look as Hessa quivered and then plunged on, "then just as I thought I couldn't take it anymore, his body went limp."

"Did he… ?" Aves asked hesitantly and disgusted.

Hessa felt herself get a little sick at the thought. "No, thank the Gods." Hessa confided, "But I was more frightened when I didn't feel his hands on me than when I did. I was afraid his laxness was a ploy to get me to turn around. So I stood there, facing the wall for a while. After a few moments, when nothing else happened, I decided to turn around."

"And?" Aves inquired eagerly.

"And… he was dead." Hessa smiled as bewilderment flashed across Aves's face.

"Dead… how?" Aves's eagerness subdued her fears as she rocked forward, completely drawn in by Hessa's tale.

"Well… I felt someone touch my shoulder." Aves's eyes widened in curiosity and fear as Hessa said this. "I think I need to explain better. I turned because I felt a tap on my shoulder, which almost made me faint." Hessa looked at Aves knowingly as she continued. "I think I may have screamed as well, but I certainly wasn't prepared for what I saw. My attacker was lying on his back with half of his skull against the opposite side of the alley." Aves gasped in horror as Hessa continued; "there was another person in the alley. I don't know how long this other gentleman witnessed what transpired, but I do know that he was the reason my attacker didn't do more to me."

"What did he look like… this mystery man?" Aves asked overcome by curiosity. "We might be able to find out who he is and properly thank him for saving your life."

With a deep sigh, Hessa confided her feelings to her mistress, "He was wonderful… and truly a mystery. All I really saw of him was his ebony hair and the alabaster skin of his arm. Yet, I know he was handsome."

"Or you hope he is." Aves played. "You know that won't help us find him."

"Aye, but we must continue on." Hessa said as she forced Aves to remember her task. "Besides, I would like to thank him myself." Hessa's voice was almost a whisper as she let the last of her words fall from her lips.

"Aye we must, or I might not have a chance to speak to my father." Aves agreed. She let Hessa have a moment to herself before they both went their separate ways.

"I'll go first and then you can follow me. Hopefully I can draw away any others still waiting for you." Hessa steeled her will against the memory of her recent attack, as well as the possibility of another, as she explained her plan to Aves. "Wait until I get to the hall, then run as fast as you can." Aves nodded her understanding to Hessa, but her features gave away her fear for Hessa as she looked at her for what might well be the last time. After another quick embrace, Hessa fled from the alley and back into the busy streets.

Aves waited, her breath came in forced gasps as the moments lurked long and burdensome. Fear for Hessa's safety came unbidden and she fought off the urge to follow immediately after her. 'There will be time enough to look after Hessa when all of this is done,' she consoled herself. Although the thought made her smile, she found it extremely difficult to wait.

'Thankfully Aves agreed to stay in the alley until I could

make it to the Council Hall.'   Hessa thought darkly. 'Unfortunately she didn't seem to know any more than I do about my mystery man.' Hessa's thoughts darted from topic to topic elusively as she forced her mind off her most recent events.   As she neared the hall, she spotted two more of Jaconis's followers.   'This is going to be difficult.' Hessa thought hurriedly since they were both guarding the main gates.

Hessa darted into the last alleyway before the council hall. She timed her movements so only one of the guards saw her. Then she waited. Her breath came in ragged gasps. 'Did it work?'

She was about to move a closer to the opening when she heard the soft scuffling of footsteps on the flagstones. She was pleased her ploy worked so well. She moved deeper into the alley as she searched for an exit she could duck into quickly.

Hessa's breath caught in her throat when noticed the alley ended a few yards away at a tall brick wall.   Panicked she searched for an opening into the alley other than the one she had used and found them all barred and locked in anticipation of tonight's activities.

The footsteps drew closer. Realization slowly dawned as she heard the second set of footsteps. 'Both guards followed me.' Hessa thought worriedly and then prayed for both Aves's luck and her own. 'At least now she can get to the Council Hall without event. I only hope there aren't any more waiting for her inside,' she worried.

Hessa tried to hide in the retreating shadows as she hoped the burgundy velvet of her gown would help her blend into the shadows enough to hide. To her dismay, the pearls sewn into her dress caught the light and caused the shadows around her to dance with her every breath. No matter how she turned, the pearls glimmered in the darkness.

She breathed in shallow puffs in a vain attempt to conceal herself. She could feel the other string of pearls along her waist dig sharply into her skin as she pressed against the wall.

"Why did I have to wear this dress?" She cursed again

quietly.

Fearing a repeat of her earlier mishap, she hung her head and tried to become as small as possible. Hessa heard them get closer. Their feet made a rhythmic beat of scuffles and patters as they approached. She wracked her brain for any idea that might help and she finally came up with one. She hoped it would work the way she wanted it to.

Hessa took a deep breath and inched along the wall farther from the mouth of the alley. At any moment, her pursuers would come around the corner and be on top of her. She waited, her breath caught in her throat as she heard their steps.

'What if this doesn't work?' Hessa thought as panic struck her again.

Pushing the thought from her mind, she lifted up her skirts slightly to allow her legs some freedom in case she needed to run. Hessa reached behind her back and loosened the thongs that held her bodice in place.

She felt it slowly loosen as more and more of her skin was exposed to the warm air around her. That was when the two henchmen saw her. She extended one of her legs while sweeping her hair from her face as they approached.

"What have we here?" The voice was deep and gruff, almost as if its owner spoke from a gravelly crevasse.

He was tall and poorly dressed. His words escaped from the half rotten teeth in his mouth as if they were trying to escape from a sewage pipe. They carried with them all of the odors of one as well. His shabby clothes were a grayish brown and it was hard to tell if they were purposefully dyed or if their coloration was due to the lack of water that they had seen.

"It would appear to be a lady... or a whore." His companion replied nonchalantly. "But judging from the quality and fit of her dress... I'd say both." His lip curled into a sneer as he looked over Hessa's exposed flesh.

Unlike his companion, he was dressed a little better. He wore an off-white shirt and black breeches. His black boots were the common work variety that went half way up his calf and ended with two small loops on either side. He wore a simple leather belt with a dagger tucked into it around his waist neatly and a soft black felt hat completed his ensemble.

His light brown hair was neatly trimmed and his clothes were clean. His black eyes darted from Hessa to his friend and back to her lithe and attractive figure eagerly as they approached her cautiously.

Hessa held her breath and waited. She needed them to get closer to her if her plan had any chance of success.

"Do you think she's in trouble?" The dry throated thug inquired. "Maybe we know her." He jested with his compatriot.

"Maybe. I thought I saw Aves, the mayor's daughter, come this way." He shrugged "But who knows. Who are you?" He called down the alley to Hessa.

"I'm just a maid who's having a bit of trouble with her dress. Please leave me be." Hessa shot back. She feared her reply would bring more unwanted attention from them.

"Is that so?" The gruff voiced thug said as he moved across the alley and into the shadows beside her.

"Y… Yes… " Hessa replied timidly as she held back her fear. Her previous encounter started to play through her head unbidden. 'This time there are two of them instead of one… ' Hessa's mind was flooded with horrid images and thoughts of what these two might do to her.

The other one moved closer as well, but on her other side, trapping her between them as he took in her body greedily with his eyes. "Well, it isn't Aves after all, although she is attractive." He laughed to his friend. "What do you think we should do with her?"

"Well… we'll help the lady of course." His sarcasm was as thick as his voice was dry. "It appears to me that she is a maid out in her mistress's poorly fitting dress. She realized that she shouldn't be wearing it and now sees the error of her ways. So, in a fit of guilt she decided to rid herself of the burdensome gown, right?"

"Definitely," the reply came almost before the question was asked. The better-dressed thug pulled his dagger free from his belt and touched its tip to her exposed outer thigh.

"Actually, my gown slipped… and I'm trying to get it back on… th… that is why I came into this alley." Hessa blurted out as she felt the sting of the dagger. She was watching the deep voiced man as he tried to get behind her. She cursed her own stupidity. Deep down she hated herself for believing that she could make this work.

"Well then… this should be easy." The gruff voiced man erupted, completely ignoring Hessa's comment. He pulled his dagger free as he motioned to her upper body. "I'll start with her top… and you can have her bottom first… then we will switch. Agreed?"

"Oh, by all means." His comrade replied as he slowly moved the tip of his dagger lightly up her thigh.

Hessa saw both daggers glint in the darkness and her breath became ragged as her heart raced. She was out of time. She realized that her plan had failed when she saw the two completely block her escape.

She tried to find a way out of her situation, but before she could complete a thought, they forced her onto the flagstones. Hessa screamed as the man in front of her pulled down quickly on her loosened bodice. He pulled her toward him quickly as he punched her in the gut and knocked what little air she had left from her lungs.

Aves saw Hessa dart into the alley as she entered the street. She moved toward the hall as she watched two men follow Hessa into the alley. She smiled slightly as she noticed that the gate to the hall was now unguarded. Panic rose in her heart when she noticed neither the men nor Hessa emerged from the alley.

Aves was torn, she could either go and help Hessa or she could get to her father's chambers. With a heavy heart, she chose to get to her father as fast as she could.

'Hessa can fend for herself.' She thought hopefully.

However, as Aves passed the alley Hessa had ducked into

she almost stopped. Aves saw a knife glint in the darkness and Hessa's dress was slack.

It was all she could do to keep moving. She locked her eyes on the ground a few paces in front of her as she ran. Aves moved her feet as quick as she could. Aves had barely opened the door when she heard it. The piercing scream came from the alley behind her and Aves knew it had to be Hessa's. Aves froze unable to move.

Aves's whole life passed before her as she tried to turn from the door and toward the alley. Hessa's scream filled her reality with a buzz of confusion. Her world shattered into a million pieces and became a completely senseless mosaic of sounds, colors and incomprehensible images. Everything around Aves was in complete chaos and she could not focus her senses onto any one thing for long without a terrible darkness creep in on her vision.

Fear pinioned her with its overwhelming power and Aves was completely helpless in its grasp. She felt a hand on her shoulder. She heard urgent voices telling her something. Still she stood in mid turn unmoving. She tried to face the alley her maid had lured two savage men into desperately. Aves saw a figure abruptly loom past her and run into the alley. The figure's red robes flapped menacingly as the wind clutched at them. The wind fanned them as if they were wild flames racing toward dry wood.

She noticed others come forward as well. Some of them she knew, although she could not recognize them. Some of them were faceless strangers wrapped in a thick fog, while others were familiar yet frustratingly unknowable as if masked by broken glass. Her mind had shut down completely.

A voice she recognized spoke to her again. Another gentle touch on her shoulder. When she did not respond, a few more words were spoken and Aves was led into the council hall.

Chapter Six: Maneuvers

A loud thumping noise filled Hessa's ears as she felt the remaining air in her lungs forced out. Her scream died away hollowly and she felt like it made no difference at all. A calloused hand held Hessa's thigh tightly and another one gripped the back of her dress. The flagstones cut into her knees and she felt the weight of one of the men on her shoulders, holding her down. Her stomach hurt and she realized one of them had punched her to force the air out of her lungs as the other one pushed her to her knees. Hessa looked up as best as she could to see what was happening.

In front of her was one of her captors. He stood with his body turned towards her and his head turned just to the left looking over his shoulder at the source of the rhythmic thumping. The other one was behind her holding onto her dress tightly with one hand and his other pushed firmly down on the back of her neck. The source of the sound was eight paces behind her better-dressed captor.

Carness, the Constable, stood squarely facing the scene. His scarlet robes of office billowed as the breeze started to pick up around them. It was as if the wind tried to match the ferocity of Carness's anger. He held a well-oiled and worn ironwood cudgel in his right hand. He rhythmically thumped it against his extended left palm. His inky black hair tossed in the breeze and caused his graying temples to appear like silver flames dancing through its darkness. His wolf-like eyes were aflame with hatred, anger and rage.

Hessa felt a wave of relief suddenly wash over her. 'Thankfully Aves told Carness I needed help,' she thought as the last remnants of her strength poured out of her muscles and she collapsed completely against her captors.

The gruff voice barked out threateningly, "Leave us be. We're merely helping this little tart just like she asked us to. Ain't we Barness?" He winked at his compatriot horridly.

"That's right. The little miss here begged us to help her. In fact… " Barness attempted to explain over his shoulder to Carness as Hessa interrupted him.

"Liars!" She scolded. She mustered as much strength as she could to refute them. "I… I asked you to leave me alone… " Her breath rushed out of her as Barness dug the hilt of his dagger into the spot on her thigh he had pressed its tip against earlier.

"ENOUGH!" Carness bellowed seeing Barness's actions. He glared at them and his image became more sinister. He raised his cudgel up and rested it on his shoulder as he freed a short broad blade from its scabbard deftly with his other hand. Menacingly he continued as he stepped closer to them. "Unhand her! When you have finished that… you will move away and place your daggers on the ground near your feet. Do you understand?"

Barness nodded and released Hessa's thigh. He then turned, keeping himself between Carness and Hessa, and started to bend down to drop his dagger as instructed. As Barness did this, the other man laughed mockingly and replied, "What if we chose differently, eh Constable?" To Carness's surprised look he answered, "There are two of us and we 'ave a hostage. Now who' s goin' to stop me from stabbin' this tart in the back and letting Barness take care of you… hmmm?"

Before Carness could reply, a voice came from the darkness behind him. "I AM… " The words were barely breathed, but everyone heard them clearly, as they danced along the wind. As the words were uttered, the man's hand fell from Hessa's side and his eyes widened. Slowly, he slumped against the wall and slid to the ground. Behind him the shadows writhed and mimicking her captor's movements.

"Who are you… ?" Hessa whispered, "and why have you saved me again?"

"In time… " His reply came softly from the shadows as his features faded into their depths.

Barness spun and lunged into the shadows howling in rage. His dagger rang out as it struck the wall and shattered, shards of it imbedded into Barness' arm and face. He fell to the ground beside his dead compatriot shrieking in pain and surprise. His target had vanished leaving no trace other than his friend's body.

Carness moved closer, shoving his broad dirk back into its sheath. With a deft swing of his cudgel, he returned silence to the alley and granted a form of peace to Barness. He turned to Hessa, huddling against the wall crying, and asked softly, "What happened here?" Hessa looked up into Carness's wolf-like eyes and mouthed a reply. He softly put his hands under Hessa's shoulders and lifted her up gently. Carness turned and carried Hessa to the council hall cradled in one arm and dragged Barness behind him by his left boot with the other arm. "We will talk more of this when you've had a chance to recover," he said soothingly.

"Aren't you going to change into the clothes I bought for you?" Halin asked Namir, his voice betrayed that he was hurt by Namir's failure to do so. Namir had not even so much as glanced at the garments in Halin's hand.

"I will change into them once we get into the Council Hall. I wouldn't want the fine clothing you bought me to be ruined on the way there." Namir said as he winked at Halin. "I know you bought these clothes to create a specific effect and I am loath to misuse your judgment."

Halin beamed with pride as the other two made their way to the attic of the smithy. Halin sprinted after them as they fled through a secret panel. The construction of the access door amazed him. He knew Tipin had not authorized it to be built and the fact it was entirely unnoticeable only added to his admiration.

They passed through the secret panel and onto the roof of the smithy quickly and quietly. From there they navigated their way to the Council Hall unnoticed.

Halin was shocked as he looked at the latticework of boards and rope lines forming various pathways amongst the rooftops of Ellsted. Somehow, Namir and Nurn had managed to place the ropes and beams in such a way their paths were practically invisible when viewed from below.

Halin tried to determine the amount of planning that they had spent on it and gave up in frustration. He could not understand how they managed to build these paths, let alone where they got the supplies. By time Halin arrived in the chamber above, the Council Hall Namir was half changed and Nurn was stepping quietly out into the hallway.

"Why do you think Jaconis had a hand in this?" Armani inquired, directing his question to Carness.

Aves and Hessa sat across from him on the other side of his desk.   Armani's chambers were expansive and well arranged. Silk tapestries hung along two of the walls and thick rugs laid across the mahogany floors. Two huge bookshelves filled the remaining walls, crammed with books, scrolls and an assortment of loose papers. Carness lounged in one of the stuffed chairs to his left and Barness was tied and gagged at Carness's feet acting as his footrest. Amusement at this sight crossed Armani's smooth features fleetingly.

"From what Hessa has told me," Carness nodded to Hessa and continued, "the two that attacked her outside the hall and the one that attacked her earlier in the market are all his cronies."

"Is the word of a maid all we have?" Armani pressed. "Although I believe Hessa, Jaconis is the son of a council member. We need something more."

Armani leaned forward in his chair and placed his elbows on his desk. He folded his delicate hands in front of his face tapping his index fingers against his forehead thoughtfully. A lock of his silvery white hair, once full and dark, fell across his face as he did so.

His motion only accented his dramatically deep widow's peak and the wizened look of his smooth face. His hazel eyes shone with a passion for life and his hatred of the situation as they flicked from Carness to Hessa and back.

"Well… " Carness started to say as Hessa cut in.

"Their target was your daughter. Can't you see I was mistaken for her?" Hessa pleaded.

Armani raised his eyebrow as he lowered his hands to his oak desk menacingly. "Did I ask you?"

"No sir." Hessa said quietly, turning her eyes towards her feet and lightly biting her lower lip.

"Then please refrain from commenting, my dear." He smiled slightly and added, "You will have a chance to tell your story, just not yet. Understand?" As he awaited her reply, Armani deftly teased the stray lock of hair back into his shoulder length queue.

Hessa nodded as Carness continued his sentence where he left off, his resonant voice carrying the same inflection and note it had before. "We also have the testimony of this cur," he lightly kicked Barness as if to make his point. "From what he told me, his 'pal' Gurn was hired by a man fitting Jaconis's description. Gurn and his mysterious employer met at the Gathering Place and exchanged money and a promissory note. This note is for use at the Gathering Place and it was signed by Jaconis. I found it on Gurn's body, as well as a pouch full of coins matching the one that Barness described." Grinning Carness looked at Armani and shot him a knowing look. "The notes and the money have been confiscated. We could use this to our advantage you know."

"I am fully aware of that." Armani agreed. "Does anyone here know why… why these thugs were paid to… to harm

Aves?" His hands were in front of his face again, clasped and trembling. A tear crept into his eyes stealthily as he asked this.

"Because I am a threat to him, father. I am a threat to Jaconis and all of his schemes. He knows this… and it seems he will do anything to have the council meeting go in whatever direction he chooses." Aves said demurely. "I know Jaconis and Daffer are planning to remove Namir as a threat to Jaconis's future as a member of the council."

"I see." Armani closed his eyes and took a deep breath before he continued. "Please, tell me again what you overheard… and how Hessa was brought into this."

Aves composed herself quickly and then ran through all of the details she had heard in her mind. After she was certain of them, Aves recited them and summed it up as briefly as she could. "Daffer was upset at Jaconis for not bringing Namir back to the Gathering Place to do his chores.

Through Jaconis's complaints, their conversation shifted to Namir's trip to Hornshir. Jaconis pleaded with Daffer not to let Namir lead it. Jaconis claimed Namir was unreliable and that only Jaconis himself was suited for the role as the expedition's leader. I know there was something else he chose to hide from Daffer, but he didn't mention anything else."

"Thank you, although you still haven't fully answered my question." Armani opened his eyes again to look Aves fully. "How did Hessa come to be drawn into this?"

Aves took a deep breath and noticed her father's frown. "I asked her to help me. I knew that Jaconis was planning on doing something to hinder Namir's plans and I thought he might try and stop me from getting to the council hall in time to be called forward." She took another deep breath and said soothingly, "I didn't want Namir to be humiliated, father, not like that and not in front of the council. If I failed to appear, it would seem like I didn't believe in Namir's ability to lead the expedition. My absence might also sway Daffer to see Namir exactly like Jaconis wants him to, or worse it might make others in the council believe Jaconis's lies."

"Hmmm." Armani said softly, more to himself than to

anyone else. "So you decided to have Hessa, your maid, do what… impersonate you?" Aves's father demanded.

Aves hung her head. "Aye, but I didn't think Jaconis's hirelings would hurt her! If I even remotely thought that she would be injured I never would have asked it of her."

"Did you actually believe no harm would come to her?" This time Carness shot the question at Aves. "Jaconis hired cut-throats and thieves!" Carness asked, astonished by Aves's naiveté.

"Aye." Aves's reply was almost a whisper. "I did and I am sorry for it." Tears crept from the corner of her eyes and rolled down her cheeks. "Please forgive me Hessa… "

Hessa leaned over and ran her fingers across Aves's face. "I will… and I do, milady."

"How should we proceed with this?" Carness's voice broke the moment purposefully with his question.

"I'm not sure. Maybe it will resolve itself." Armani nodded his head and laid his hands on his desk once more. As he did this, he shot a knowing glance to Carness. "But let's be prepared. When Namir is called forth, take no chances. Do the same for those to accompany him on the trip. I want to make sure there are no more surprises today unless I am the one to instigate them."

"What if Daffer tries to revoke his approval of Namir?" Aves asked demurely.

"I will deal with that if it happens." Armani's eyes glinted fiercely as he said this. "Make sure to inform Allair of the plot… and Saril if you are able. We cannot afford to let Jaconis win by using these underhanded tactics; otherwise he will become emboldened in the future." He directed his next few comments to Carness, although he looked at everyone as he said them. "As for this vagabond," his eyes falling upon Barness, "chain him up until they leave and then flog him. I want him to fully regret his part in this."

Carness nodded and asked after both Aves and Hessa had left, "The one thing that still puzzles me is the shadow walker. Who is he and how did he know where he was needed?"

"That I don't know, although I would like to." Armani agreed.

"Does anyone else have anything to share?" Armani's smooth voice rang throughout the hall.

His silvery white hair cascaded down to his shoulders and spilt over the black robes that indicated his position as both the Chancellor of the Council and the Mayor of Ellsted. He looked across the hall at the other council members and waited patiently. His fiery hazel eyes scanned their faces as he searched for any sign of their thoughts. After a moment, he waived his staff of office and banged it on the flagstones beneath his feet.

"Then the matter stands." He turned to the petitioner, one of the many shop owners of the market, he announced in a diffident tone. "When the Constable recovers the lost lamb it shall be returned to you. If Carness determines it was slain or irretrievable, the council will reimburse you for your loss." This being done, he motioned for the plaintiff to leave. He lowered himself into his seat and motioned for the next piece of business to be announced.

Allair stood; her neatly trimmed green robes hugged her petite frame following every curve of her body in tasteful contours. Her green robes indicated her position as the council Envoy. They were tailored to fit snug and thus project an air of diffidence to those about her.

Allair's long chestnut hair silhouetted her face as she read from the scroll of registry. Her deep brown eyes darted from the scroll to play across the faces of the council members and the general assembly as she read.

"The next order of business, Chancellor, is the decision whether to grant Namir permission to lead the goodwill expedition to Hornshir." Her silky voice hung in the air as the tension in the room rose.

Each of the councilors fidgeted and the people that lined the upper balcony murmured amongst themselves. She knew her husband had told her the issue was a terse one, but she had no idea the weight it bore until now. She sat fluidly as Armani rose.

Clearing his throat, Armani addressed the council regally. "We have put this off for far too long. A week has passed and we still have not come to a decision on this. The allotted time has now passed again; we need to choose. Do we allow the expedition or not?"

His question lingered as if floating on the waves of tension filling the chamber. He looked from one councilor to the next and decided to give the floor to any wishing to voice their thoughts.

"Anyone wishing to speak their thoughts on the matter can do so now." He lowered himself into his chair again.

He hoped to sit for a bit longer this time. His face was cast in shadows as the fading sun moved across the main windows of the chamber and played along his widow's peak forming an ominous air about him.

Daffer stood and as he did a dismal shroud of hatred and scorn hung about him, "I am against this for one reason alone. I fear that Namir's recent actions prove his inadequacy to lead this expedition." He glowered around the room as if challenging anyone to defy his statement.

Allair rose to his unspoken challenge. "What actions are you speaking of? The last time this topic was broached you supported it. Why the sudden change of heart?"

Daffer glared at her as if she did not belong among them. His grey robes indicated that he was the Leading Merchant of Ellsted. They fluttered across his burly frame in the cool breeze that wafted from the windows as he retorted.

"Throughout this week he has shirked his chores and other duties time and again. From these recent actions, I'm afraid he would do the same or worse on this expedition. What would become of this much needed trip if Namir shirks this important task altogether? As far as I am concerned, he has recently proven himself incapable of being relied upon." He placed his meaty hands firmly on the rail in front of him and as he glowered at Allair as he leaned heavily upon it. "This trip is far too important. Not only is it an opportunity to build new alliances for our town, but we need supplies to last the winter! Far too much is at stake to allow it to be bungled by that undependable cur!"

"And who would you choose to lead it?" Saril asked softly. His stooped and mousy frame sat collapsed in his chair. His bluish white robes, the robes of the Healer, floated about him. His sightless misty blue eyes gazed around the chamber and his thin grey hair blown by the light breeze formed a whitish-grey halo about him in the fading light of the sun.

"I feel my son, Jaconis, should go in his stead." Daffer's declaration forced the chamber into silence. "Though I would be deprived of his skills and services while he was gone, I can think of none better to spread the news about our fair and none more reliable to bring the appropriate supplies home from Hornshir."

"Is this desire for the betterment of Ellsted or for that of your son, Daffer?" Armani inquired archly.

"Are you accusing me of having a hidden agenda?" Daffer bellowed; his cheeks filled with color as his anger rose.

"I am just unclear if you are posing your son as the head of this expedition to raise him higher in the eyes of the local merchants or if you truly have the best interests of Ellsted in mind with your proposition. I believe the question to be a fair one." Armani shot back at Daffer defiantly as he saw Carness rise to his feet.

As he rose from his chair, Carness calmed both the spectators in the balcony and the councilors as well. "None would dare accuse you of owning enough ingenuity to possess a hidden agenda, Daffer."

Carness's taunt made Daffer flinch as if struck and elicited a chuckle from the general assembly. Carness stood in his dais across from Daffer's, his scarlet robes rippling across his wiry chest. His golden brown eyes dared Daffer to test him and make his duty as the Constable needed.

Seeing Carness's ploy Daffer offered a truce by saying,

"all I am saying is that Namir has proven to be undependable at smaller tasks. Why reward someone that shirks smaller tasks with a greater one to bungle?"

"Well spoken," Carness's black crested head nodded. He turned to Armani and stated, "Chancellor, I feel Namir needs to be called before us to address Daffer's charges."

Armani rose to his feet again, leaning his tall body heavily against his staff as he did so, and assented. He was well aware that these tense sessions were taxing to his health, but knew of little he could do to end them without sacrificing his position as Chancellor.

"I hereby call forth Namir. Madame Envoy, please bring him before our austere body." He threw his arms wide and motioned for Allair to summon Namir into the council's presence.

She rose obediently; her deep brown eyes scoured the balconies as she probed the faces that looked at her for Namir's. 'He should be here already,' Allair thought slightly disturbed. She focused her vocal skills and called out to the crowed assembly.

Her resonating voice pealed from the walls in rushing waves of sound. "Namir, make you presence known before us!"

As soon as Namir was fully dressed, he stepped out into the hallway after Nurn. He looked down the hall to the three doors opening to the council chamber's balcony.

"Just as I thought," Namir muttered darkly as he saw three of Jaconis's friends standing guard at each one. He calculated the odds of getting past them and decided they were not in his favor. Instead, Namir led Nurn and Halin up the stairs to their left to see if the next floor was any better. Like the first, Jaconis's coterie was there as well. Halin muttered silently, Nurn grumbled and Namir pressed on. They skipped the next floor for similar reasons.

"What will we do if there are people blocking the top

level?" Halin whined.

"What we must," Nurn replied shaking his head, "although I don't relish the thought, especially for such a small matter."

"This matter isn't small," Halin snapped before he realized what he just said. "I mean it's important for this trip to be made, isn't it?" He added trying to lessen his lapse in judgment.

"Aye," Namir stopped and turned to face his friends. "It is important, but what Nurn means is that it isn't important enough to kill someone. Moreover, I refuse to let that happen. We must find a way into the hall otherwise all we have done will be wasted." His determination settled around him like a mantel as he pressed on to the last floor.

He knew the passage would be small and tight for Nurn, so maneuverability would be extremely limited.

He turned to Nurn and devised a quick plan. "Nurn, you go first. It's very unlikely anyone outside the hall will try to stop you. If they do, simply move them away from the door. Halin and I will slip into the hallway behind you. If things are bad we will go through the door as you pass it, then you can follow us in once we get inside. If all goes well, however, you will be able to step through the doorway and onto the balcony first. I'll follow close behind you and Halin will take up the rear and enter on my heels. This way, no matter the outcome, we will all be in the council chamber and ready to appear in front of the council unmolested."

Nurn nodded. The plan sounded good enough to him. He turned to Halin and whispered, "This is why Namir is in charge. You would do well to learn from his skills and attempt to mold yourself to be more like him." Stepping away before Halin could reply, Nurn made his way to the door and was through it before Halin could blink.

Chapter Seven: Choices

Allair's voice was just starting to fade as Namir's reply erupted from the uppermost balcony. "I am here!" Namir exclaimed as he strode forward to the railing partitioning the balcony from the air above the council members. A slight murmur rose from the gathered masses and Daffer's face darkened as Namir framed his next few words. "And, if would please you, I will vault down into your austere presence." He proclaimed so all within the chamber heard.

Looking to the Chancellor for guidance, Allair held up her hand to stay Namir's actions as well as his tongue. Seeing Armani nod his head once, she lowered her hand and spoke. "You are to come before us, though leaping the great distance is not required." She smirked at the absurdity of Namir's statement. As much as she might like to see, certain individuals throw themselves from the four levels above her onto the recessed floor below her and Namir was not numbered among them. "Since the Chancellor himself has demanded you appear before us, let none bar your way or restrict your approach. Else they will have to deal with the Constable's justice and wrath." That being said she sat down in her comfortable chair and awaited Namir's approach.

As Allair sat, Carness rose again. Striding to the front of his dais he proclaimed, "Unbar every portal to the balconies and the main chamber. I would see everyone standing outside the doors come in and be seated prior to Namir leaving of my view!" His voice boomed throughout the hall as he took his bow from off of his shoulder. The newly lit torches threw a dancing beacon across his features as the light played amid the graying hair on his temples. Carness's ominous look made everyone in sight shrink into their seats to hide from his icy stare.

The doors flew open instantly as if Carness had moved them by the force of his will. Before the doors were fully open, several men stepped through and found seats hurriedly. Three men entered from each of the thirteen doors. Carness looked hard at each of them and scrutinized their features while memorizing their faces. They would all be part of his investigation into today's incidents once the council session was over. After he felt comfortable with his inspection, he motioned for Namir to descend from the upper balcony.

Namir obeyed Carness's gestured order. As he left the balcony, Halin and Nurn followed close behind. The three of them descended the winding stairs to the second floor, there Halin and Nurn let Namir continue to the main chamber alone. The brothers made their way into the main audience gallery and found seats near the back. As Halin sat down he looked at Nurn and saw the deep lines of dread etch a veritable map of intricate lines onto his face. Halin closed his eyes and took a few deep breaths to relax; then he opened his eyes and took in the scene unfolding before him.

The whole time Halin was getting comfortable, Nurn scanned the assembly with a pensive eye as he tried to find any possible sources of trouble before it arose. Nurn knew Carness would be doing the same thing, but if he had learned anything from the Constable's lessons over the last few years, it was that one man alone could not stop every threat by himself no matter how skilled he may be.

Namir walked the cold corridor to the main entry hall alone. His thoughts turned from today's ordeals and intrigues to the trial that lay ahead; one of many trials. Namir knew that if he was being called in front of the council, someone had contested the choice of him as leader of the expedition. 'If I only knew what Daffer and Jaconis were planning.' Namir was completely lost in his thoughts as he arrived at the open chamber door. He strode through it before he realized it and all thoughts about proper etiquette and protocol he needed to show were instantly lost. He remembered these things several moments too late as Daffer bellowed down at him.

"See? The whelp has no manners! Is this the kind of person you want to represent us to the Council of Hornshir?" A dark look played across his face as he smiled a sinister grin.

"Indeed, it might prove detrimental to have such a headstrong boy guard our reputation," interjected Saril unasked. "One so brash may cause more problems than we need in these hard times."

Namir cried out, trying to project his voice above the clangor caused by Saril's statement to make sure that both the council and the general assembly heard what he had to say. "I meant no disrespect, elders. I was in such haste to respond to your summons that I forgot myself. Please forgive my transgressions." He lowered himself to one knee and stooped his head as he waited to be addressed.

Carness smiled approvingly as his golden brown eyes turned to meet Armani's. "I accept his petition, although I know it is not for me to decide." He smiled a wolf-like jeer towards Daffer. "Since it was made to the whole assembly I declare a vote. Chancellor, I support Namir's apology and place it before the council to see its recognition."

Nodding solemnly Armani stood and filled the hall with his voice. "All in favor of this boy's apology make your signal now!"

Silence reigned in the chamber. No one dared speak as the town fathers weighed their responses. All present knew this was more than a simple vote, Armani could simply accept the apology if he wished, such was his right as Chancellor. This was a cleverly played maneuver to show any alliances between members of the council and members of the general assembly.

Everyone knew the expedition was needed, that much was undeniable. The expedition's leadership remained uncertain. The expedition could fail if the wrong person led it and the time had come to choose who would insure the fate of Ellsted. The chosen leader may even be weaned for service in the council; a much vied for opportunity. With the prestige of establishing trade with Hornshir and the power of a council seat as a possible outcome, the leader of the expedition would be financially secure for the rest of their life. Tension mounted and the air became brittle as the council members motioned their responses.

Armani's hazel eyes darted from one member of the council to the next carefully weighing each person's response, he noted that many of the others did the same. Clearing his throat he boomed, "Madame Envoy, make a tally of the replies and record them in the order I call them."

Allair nodded and replied dutifully, "Aye Chancellor, as you command." She picked up the book resting at her feet and carried it as well as she could with one hand, her other one still holding her response to the vote rigidly. She strode over to the podium a few feet from her chair and opened the book with her only free hand. She deftly lifted the pen from the inkwell and prepared to record the votes.

"Let us begin then." Armani snapped and turned to look over the audience. Addressing them he stated, "Please be silent during the tally." He maintained the necessary pomp knowing full well the comment need not be said. The hall already bore the silence of the dead and none would interrupt such an important moment.

"Madame Envoy." He barked for her to begin the record as he turned to the first council member.

"Note Daffer has declined the boy's apology." He looked into Daffer's drab brown eyes, his grubby hand held aloft balled into a fist signifying his choice.

Armani then turned to Saril and his spirit fell as he noted his fist held aloft in a similar fashion, "as has Saril."

He slowly turned to Allair holding his breath. He knew the vote would be close; he just hoped she had not defected to Daffer's side. He breathed easier as he saw her delicate hand outstretched and her palm opened. Armani took delight in seeing her smooth fingers arch away from the ceiling as she held it there for all to see, defiant of what others may think of her. He turned his gaze to her eyes and allowed himself to get lost momentarily in their depths. He felt some of the weight lift from him as he called out, "Allair chooses to accept."

Tearing his eyes from Allair, he turned to face Carness and assessed his choice. Carness stood with his shoulders square and his arm outstretched in the same fashion as Allair. This was no surprise. Armani mused over the thought of Carness being Chancellor; it was a close race, too close in fact. 'Carness does appear more regal than I and he always seemed aloof.' He pulled his thoughts back to the task at hand as he intoned, "Let it be noted that with Carness's acceptance the council is tied. It comes to my vote and the vote of the general assembly then." Armani turned to the first row of the balcony and looked at the four heads of the assembly. "Please announce the decree of the assembly." He commanded trying to seem as aloof as Carness did.

The four men stepped to the edge of the balcony and each extended their hands to cast their vote. They wore the earthen brown robes that marked them as the elected members of the assembly. Armani's heart sank a little as he saw the first two hands, each one held in a tight ball indicating their disapproval of Namir's apology. Nervously Armani looked to the second set of assembly heads and was relieved as he saw their palms outstretched in compliance.

"Madam Envoy, please note that the assembly is equally divided in this as well." Armani paused to increase the effect, he then lifted his own arm aloft holding his palm up and his fingers outstretched. "Madame Envoy, please record that with my vote the council has decided, seven votes in favor and six against. Namir's apology has been accepted." He waited until he heard Allair's pen stop scratching its way across the page before saying, "Now we can move forward." Facing Namir, he motioned for him to rise and move forward. "Namir, you have heard the concerns against, have you not?" He inquired.

"Aye," Namir nodded as he regained his feet.

"Then answer us this. Why do you feel the council should send you on this errand," noticing the slight confused look on Namir's face, Armani expanded the question, "since Daffer believes that you are not capable to focus the needed attention on this task." Armani looked at Daffer and Saril in turn noticing their approval of the question before returning his gaze to Namir and allowing him to respond.

"I feel this way because I am the only one that can assure the expedition to Hornshir will succeed." Namir thrilled as he heard the assembly gasp. He knew Jaconis would take offense to this remark, as would his lackeys.

"What makes you think that you won't disregard your task, like you have so many in the past few weeks?" Daffer bellowed, cutting Namir's chance of explanation short. His face was red and everyone could tell he understood Namir's comment was meant as a slight to his son.

"Daffer, hold your-" Armani started as Namir cut him off with another response.

"Uncle, I am aware I have set some of my chores aside throughout these past two weeks. However, I never failed to finish them, save when others finished them by the time I returned. I did forgo them for a good cause, however." Namir tried to explain what his intentions were when Carness stepped in.

"Namir... Daffer... " Carness looked each of them squarely in the eye as he said their names. "This is neither the time nor the place to air issues best dealt with in private. Namir, although you originally had leave to speak, you lost that when Armani spoke again. It would behoove you to be less petulant and notice what is occurring before you start explaining yourself." Carness turned his attention to Armani and continued, "The floor is yours Chancellor."

"Thank you Constable," Armani nodded his thanks to

Carness as he replied. "Now," Armani glared at Daffer as he continued, "Daffer. While it is true that you are the merchant elect on the council, not even you, a council member, have the authority to interrupt someone who is giving testimony to the council. Since I have never had to force this before I loathe to now, however if you cannot hold your tongue I will be forced to exclude you from the meeting and this decision. Is that clear?"

Daffer felt repulsed by the thought of answering to Armani. He had never liked him before and now he hated that he had to listen to this gibberish. "I understand." Daffer agreed. His face was still red as he took his seat.

"I am glad we are clear on this." Armani nodded as he turned his attention to Namir. "Please consider your next words carefully, Namir. I believe you and Daffer have issues to discuss after we are done here, so let's leave those issues alone. Understand that my statement to Daffer bears directly on you as well." Armani's icy stare forced Namir to direct his gaze down as he kneeled. "If you try to divert the line of questioning from what is asked you will not only be escorted out, but you will be replaced on this journey. Do you understand?"

"Aye," Namir assented.

"Good. Now, continue where you left off. Other than your belief that you are best suited to lead, why should the council chose you for the task?"

An impish grin spread across Namir's face, "Your right Chancellor, I should not have tried to make this about myself." Namir glanced from Armani to the rest of the assembly as he stood. "I am not here to boast of my prowess and various skills and I did not intend that only I can lead this expedition successfully because of a trait I possess. Instead I meant to say the main quality I have is that I know who to place my trust in."

"And who would be on the list?" Allair asked as she penned the meeting notes in the smaller tome.

"If allowed to lead the expedition to Hornshir, I would

choose those more trustworthy than myself to accompany me." Namir directed this more towards Daffer than to the assembly.

"This expedition is not for one person to perform alone; instead it truly belongs to several. Like in all things, a group of people needs a leader to guide them in their tasks and I would be that leader solely because of the research I have performed and the contacts that I possess. As for who is needed for the expedition to succeed, I would take Nurn for his strength, in case anything should happen along the way there and back. Halin is my second choice. Not only is he Nurn's brother, but his taste in clothing and knowledge of the finer aspects of merchandise and wares is impeccable and second to none. The third and final person I would choose is Aves, the esteemed Mayor's daughter. I would ask her to accompany me for more than her pleasant demeanor." Namir paused to allow his choices to sink in before he continued with his reasoning.

"Being the Mayor's daughter, Aves is the closest we have to nobility here in Ellsted. A citizen of her rank and stature could only aid us in our task. She would help our mission appear as sincere as it is intended to be. Plus the diplomacy that she has been trained in may prove extremely valuable. Not to mention her ample ability to get what she wants." His steel blue eyes played over the crowd as he said the last part. He was hoping to catch a glimpse of Aves in the crowd, yet failed to do so in the short time he had.

"What of the concerns of the Gathering Place and the rest of the merchants?" Daffer blurted before the Chancellor could continue his own line of questioning. "I see that the blacksmith has his due and the mayor as well, but what of the rest of us? Shouldn't we have a say in who represents us?" The hall became alive at this. A roar issued forth from many throats as Daffer glared at Namir hatefully and smugly.

"Silence!" Carness's voice shook the walls like a thunderclap. Once again, an oppressive silence took hold of the chamber. "Let the Chancellor speak!"

"Thank you, Constable." Armani nodded his appreciation to Carness and probed, "An interesting list of followers to choose, though a wise one none the less. However, Daffer does have a point. He may be rude, but he speaks truthfully. Do you have a reply for this Namir?" He let his gaze rest upon Namir so all were aware that only Namir had permission to speak. Any others that attempted to would be dealt with swiftly by Carness, whether they were members of the council or the assembly.

"I am confused by my unc… by Daffer's concern." Namir confided. He looked around the room again searching for some sign of Aves. He was about to give up, when he finally saw her and was startled by what he saw. "I had hoped he would see me as his emissary, but it looks as if that is not to be."

Beside Aves was another woman, both were of the same build and both looked stunning in their expensive dresses. The only difference between them was their hair color and even that was hard to tell from a distance. Namir stared at the two while he spoke and noticed Aves reveal the identity of the other lady to him through gestures. This forced Namir to smile despite himself.

'This just might turn out good after all,' he thought as he continued.

"However, if Daffer wishes a different person to account for his interests, then so be it." Namir continued. "I can think of another who could serve that purpose adequately. Before I reveal this person, however, I wish to insure that everyone understands what my role in the expedition will be."

He saw a look of triumph shimmer across Daffer's motley looks, when he had agreed to let someone else replace him, only to be followed by a sullen glare as he continued his sentence.

"All present should be aware, by now at least, that I am not from Ellsted. I was born in Hornshir and know its ways better than anyone present can claim to. This will prove useful for the expedition. Likewise, since I am from Hornshir many there may decide to trade with us based solely on this fact. With this said, I will now declare the person that I would choose to replace me as merchant's emissary, if I may?" He looked at Armani as he said this attempting to keep the conversation free from interruptions.

"You may." Armani assented.

"I would choose her." Namir gestured toward Hessa. As he did so, the crowd moved away from her as if she was a dangerous beast.

Armani raised an eyebrow and the rest of the council stared at Hessa stunned. "Do you know who she is?" Armani inquired with mirth in his voice.

"No. And I don't care." Namir lied. "I choose a stranger so that none can protest my choice. She would appear to be of some elegant upbringing, however, which may work to our advantage. Did I make a poor choice, Chancellor?" Namir attempted to look innocently up at Armani and knew full well that he would fail.

"Maybe... maybe not, young Namir." Armani grinned very wryly and deeply as he turned to look at Daffer. "What say you to this? Do you accept this selection as an acceptable emissary?"

The silence became unbearable as the cogs in Daffer's head were forced, once again, into motion. He finally spoke as a look of relief spread across his face. "No, I don't accept her. She isn't an acceptable emissary." He smirked at Namir then and added, "I do not know her, and therefore I cannot be sure she will have the interests of the merchant population at heart." His face shone with triumph as he continued, "Truth be had, this is the first time I have ever laid eyes on her."

"That is untrue." Armani said lightly. "She is my daughter's maid." His pride soared as he realized that none of the assembly had recognized her. "Be that as it may, Daffer has expressed his decision on this and since his realm is the welfare of the merchants, I cannot allow her to be your replacement in this expedition, Namir."

Namir bowed to Armani and lowered his head as he replied. "Then may I ask Daffer to select another to be the emissary, though I feel your daughter's servant should accompany us as well."

"You may," Armani acquiesced. "Daffer, enlighten us to your choice and your reasoning behind it. Know this; no matter whom you select, Namir will lead this expedition to Hornshir. Your choice's only duty will be to protect the interests of Ellsted's merchants. Do you understand?" He shot an imposing look at Daffer, though he was not sure if Daffer was intelligent enough to understand it.

"Aye, I understand." Daffer answered with no apparent hesitation. He brushed some of his oily grayish brown hair away from his forehead as he gathered his thoughts. Everyone knew thinking was not one of his strong points, and he proved it to them yet again. By time Daffer had arrived at his choice the crowd had already anticipated it. "I would send Jaconis. Not only is he my son, but he is well versed in the merchant's affairs here in Ellsted." He looked smugly at Armani as he said this.

Armani stood with a thankful look on his face, glad that Daffer's ordeal had proven much shorter than normal. He then addressed Namir saying, "Do you have any objection to this?"

"If I did, milord Chancellor, would it have any bearing on Jaconis's inclusion in the expedition?" Namir beseeched with his head still drooped.

"No." Armani's reply rang through the silent room.

"Then I have no need to voice an objection. May I prepare my team for our departure now?" Namir asked.

"Soon, do not become overzealous, young Namir." Armani turned and looked over the assembly.

Once he was satisfied with what he saw, Armani spoke to Allair, "call forth the members of Namir's 'team' to appear before us. I wish them blessed before they make ready for their trip."

Allair nodded and then called out their names. "All those whose name I call step forward and receive the blessing of the council!"

As she stated this murmurs broke out through the chamber. Many took this opportunity to leave the proceedings, while others gossiped about the expedition's eventual outcome. There were as many bets that the expedition would fail, as there were hopes that this band of young adults and children would be able to accomplish their goals.

Allair's elegant voice rang through the growing din of the room calling one name after another of Namir's chosen companions. "Nurn come forth. Halin as well. Aves… bring your maid Hessa with you as you approach. Jaconis do not tarry." Allair's words were joined and parroted by many others before the small group was all collected and gathered.

Nurn was the first member to rise. He stood and completely stretched each of his tense muscles in turn. He then beckoned to Halin and made his way to the aisle and out the open door easily. While he descended the flights of stairs that led to the council's entry hall, Nurn remained somber and collected. He mused to himself several times that Halin needed to relax before going in front of the council and then said a silent prayer to his goddess Tumere, his people's goddess of the woodlands and vengeance, before he mentally returned to Halin's incessant bantering.

"Do you think Jaconis will cause much mischief in Hornshir?" Halin pestered.

"That remains to be seen. Worries like these are best left to Namir." Nurn scowled at the thought of traveling with Jaconis, he would rather sleep with a viper than turn his back on Namir's cousin. "What I do know is that Jaconis will have to be kept busy while we are in Hornshir."

"Why?" Halin pondered, his tinny voice echoing down the stairwell.

Sighing deeply Namir replied, "Because the trip has a more personal significance for him than he has shared with the council." Nurn walked a little faster allowing Halin some distance with which to think about his last statement. It was not until they were almost to the first level of balconies that Halin became too frustrated to remain silent.

"Meaning?" Halin pressed. His gate was exaggerated in order to keep pace with his brother making him appear more awkward than he already was.

Nurn stopped; the door to the first level of balconies stood wide with people moving back and forth through the hallway beyond. He turned to Halin and whispered, "It deals with his past. I cannot say more for the walls have ears. Let's be done with this for now and make haste to Namir's side." Nurn's tones came out unevenly and sounded more like growling than speech. The best Halin could do was nod in agreement.

'One of these days I will understand Nurn's mood swings.' Halin thought as they continued down the passage. "One last thing," he added quickly.

"What?" Nurn snapped.

"Do you think I look presentable enough to appear before the council?" Halin asked mockingly while he smoothed out the creases in his pants with his left hand and flattened his collar with his right.

Nurn grasped Halin's collar and thrust him down the stairs chuckling. "Aye, you look just like the preening peacock that you are." He shook his head mirthfully as he followed Halin's stumbling form.

Hessa turned and looked into Aves's eyes in disbelief. Stunned she asked, "Why must I go in front of the council? I don't understand this decree, milady."

Smirking Avis answered as she rose to her feet, "It's alright, Hessa. You can accompany me to Hornshir for my safety… or to be a thorn in Jaconis's side. Either way it will be fun; that is if you're ready for some adventure." She tugged lightly on Hessa's sleeve as she urged her to her feet.

Nodding to Aves's statement Hessa stood and commented, "If I had a say neither of us would be going. I know you care for Namir deeply and would do anything for him… "

"Don't say it! Don't you dare say it!" Aves cut in; her anger visibly welled up in her eyes. "It isn't foolish… and I don't like him as much as you seem to think." She turned only after she was positive Hessa was standing. She paused and waited for Hessa to join her before she stepped through the door and into the hallway beyond. Aves made sure to gather Hessa's arm in hers when she ventured out into the hallway.

"Are you feeling faint, milady?" Hessa inquired concerned.

"Aye." Aves looked into Hessa face with a wry grin as she continued, "Actually, I just wanted to ensure that you don't flee, my dear." She winked and then continued through the doorway that led to the stairs. Whispering she said, "And don't call me milady again… alright?"

"Aye." Hessa replied sullenly. "What would you have me call you then… sister?" Hessa's sarcasm was very plain to Aves and it stung a little. Hessa had been raised as Aves maid and companion. This meant in many ways they were very much like sisters, yet in many more they were not.

"Of course not… " Aves said as she tried hard to sound mirthful. "Then again, aye. It will do… Call me sister… or even, cousin. Yes call me cousin or by name while we travel. It will make the trip more interesting. It may make it safer for us both if people think that we are related." A spark gleamed in Aves's eye as she confided this to Hessa quietly. "And I'll do the same. I'll call you either by your name or cousin. Agreed?"

"Alright. It may prove interesting, milady." Aves scowled as Hessa said this. "I mean… it may prove interesting, Aves."

"That's better." Aves's mood lightened as Hessa corrected herself. "Now let's get down there before Jaconis does." Hessa nodded as the pair hurried down the stairwell.

Chapter Eight: Plans

Jaconis fumed as he rose to his feet. Things were not going as he had planned at all. Seeing Aves and Hessa take their leave of the gallery, he decided to stalk after them in an attempt to learn what secrets they guarded from him. He wondered how Aves had managed to make it to the council hall past all of his henchmen.

'Which of my underlings failed?' The implications infuriated him more than the thought of his father's incompetence.

At least Daffer had taken the bait and chosen him as their representative. It was not the leader of the expedition… but it was an important position… and should anything happen to Namir en route to Hornshir, he would exert his authority to gain command of the expedition at that point. He grinned deviously as he gained on Aves and Hessa. He noticing the way the two of them walked… holding each other in confidence he realized he needed to gain one or the other's trust in order to bring his plans to fruition.

Jaconis motioned to the door as he passed each of his goons. The first just looked at him in confusion, but the one to his left seemed to understand. He shook his head and realized he needed to get a better class of underlings.

Jaconis hurried along feeling the need to keep Aves and

Hessa in sight. He was taken completely by surprise when Tali stepped in front of him. Were it any other time he might have welcomed her intrusion, but not now.

Tali's long brown hair glistened with fragrant oils, jasmine and rose. His breath caught in his throat as his eyes traced her glistening hair down to the exposed cleavage that lay before him. Nervously he looked up into her deep brown eyes.

Memories of their first meeting last summer burned into Jaconis's mind. Tali had accidentally wandered into his chambers mistaking them for her own. It was an awkward encounter, but a pleasurable one. Unfortunately, for Jaconis she had insisted on leaving before he could convince her to stay the evening.

Jaconis was brought back to the present as he felt her lips on his. He refocused his eyes on her and noticed she had leaned forward and gently placed her lips upon his. He slowly moved his arm around her waist and held her like that for some time. All of his worries faded from him at her touch and he felt almost like he was in heaven. All too soon, Tali pulled her sleek and scantily clad body away from him and out of his embrace. Jaconis felt compelled to stop her, so he reached out and grabbed her arms firmly.

"Don't you have to be somewhere, dearest?" Tali's voice was deep and alluring as she asked her question almost innocently.

"Aye… though I long to linger here… " The thought of possessing her filled his every thought as he licked his lips gingerly.

She nodded seductively and spoke, "I long for the same, but it is not to be. At least not yet." Tali smiled flirtatiously at Jaconis as she slowly continued in her husky voice. "The council has called you and asked you to hurry." She chided Jaconis and rebuked his advances again as he tried pulling her closer to him, much to his spite.

"Why did you hinder me then?" Jaconis's inquiry held much of his passion for her… and his pain at her rebuke.

Tali's soft laugh caused her breasts to heave tantalizingly.

"Two reasons… first, I have never kissed anyone summoned by the council before." She winked at him as she enjoyed his astonished look. "The other is because I noticed things didn't seem to go quite as you would have liked." Seeing Jaconis wince she added almost to herself. "I knew I was right."

"Get to your point!" Jaconis said abruptly, still unable to take his eyes off her.

"I was just wondering if it was your plan that had been flawed or if it was your help." Tali gazed into his emerald eyes anxious for his reply.

Jaconis's reply rumbled from his throat in a low growl hatefully, "My plan was perfect… at least it should have been!"

"Just as I thought," she smirked. "It seems that I have a very attractive bargain for you then, my dearest Jaconis." Tali licked her lips as her gaze met his. Jaconis shuddered before her in anticipation. His torment was exquisite. Before she lost her hold, she continued. "You need me… and what I can offer you."

"I… I… In what way? What do you mean by this?" Jaconis stammered.

"You need someone with intellect… " Tali pulled him closer and breathed the rest upon his throat. "Someone crafty enough to improvise and make plans in your stead, should you be… unavailable. I can do this… if it pleases you."

"Wh… What would you ask in return?" Jaconis held his thoughts steady although the rest of his mind strayed.

"Just a part of your profits." Tali's matter of fact tone jolted Jaconis to his senses abruptly.

"How much of a part?" Jaconis asked shrewdly.

"As much as I deserve… I would do anything for you to succeed," Tali purred.

"Anything?" Jaconis's question welled out unbidden.

"Aye… " Tali thrust against him, "… anything."

Jaconis gulped for air abruptly as visions of Tali's naked form pressed against his in the rhythmic pulse of his passions flashed before his mind's eye. He nodded slowly as he shut out these carnal thoughts. "Then you are welcome to it. Meet me at the Gathering Place this evening. We'll discuss the matter further then."

"Any orders for me now… aside from that?" Tali mused shrugging her shoulders so more of her cleavage would be exposed as if by accident. She was pleased when she saw Jaconis's body betray his desire.

"No… nay… aye." Jaconis stammered. Seeing Tali's mirth at his stammering he took a deep breath and continued. "Aye, please go out to my gathering fold and have them ready to follow the other members of the expedition as they depart. I want to know what they are planning on bringing and which route they plan to take to Hornshir. I want to have surprise as well as knowledge on my side."

"Very well." Tali chastely kissed Jaconis's cheek then turned abruptly to leave.

Jaconis slyly grabbed Tali's arm and pulled her back around and into his arms for a deeper show of affection. Tali's cheeks turned crimson as she pulled away from him and fled. He stood there and watched her leave as a broad grin split his lips.

Tali felt Jaconis's eyes on her as she made her way over to the door on the opposite side of the hall. She felt his stare through the throngs of people attempting to leave the hall and she enjoyed every minute of it.

It was the yelp of surprise that caught Nurn off guard. He had just passed the doorway to the first level balcony when he had heard it. His hackles rose as he bounded around the corner ready to defend his brother from some of Jaconis's goons. However, in his haste he did not notice Halin was not as far around the corner as he thought. Nurn stumbled over Halin and pushed Aves down on top of his brother. Nurn barely caught himself as he fell headfirst down part of the stairway

At the sound of Aves's and Halin's combined yelp, Hessa dodged neatly to the side just in time to witness Nurn's foot get momentarily caught in the back of Halin's shirt.

Aves slowly regained her feet. She turned to Halin as she took in the situation and asked, "Are you quite done accosting me?"

Blushing and unsure of what to say, Halin stood slowly and apologized without looking into her eyes. "I am sorry, milady. I meant no offense. My brother and I were… "

"Don't worry about it." Aves's eyes were filled with delight as she realized to whom she was speaking. She chose not to turn and see how close his brother was to them. "I'm just curious if this is how you always meet the fairer sex?" Seeing Halin's blush deepen she continued. "I mean, first you didn't move out of my way in the market earlier… " Halin gasped as Avis said this. "… aye I noticed you. What's more is that I remembered the encounter." She winked at him and continued, "and now you throw yourself at me as I make my way to the council chamber. If I didn't know any better, my dear Halin, I might think you wish to despoil me." Mirthfully she gazed at him as if she expected a reply.

"I'm sorry, Aves." To her surprise, Nurn replied from behind her instead of Halin. His voice boomed throughout the staircase as he continued. "I must have pushed my brother harder than I had thought. I deeply regret that my actions caused you ill."

Now it was Aves's turn to blush. She tried unsuccessfully to hide it from Halin's view as she turned to face Nurn. "It is quite all right, milord." She curtsied quickly and rushed to Hessa's side. Aves made a show of checking Hessa over to see if she had been harmed in the mishap.

Seeing her lady's reaction to Nurn, Hessa remarked quickly in the hopes of changing the topic of the conversation, "I think we should hasten to the council before Jaconis stumbles upon us as well."

"Aye." Nurn and Halin agreed in unison.

Hessa nodded at them and then took Aves's arm in hers. When the two of them were settled and ready, Hessa bade Nurn and Halin to follow them as she turned to continue down the stairs. Halin and Nurn fell in step easily behind the ladies as they descended the final stairway to the main council chambers.

As they entered the chamber, Aves let go of Hessa's arm and quickly made her way over to Namir. She pulled him close to her and held him in a fierce embrace as the others approached.

Leaving one arm around Aves, Namir turned to face the others. A smile was firmly set on his handsome face as he welcomed them. "Thank you all for joining me so swiftly." His grin deepened when he noticed Jaconis was not amongst them. "Shall we continue this then?" He asked the council as he turned to face Armani.

"Aren't you forgetting someone?" The voice cut out of the darkness swiftly; its bitterness stung like the edge of a knife. As the assembly tried to discern its source, Jaconis stepped from the shadows and laughed at them mockingly.

Begrudging Jaconis his entrance, Namir turned again to Armani. "Milord Chancellor, now that my party is fully assembled, may we gain the council's blessing?"

Armani acquiesced by motioning for the group to draw closer. "Saril, please come and bless this group. I wish to do all we can to insure their successful return." Armani waited for them to gather in front of his dais before extending his staff above them. He waited as Saril cleared his throat and readied himself before he motioned for the rest of the council to extend their hands towards the group in prayer.

"May the great light guide you and Ea take you under his wing. Oh mighty Ea, the Lord of the sweet waters and the Patron of wisdom, magic, and healing, please guard these, Your children, and keep them safe on this expedition. Please let all those that would hinder them find Your wrath and may Your knowledge aid them by granting them speed in their tasks and trials to come." Saril intoned quietly. He swayed with every breath and leaned heavily upon the rail before his dais. "With this said, consider yourselves blessed. Please go about your preparations and keep Ea's light in your hearts." All heads came up at this point, save for Nurn's, and the group made ready to leave. Saril, feeling Nurn's reverence, called out to him. "Nurn, your reverence is well placed, but now is the time for your departure. Please keep Ea's light in your heart and make your way out of here with the rest of your compatriots."

Nurn raised his head slowly as his thoughts played darkly over his face. Nurn did everything he could to stay his tongue as Saril spoke to him of Ea and His blessings. Deep down Nurn knew that Ea's blessings were no more than mists compared to Tumere's will, but he decided not to speak of this to Saril.

Instead, he looked up into Saril's clouded eyes and remarked curtly, "Of course Healer." Nurn then looked over to Namir and motioned for his attention.

Namir, completely rapt in his effort to get Jaconis to agree with his plan, noticed Nurn's signal and moved over to him after he quit Jaconis's presence uneasily. "Aye?"

"I will go out first, if I may." Nurn glanced at Jaconis and let his features reflect the contempt he felt for him. "I may be able to find a suitable place for us to meet."

Namir nodded at Nurn's suggestion and rubbed his chin in thought. "Agreed. However, go to the stairs first to secure us a section free from outside eyes and ears." Nurn nodded and left the council hall.

Namir raised his voice above the group's growing din as he turned to the rest of the party, "Friends, gather round!" He saw Jaconis's glare at his remark and noted that although Jaconis knew that he was no friend of Namir's, he did not hesitate to join the huddle. "Let us quit this chamber and meet in the hall outside to make our plans for tomorrow's departure."

"What is there left to plan?" Jaconis's smooth voice flowed over them like fresh oil.

Smirking, Halin interjected, "Where we can toss you for starters." Feeling proud of his wit, he scanned the small group for their reactions to his little barb. His mirth drained slowly as

Namir's scowl was followed by Aves's and Hessa's grim frowns.

"All humor aside," Namir let the weight of the moment build, "we need to discuss the route we are going to take in the morning as well as the provisions each of us need to arrange for. We also need to decide on the time of our departure."

"Fine by me. The sooner we're done the faster I can attend more important affairs." Jaconis retorted alternating his severe glare from Halin to Namir and back.

Namir immediately disregarded Jaconis's snide remark and turned to leave the council's presence. He paused to see if there would be any more comments from the council before the group departed. When none came, Namir led them into the hallway where Nurn waited patiently. He waited until the others arrived. Namir watched as Aves and Hessa walked up arm in arm. In the dimly lit hall, they appeared very much like sisters.

'Maybe Halin and Nurn can both have what they desire,' he thought.

Seeing Jaconis following them closely, yet far enough away that he could keep their assets in his view quickly brought Namir back from these thoughts. He knew Jaconis entertained vile thoughts that involved both of them and himself by the look in his eye.

'Hopefully Nurn doesn't see Jaconis's face,' Namir brooded to himself. 'The last thing we need is to have one of us brought up on charges for murder.' Lastly Halin made his way, making sure the main doors to the council chambers were closed behind him granting them the privacy Namir wanted. Namir smirked as he thought about Halin as a sentry. 'Hopefully I'll have a chance to build Halin's skills on the way to Hornshir.' Namir thought quickly as he felt his elation drop a little with the thought of forcing the boy to lose some of his innocence.

Once they were assembled, Namir walked to the center of the hall. "We need to get some details worked out before we run into any problems on our trip. First, I am the leader of this expedition. This means my word is law while we are traveling to and from Hornshir." He waited calmly for Jaconis to say something… anything, but to Namir's amazement, he did not. "That being clear," he continued, "the only other thing that I want to inform you of is our path to Hornshir. We will start by meeting on the hilltop to the south of town just after day break." Namir ignored Jaconis's grumble of disapproval and continued before he could raise an objection to the plan. "From there we'll follow the river as far as we are able to and ford it at our first opportunity."

"Why don't we just take the ferry north of town?" Jaconis inquired.

Namir shook his head. "It has set hours of operation, and unless you are eager to sleep tonight on the road, the first available time to cross is noon. Judging from the importance of this expedition, time should not be wasted."

"Then let's go now." Jaconis grinned mischievously at Namir's hesitance.

"No." Nurn deftly cut Jaconis's idea short. "Tell me, have you readied your supplies, Jaconis?" Nurn's deep voice rolled over all of them filled with hatred and scorn. "Better yet, have you bothered to survey the route on both sides of the river in anticipation for this expedition?" Seeing Jaconis's face turn scarlet, Nurn continued. "I thought not. This is why the Chancellor chose Namir to lead us. Now, we will do as he says. No questions and no grumblings!" The threat in Nurn's deep voice was palpable, even Namir felt cowed by the big man's intentions.

Jaconis cringed away from the promised pain of Nurn's threat and agreed swiftly. "I'm sorry." With his head hung he continued. "I was simply unsure of Namir's choice. I am not used to him being prepared… "

"Enough." This time Aves stopped Jaconis's ranting. "Everyone is tired and all this baiting is completely unnecessary. Leave it be, Jaconis." Her hazel eyes flashed with anger in the gathering gloom of the evening.

Namir cleared his throat to get everyone's attention. Once

he was certain everyone was paying attention, he continued. "Go home and prepare your things. I will see you all in the morning. Make sure to speak to those you hold dear and to your masters as well. Pack your own supplies as well as the items for barter and trade by daybreak. I'm afraid sleep will be scarce for all of us this evening, but time is of the essence." Namir turned abruptly and walked off. After Namir had vanished into the darkness, Halin glared at Jaconis then took his leave. Aves and Hessa strolled off and left Nurn and Jaconis alone in the hall.

"Namir asked me to tell you that he will not be back to Daffer's residence." Nurn's voice echoed in the hall menacingly.

"You mean he is not going to stay there tonight?" Jaconis inquired slightly surprised.

"I mean he will not be back ever." Nurn said with an ominous and oppressive tone. As his words rang through the hall he stepped off in the same direction that Halin had gone and he took the only torch with him.

Jaconis stood in the gathering darkness for a while as he brooded before he too walked out of the council hall. He quickened his pace as he thought about his meeting with Tali. 'Hopefully she's waiting for me already.' Jaconis hardly noticed the road or the growing shadows as he sped towards the Gathering Place. His only thoughts were of Tali and her generous offer, 'Finally I'll have someone talented working for me… and I know exactly how to use her talents.' He smirked as he walked into the inn's main room.

The fire roared and he felt comforted by the warmth as he looked across the room. It was full of people eating and drinking, each one complained about their tasks or boasting of their day's profits. Everyone vied for the attention of the whole room and each had a mug of ale in hand, as they either spoke or listened.

The smell of freshly roasted deer cut through the odor of the room packed with hot and sweaty townsfolk. The most common discussion seemed to be Namir's expedition, or so everyone was calling it. Many of the older folk claimed Namir would come back bearing all of Hornshir's riches on his back or embellished on what the trip to Hornshir would be like. The younger men and women in the inn lamented the fact they had to stay here and work, while Namir and his friends were allowed to go on this grand adventure. As Jaconis passed each of the boisterous drunkards, his mood became darker.

Disappointment was not a feeling unknown to Jaconis. In fact, he was used to being left down by everyone close to him. His heart fell when he noticed Tali was not waiting for him in the main room. His hopes and dreams slowly faded as he scanned the crowded tables and booths and heard no mention of himself in the conversations that he was able to overhear. Jaconis paced the main room of the Gathering Place throughout the evening, muttering as he did so, and tried to drown his depression in the watered down ale his father served. Jaconis eagerly glanced at the door every time it opened half-expecting Tali to make her way into the inn from the chilly night air.

At midnight, he sulked up to his room half drunk. He did not bother to take a lamp with him. He stumbled up half of the steps and ran into several walls before he gained the privacy of his room. The last bastion of Jaconis's hope was dashed as he opened his door and noticed his room was devoid of any human life. He quickly stripped off his clothes and threw himself onto his feather bed. He vowed bitterly to get revenge on Tali for her treachery and within a few minutes, he was asleep.

Dreams of Tali and her promises filled Jaconis's thoughts. He felt her breasts against his exposed chest… the silky luxuriant feeling of her hair as it brushed against him… her full lips on his bare skin both tingled and excited him. The way her laugh tantalized him and how her smile vexed him… all of this mingled with her scent and wiles. "Why can't I escape her?" Jaconis repeated as he tossed and turned in his sleep.

Jaconis awoke and screamed. His body ached and a light sweat covered him. It was still dark. His mind whirled with visions of Tali mingling with those of Aves and Hessa. There was blood as if some sort of battle had taken place. At first, he thought that the Gathering Placed had burned down. Smoke from the fire in the main hall filtered through the floorboards. Jaconis calmed himself down and forced his mind to realize he was in his room. He carefully gauged his surroundings. The temperature was wrong for the inn to be on fire. He lay back down and panted mercilessly as he tried to remember his dreams.

Several long moments passed before Jaconis noticed the weight in bed beside him. A light caress on his outer thigh and across the small of his back stole him from the lingering remnants he had managed to recall from his dream. Moonlight danced across the room and bathed Jaconis in its silvery sheen. He slowly turned, not knowing what… or who… to expect.

Jaconis held his breath. His eyes moved quickly up from the foot of his bed. He slowly scanned the pools of shadows cast by the moon's delicate glow. His eyes grew more accustomed to the silvery blue darkness as Jaconis noticed his bedding in complete disarray. He assumed it was from his nightmare and continued his assessment of his bed.

Jaconis's eyes were drawn to the shape of a woman's calf half exposed before him in the inky darkness. He traced it up to the woman's neck. Her thick curly hair enticed him. Jaconis continued to gaze along her glistening body. He gently reached over and ran his fingers along her lightly covered hip. A light gasp tore his eyes from her full hips up to her face. Realization hit him all at once.

'How much of my nightmare was a dream and how much was reality,' Jaconis wondered as he caressed Tali's cheek with his free hand.

He slipped the fingers of his left hand along her thigh and grinned as Tali writhed. Her lips parted and her breath became ragged. Somewhere deep inside of him, Jaconis felt that this was somehow wrong, although he never could remember feeling this way before about anything.

He struggled with himself, Jaconis finally decided not to pursue this. Instead, he kissed her once very passionately on her lips, then drew the covers over both of them and held her close. Jaconis's dreams were more peaceful than normal, yet in the distant recesses of his mind, he saw something looming over him… something dark and ominous.

Chapter Nine: Encounters

"Which is worse? Eh, Namir?" Aves's voice rang out and filled the vale that they were camping in as the small groups' peals of laughter echoed with it.

"You're babbling." Namir looked Aves directly in the eye as he tried to keep his mirth in check.

"Namir, that wasn't one of the choices." Hessa argued. "Come on… please." She did her best to look innocent as her chemise pulled tightly over her ample body. She had folded her wet legs under her chemise as well to make it a little less revealing.

"Very well… if I must." Namir took a quick look around them to make sure that the others were out of earshot before he continued. "I'd have to say Jaconis's complaints are worse, though Halin's endless questions are harder to bear. Now that I've said it, leave me be until they get back." Namir turned and stalked back to the river. He hoped that they would remain by the fire and leave him alone with his thoughts.

"What should we do when Nurn and Halin get back?" Aves shouted after Namir as he left.

He turned back towards them slowly. If the ladies could have seen his face, they would have shrunk back from him instantly. Still rankled he replied, "Have them quell the flame and ready their packs, we'll leave as soon as I get back."

"And what if Jaconis should return first?" Hessa

mimicked Aves's tone and demeanor as best she could. This not only annoyed Namir at times, it also proved difficult to tell the two apart.

Namir stopped in mid turn and snapped without sparing a glance, "Aid him in readying the game. That is if he has caught any."

'Nine days on the road so far and no sign of a good fording place.' Namir ignored their further attempts at conversation. Instead, he let his mind race back over their journey. 'It seemed to have started out so well too.'

Once he left the council hall, Namir had fled Ellsted and slipped past the sentry Jaconis sent after him effortlessly. After that, he made his way back to Tipin's Smithy. He remembered the feeling of warmth as he came back in through the panel in the roof. There he found Nurn and Halin waiting for him. The night seemed to be alive, as if there was a spark of adventure flying free in the air itself. It was a very refreshing feeling and the three of them enjoyed it as they spoke. They had a brief conference to find out if they had been followed as well. When they confirmed this, he gave them the provision list he needed them to pack for him and gave Halin the last of his money to repay him for the clothes he bought for him. Since the brothers were followed, Namir decided it best to avoid making contact with Hessa and Aves. Instead, he went to the meeting point and sleep there.

The night seemed to drag on forever. Namir felt as if it was the longest night of his life. The feeling he was followed haunted Namir's every step, yet every time he turned, there was nothing behind him but pools of shadows and darkness. Once or twice, he thought he actually saw something move, but Namir could not decide if it was real or just his weary eyes playing tricks on him. Namir stood at the base of the hill for a while arguing this point until lethargy forced him to fall asleep where he stood. He was able to rouse himself after a few moments and made his way to the summit of the hill where he fell asleep instantly. Namir passed out in his favorite nook, the one in which he greeted the dawn every day.

He awoke as the first vestiges of the morning sun burned across the sky and set the clouds aflame with hues of orange, yellow and gold. Namir had often wondered how it would feel to wake up to the rising sun above him and now he knew. It felt exquisite. He sat motionless. He felt as if his movements would steal the moment away from him. After a far too brief period had passed, sounds from the base of the hill slowly made their way to him and drew Namir from his indulgences.

Namir remembered descending the path toward the base of the hill where he saw Jaconis already waiting for him. Disgusted, Namir decided to wait for the others to arrive before he revealed himself to Jaconis.

'With any luck Jaconis didn't see me yet and I can surprise him with my entrance.' Namir mused to himself.

While he waited, Nurn and Halin arrived. The brothers, thick in mirth as usual, walked up playing some sort of game. Namir wondered how they always came up with so many different games. It was as impossible to keep up with the rules they would take turns spouting off, as it was to learn the various strategies well enough to be any good at them. Both brothers laughed raucously as they crested the small rise and came upon Jaconis sitting on a stump. Namir smiled as he saw Nurn and Halin.

'It will definitely be a good trip with them as company,' Namir decided from his hiding place. He lingered longer than he planned just to see what the brothers would do to Jaconis.

Almost immediately, Halin approached Jaconis and, while grinning, held out his hand in greeting. Jaconis hesitated for a few moments while he looked at the tawny haired youth and appraised his intent. Finally, Jaconis succumbed to Halin's jovial demeanor and clasped his arm in greeting. From where Namir sat, he could tell Jaconis's greeting was impartial and had none of Halin's warmth to it. Soon it was evident to Namir that both Halin and Nurn noticed Jaconis's lack of warmth and neither seemed particularly happy by it.

Nurn waited patiently as his brother settled himself on a nearby rock and Jaconis resumed his perch on the stump before he walked over to him exactly as Halin had. Jaconis looked up as he saw Nurn approach and he reacted in the same way, though a little more reluctantly. As Jaconis clasped Nurn large wrist, still with a look of indifference that bordered on loathing, Nurn tightened his grip.

The look on Jaconis's face was well worth the wait. He saw his cousin's eyes widen with shock and a look of extreme discomfort spread across his face slowly. Jaconis's mouth fell open noiselessly when Nurn leaned forward. Namir could not tell what Nurn had said, but he could tell it was something that upset his cousin. Jaconis immediately fell to his knees and placed his head to the ground in abject humility.

'Whatever Nurn told Jaconis must have made quite an impact.' Namir thought jovially.

Namir started to stir from his hiding place as he saw Nurn slowly drop to his knees and closed his eyes as well. Watching the two of them sit there held Namir's attention until the sound of hoof beats roused Nurn and Jaconis from their prayers.

A feeling of astonishment washed over Namir again as he recalled Aves's and Hessa's arrival. Not only were they dressed as poshly as nobles, but they rode in a splendid carriage as well.

Namir remembered exactly how they looked. Both girls were dressed in matching gowns and bore enough a resemblance that they could have been sisters if not twins. Their russet dresses offset the red hints in their hair and the hazel hue of their eyes. Separately each of them was stunning, but together they were breathtaking.

After the carriage halted, the driver vaulted down in one fluid motion and opened the carriage door. His movements were graceful. He was so fluid that the low bow he ended them with seemed to be the most proper way to stop. Namir chuckled to himself as he remembered watching Jaconis, Nurn and Halin bowing to Aves and Hessa as well.

It was not until Aves had risen from her seat in the

carriage and stepped out that the three of them realized she was their party member and not a visiting member of the royal family. They quickly remembered themselves and ended their bow abruptly. Only Nurn rose without a reddish flush of to his face.

Namir knew Armani owned a carriage from the many tales Aves had shared with him when they were younger. Even so, he had convinced himself all of her stories were creations of her imagination. When he had asked why her father never used it, Aves assured him that it was unnecessary to use one in Ellsted due to the small size of the town. Now Namir was proved wrong in a very beautiful and grand way.

The carriage the girls had arrived in was wonderful. It was crafted lovingly out of a sleekly polished deep red mahogany. The brass wheels had been buffed to glisten perfectly in the gathering sunlight. Overall, the design of the carriage was slim, yet functional. It was open to the air without any type of covering to restrict the gentle breezes for which the three rivers were known. This allowed the passengers to enjoy the softly scented gusts of wind as they came across them.

The carriage was large enough to accommodate four passengers and had room for two more on its boards as drivers. To make the ride even more wonderful the carriage was drawn by two beautiful mares. Both mares had a deep chestnut hue which matched the carriage's reddish gleam and the black socks and mane of the horses accented the carriage's brass fittings nicely as well.

The carriage was designed as more than just a pleasurable way of traveling, however, there were ample storage racks below the main deck and along the back end, all of which had been filled with chests and barrels full of provisions for the group. In all, the carriage was the single most expensive thing Namir had ever seen in his life.

Namir remembered the anxiety he felt as he tried to make his way silently down the path. He maneuvered stealthfully to the crest of a small rise just above the group. This reawakened old aches and pains as he recalled that the sun was almost in the perfect place for his dramatic entrance. He heard Aves ask the others if anyone had seen him yet and Namir knew he had to make an appearance soon or else they might start searching for him. He decided it was time to make his arrival.

The look of wonder spread across their faces as his shadow fell across them, especially Jaconis's. This was a memory he would cherish forever. The sun had felt as wonderful on his back then as it did now. The cool ripples of the water around him only strengthened his recollection of the cool morning breeze blew across his face that morning nine days ago. He waited a few moments before he descended the rest of the way to the amazed group.

Once he arrived, Namir was immediately barraged by their questions and demands. He waived most of their concerns aside briskly; although Jaconis's sardonic tone forced him to address many things that he wished not to mention. Namir felt his anger flare again as the heated debate replayed itself in front of his mind's eye.

"Are we to take someone with us that the council doesn't know about?" Jaconis's demand had brought all other conversations to a halt.

"Would you prefer to walk all the way to Hornshir?" Retorted Namir coolly, though a hint of venom had noticeably seeped into his voice.

"I am not saying that!" Jaconis challenged.

Nurn's rebuke had come swiftly. "Then say what you mean and be quick about it!"

The menace in Nurn's voice rumbled violently across the little clearing as the driver spoke up. He was a timid man and barely stood as tall as Aves. "I was asked only to bring the ladies here and to instruct one of you in the carriage's operation. Once that is done I am to return to Ellsted."

"And who ordered this!" Jaconis shot before Namir had the chance to reply.

"That is enough from you Jaconis!" Namir looked calmly into his cousin's emerald eyes. "Don't force me to have Nurn silence your tongue. I believe he has already taught you some humility today." Namir had paused for a moment to enjoy Jaconis's look of shame before he continued. "Are you so eager to learn this lesson again so soon?" He stared Jaconis down and waited until everyone else quieted down as well. Namir turned to the driver and asked. "Please continue. I am sorry for my cousin's brashness, though he does have a valid question. I would love to know who to show my gratitude to for this most generous gift."

The driver smirked at Namir's word play. "Armani of course. But I thought you already knew that much, milord."

"Aye, the thought had crossed my mind that he was the one who gave us this boon." Namir looked over to Jaconis smugly for a moment before motioning to Halin and Nurn and continuing. "Please teach these two your craft. I believe we will do better to have two learn how to handle the carriage than just one." Nurn and Halin immediately rose to their feet and stepped over to the carriage driver.

"So be it." The driver bowed and took them aside.

Namir relived his disgust at being delayed for most of the day, but he felt the speed of the carriage would make up for the minor delay. What troubled Namir the most was Jaconis's reaction to the carriage.

'Why must he always make things difficult for us?' Namir brooded as he mulled the scenario over in his mind again. 'Somehow I will either have to rid myself of Jaconis or get Jaconis to stop making things harder than they need to be.' Neither of these ideas appealed to Namir in the slightest.

"Namir!" Nurn's voice shattered Namir's brooding by its urgency.

Namir had waded out of the river and spun in the direction of Nurn's voice before he realized what he was doing. He waited only a few seconds as he spotted the movement in the bushes that indicated where Nurn was before he called back, "Here!"

Nurn broke through the brush and almost pushed Namir

back into the river as he gained Namir's presence suddenly. Still panting Nurn gripped Namir's shoulders ruggedly. "I wanted to tell you myself."

"What is it?" Namir stood there as he moved both of his hands underneath Nurn's shoulders to prop him up as if he were Nurn's sole means of support.

"I couldn't find the horses." Tears came to Nurn's eyes as he confided this. "I looked as far as I dared to alone, but found no trace of them." Nurn slumped fully giving his weight over to Namir to support completely defeated.

"It's alright, my friend. We can get by on foot if we need to." Namir reassured his hulking friend as best he could. Bitterness crept into his heart as he thought about yesterday's incident. "Go back to the others. Help Aves and Hessa gather up what's left of our supplies. Hopefully Halin can find some trace of the carriage and the rest of our provisions."

Nurn rose slowly as Namir watched him lumber back through the brush leaving him alone again with his thoughts. Hatred welled up within Namir as he watched Nurn make his way back to the others. His agony was complete. Namir picked up a rock and threw it into the shallows of the river as hard as he could.

'I know Jaconis had a hand in this somehow,' Namir thought to himself angrily, 'if only I could prove it.'

He let another rock sail into the clear water. He closely followed it with another. He needed to cool off. His mind wandered back to the attack as he waded back into the river.

It had been the end of the eighth day and Namir was pleased to have been proven right. The carriage did aid them in their travel to Hornshir. Everyone had been in a spirited mood and the sky was clear. Nothing could have gone wrong. The day passed much like the seven before, uneventfully. Halin entertained everyone with the songs and tales his mother had taught him. Even Aves helped pass the time by accounting some of the stories she overheard from her servants and her father's guests. Overall, it proved to be a very pleasant trip.

In the evenings Nurn and himself would help Halin understand how to fight, although most of the time it seemed pointless. Halin was just too lighthearted to take the training seriously. The only one that seemed bothered by anything was Jaconis. For some strange reason the farther they went from Ellsted the more irritated and distant Jaconis became. Namir remembered thinking that it was just homesickness and paid no real attention to Jaconis's brooding.

They had gained at least three days of travel for every day they spent using the carriage. Within the first day, although it was nearly spent by time they had left, the group had made it to the first hollow Namir had selected for their refuge. By the end of the sixth day, they were almost half way to Hornshir.

The lack of a good ford bothered him, however, and Namir made a point of going to the river at every stop in a vain attempt to find some sign of a good ford. The main problem they had to overcome was the carriage. It would flood if they had taken any of the earlier fords they passed and the farther they went the less likely it was they would find a suitable ford.

Namir lingered at the river grappling with this problem while the rest of the group prepared the evening meal and the fire. By time Namir rejoined them, a raging fire was blazing forth in the middle of the glen and a number of makeshift beds lay scattered around it. Halin was singing a haunting tune while Hessa cooked some sort of stew. Nurn just finished the bedrolls as Namir approached him.

The thing that bothered Namir the most was the neither Aves nor Jaconis was anywhere nearby. He quizzed Nurn about this and was assured they were feeding the horses on the other side of a row of bushes. Namir recalled feeling uneasy about it still, but he allowed himself sometime to relax and to listen to Halin's song.

In the back of his mind he knew something was wrong, he just did not know what. Namir made a mental note to himself to ask Aves about their absence when she returned and allowed himself to get lost in the words of Halin's song.

Shadow Dance

Namir could still hear the lyrics of Halin's song perfectly as he recollected the incident. Halin's voice was a light tenor in the light breeze of the evening and was oddly accompanied by the crackling flames and insects heralding the arrival of dusk.

"Gather around to hear my tale,
The only tale left to tell.
Feel the mists of your shore
Rising up from hell.
Wanton beasts in a row,
Nothing there left to lose.
Death comes for your coward heart,
Forming up the noose.

Fire and wind in the night
Tell me what you feel is right.
Wind and rain in the morn
Whisper of secrets forlorn.

Hail and water falling down,
Only your hope can survive.
In the dream your answer comes,
Bringing you back to life.
Come with me and see the fate
That lies for you in the light.
Bask in the glory of his wrath;
Whose is the power of might?

Fire and wind in the night
Tell me what you feel is right.
Wind and rain in the morn
Whisper of secrets forlorn.

Thunder claps and clouds will roll,
Gathering for war.
Winds will howl and the sky will fall,

Ripping the veil as before.
Mountains move and march into
The waiting ranks from above.
The trees move last and these
Perilous things begin to shove.

Fire and wind in the night
Tell me what you feel is right.
Wind and rain in the morn
Whisper of secrets forlorn.

Darkness itself arraigned to fight,
The battle of great woe.
In the end its power was slight,
Light proved the greater foe.
Peace was bought through bloodshed
Of the earth and the sky.
How can we hope to live
Without ever knowing why?

Fire and wind in the night
Tell me what you feel is right.
Wind and rain in the morn
Whisper of secrets forlorn.
Whisper of secrets forlorn."

Aves's scream first roused Namir from Halin's compelling lyrics. At least he thought it was Aves that screamed. Namir recalled the feeling of dread overcome him as he leapt to his feet and found himself racing Nurn toward the sounds of a struggle. Thorns tore at his pants from all directions and his arms were gashed and smeared with blood when he finally erupted into the clearing. The first thing that he noticed was Jaconis lying bruised and unconscious where the carriage should have been. Nurn found Aves a few feet away and on the other side of a small group of shrubs.

Namir shivered at the thought of how she looked. She lay

in the dirt all bloody and lifeless. In many ways, she resembled a very battered and discarded doll with her limbs splayed out in all directions. Aves's skirts were hiked up and torn to shreds and welts were raised across her cheeks, arms and exposed thighs.

Namir let his mind focus on his two unconscious companions that were missing. He reflected on how he turned his shirt into make shift bandages for the two of them. At the time, it seemed natural enough to him, but now he was sore pressed for clothing. Either way, he chose to cut his shirt into strips as he bandaged Aves's most brutal wounds before he moved on to Jaconis to tend his injuries as well. Namir believed Nurn told Hessa and Halin of the attack.

A part of him hoped that Nurn was not just standing there watching him work, but that he was doing something productive. It was not until Nurn took him by the shoulders and shook him lightly that Namir noticed he had finished bandaging both Aves and Jaconis. He also realized that the two of them had been carried to the fire and he sat alone in the darkness.

Namir remembered the feeling of numbness steal across him as the situation registered to his brain. Several hours passed before Namir regained most of his senses. He still felt that a part of him was lost in the attack. By the time that Namir finished caring for his injured companions, any and all hope of tracking the thieves had fled with the last vestiges of daylight. Nurn had assured him that they searched as hard as they could. At least they had until Hessa demanded they help her get Aves and Jaconis over to the fire.

Once that was done, Hessa fell to preparing the group's evening meal and Halin stayed with Aves and Jaconis in case they awoke. That left Nurn free to find Namir and see why he had not returned to the fire as well. Namir understood Nurn's fear that he might have been attacked as well and quickly agreed to return to the fire with him.

Aves was the first to wake. Not only was she disoriented, she was also sore all over. Namir hoped she could give them some idea of who attacked them or at least which direction they had come from.   However, Aves could not remember anything about the attack. It was as if her memory was limited strictly to Jaconis telling her he found a berry bush beside the horses. She distinctly remembered turning around to walk over to him. Nothing else, it was all blank from that point to when she woke up near the fire. Aves's only memory of any sort was a quick wash of color and blackness.

Jaconis was no better.   He was extremely angry and belligerent, but he had no recollection of what had happened either. He claimed he had just found a berry bush and wanted Aves to help him determine if the berries were poisonous. Jaconis emphatically remembered calling Aves over to him and as he turned to see if she had decided to come look, a black figure moved forward and struck him across his forehead with something hard.

The only other thing Jaconis was able to remember was hearing the horses neighing frantically as he fell into unconsciousness. Jaconis described hearing the horses as he related feeling someone hitting him many times, as he was falling into unconsciousness. At first Namir wanted to verify this part of his story, but Hessa had pointed out that the type and number of wounds that Jaconis had received validated his story perfectly.

'As if the attack wasn't bad enough, the berries Jaconis had found actually were poisonous.' Namir fumed as he sank beneath the surface of the river.

He shuddered as he felt the icy cold water of the river slowly rise over his head and brought him back to his senses again. Namir floated in place. He hoped to find a solution to their problem, any solution.

'We can continue without the carriage and horses. We planned to do this from the beginning,' Namir conceded to himself. 'It's the loss of the supplies that's the problem.' He knew that they needed to have access to the goods that they brought to trade in Hornshir. Without them, and the rest of the gifts that had been sent to gain the trust of Hornshir's council, their success was not certain. All of these things had been on the carriage. Recovering from the loss of these gifts and trade goods would be impossible. 'If I could just figure out which direction the carriage was taken.' Namir brooded as he returned to the surface of the water and made his way to the shore.

Halin sulked as he followed the ruts of the wagon's wheels into the forest. 'Why was I chosen to track the wagon,' he complained to himself in his own mind. Halin pictured Namir answering this question easily. 'Because you are not skillful enough to track down the horses,' or, 'because you are useless with the injured.'

There were probably a million other reasons that Halin did not know of as well, but he really did not want to know the answer. Instead, Halin allowed his thoughts, and his imagination, to carry him further from his task as he wandered through the woods. He managed to wander quite a distance from their encampment before he stumbled over an exposed root and fell face first to the ground.

Halin slowly regained his footing, keeping his imaginary conversation with Namir going the whole time. He meticulously brushed the dirt and twigs from his clothes as he stood and added his clumsiness to the already lengthy list of why he was the one selected to track the carriage. It wasn't until Halin finished brushing the last vestiges of fresh dirt off his boot that he noticed this section of the trail had been recently brushed clear of any marks.

This realization abruptly ended his imaginary debate with Namir and turned thoughts to his lack of weapons and fighting skills. "Why couldn't Nurn and Namir have taught me more?" Halin whined quietly to himself as he snuck along this new trail. He argued with himself about going back to get the others or continuing on his own. After several long moments of deliberation, he decided to continue on without them. "Besides, this way I can let them know more about what happened to the carriage and not just return empty handed," he mused.   Halin prowled along this new pathway and was encouraged when he saw ruts from the carriage appear over a little hill several paces from where he had fallen.

"Obviously the thieves think their pathetic attempt to hide their trail will elude us," Halin snickered to himself.

His hopes soared, 'it'll be just a matter of time before I come across them now. Should I go back and get the others… or should I attempt to find the location of these marauders?' He mused again silently.

Halin recalled the argument he recently had with Nurn back from the recesses of his mind. He could feel the confusion it caused him again. Halin's knees started to buckle, so he sat down to puzzle out the correct choice. It was getting dark and the longer he waited the darker it would get.

He did not want to lose the tracks completely, but he also did not want to come across the carriage thieves without either Nurn or Namir to back him up. Halin rolled the decision around in his mind before he finally chose his course of action. Although it had taken him longer than it would have taken either Nurn or Namir, he felt confident that he had come to the right choice.

'Nurn would probably continue on. He would also be able to bring the carriage back single handedly… if only I was as strong and talented as he is.' Halin thought bitterly.

A few moments later, he focused on what Namir might do and he finally decided that Namir would be able to bring back the carriage by himself as well, but in a different way. This left him only one choice… he was going on and would not return unless he was successful. Besides, this way he could prove to the whole group how useful he really was.

From what Halin could determine, the trail led away from the river that separated them from Hornshir. He moved as fast as he dared to without running. This way he could move quietly and avoid detection, but still be able to gain a little more time on the fleeing thieves. Halin was determined not to miss any signs of their passage, so his travel proved slower than he would have liked.

Although the main ruts were evident and clear, the brigands might attempt to lay a false trail or to disguise their true path. Halin was certain that he would either come across the bandits or find that he had been following a false trail at each and every bend he came to. The farther he went the more certain of this he became. Halin followed the trail farther from his own encampment than he had originally planned to, but he did not care.

He knew that if he managed to find the carriage, his absence would be vindicated no matter how much time it took him. His steady stride beat its rhythm in his ears like the beat of a great song and he let his mind get carried away with it as he stalked along the carriage's path.

Halin was startled again as he stumbled over an upturned root that grabbed his boot as he passed a thickly overgrown area of the woods. As Halin fell to the ground, his surprise increased when the bush next to him moved on its own. Halin attempted to get up quickly, but his hands found only fresh mud and loosely packed dirt. His grip on the ground slid from him as he twisted around to get better footing.

Every effort failed to do anything except to produce a dull thud as his body struck the ground repeatedly.   After several attempts, Halin determined why his attempts failed. The loose dirt below him was turning to mud. He figured that a spring had started to gush into the soil somewhere nearby and it had created an ever-growing mire that he was laying in the middle of it.

While Halin was struggling against the rising mud, he felt a sharp pain blossom in the center of his back. He felt what little breathe he had left forced out again. Halin quit moving entirely. Something pressed into his back and its weight made it impossible to stand.   He hoped that if he quit moving whatever had landed on him would go away.

Halin laid in the rising mud and brine confused and afraid. How long he had lain there prone and defenseless was beyond him. The only thing Halin was aware of was the dirt in his mouth and clothing, the pressing weight of whatever it was that pinned him to the ground, and his bruised pride. The mud rose to cover his nose and Halin tried again to determine what was on him. He forced himself to focus his full attention on it, as he did he noticed the sun had set and the early hours of night were upon him. Whatever it was on his back settled itself firmly where and was extremely hard.

'It could be a branch that fell on me… or a rock… or… ' Halin felt his mind wander a little as a new pain sprouted in the back of his head. He saw the darkness of oblivion loom before him and he fell into its welcoming embrace swiftly.

Consciousness flooded a new sense of pain back into Halin's body as he awoke. Slowly he realized that he was lying on his back and the thing that dug into the small of his back was a rock. Halin moved his head slowly to the side and felt the pain get worse. It did not matter which side he moved it.

He decided to stop moving his head, but that did not help either. All he could see was the blackness. Halin knew his eyes were open. He also knew Nurn would have figured out where he was by listening to the noises around him or the amount of light. Halin strained to see or hear anything. He chided himself mentally as he failed each attempt to sense a sound or light of any sort. One of his senses just had to give him some idea of his predicament.

The urge to scream slowly stole its way over Halin's mind as he lay there in the darkness and if it was not for the sharp throb that pounded inside his skull, he might have. More time passed as a low buzzing noise forced itself into his realm of sensation. He was unsure if the monotonous buzz in his ears was worse than the accursed blindness he was experiencing, but he knew he could do without either of them. Halin resolved to lie where he was and to be as still as possible. He also decided that the incessant buzzing and the blindness were equally as bad.

'Hopefully this will pass soon.' He thought to himself, the sound of his own inner voice causing new ripples of pain in his head. 'If not I'll just die. Then I might be able to get a sense of my surroundings.' Even his own sarcasm failed to raise his spirits. Completely depressed at his own failure Halin succumbed once more to the euphoric escape sleep offered him from his pain. 'Hopefully it will subside.' This last thought passed through Halin's mind as he drifted off to sleep.

Chapter Ten:
Survival

"You didn't have to enjoy it so much." Jaconis fumed after he made sure no one followed him.

"But it was so much fun, my beloved." Tali leaned over and kissed Jaconis's bruised cheek lightly. "Besides if I hadn't made it look so real, Namir and the others would never have been fooled. Now we wouldn't want that… would we?"

Tali's playful tone and demeanor forced Jaconis to grin. "Can't you take anything seriously?" Jaconis put his arms around Tali's soft back and pulled her down on top of him as he kissed her deeply. "Though you are a devious one, I'll give you that much." Jaconis ran the back of his hand along Tali's cheek and jaw lightly.

"Part of my charm is my lack of concern for anything that happens around me." Tali winked at Jaconis as she pulled away from him. Then, as if she thought better of leaving him, she kissed his lips playfully. "Another part is my sexual appeal… wouldn't you agree?" Tali arched an eyebrow and waited for his response.

"That's the part that I wouldn't trade for anything. Now… when I leave, have Barness go back over the trail. I want him to make sure no one finds your little nook. Namir has both Nurn and Halin looking and although Halin isn't too adept at tracking, one of them is bound to notice Barness' initial attempts to cover the carriage's tracks." Seeing Tali nod in acquiescence he continued. "Where are Canges and the others?"

"Hunting," Tali looked disappointedly into Jaconis's eyes. "Does this mean you are leaving so soon?" Her left hand caressed Jaconis's groin while her right one played with his hair.

"Not yet… there is still something here that I need to attend to." Jaconis reached up and ran his fingers through her silky hair. Then he pulled her face to his and kissed Tali passionately.

As the heat of their passion rose, the wind about them mirrored it. Soon the breeze, which had lightly frolicked around them moments before, fiercely whipped about them in a complete frenzy. Tali leaned back and pulled away from Jaconis's grip. Jaconis drooled as he looked up at her lightly bronzed and toned chest and arms.

Tali smiled as he did so. She flung her head back and allowed the growing wind to ravage her hair. Tali looked like a wild vision of ecstasy and passion and Jaconis enjoyed every breathtaking moment of it.

Tali grinned down at Jaconis coyly; she enjoyed the look of ardor on his face. Jaconis tried to rise up to her, but she forced him back down to the floor of the carriage easily. Both of them knew Tali was in control and that she would not relinquish it any time soon.

Jaconis marveled at how much he enjoyed her as she forced herself on him. Every time he tried to resist, she forced him to comply by striking him lightly.

'Tali is truly remarkable.' Jaconis thought voraciously as his desire for her ate away at the dark recesses of his mind.

Tali allowed Jaconis to lean up and kiss her once before she struck him across the face and pushed Jaconis back down onto the floor of the carriage. Tali slowly moved up his body, playfully exploring his taught and lean frame. Her warm kisses flowed over him as she meandered her way up to his neck. Jaconis's hands wandered as she kissed him. Everywhere

Jaconis's hands touched was warm and soft, yet the flesh held an unyielding quality to it.

Tali's teeth found the side of his neck as he pulled at her and Jaconis reacted exactly as Tali thought he would. She knew the pleasure this would bring so she sank her teeth deeper into his neck. Tali hoped she had timed her final bite right as she felt Jaconis spasm beneath her again.

This spasm came at the perfect time and it allowed Tali to sink her teeth into Jaconis's neck hard enough to bring his blood welling greedily to the surface. Tali suckled at his blood greedily and giggled as she felt its warmth spread across her lips.

Jaconis felt the pleasure of her bite mingle with the intense pain of the wound. His body writhed in both a horrific feeling of ecstasy and the mind numbing agony as he felt Tali's tongue moving through the open wound. Several moments passed before he could do anything other than writhe in the intense moment. Then, without warning, Jaconis screamed as loud and as hard as he could.

Birds rustled overhead as Namir and Nurn toiled with Jaconis's unconscious body. Namir cursed his cousin's ineptness with every breath as they struggled to get him safely to their camp. 'How could he be stupid enough to carry dead carcasses with him while hunting?' Namir wondered. "Although the forest is sparse, only a fool would forget that wolves live and hunt nearby," he muttered quietly.

"What was that?" Nurn asked; the fatigue in his voice was palpable and undisguised.

"Nothing." Namir lied. "We should rest. Let's put Jaconis down over there." Together they delicately laid Jaconis's makeshift litter down between two trees. They nestled it amid the branches to keep it off the ground. Once they had this done, Namir stretched and asked Nurn, "You don't think a wolf did this, do you?"

Nurn slowly shook his head. "No. A wolf wouldn't leave

the body behind… they only kill when they are hungry." He turned the matter over one more time in his head as he worked over every little detail. "I don't think it was a bandit either. Jaconis's dagger was still on him and was not drawn. His clothes were also on him and, aside from his blood, they were left undamaged." Nurn paused as he relaxed his left shoulder and rubbed it gently with his right hand. "Both his clothes and his knife are too well made for a bandit to leave behind; even if the clothes did get a little bloody."

Nurn sat there massaging his other shoulder as he said this. Then he rubbed his eyes to ward off sleepiness. He knew his endurance was visibly taxed, but he also knew they needed to get back to the camp as soon as possible.

"So… we can safely assume that whoever, or whatever, attacked Jaconis also attacked Aves… " Namir shook his head "and more than likely stole the carriage and horses." He sighed deeply. "This makes no sense. Why would anyone leave witnesses behind? Why not kill them outright the first time. What's more, why leave one of the original witnesses alive after a second encounter when they found Jaconis alone?"

Nurn sprang to his feet as his face lost all color. Fear rode stiffly behind his eyes as he faced Namir abruptly. "What if Jaconis's attackers thought they had killed them?"

Namir looked at Nurn confused. "Alright, so they thought they had killed them… but when they stumbled across Jaconis again wouldn't they make sure he was dead this time?"

"I think they left him for dead. They were in a hurry." Nurn said as he hurried back to the litter.

"Why? Why would they be in a hurry?" Namir matched his friend's pace but was still confused about Nurn's intent as well as his odd actions.

Nurn turned to Namir while he reached for the litter's handles. He seemed to be completely refreshed. "Because Jaconis's attackers knew that he would not survive a wound like that unattended. And since he survived then the girl they had attacked might have survived as well."

Comprehension slowly sank into Namir's skull. "Aves."

He said slowly. "They went to find her before she could find help." Namir lifted his end of the litter and they ran as fast as they could manage. Each of them hoped to reach the girls before the bandits did and knowing somewhere deep inside that they would not.

Namir's breath burned in his chest as he ran. He struggled in vain to keep up with Nurn's impossible pace. As he ran Namir's thoughts grew darker and bleaker with each stride. Scenes of vile actions and bloodshed filled Namir's mind with grotesque images as horror and fear mingled together. Although he was amazed at Nurn's strength, Namir lost himself in the images that plagued him. It was not until he heard Nurn bellow to move that he realized his folly.

"Get up! I can't pull both you and Jaconis all of the way back to camp no matter how strong I am!" His breath was hot and sweat poured from off of Nurn's brow in rivulets.

As Namir's mind pulled itself back from the horrors that plagued him, Namir noticed he was sprawled out on the ground. From the amount of dirt caught in his boots and spread all over his pants, it was evident that Nurn dragged him for quite some time before he complained. Namir's were mercilessly torn and his arms were gouged several times by passing branches and thorns.

'How is it that Nurn didn't stop,' Namir wondered.

He looked at Nurn apologetically as Namir stood and lifted his end of the litter once more. No words passed between them. None were needed. As soon as Namir lifted his end of Jaconis's liter, they set out again at the same impossible pace. This time they were both silent and focused on where they were heading. Namir felt his hope bleed away from him with every step as they closed the distance to their camp.

As the two young men entered the clearing and strode into camp, Namir realized that the camp was exactly as his imagination had depicted it. There was blood everywhere and nothing moved, not even the wind dared stir the branches. Even the patches of grass that had managed to poke up through the freshly dried blood stood deathly still.

The thick metallic stench of blood filled their nostrils and weighed down the air around them. The forest was already humid enough without this grizzly scene. Now the air was full of sweat and blood. Their clothes stuck to them instantly as they walked into what was left of their campsite.

Namir felt a part of him die as he thought, 'I led them here. Me. Now they're all dead.' He looked over at Nurn, his big meaty hands hung limp at his sides and a look of pained disbelief covered his already weary face. 'How could I have brought this on them?' Namir wondered to himself.

As the two of them looked around their violated encampment, Namir realized they had dropped Jaconis's litter when they came into the camp. Namir took a moment and looked down at his cousin's body. He tried hard to see Jaconis's injuries as a product of his own hand, but failed to.

The blood soaked through the bandages that lightly covered Jaconis's neck as Namir looked at him pitifully. 'What have I done?' Namir thought again before he too crumpled like the broken twigs and trampled grass all around him.

The movement was faint at first. There was a soft rustle of leaves against stone and then nothing. Nurn noticed it first, but he chose not to react to it. Instead, he closed his eyes and prayed to Tumere, the goddess of the woodlands and vengeance... his goddess, the goddess of his people.

"Grant me the strength to act and the peace of mind needed to fulfill my dark task." His words fell from his mouth in whispered threads as he took care to allow only Tumere and himself know his wishes.

Then he waited quietly for his prey to move again as he crouched perfectly motionless. It was as if he was still locked tightly in the grip of his prayer. He did not have to wait long.

Mere moments later a second rustle of leaves and a slight movement of pebbles came from the rocky slope to Nurn's left. This one was more persistent than the last one had been and told more about the location of whatever it was that made it. Unlike the first noise, this one was close and loud enough that

Namir, still caught in his fit of self-loathing, noticed and turned to glare at its source. Namir slowly rose to his feet, a little unsure of how long he lay beside Jaconis's unconscious body and made his way towards the sound boldly.

He was not trying to hide his approach as he closed in on where the noise came from. His face and demeanor were bleak and seemed to be cast from steel. It would be obvious to anyone who saw Namir that he was determined to end the disturbance one way or another.

As Namir stepped past the last clump of gore infused brush, Nurn reached up and placed his left hand onto Namir's chest. Nurn easily held Namir back and gave him a quick hand signal. He then shoved Namir backwards to get him far enough back that Nurn could still operate in relative stealth. Nurn assumed Namir understood that he should walk back to where he had just been.

Nurn's actions surprised Namir at first, but realization of Nurn's plans seeped into his mind quick enough for him to discern Nurn's intentions. Nurn wanted it flushed from the bushes, whatever it was. He also wanted to keep surprise on their side. Namir nodded his assent, turned mostly away from the bush, and relieved his bladder. As Namir did this, he watched Nurn lift a good sized rock from the ground and meticulously clean the dirt and debris off its surface.

Namir noticed Nurn moved as if he was numb and devoid of all feeling. This bothered him and Namir could not understand why. When Nurn finished, he deftly rose to his feet and made his way soundlessly to the bushes. Once there, he resumed a low crouch in the darkest shadows and waited for a sign that his prey was where he thought.

A third rustle came from the bush shortly after Nurn steadied the rock. Namir watched closely. He saw a hand on the ground at the base of the bush. 'Either the person doesn't think we heard him or they're not that skilled.' Namir mused to himself as he finished answering nature's call. In the time that it took Namir to pull his breeches back into place, Nurn had made his attack. Nurn hefted the stone at his target easily.

It sailed straight into the thick branches of the bush and broke them as it passed. The stone's arc ended very quickly with a dull hollow thud followed shortly by another thud moments later as the person collapsed.

As soon as Namir saw Nurn's rock fly, he strode towards the fight as fast as he could. Namir was only a few paces away when he saw Nurn vault over the shrubbery. Nurn's actions were a blur as he leapt over the bush and landed on the unconscious form of his target. Namir was amazed at Nurn's speed as he strode towards him. By time Namir was where Nurn had been standing, Nurn was already raising his victim high above his head triumphantly.

What happened next threw Namir into even more confusion than he already felt. Nurn stood triumphantly as he held his victim above his own head easily. He slowly turned to get a good look at his prey's face when Nurn collapsed as if an arrow had struck him. It was all Namir could do to stay on his feet as he drank in Nurn's reaction.

Namir rushed to Nurn's side as soon as his senses quit spinning. "What happe… " his voice, filled with anger and dread, caught in Namir's throat as he saw Halin's unconscious body cradled gently in Nurn's arms. Blood was flowing freely from a gash on the left side of Halin's face and his arms and legs dangled limply as if he were a discarded doll.

"I didn't know it was him." Nurn's voice faltered as if his tears were stronger than his will. "Help him… please Namir… please don't let him die… tell me he isn't dead." The break in Nurn's voice tore at Namir's heart. His large friend continued talking, saying the same things repeatedly. Tears mingled freely with Nurn's sweat as he looked down at his brother. "I… I… I didn't mean to… I… I didn't… didn't mean to do… to do this… " Nurn's tears flowed unchecked as he held Halin's limp body tightly against his chest.

"Set him down," Namir ordered to no avail. "NURN! I SAID SET HIM DOWN!" Namir's voice rang through the woods violently, like the rumbling of distant thunder and Nurn did as he was told. Namir completely regained his senses as he loosened Halin's clothing and elevated his head. Namir tore Halin's sash off him quickly and opened it, careful not to get the inside dirty as he pressed it against the flowing wound. He then gathered a hand full of leaves and pressed them against the make shift binding to create enough force to stop the bleeding. "He needs water."

"I'll get it." Nurn decided solemnly. Nurn stood for a moment then started to walk back towards their camp.

"No Nurn. The river isn't too far from here, get the water from there. It will be cleaner." Namir instructed as he saw Nurn's lifeless face look at him almost questioning. 'This hasn't been easy on him.' Namir realized as his friend lumbered off towards the sounds of the river. Namir forced himself to watch Nurn's actions until he had grabbed their wineskins and step out of his range of vision. 'I am going to have to find some harabola root to give Nurn to help him relax tonight,' Namir thought as he turned his attention back to Halin.

Namir scoured his memories for the knowledge he learned from Saril seven years ago. He vaguely remembered Daffer carrying him to Saril's home every morning so the inn could have a healer of its own. The long days spent learning the properties of root and ash seemed far away and the more useful the knowledge was the harder it was to recall. The hard labor he had to perform to teach him about the need for medicine and its uses was the easiest to remember.

Even the day Saril and Namir plotted to end his public tutelage and embark on one of their own devising proved far easier to bring back than the proper barks needed to close wounds quickly. After much delving, Namir was finally able to unlock these lost memories. So much had happened between then and now that begged for resolution, but Namir was able to sift through those burning coals enough to let the needed knowledge flood back into his mind.

Namir's hands moved deftly over Halin's unconscious body. It was as if his hands had a life of their own. As if they had never forgot what needed done. Namir repeatedly caught himself longing to have Saril there to confer with about a sprig of moss or a cut of leaf. It was not that Namir thought Halin was in any danger in his own care, he just wished to have the companionship and experience Saril would have been able to give him.

"Thank you hebasii Saril," Namir muttered quietly, more to himself than to anyone else, as he finished binding Halin's many wounds. Namir had noticed that there were too many fresh wounds for Nurn to be the only cause of Halin's suffering.

"Heb-a-see who?" Nurn asked from behind Namir as he stood there with three full skins of water. He had regained some of his old self as he stood silently behind Namir and watched him tend to Halin's wounds. He noticed Namir crack open several different roots that lay nearby and finally collect some of the sap to spread across Halin's chest and arms. That was when Nurn realized he had not been the only one to hurt Halin. With this realization came anger and a burning desire to know more about what happened to Halin before they found him.

"Never mind," Namir said tiredly as he fell back to his work. Namir had Nurn help him rinse out both of their sashes and replaced Halin's blood soaked one with Namir's. Namir then trickled water into Halin's mouth and showed Nurn how to do this by wetting Nurn's sash and wringing the water out of it slowly into Halin's mouth. After he was certain that Nurn knew what to do, Namir stood to leave.

"Where are you going?" Nurn reached out and held Namir in place by his shoulder.

"I must gather a few things." As he saw Nurn's questioning look, Namir continued. "There are some herbs and roots I saw near the river earlier. I might be able to make them into a tea or, if we are lucky, into a salve to help Halin." He felt Nurn's grasp slip off his shoulder.

Namir took Nurn's receding hand and clasped wrists with him. "Halin is going to be alright, Nurn. I know you are worried, but he will live. I can promise you this much." He released Nurn's big arm and turned to go.

After he took a few steps, Namir stopped and looked back over his shoulder at Nurn as commented aloofly, "I think we should build a fire. Why don't you build one while I am gone? Then we can move Halin and Jaconis near it so they can stay warm tonight. It might also be good to roast some of the game we found with Jaconis. I will be back soon." Namir saw a familiar grin slowly spread over Nurn's face as he had mentioned the game Jaconis caught. Namir enjoyed the sight for the few moments it lasted before Nurn's fear for his brother's condition stole it away.

"What of the others?" The concern in Nurn's voice stopped Namir cold. It was as if Namir had completely forgotten about the girls.

Namir turned towards Nurn again and weighed his words carefully before he spoke them. "We'll look for them when I get back. Right now I need you to care for Jaconis and your brother." He said motioning towards Halin and Jaconis.

'How am I going to tell him of my fears?' Namir thought bitterly as he held his tears in check. 'What words can I use to get him to believe that Aves and Hessa are dead?'

Nurn nodded as Namir turned and left. He watched Namir make his way toward the river and out of his sight before he gathered enough wood to make a fire. When he ran out of easily gathered wood, Nurn turned to the nearest copse of trees. He selected one that looked like it had been dead for some time.

Then, praying to Tumere, he ripped it from the ground as he muttered, "Give… me… strength… !"

Nurn staggered backwards under the weight of the tree he held tightly to his chest. He turned enough so the tree could fall between the others without binding.

Nurn sat down on the fallen trunk and wiped the sweat and tears from his face with the back of his hand. 'We really need an axe.'

The thought of this made him smile. He saw Tipin standing there again, asking him if they had everything that they needed before he left and he had said yes.

'What a fool I am… a stupid careless fool.' Nurn thought as he started tearing the tree apart with his bare hands.

He grabbed an exposed piece of wood here or a protruding branch there and with the sheer force of his muscles, he ripped the tree into manageable chunks of woods and bark. As Nurn bent to his task, he prayed to Tumere for aid and guidance.

Once Nurn managed to dissect the tree, he turned his attention to Jaconis and his brother. It was hard for Nurn to fight his desires and move Jaconis first. Unfortunately for his pride, Nurn had to admit that Halin was more stable than Jaconis. He also realized that he had all but neglected Jaconis since he had attacked his brother.

Nurn moved purposefully over to Jaconis and lifted him as gently as he could manage. He let the end of the litter that supported Jaconis's legs drag on the ground as he pulled it over to where he was going to build the fire. After Nurn had muscled Jaconis into as comfortable of a position as he could, he went to Halin's side and lifted him delicately afraid to cause any more injury to his little brother than he already had.

Nurn attempted to float on the air itself as he carried Halin to the bed of tree branches and fronds he had constructed for him. He laid Halin down in this makeshift bed and took great care to place him in the same position that Namir had left him. Nurn gingerly propped Halin's head on a pillow of grass, leaves and bark he made for him.

Not only did Nurn have a good-sized fire lit in a circle of stones by time Namir had made his way back from gathering his herbs and roots, but he also managed to get two birds and three rabbits cleaned and spitted. Namir was greeted by the warmth of the fire and started to dry what little herbs he was able to find as he breathed in the aroma-laden air filled with the sweet scent of roasting meat. Nurn knelt beside Halin lost in prayer as Namir made himself comfortable next to Jaconis and started changing his bandages.

"The fire looks good and the meat smells wonderful as well." Namir smiled as Nurn opened his eyes somewhat surprised by his presence. The fact that Nurn did not flinch at the sound of his voice impressed him. It meant that Nurn had heard his approach, but decided to let him get close without giving away his knowledge of Namir's presence.

"I was busy while you were off picking flowers." Grief etched into Nurn's face as he replied. Although Nurn's tone bore the soft notes of sorrow in it, there was a hint of jest as well.

Namir placed his hand on Nurn's shoulder reassuringly. "Fear not. Halin will live, that much I have promised you." Seeing Nurn's doubt he added, "His skull is uninjured and only a small patch of skin was cut free. He lost some of his hair with it, but it will grow back. The worst that will happen is he will have a scar to lie to the ladies about." Namir did his best to cheer up his friend, but was not sure if he succeeded.

"Are you sure?" Although Nurn was troubled, Namir was heartened by a slight smile that had found find its way to Nurn's lips.

"Aye, but I do have some bad news as well." Namir saw Nurn's smile fade as he steeled himself against anything that he might have to hear. Namir paused to allow a little more tension to build before he continued. "I fear Jaconis will fare just as well as, if not better than, Halin." Namir had to cut his response short because he could not contain his laughter any longer and neither could Nurn. When the two of them managed to regain some of their composure, Namir continued. Namir still chuckled softly to himself as he added, "we might not fare so well, however, unless you can get that meat finished and ready for us."

Nurn laughed raucously again as he fell to the task of cooking the meat. Namir steadied himself as well after another bout of laughter and tended to both Jaconis and Halin as he waited impatiently for the food to be finished.

'Which was worse?' Aves simply could not decide. 'Would it be this bad if we'd given up and died?' She thought tiredly to herself.

Her muscles were cramped from being in such close quarters for so long and her breath was barely coming in labored gasps. Hessa was close enough for her to reach out and touch her, but Aves knew better than to move that much.

'He might come back.' Aves's mind raced. She tried to sort everything out in her mind again as she tried to let the night play over again.

Unfortunately, she was tired and too exhausted to think. Aves felt foiled by her own limits as she realized the best she could do was remember his comment.

"YOU TWO, THERE IS A CAVE JUST PAST THE TREE LINE. HIDE THERE AND LET ME HANDLE THEM." His voice was no more than a whisper, but both of them heard him perfectly.

He stood in the shadows twenty paces from them, yet it seemed as if he were right next to them. The oddest part was the fact that he did not seem threatening at all. This, in itself was miraculous, because he held a very threatening blade. Its long metallic black length was serrated and it ended with a barbed tip. Aves had not seen many swords in her life, but she knew each one made for a purpose. His sword was created for pain and Aves was not sure what she should make of him.

'Who is he?' She wondered again as she shifted enough to allow blood move through her limbs.

Hessa shifted in the darkness as well. The cave was just large enough for the two of them to huddle into it with no extra space around them. Hessa had almost not made it into the cave at all. She waited for Aves to enter and get situated before she crawled in behind her. Aves listened to Hessa's breath come and go in a very rhythmic pattern. It taunted Aves's eyelids into closing several times against her wishes.

Aves fought the drowsiness that crept over her for a while, but her exertion mixed with her healing wounds sapped all her strength. 'Hessa seems so relaxed and trusting about this man.'

This simple fact bothered Aves extremely. 'Why did Hessa trust him so much? Why did she just nod and force me to go with her without questioning his plan?' Aves's brain swam. She was exhausted and these thoughts pummeled her mind relentlessly.

Outside the sounds of battle continued to send its deadly song through the rocky walls that surrounded them. Cold steel on wood, metal against flesh, these sounds mingled with the grinding sounds of stone against stone as corpses thudded to the ground and created an ominous rhythm. The worst part of this concert was that each movement was marked with the stench of blood and the screams of agony.

The silence that followed the close of the battle was as deafening as the screams had been. Once the clangor died away, there was nothing, almost as if everything had died or simply vanished. No birds chirped. No insects filled the night with their song. Not even the wind dared to disturb the evening with its ramblings. There simply was no sound at all. The world outside of the cave held its breath as if it observed a moment of silence for the dead. Amidst this silence, Aves found peace. She let the darkness seep into her consciousness and allowed the peace of oblivion to consume her mercifully.

Aves slept through the soft sounds carried on the light breeze of something living coming once again into the clearing. The brief struggle between the brothers passed without her notice and even the noises of a desperate and worried man scavenging through the woods and uprooting trees did not disturb her sleep. It was not until someone tugged hard on her arm that Aves awoke.

"What is it? What do you want?" Aves snapped, her voice was hoarse and caused her throat to itch and burn.

"We need to go." Hessa whispered in her ear. Her voice was just as hard and gravelly as Aves's.

"Why?" Aves let her words come out at their own speed without forcing them. She hoped it would spare her throat some discomfort.

"Can't you smell it?" Hessa finished as she pulled Aves

out of the cave.

"Fire!" Alarmed Aves tried to move away from the cave and fell as soon as she put weight on her leading foot.

"Aye… but there's more. Someone's cooking with it." Hessa's words made Aves's stomach grumble with hunger. Hessa turned to see if Aves was all right and helped her to her feet as she mentioned the food.

"Do you know who it is?" Aves's fear was apparent.

"It's not them… aside from that I don't know." Seeing Aves's stern look, Hessa continued not allowing Aves to speak again. "The last two times I've seen him none were left to oppose him. I really don't think this time it would be different. Besides… whoever has the fire also has food… hopefully they have enough to feed us too." Hessa moved a little closer to Aves and braced against her in case Aves tried to move on her own again.

"After what happened I wouldn't trust it." Aves said slowly as she let Hessa get used to her weight. She grabbed a nearby tree for assistance and slowly eased her weight against Hessa's sturdy shoulders. "If you can help me… or wait long enough for my legs to wake up, we can go see."

Hessa nodded in agreement and helped Aves hobble towards the clearing. They were halfway from the edge of the clearing when Aves's legs were awake enough to support herself without any more assistance, a yard from it when she found the strength she to run.

Chapter Eleven: Gifts

"… and then everything went black." Halin's voice rose to indicate he was done as he bit into a leg of rabbit. He leaned lightly against a stump as he finished recounting his tale. "What about you Jaconis? What happened to you?"

Clearing his throat Jaconis started to relate his own misadventure. "As you all may have guessed, I am not the best at setting snares." He let them laugh before continuing. "However, this time it wasn't my snare work that got me. Just as I had caught my second bird, I heard a horse's neigh. I thought I might have stumbled upon the place the bandits had taken our carriage when I came across one of them. He was almost as tall as Nurn and at least twice my build." Jaconis paused for dramatic effect. "Unfortunately he saw me before I saw him too clearly… " A brief noise interrupted his sentence followed closely by a shadowy figure that darted into their midst abruptly.

Nurn was on his feet before Namir could think and seemed ready for anything. He reacted as the dark shape burst out from the cover of the tree line. No one had a chance to move before Nurn leapt upon their assailant and easily forced it to the ground. Whoever the person was, it shrieked as Nurn collided with it. The force of Nurn's motion forced the two of them back along the assailant's path and into the thicket beyond.

"You two hide yourselves," Namir shouted to Jaconis and Halin as he ran after the two figures so he would not lose sight of them.   Namir hoped Jaconis and Halin would be safe without either Nurn or himself to protect them until they could determine who their attacker was. Namir arrived just in time to see another person step from the shadows and start to swing a thickly gnarled branch at the back of Nurn's head. There was something immediately familiar about the person with the branch, but Namir could not place it.

"STOP!" Namir yelled as loud as he could. He hoped he could surprise Nurn's attacker. Everyone froze. As soon as Namir's words died, he saw the person behind Nurn drop the branch and step backwards, both of her arms extended to show that she was not a threat.

Nurn heard the noise of the branch hit the ground and relaxed a little. 'At least now I don't have to worry about getting hit in the back.' He thought, somewhat relieved, as he looked down at the person under him.

Namir moved closer in order to see everyone a little more clearly. The first thing that caught Namir's attention, however, was not the lady who was going to attack Nurn, but Nurn's laughter. The next thing Namir heard, once Nurn was a little quieter, was the muffled comment made by his captive.

"What is it with your family? Do all of you get some sort of sadistic joy out of jumping on top of me?" Aves's voice came to Namir's ears harsh and forced.

"No… I am sorry." Nurn apologized as he tried to talk between laughs. Conversations with women were not one of Nurn's strong points and now he had to try to get out of an embarrassing one. "I just thought… " Nurn started.

"You thought nothing! Can you please get off me?" Aves demanded.

Hessa smiled and giggled softly. She was amused by Aves's plight. 'Normally she wouldn't want him to go,' Hessa thought to herself. "Namir… please tell me you have water." Hessa's ragged voice tore through the humorous situation as she turned to face Namir and stepped out of the shadows behind Nurn.

Namir looked first at Aves then at Hessa happily amazed. They were filthy, but alive. Their clothes and hair were matted with dirt and sweat. "Aye," he managed to say. "I can be right back with some." Before he left, Namir walked slowly up to Hessa and gave her a long hug. He could feel Hessa tense up as he touched her, but he did not care. Namir was just too pleased that they both lived. He let go of Hessa gently and turned back towards the clearing. "You both had best wait here so I can make sure Jaconis and Halin know we are all well. I would hate to have a repeat of Nurn's performance." Namir smiled as he left them and wondered if Nurn and Aves would still be lying on the ground when he returned.

Namir was amused to find that they had not moved as he ran back with a water skin clutched tightly in his hand. He went first to Aves and slowly poured some water into her mouth. It was difficult to reach around Nurn's huge form, but Namir managed. As Aves finished, Namir whispered into Nurn's ear,

"You might want to let her up now... there's no telling what will happen if the two of you get too comfortable in that position." Namir smiled as Nurn's face turned a bright red. After he ensured Nurn had not sustained any injuries, he walked back to Hessa and offered her some water. "Drink it slowly," he said calmly. He knew he did not need to tell her this, but after everything that had happened, he decided not to leave anything to chance.

"I know as much about healing as you, milord." Hessa took the skin from Namir and drank from it slowly.

"Of course you do." Namir said as he noticed Nurn and Aves back on their feet. The most interesting thing he saw was that they remained within close proximity to one another. "Let's get back to the others. Just now I find myself very weary of surprises." He suggested as Hessa finished her drink. Namir heard them all mutter in agreement, as the three of them followed him back into the warm embrace of the fire and their encampment.

The next three days were spent tending to Jaconis's and Halin's wounds. While Namir and Hessa were busy with that, Nurn and Aves foraged for food and supplies. Hessa had deemed it necessary that Jaconis and Halin sleep in actual beds instead of on the cold moist soil they had found. Nurn tried to convince her they would be fine if he collected some branches to lay on, but Hessa refused the idea.

Instead, both Aves and Hessa insisted they build a shelter for all of them to stay in while the two healed. The fourth day found Namir and Nurn gathering wood. Two nights later the shelter was finished. It was sturdy enough to block the light gusts that came with nightfall and provided adequate shade throughout the long warm days. The nights, though chilled, were warm enough with the added heat from the fire. The days of convalescence passed slowly for everyone.

Six more days flew by uneventfully. Namir finally gave up hope of finding the carriage and the rest of their provisions. Instead, he told Nurn and Aves he was going to send word to Armani about the attack as soon as they reached Hornshir. Namir made sure not to let either of them hear the concern he felt that they might not even make it to Hornshir in their present condition.

The rest of the journey to Hornshir was more brutal than the days lost to healing and survival had been. Thankfully, both ladies decided to bath in the river before they had set off at dawn. This was one of the only pleasant occurrences. The main issue was their speed of travel. Jaconis, Aves, and Halin needed to rest frequently due to their injuries. The only thing that seemed to go in their favor was there were no further incidents. They even found a good spot to ford the river, although it did take them a considerable amount of time to cross it.

As they trudged along the track they had found, the hours gave way to days. From what any of them could tell, they were no closer to arriving in Hornshir then when they had started.

Jaconis's constant complaints only shortened Namir's patience and made the days seem longer than they were.

They endured five miserable days of the sweltering heat before the weather let up and granted them a cool day of rain. Not only were they hot and tired, but they had run out of rations. Although Nurn was an excellent hunter, even he had a hard time finding enough for them to eat while they traveled through the sparse forests along their path.

On the eve of the twenty-first day on the road, the sixth day since the attack, they arrived at the gates of Hornshir. The thick dirt encrusted walls loomed above them as the sun slowly sank behind the hills. Hornshir's black gates were closed and bared for the night. This prevented any of the wandering criminals from getting into the city to cause havoc.

An occasional flicker of torchlight played across the ramparts some thirty feet above them and the smooth walls offered no means of access. They were constructed to ward off any unwanted entry in times of war. All of the stones had been perfectly aligned to create one sheer surface. Campfires dotted the plains just outside the walls. They sent their flickering light across the low plains like fireflies in the gathering gloom.

"Now what are we going to do?" Halin looked at Namir inquisitively.

"There is nothing we can do, but wait. Let's build a fire and settle in for the night." Namir motioned towards the nearest stand of trees. "We should camp over there; I don't feel comfortable camping in the open."

Nurn nodded his agreement. As soon as they arrived in the cover of the trees, Nurn busied himself with building a fire to stave off the chill of the late summer night. After the fire was built, Namir helped Halin and Jaconis over to it. Hessa lead Aves over to it as Nurn coaxed it to life. Once everyone was settled, Namir unpacked the last of the provisions. Hessa busied herself by readying the water and what few herbs she had gathered along the way.

"This won't go far." Aves voice was tight and her young face was creased with too much worry for her young age.

Namir walked over and looked over the scarce remains of their provisions. "Nurn, we need to gather food." He called over his shoulder easily.

"Will the others be safe?" Nurn inquired as he strode over to Namir's side.

"This close to Hornshir's walls… they should be." Namir replied as he mentally calculated the actual distance to Hornshir. "Besides, there are other encampments nearby. I'm sure that if anything happened to them, the people at the other camps would help," Namir reassured Nurn as he motioned toward the other fires that spotted the hillside and plains surrounding Hornshir's gates.

"Fine, then let's be off. The sooner we leave, the sooner we will be back." Nurn grunted tersely as he secured his knife to his hip.

Namir turned to Hessa and Aves and instructed, "Cook the rest of the provisions and divide the meal between you four, Nurn and I will come back with food to eat for breakfast."

"What will you and Nurn eat?" Hessa asked quietly almost afraid to hear his reply.

"We will eat what we catch." Namir forced a smile to his lips. "And if we find nothing tonight then a little fast won't hurt either of us until we can get into Hornshir tomorrow."

When Namir was ready, the two friends made their way into the sparse forest. The two of them easily fell into step with each other and soon they were moving like shadows as they flitted from one tree to the next. Silently they stalked through the forest as they tracked anything that moved. The long hours they had spent as children hunting in the forests around Ellsted and amongst the town's nighttime streets now proved their worth as the two moved in complete unison.

Even Nurn's large frame moved nimbly through the undergrowth without disturbing the brush that lined the path. Several unproductive hours passed as they hunted in vain. After three hours, they decided to increase the range of their search. They would move farther from their camp, but both swore they would reserve enough strength to sprint back to their companions if they heard the slightest sounds of a fight.

Nurn moved ahead of Namir when something about the trail caught Namir's eye. He stopped and waited for Nurn to notice he no longer moved. Only a few moments passed before Namir was able to direct Nurn's attention toward one of the side trails. Nurn's black eyes glinted in the dark as he walked back. The way the light reflected off his golden skin at night made Nurn's eyes appear as if they were bottomless pits in his skull and Namir always found it unnerving.

Nurn's face did not change as he saw the tracks Namir indicated. Instead, he bent down low and looked them over. When he stood back up, he looked at Namir and signaled they were definitely wheel ruts. They used signs to quietly converse with each other as they decided to follow this new path. Nurn led, as they started down the new path like wraiths eager for a kill.

Anxiously they darted from one side of the path to the next as they snaked their way along it silently. Halfway down the path they switched positions. Namir took the lead to act as a scout with Nurn following behind to ensure no one flanked them.

They followed this new path for a half hour when Namir stopped and motioned for Nurn to approach. As Nurn ghosted over to him, Namir pointed to a carriage in the clearing ahead of them. "I think that it is our carriage." Namir breathed lightly as he allowed the slight breeze to carry his words effortlessly.

Nurn looked into the clearing and nodded. Their carriage was less than fifteen paces away from them. Nurn closed his eyes and listened. He heard the horses' soft whicker, but nothing else. After Nurn satisfied his senses, he pulled his knife free from his belt and pushed it into the ground silently. Seeing Namir's confused look he motioned for Namir to do the same with his own. When Namir let go of his knife, Nurn deftly rubbed dirt onto the blades as he pulled them one at a time from the ground.

He eased the dirt into his hands and quickly worked it into

the highly polished steel to remove the gleam from them. Namir smiled fully appreciating the way his friend thought as he watched Nurn's labor.   Once he was finished, Nurn motioned to the carriage. "I'll go get the horses and bring them to the carriage, while you take care of the supplies." Nurn's voice was like settling gravel as he spoke quietly.

"No." Namir whispered as he shook his head from side to side. "First we need to make sure that the people who attacked us won't be able to do so again." Namir saw the flicker of hate in Nurn's eyes as he nodded in agreement.   "We will both move in together.   We'll enter their camp from under the carriage so we can surprise them easier."   Nurn nodded his ascension again and then they melted into the shadows once again.

Namir scurried under the carriage as quietly as possible and scanned the area on the other side as Nurn settled in beside him.   As he waited for Nurn to arrive, he looked over the empty camp one more time.   He was completely baffled. There were no tents and no fire pit.   It was as if the thieves started to set up their camp and then decided to leave without the carriage, horses, or supplies.

Namir was so engrossed in searching the camp with his eyes that he almost cried out when Nurn placed a hand on his arm to get his attention. Namir looked apologetically at Nurn as he gestured that they were alone. The two of them moved out from under the carriage slowly as they surveyed the clearing again. Nurn checked the carriage to make sure no one lay in wait for them, while Namir checked to see if there was another campsite close by they had not noticed. Neither of them felt the eyes that watched their every move as they performed their search.

"There is no one here," Namir confided after a few moments of searching. His voice caught somewhere between a whisper and a bark.

"Here either." Nurn agreed, speaking a little louder than Namir had.   "Though all of the supplies are here, as are the horses," Nurn shook his head confused.   "It almost looks like the horses just wandered here of their own, but it makes no sense." Nurn's voice crept from a gravelly whisper back to its normal volume.

Namir sighed. "I don't understand it either." He shrugged. "Let's get the horses hitched up and get back to the others. We have been away long enough. These provisions will be enough to ease our hunger as well as everyone else's fears."

"Aye, that they will" Nurn said as he went off to gather up the horses.

While Nurn gathered the horses and hitched them to the carriage, Namir did another quick check of their possessions. 'It is all here.' Namir thought to himself utterly confused. 'Why would they go to all of the trouble of stealing our possessions and attacking us if they were just going to leave them unguarded? It makes no sense.' Namir climbed out of the carriage as Nurn vaulted up to the driver's boards.

The trip back to their encampment went slower than Namir thought it would. The darkness impeded them more than he had expected and Namir did not dare to light the lanterns in case the bandits were somewhere nearby. Several minutes passed as the two of them discussed using the lanterns to make sure the horses did not step into a hole or stray too far from the road. Nurn finally agreed with Namir that although the lanterns would allow them to travel faster, it would also make them more of a target in case the bandits camped nearby.

Either way, Namir felt safer in the darkness. He agreed with Nurn that he should walk in front of the carriage and guide the horses past the ruts and holes in the rough track, while Nurn sat on the boards and controlled the horses. This made the trip extremely long and tedious.

By the time they made it back to camp it, was almost dawn and the fire had long since burned out. They decided not to wake the others as they entered their encampment. Instead, they both unhitched the horses and groomed them as quietly as they could manage. Once the horses were cared for, Namir and Nurn inventoried the goods for a third time to see if anything was missing. They sated their hunger on some of the dried rations packed in the carriage.

"The cask of mead seems intact and untouched." Namir revealed quietly.

"As are the knives and spear heads my father sent." Nurn answered. "All of the bolts of cloth Aves stored with them are here as well. What of the grain?"

"It is mostly here. It does look like some was removed, but we have enough left to show Ellsted's good intentions." Namir replied as he replaced the grain cask's lid.

Nurn put Tipin's blades and the three bolts of cloth back under the driver's board as Namir retied the casks to the back of the carriage. Once these things were done, both of them made their way to their bedrolls and attempted to get whatever sleep they could before they had to wake up and face the others. Namir decided to sleep in the carriage to ensure it did not wander off somehow, while Nurn slept near the horses for the same reason.

Morning came too quickly for Jaconis. His body ached all over and his head swam mercilessly. Worse still, his stomach cramped from hunger due to the scant meal he ate the night before. Jaconis slowly lifted his aching head and saw the carriage sitting in the middle of the camp.

'I wonder where they found it.' Jaconis thought as the realization of this discovery startled him fully awake.

The horses neighed close to where he lay and he could smell the sweet aroma of breakfast. He noticed that Aves had settled herself into the carriage with Halin close beside her, but Jaconis could not see Namir or Nurn anywhere. He knew his plans had gone drastically astray, but this new turn completely unnerved him.

"Where are the two heroes?" Jaconis asked sarcastically as he slowly propped himself up into a sitting position.

"Getting water for the horses," Hessa answered as she stirred a pot of potatoes that simmered over the fire. "I used the last little bit of water we had for breakfast.

"How… Where did they find the carriage and the horses?" Jaconis asked hesitantly. To his dismay, Hessa merely shrugged as she continued cooking.

"Breakfast will be ready soon." Hessa informed him. Jaconis grimaced as she ignored his previous question completely.

"Thank you." Jaconis replied as if distracted by his thoughts. "And the supplies… are all of the supplies here as well?"

"I think so," Hessa said curtly. "Is that all that you are concerned about, Jaconis?"

The tone in Hessa's voice bordered on scolding, which greatly amused Jaconis. "No. I'm also concerned about how your food will taste." Jaconis smiled mirthfully into Hessa's disapproving stare.

"You were the only one to add stuff to the pot right? I mean Namir didn't manage to put something more into it… did he?" Jaconis knew his questions would irritate Hessa more than anything else he could do, so he indulged himself.

"You are truly impossible," Hessa chided him. "But you'll have an answer to at least one of your concerns soon." Hessa ladled a boiled potato into a bowl for everyone and then added some eggs and bacon as Namir and Nurn walked into the camp.

"So… where did the two of you find the carriage?" Jaconis pestered Namir and Nurn as they walked past him on their way to the horses.

Jaconis started to grumble when he realized that the only answer he would get was Namir's knowing grin and a derisive snort from Nurn. "I was just wondering," Jaconis muttered darkly into his bowl as he scooped some of its contents into his mouth.

"Well?" Hessa asked. She hid her amusement at the reaction that Jaconis received.

"Well what?" Jaconis spat, spraying some of his breakfast into the fire.

"Does it taste good enough for you, or are you going to

spit the rest of it into the fire?" Hessa asked bluntly, getting more irritated with Jaconis as the morning progressed.

"Yeah it'll do." Jaconis muttered, completely losing his desire to make Hessa angrier.

"If it tastes half as good as it smells I'll consider it a feast." Halin added just to spite Jaconis. Halin slowly propped himself up in the carriage as Hessa carried bowls for him and Aves. Halin winced slightly as he took his bowl from Hessa.

The morning passed too slowly for Namir. Between Jaconis's complaints and Halin's whining, everything seemed to take longer than it should have. "I know Jaconis had something to with the carriage's disappearance," Namir confided to Nurn as they lowered the barrel they had turned into a water trough for the horses. "Judging from his questions this morning, I don't think that he had anything to do with us finding it."

"Aye." Nurn replied, wiping the sweat off his forehead with the back of his arm. The temperature was already rising and the sun had barely risen. "Although I did doubt his involvement until this morning… to think that anyone would go to such lengths." Nurn shook his head in confusion as he emptied a few more water skins into the trough.

"Jaconis is an odd one," Namir agreed. "But I don't think he meant for things to happen quite like they did."

"What do you mean?" Nurn asked as they finished filling the trough. He moved out of the horses' way as they drank and he took a seat on a nearby stump.

"I think Jaconis may have gotten involved with a tougher group than he anticipated. I also think he is no longer fully in charge." Namir smiled as he thought about it. "It was his injuries that tipped me off to it. The later ones were nearly fatal, too fatal for even Jaconis to agree to sustain willingly no matter how much he wants to succeed."

"True. But if Jaconis isn't the person planning things, then who is?" Nurn's question went unanswered. A loud rumble pushed through the undergrowth. Both of them heard sounds of something approaching and it worried them.

"Wait here, I'll go and see what's happening," Namir barked as he raced over to the nearest tree and scaled it. Namir vaulted from branch to branch, slowly making his way to a decent vantage point.

It took a few moments for his eyes to adjust to the sudden exposure of light gleaming off the dew-covered leaves around him. When they did, he saw a dark seething area near the gates of Hornshir. Namir struggled with his thoughts about what it might be as his mind sorted through all the possibilities. It was not until Namir heard the cacophony of people striking their camps and moving in large numbers towards Hornshir that he realized the gates were open. Then it dawned on him that the seething area was throngs of people trying to gain entry into the city.

Namir shimmied down the tree as fast as he could and then ran back to the clearing where he had left Nurn and the horses. Still panting from his exertion, he motioned to Nurn. "We need to go or we may not get into Hornshir today."

"What do you mean?" Nurn looked at Namir confused. "What's coming?"

"Nothing is coming." Namir snapped as he gathered his breath. "What we hear is the line of people trying to enter the city. The line is forming as we speak. The gates are open and if we delay too much longer, the line may be so long that we will not be able to get into Hornshir. It amazes me that we didn't enter the line as soon as we left Ellsted." Namir brooded as he thought of the length of the line he had seen.

"It can't be that bad, but you're probably right. I'll gather the horses and meet you back at camp." Nurn offered.

"Aye. By time you get there I'll have everything loaded and ready to hitch the horses up." Namir informed him. "At least we will have the carriage to wait in." Namir said over his shoulder as he vanished into the tree line again.

After a half hour of work, Nurn finally managed to get the horses ready and back to camp. Namir proved true to his word, as soon as he returned to camp he told the others his plan and started to strike camp. Namir had just finished stowing their provisions when Nurn led the horses into the camp. Namir situated the others into the carriage so that Jaconis and Halin were sitting just behind the driver's boards with Hessa and Aves facing them on the backbench.

When Nurn made it to the carriage, Namir dropped from the boards and helped him hitch the horses to the carriage. After some quick instructions from Nurn, and some lighthearted ridicule from Halin, Namir and Nurn managed to get the horses hitched up with little difficulty. Nurn steered the carriage back onto the road leading to Hornshir.

Not only was the line to get into Hornshir long, but it was extremely slow moving. After four long hours spent under the baking sun it seemed like they had barely moved any closer to the gates. However, once the gypsy caravan that had been holding up the line entered the city, the line moved quickly.

They just made it to the actual road leading into Hornshir when the breathtaking view hit them. Their first glimpse of the city beyond the gates was marvelous. Hornshir was made up of tall elegant looking buildings as far as they could see. These buildings were cut from slate and marble and, at a distance, had the look of being sculpted out of the living rock.

From their vantage point outside the city gates, they noticed short squat wooden shops mired the taller buildings with a sense of revolting squalor. These shops seemed to be in direct opposition to the splendor of the buildings that rose above them magnificently. While the taller buildings seemed elegant and pristine, the wooden stores and businesses that sprawled out before them had a thrown together feel about them and seemed very run down.

The shops extended from the base of the towers to the base of the walls. Protruding from these shops were canvas tents and free markets. These were mostly gypsies, but some were from other lands trying to sell their wares. Merchants of every type hawked their wares, which ranged from vases to slaves and everything in between. The streets teamed with people and livestock. Surrounding all of this were filth-covered cobbles, it was as if the inhabitants did not care about the cleanliness of their city.

"Not a sight for sore eyes," Halin whined as much from the sight of the filth as from the stench that surrounded them.

"Aye." Nurn agreed. "That it isn't."

"What do you mean?" Namir inquired. "It's teaming with life! If that isn't a good thing, what is?"

"Something cleaner maybe?" Jaconis shot sarcastically at Namir. The putrid scent hit all of them an hour before and Jaconis had been complaining about it ever since.

"What say you, girls?" Namir asked hopefully since he was obviously out numbered.

"It is different." Aves offered tactfully.

"Well, I like it." Hessa added. "Sure it smells foul and seems dirty, but that can be tolerated. Just think of all the possibilities Hornshir holds. And those buildings… the tall ones… just look at how beautiful they are." Hessa added amazed.

"I'll be the first to admit that Hornshir is rather breathtaking." Halin said jovially, as he pantomimed holding his breath. This caused everyone to laugh a little bit.

The sun was setting as they finally approached the gates. They were all talked out and completely worn out from the day's wait. The growing consensus amongst them all was the hope that they would enter Hornshir before the gates closed.

When Namir saw the guards inspecting every cart his breath caught in his chest.   He knew the feeling was unwarranted, but he could not help the sense of dread that passed over him as they moved closer to the front of the line. Even though there were still a few carts and people ahead of them, to Namir it seemed like the guards were intent on him and no one else.

He could almost feel their eyes cutting into him. Namir suddenly understood why Carness did not want to have other guards in Ellsted. It was because they made the place feel unwelcome instead of making it feel safe.

The dwindling light glinted off metal studs and accentuated the deep chestnut brown leather of the guard's armor as he approached their carriage. "What business do you have in Hornshir?" The gruff voice barked at them. His hardened demeanor matched his studded leather armor perfectly, cold and devoid of compassion.

Namir spoke before anyone else could. "We are emissaries from Ellsted and we are here to speak with the mayor of Hornshir and his council." Namir recited the lines Armani taught him verbatim.

"What if the mayor is too busy and won't see you? What then?" A different guard made his way to Namir's side of the carriage as he asked his question. This guard wore all metal armor, slightly rusted and battered. His stride held more purpose and his voice was cracked from overuse.

Jaconis stifled a yelp as Hessa kicked him in his shin. "Then we will wait here until he is either free to see us or until he changes his mind," Namir replied coolly. "Although we mean to wait within Hornshir's walls instead of without," Namir directed this last bit at the second guard instead of the first one.

"You're presuming a lot aren't you?" The first guard said before he was motioned to silence by the second one.

"Is that a demand or a request?" The second guard asked.

"Both." Namir replied. "We have wounded amongst us badly in need of a healer. I fear they will not live long if we are forced to wait outside of the walls. I know your guards patrol the land around Hornshir, but since we were attacked on our way here I doubt our safety outside of these walls would be ensured." Namir finished as if challenging anyone to refute him.

"Well said." The second guard nodded. "What are your names?"

"What's yours?" Halin piped up before Hessa could restrain him like she had Jaconis.

The second guard laughed quietly and smirked as he replied, "I am Faris, captain of the guard, now may we continue the entry with no interruption?"

"Aye," Halin replied quietly.

"Good. Now, what are your names?" Faris asked again.

Chapter Twelve: Trials

The raucous din of the Flying Muses made it hard for Namir to think. He sipped his ale and reflected upon the trials he had to face. He heard Nurn's laughter mingled with Halin's tinny voice and knew there was a story being told. Aves and Hessa were probably off enjoying the market, trying to decide what they should buy, or they had sequestered themselves in their room to get ready for tomorrow. Either way they would not be bothering him with their problems right now. Belanui was fast approaching and within a few weeks they would have to be on their way back to Ellsted, at least some of them would be.

"So, what is the plan?" Nurn's booming voice drew Namir once again from his thoughts and back into the present.

"Eh?" Namir questioned, completely unaware of what Nurn meant.

"The plan for tomorrow?" Nurn reiterated.

"Ah… that plan." Namir nodded as he looked into his mug. "Well, I was going to have Aves, Hessa, Jaconis and you gain an audience with the mayor tomorrow."

"What about you and Halin?" Nurn's eyebrow rose as he asked this.

"We are going to wander through the town and spread word of Ellsted's Belanui's Festival, of course. Then, in the evening, all of us will meet back here to discuss how everything went." Namir stated plainly. "Make sure that you take the wares with you, all of them. I want the mayor to know our proposal is made with only good intentions."

"Shouldn't we take a few days to allow Aves, Halin and Jaconis more time to recover?" Nurn inquired.

With a deep sigh, Namir reluctantly agreed. "Very well. If they need the time then so be it, but by this time next week you need to be focused on the trade meeting with the mayor. No matter what the rest of you do tomorrow, I am still going to spread the word of the fair while I wander around the city. Tell everyone else what our plans are when you get the chance, I'm going to see if I can find a healer." Seeing Nurn nod in agreement he added, "If you see Aves or Jaconis, have them go back to their rooms immediately. I'll have the healer meet them there."

"Aye." Nurn said as he rose and then disappeared into the throng of people around them.

As Namir saw Halin approach as he finished his second ale. "I understand you want me to accompany you for something?" His voice was as tinny as usual.

"Aye, but not now, in the morning. No, better yet, in a week." Namir nodded. "For now, go to your room and wait for the healer. I will bring him to you and then you can take the rest of the week to heal. After that meet me here and I'll tell you what we are going to do." Namir looked at Halin for a few moments just to make sure he had understood him before Namir rose to leave. Namir walked to the door and stopped by the large man sitting just inside and asked, "Where can I find the nearest healer?"

The big man looked into Namir's steel blue eyes and then pointed towards the wall on the other side of the room, "Go out to the street and go that way. After you get four blocks you should run into him." The man's breath reeked of ale and spirits, but Namir nodded his understanding and walked out into the street.

The wind blew lightly against Jaconis's back as the sun slowly set. The cool night breeze was a pleasant feeling after being forced to stay in a hot room for the last few days.

'I wonder how they managed to retrieve the carriage.' Jaconis's thoughts meandered back to the events that happened before they entered Hornshir. As he mulled over the discoveries the group had made he was startled awake by a realization. 'How did Namir and Nurn retrieve the carriage and why are they keeping it a secret from me?' The point was moot now; they had retrieved it and they had entered the city with it. Hopefully he could find Tali and get some answers. 'How did Tali mess this one up?' He mused. 'Everything was going perfectly.'

His thoughts raced through his mind as he calculated one possibility after another. He wound his way through the maze-like streets of Hornshir as he puzzled over it.

"How can anyone stand to live here?" Jaconis cried as he narrowly dodged a stream of waste flung from the balcony overhead.

"Very carefully, I'd guess." A voice purred from behind him.

Jaconis jumped, much to his watcher's amusement. He spun around to face the person that had snuck up on him and felt his face grow pale when he saw the voice's owner. "How… Where… ?"

"I followed you from a distance… I think that's what you wanted to know." She said as she arched away from him in a deep stretch.

"No… I mean aye... I mean… not really." Jaconis replied as he stumbled on his words. "What I meant to ask was how did you manage to lose the carriage?"

Tali raised an eyebrow in irritation at his question. "I didn't lose it. I decided to give it back to them, so I placed the carriage in a very noticeable place. There is a difference." Her soft lips settled themselves into a pout as she finished speaking.

"Besides, you wouldn't be able to succeed in Hornshir without the carriage… right?"

"Maybe… maybe not." Jaconis frowned as he rubbed the bandages around his neck lightly in order to draw her attention to them. "Did you have to do this?"

"Maybe… maybe not." Tali mimicked his tone perfectly; a dark gleam lit her deep brown eyes mischievously.

"Just answer me… why?" Jaconis was growing impatient and Tali knew it.

"Since Canges had captured Halin… I thought it might look better for you if we made another raid." Tali soothed. "But it didn't turn out as I had hoped."

"What, exactly, did you hope for?" Jaconis demanded.

"Not the bloodbath that I received!" Tali's glare withered Jaconis where he stood. "It wasn't supposed to have happened that way at all. I envisioned a small encounter, just wounding the girl enough to make sure the others would not come after the carriage again." The look in her eyes shifted from anger to dread subtly as she recounted the tale of what happened for Jaconis's benefit.

"I had Canges follow Namir and Nurn, so we would know when they had found you. The rest of us were prepared to pay a quick visit to the ladies upon his signal." She took a breath and continued before Jaconis could stop her. "Everything was going smoothly. We followed the girls into a clearing and we moved silently to encircle them so they wouldn't hear us and to ensure that they couldn't run away. I made sure all of your men did just as I had told them. We were just a few steps behind them, when I decided to stay closer to the trees than the others did. I think that is why I survived and they didn't." Her voice faltered. Jaconis reached for her, hoping to ease her pain… to shelter her in some way from her memories, but Tali pulled away from him before his hand could even brush her skin.

"I never quite saw it… the thing that killed them. We'd just entered the clearing," Tali's eyes became vacant as she recalled the events nervously. "The whole place was silent.

There were no noises at all. Then a shadow flickered past me. It moved across my path right in front of me. I turned to follow its movement when I saw the first one, Hetkinen, fall. All there was left of him was a column of blood gushing its way towards the sky from his severed throat."

Her body shook violently at the memory. Jaconis grabbed her and pulled her tightly against him, as if trying to stifle her memories, but she continued oblivious of his actions. As she did, her voice grew hollow and seemed small and distant.

"I really didn't see what hit them… any of them. One after another they fell, all of them dead. Some died quick, but all of them died quietly. It was very surreal. The only real sound I can remember hearing was the sound of laughter. At least I think it was laughter." Tali shook again and Jaconis held her tighter. Her breath escaped in shallow puffs as she continued. Her voice was so quiet that Jaconis was forced to put his ear directly against her lips in order to make any of her words out.

"It was as if the wind laughed at us, like it mocked us and our trivial concerns. I saw our attacker only once throughout the whole fight. It flitted… no he flitted from man to man with his dark blade cleaving through their flesh and armor as if they were merely shadows strewn before the primal rays of the sun. He was elegant, yet dreadful. I saw him and he smiled at me. He winked one of his ebony eyes and wrought his fine white lips into a hint of a smile. And then he spoke… " Her body was wracked again violently and she slumped into Jaconis, her full weight forced Jaconis to his knees. Her eyes sought out his and she forced out the rest as if her life depended on it.

"He told me, 'CHILD, YOU ARE MY MESSENGER. DELIVER ME UNTO THEM… OR I SHALL DELIVER YOU UNTO YOUR DOOM!' I think he came closer to me … but I fled. I ran away from him and the clearing as fast as I could. I paid no heed to the forest or the path I was on." Her voice cracked and she once again slumped against him motionless.

Jaconis held her silently for a while, rocking her gently

back and forth in his embrace while he soothed away her fears. When she appeared coherent enough to continue their conversation once again, he brushed her hair away from her face and urged Tali to resume where she had left off. "I assume, then, that is why you chose to leave the carriage outside of the city?"

"Aye." Tali pulled herself out of his arms slowly. "I left it where they might find it… if they looked. And it seems they did." A slight hint of confidence returned as she finished her statement.

"Who was the man from the shadows referring too," Jaconis probed a little too eagerly as his curiosity bested him.

"I… I don't know." Tali lied trying to sound scared. She knew Jaconis had probably seen through her ruse, but she did not care. 'He can't find out about them yet.' Tali swore to herself silently, 'at least not until I can be certain of him.'

"Fine, we can talk about it later." Jaconis responded, obviously unsure of Tali's answers and motives.

The ale slid down Namir's throat and it washed the unpleasantness of the week down with it. His muscles ached and he could feel the stiffness of unused muscles start to set in painfully all over his body. It never occurred to him before how tedious and tiring his task would be once he had gotten down to it. The days that he spent walking along the streets to spread word of Ellsted's rapidly approaching Belanui's Festival wore away at his stamina.

The blowing dust carried in on the warm winds of late summer combined with the unfriendly animals he had encountered made the days long as well as a little exciting at times, unfortunately there was only so much excitement one person could take. Not to mention the stench of the streets was as over powering, as it was revolting. There were too many people and animals in it at all times. 'I need to take a break from this soon.' Namir thought as he lowered his mug. He thought about tomorrow's tasks and felt the cold grip of melancholy grab his heart.

"I can hardly wait until we are done with all of this." Halin whined completely exhausted after his first day of walking the streets with Namir.

"You know. It's going to a lot take more time than this, right?" Namir confided to Halin as he sipped at his ale again.

"It is?" The break in Halin's voice was as audible as the one in his will. It was obvious that something inside of him was crushed completely.

Namir fought his own emotions as he looked at Halin's shocked look. It was a struggle to decide if the look on the boy's face was more entertaining than the hurt sound in his voice or not. "Aye, it is." Namir sighed. "Just as soon as Aves wraps up her negotiations and Jaconis finishes composing the new trade agreement between Hornshir and Ellsted the real work will begin."

"What do you mean by 'real work'?" Halin gulped as he struggled to get the question out of his mouth.

"Well, the real work will be loading the wagons for the trip home. But it won't be just loading the wagons, it will mean arranging the supplies we obtain in a way that all of them get to Ellsted safely." Namir finished another swig of his ale before he continued. "Once all of that is settled, we need to decide who goes back to Ellsted and who stays here to ensure that word of the festival stays alight in the minds of Hornshir's citizens." Halin groaned and paled visibly as Namir continued listing the tasks. "But not to worry, I figure we have at least half a week before any of the real work begins. Here take this and get us two more." Namir handed Halin his empty tankard and motioned towards the bar.

"By the way, who is paying for all this?" Halin ventured, a little afraid of his answer, as he motioned to the surrounding inn.

"Why, the kind citizens of Ellsted of course." Namir winked and turned to look at the dancers as they performed on the stage nearby.

Halin made his way to the bar brooding as Namir's answer

mingled with darker thoughts. He knew that the rooms were not cheap here and neither was the ale the group had consumed. He was very unsure how long their funds would last. Halin hated to second-guess Namir, but he had heard the Flying Muses was the best Inn in town for artists and their ilk. This meant that although the atmosphere was very congenial to working on artistic endeavors, it was also expensive.

"Do you remember back in Ellsted," Halin broached the subject hesitantly as he returned with their drinks, "when you told me you and Nurn might teach me a few things?" Tears misted into his grey eyes unwanted.

"Aye," Namir replied to Halin's question completely distractedly by the ladies' routine he was watching.

"Umm… when do you think we will have time for more of it? I mean if we have extra time, that is?" Halin asked hopefully as he stumbled over his words. Halin did his best not to sound too eager, but he knew that some of his dread had crept into his voice.

There was something in Halin's voice that caught Namir off guard and jarred his mind back to their conversation. An edge that Halin never had crept into his voice and it startled Namir. "I'm not sure." Namir rubbed his chin absently as he motioned to the barmaid for yet another ale, completely unaware of the one that Halin had set in front of him. "Maybe next week we could manage some time, after things calm down… or possibly the week after."

"No sooner?" Halin interrupted, still trying to hold his fear in check. Halin's voice carried a tinge of pain in it, almost as if he was hurt by Namir's words.

"No. Next week would be the soonest. We do have duties that we must make sure are finished first. Why are you so concerned about it?" Namir's curiosity was peaked now and he waited hesitantly for Halin's response.

"Oh, no real reason." Halin lied. "I was just hoped for a diversion from our duties."

"I wish it could be different for us." Namir said as he laid a comforting hand on Halin's shoulder. "I wish the way here had proved less eventful and adventurous for us." A tear fell slowly from Namir's left eye and it meandered its way across his cheek and down to his chin.

"There's nothing I would have traded for it." Halin looked into Namir's glistening eyes as he said this. "Although it was tough and most of us barely survived. I wouldn't have forgone a single moment of our trip. I just wish I could have been of more help... "

Shaking his head to stop Halin in mid-sentence, Namir replied, "Stop... there is no use in blaming yourself. Nothing else could have been done differently, although I still lay awake at night trying to find a different way that we could have gone... a better path at least... or anything that might have made things turn out better."

"Could haves can fill a well." Nurn's bass voice echoed Namir's thoughts perfectly as it filtered through the crowded room.

"Nurn!" Halin leapt to his feet and embraced his brother heartily.

"How did the meeting go today?" Namir probed.

"Aside from Jaconis's attempts at conniving more out of Hornshir's Council of Elders in exchange than they are willing to give, they went well. Aves proved to be very shrewd and knowledgeable in Hornshir's local politics and Hessa has shown herself as a valuable mediator between Jaconis and Hornshir's Council." Nurn said all of this as he deftly sat down in an empty chair he managed to pull to the table from another table that sat a few feet away.

Absentmindedly he lifted the tankard from the table in front of him to his lips and drew deeply from it as the barmaid approached them.

Before the barmaid could rebuke Nurn for drinking someone else's brew, Namir interjected mirthfully. "It's fine. Please bring us three more; we have a need to wash the day from our throats. By the way Nurn, where did Aves get off to?"

As the barmaid left, Namir noticed the two mugs of ale on

the table and smiled somewhat ashamed. He picked up his mug and drank deeply as Nurn reported his information to Namir.

"Hessa and Aves went directly to their room to bathe." Nurn grumbled somewhat dejected.

"And Jaconis?" Halin piped up as he drew himself into the conversation.

"He went to peruse the market." Nurn finished the remaining ale in his tankard just as the barmaid arrived with three more. "Here you are." He winked at her as he placed the tankard into her delicate hand.

"I think you are enjoying this a bit too much, Nurn." Namir snickered at Nurn's antics.

"Someone has to. Besides, if we're going to be here for another year or so we may need to make a few friends." Nurn's grin grew wider as he saw Halin's face fall in a look of horror and astonishment. "Don't tell me he doesn't know yet." Nurn said to Namir mockingly.

"Aye, he doesn't." Namir admitted somewhat abashed.

"What don't I know?" Halin's question was more of a plea than an inquiry.

"That a decision has been made." Nurn confided to his brother with a somber air about him.

"A decision about what?" Halin's features contorted even more in confusion as he tried to piece together what they were talking about.

"I'll need you to swear a vow of silence before we can tell you anything else." Namir looked at Halin sternly as he desperately held in his laughter.

With a deep sigh, Halin nodded his agreement. "I'll swear to anything you need me to, if it means that I'm no longer left out of your plots and schemes."

"Did he just say what I think he said?" Namir asked mockingly as he awaited Nurn's reply.

"Aye he did." Nurn's smile subtly changed from one of mirth to that of appreciation.

"Well then, I think that deserves a drink before we

formalize his oath." Namir winked to Nurn as he raised his tankard for another draught. Confused, Halin raised his tankard with them although he still felt like he was being excluded.

"And what's to celebrate?" Jaconis cooed from behind Halin as he crossed the room to their table.

"Nothing much." Namir confided to his cousin with a knowing gleam in his eye. "Halin here just volunteered to spread word of the fair in the market tomorrow… alone." He could not help but allow a wolfish grin to cross his face when he saw Halin almost choke on his ale.

"Is that so?" Jaconis asked as he directed his attention to Halin. His disbelief was as palpable as his unasked question.

"Aye." Halin muttered as he saw the dark look shot at him by Nurn. "I just tried to breathe my ale though, not a pleasant thing to do and I wouldn't recommend it… even to you"

"Breathing is a thing that is best left for air, brother." Nurn intoned trying to change the topic from their festivities.

"How did your day go?" Namir asked as he picked up on Nurn's subtle change in conversation. This forced Jaconis into the conversation on a rebound as well as on the defensive.

"It went well." Jaconis sighed. "But it would have gone better if Hessa hadn't been present." He started to sit down, but was stopped by Nurn's sudden stretch. Jaconis watched as Nurn put his feet into the only empty chair at the table and then met his eyes as if a challenge. "She's a tad infuriating. Whose side is she on anyway, Ellsted's or Hornshir's?"

"Both." Nurn growled. His temper, still obviously frayed from earlier. "She is trying to do what is best for both cities. That is something you don't seem to understand."

"What do you mean by that?" Jaconis rebuked Nurn's statement vehemently. It was clear to everyone that Jaconis was somewhat taken aback by Nurn's tone.

"What I mean is that it's ultimately in Ellsted's best interest if Hornshir can maintain the trade agreement once it has been accepted. If the agreement proves too much for them, they will stop abiding by it." Nurn spat as his muscles tensed.

Namir reached over and put a hand on Nurn's forearm to keep him in his seat, but he was unsure if it was going to work.

"I expected you to side with her, Nurn. You have been casting your lot in with her ever since we left Ellsted." Jaconis sneered at him as if Nurn were some sort of cur to be shunned or mocked. "But I was seeking Namir's opinion and not yours."

"Well, it seems that I am going to side with Hessa and Nurn on this as well. Although it is a bit of a surprise to me that you would even want my opinion on this matter, since I have no voice for the merchants of Ellsted's needs in this that is." Namir stated coolly as he locked eyes with Jaconis defiantly. "Besides, I know how you and Daffer can get when it comes to profits… "

"What does that mean?" Jaconis ruptured indignantly. Namir could see that Jaconis was at his wits ends as well.

"Just what I said," Namir smiled as he saw Jaconis's face flush with anger.

'If only Jaconis had the nerve to do something.' The thought flitted through Namir's head quickly as he continued where he had left off.

"Both of you tend to be short sighted anytime there is money to be made." Namir shot back at Jaconis putting him on the rebound again. "I've found that it is sometimes best to have things develop into your favor instead of forcing them to." Seeing that Jaconis was still confused about what he meant, Namir decided to change his ploy. "Let me try and explain this in a different way, cousin. There are times when it is best to make a meager profit in order to gain a steady income from something, than to get a small sum all at once. Time can change the meager income into a greater benefit."

"If you say so… but I disagree." Jaconis fumed. He knew that Namir was trying to make a fool out of him and Jaconis did not want to give him that satisfaction. "I need to go and wash the day from me. Good bye." Jaconis turned in a huff and stormed away, leaving them to their mirth.

"Let the wind take your cares, Jaconis." Namir called

after him as Jaconis fumed across the room and over to the stairs. "Finally." Namir turned back to Halin and Nurn as soon as he was sure that Jaconis was out of earshot. "That is why I sit here." Namir quietly told Halin as he motioned to the distance from them to the stairs and the proximity of the musicians.

"And I thought it was just because you have a better view of the dancers." Halin replied jokingly.

Namir smiled at Halin's jest. "As for you spreading word of the festival tomorrow alone… I really am going to ask that of you."

"Why?" Halin asked a little shocked.

"For two reasons. The first is that Jaconis is now expecting it." Namir paused as he drank down the last of his ale. He slowly lifted the other tankard in front of him to his lips before he continued to speak.

"And the second?" Halin appealed, unintentionally cutting off Namir's train of thought.

"To further our stay in Hornshir of course," Namir's flat tone was severe and somewhat sterner than Halin had expected. "You see, Jaconis didn't bother asking me what I'd be doing while you spread the word about the fair. This will free up some time for me to pursue accommodations for us as well as future employment. If we are going to be here for a while, we'll need to find some way to provide for ourselves."

"I guess that I can understand that." Halin pouted as he gave way to Namir's judgment.

"Our father has provided well for us." Nurn confided to Halin. "We have enough gold to last for a few months, longer if we're careful." He placed his hand gently on Halin's shoulder. "But we need to learn to be self-reliant as well."

"Who else is staying?" Halin asked as he started to cheer up a little.

"It'll just be the three of us." Namir replied after he finished the last swig of his ale. "I haven't checked with Aves or Hessa, though and I might not. I'm sure Aves's father wouldn't like his only daughter staying in Hornshir instead of returning to the safety of his home."

"Are you certain?" Nurn asked. "He did surprise us with the use of his carriage after all."

"Aye that he did," Namir started to raise his hand in order to beckon for the barmaid, but Halin pulled lightly on Namir's sleeve to stop him.

"I don't think that we need anymore. Otherwise we won't even be able to stagger to our rooms." Halin grinned at Namir stupidly as he successfully over exaggerated his drunkenness.

"Very well, let's go then. We can talk about this tomorrow." Namir attempted to stand and swayed for a moment before he sat back down. His second attempt faired a little better because Nurn had reached out a hand to steady him.

"Aye Namir, I think Halin was right. You've had a little too much for today. Tomorrow is another day." Nurn commented as he stood and helped Namir and Halin over to the stairs. 'One of these days these two will learn their limits,' Nurn thought bemused as he all but carried them to their rooms.

Chapter Thirteen: Doubts

"Tell me again why we have to put up with him!" Aves exclaimed darkly as she sat in the sudsy water of her bath.

"Because he was selected by the council as the head of Ellsted's merchant affairs while we are in Hornshir." Hessa retorted bitterly. "Although they never said he had to make it back to Ellsted alive." She shot back at Aves playfully in an attempt to break Aves's foul mood.

"Oh what dark dreams are you trying to inspire in me?" Aves splashed water at Hessa from her tub.

"Only the ones that promise to get you into a better mood." Hessa replied. 'Finally. I have been waiting for Aves's mood to change.' Hessa's thoughts whirled through her head as Aves's stood up and stepped lightly from her tub into Hessa's. "It isn't big enough for both of us you know." Hessa complained when Aves leaned over her.

"I know." Aves said playfully. "I was just getting my towel." She stood upright again and gingerly stepped from the tub while she tried to dry her foot and leg before she stepped onto the cold wooden floor of their room.

"And here I was hoping you found my company that alluring." Hessa lamented sarcastically.

Aves acted shocked by Hessa's comment and replied wittily, "What evils are you speaking of?" She tried to hold back her laughter as she continued, but a few giggles slipped out against her best efforts. "Although I must admit that the thought had crossed my mind on a few occasions."

"Eh?" It was Hessa's turn to be surprised and she blushed.

"Well… you are so good at bathing me," Aves winked playfully at Hessa as she found new conviction in Hessa's embarrassment. Aves contained her laughter as she saw Hessa squirm a little at the new direction of the conversation as she continued, "and it was a little thrilling back in Ellsted to have someone else in my tub with me." Aves smiled coyly at Hessa as she watched her blush flood down from her face and spill onto her bosom.

"I… I never... never knew you thought like that." Hessa exclaimed completely embarrassed.

Hessa's comment bypassed Aves's newfound convictions and she burst out laughing. She giggled playfully as she blurted, "Oh you are such a card love. I can't say honestly that the thought didn't pass through my mind before, but that is was all that it was. A thought, please don't worry about it." Aves said as she tried to sooth Hessa's shock and dread.

"Who said I was worried?" Hessa commented as she tried to regain her composure. Hessa sighed deeply before she changed the topic of the discussion, "What is your problem with Jaconis? Why do you let him bother you so badly?"

"Why shouldn't I?" Aves answered. "He's a pig and he's greedy to boot. I was there remember? I saw how he looked at you as we traveled to the council hall. He had the leering look of a jackal before it eats its prey. Not to mention how angry he got when you interfered with his plans with Hornshir's council before he really had a chance to pursue them."

Hessa giggled, delighted at the memory of her exploits as if she was hearing about someone else. "Aye, it was a fun day in that respect. Did you notice the look on his face when I advised the head elder of Hornshir to regard Jaconis's words with doubt and to weigh their true meaning before he replied? It was completely priceless!"

"That it was." Aves smiled as she wrapped her towel

around her hair. She heard Hessa rise to leave her tub and deftly moved out of her way to give her enough room to maneuver. "Let me help you." Aves offered. Before Hessa could argue, Aves stepped over and placed a towel around Hessa's waist. Aves's hands moved swiftly over Hessa's sides as she dried her former maid diligently.

"I can do this by myself you know." Hessa commented.

"I know that, silly. I just wanted to see how it felt to be the servant instead of the mistress." Aves smiled up at Hessa and sat down at her feet. Once she was settled, Aves reached up and dried Hessa's legs.

"Why?" Hessa asked somewhat confused.

"Haven't you ever wondered what it would be like to be the mayor's daughter?" Aves asked Hessa as she finished drying Hessa's calves and feet.

Hessa closed her eyes and enjoyed the feeling of being pampered as she answered Aves's question. "Aye, I have often wondered that. But that isn't how things are." She steeled herself against Aves's ploys and stepped away from Aves quickly. She strode over to her bed leaving Aves on the floor by the tub alone.

"I'm sorry Hessa. I didn't mean to upset you. I just wanted to see how it felt… to know what you go through… to experience things a little differently." Aves confided, "I'm sorry if I upset you."

"I know what you were doing… and I'm not upset." Hessa drew her nightshirt on over her head and then turned to face her mistress.

She took in the hurt look on her face. Aves's body was slumped as if she had been physically struck. She sat in a small puddle of water that had splashed out of the tub and she looked up into Hessa's eyes with a lost and wounded stare. "Stand up and let me dress you." Hessa said as she allowed a small smile to crease her lips.

"No." Aves replied obstinately.

"Why not?" Hessa asked, a little surprised by Aves's answer. She grabbed Aves's nightshirt off the bed. With nightshirt in hand, Hessa turned and walked over to Aves.

"Because I offended you, that's why not." Aves retorted.

"Forget about it, please. Besides Jaconis made me feel worse today, but I'm not sulking about it, am I?" Hessa returned somewhat jovially.

"No… I guess not." Aves stood up grudgingly and lifted her arms to make it easier for Hessa to pull the nightshirt over her head. Once Hessa was finished fussing with the nightshirt, Aves walked over to her own bed. "Besides we've had a hard day and another one lies ahead of us." Aves said glumly as she climbed under the covers.

"Forget tomorrow for now." Hessa cooed to Aves soothingly. "The next few weeks will prove hard enough without us dreading them before they even happen." Hessa let Aves get comfortable under the covers before she crawled into bed.

Hessa lay quietly and listened to the steady rhythm of Aves's breath. She struggled with her own thoughts as she noticed her mistress drop off into a deep slumber.

'Aves, how are we going to survive?' Hessa thought to herself as she drifted off to sleep as well.

"So where are you heading to this morning? Halin asked Namir curiously, as they left the Flying Muses.

"Here and there." Namir answered as he glanced around quickly to see if anyone had followed them from the inn. Once he was certain that they were alone, he continued, "Why? Is there something bothering you?"

"Well… not really." Halin lied pitifully. He attempted to sound convincing in his lie and he knew he failed badly.

"Good… so out with it then." Namir's cool gaze became steely as he looked Halin directly in the eyes. "I have the feeling there is more to the questions that you asked and your odd behavior yesterday than you told us. So now you need to tell me… please."

"I will… but not here." Halin whined in response. He felt

trapped, but he did not know how to get rid of the feeling. "I think that it would be best if I told you what was bothering me when we are completely alone."

"Fine," Namir agreed a little disturbed by Halin's uneasiness. 'This isn't like Halin.' Namir thought to himself swiftly as he continued his sentence. "Meet me here, at the Flying Muses, for lunch and we can discuss it then… that is if it really can wait that long… " Namir reassessed Halin's nervousness and he was certain that it did not bode well. Something bothered Halin badly and Namir wished he knew what it was.

"Agreed," Halin agreed gloomily. "So… we're to be back here at noon then?" He was unable to hide the nervous twinge in his voice.

"Aye and try not to be late." Namir said laconically over his shoulder as he made his way through the crowd.

Halin watched Namir vanish into the crowded streets as the throng of people engulfed him. 'Why didn't I tell him?' Halin pondered morosely.

As soon as Halin was certain that he was alone again, he plunged into the busy streets and made his way to the market.

'I know that Jaconis is following me… I can feel it.' Halin mused. 'Here I am completely unable to protect myself from him. Why didn't I just tell Namir about my fears?' Halin peered over his shoulder cautiously as he tried to catch a glimpse of Jaconis.

Deftly Halin dodged the hawkers and peddlers in an attempt to get Jaconis to slip up and reveal himself. He made sure to nod to the merchants curtly so he did not offend them as they threw out their well-rehearsed deals. Halin noticed a shadow that seemed to dodge just outside of his view as he wound his way through the unfamiliar streets.

'Someone really is following me. Why can't he just leave me be?' Halin thought grimly.

Halin ducked into random shops and locations in a vain

attempt at catching a glimpse of his pursuer. He did his best to blend into the crowd as he exited each store and he focused on not calling attention to himself, but it did not seem to help. Every time Halin glanced behind him, there he was just a pace or two back. He felt trapped.

"Why couldn't the trip here have been smoother?" Halin cursed as he ducked down a back alley at random. He breathed a little easier when he noticed that the alley had a few corners that led to darker places where he could hide. "Just don't get lost." He muttered to himself as he threw himself around a corner blindly.

"Getting lost is the least of your concerns, boy." The rugged voice that erupted behind him sent chills up Halin's spine. Not only was it not Jaconis's voice, but it was gruff and cruel sounding.

Halin almost ran into a wooden fence in front of him that bisected the alley before he saw it and stopped. It was then that he heard the person move behind him, closer than before. Halin realized that the fence blocked his path completely at the same time he noticed how close his pursuer was to him. These realizations only added to Halin's surprise and fear. Panicked, he turned to face his pursuer. He believed that he was prepared for anything, but he was wrong.

The image that met his eyes came straight out of one of his nightmares. His assailant stood easily two spans taller than he did and its chest was covered with glittering metal chains that had been fashioned into armor of some sort. Rising above the chain mail was a bestial fur covered face. Halin's eyes widened with fear as he looked from the metal to the matted furry features of the thing. Its breath came in puffs of steam as it looked at Halin and smiled to reveal its sharp wolf-like teeth.

"Wh… Wh… What ar… are you?" Halin managed to say before his voice completely abandoned him in fear.

"I am your deliverer." His assailant rasped, its voice sounded like metal scraping across stone. Halin stared unable to speak as the beast drew closer to him. "Well, aren't you going to ask what I am going to deliver you from?" Its mirth was written plainly across its features. It was definitely enjoying every moment of Halin's fear. "You should already know, but in case you have forgotten, I am here to deliver you from your wretched fate." It breathed a huge cloud of steam directly into Halin's face as it loomed above him. The vile stench drove Halin to the ground as if he were struck.

"I'm not sure who you are, but I suggest that you leave him alone!" Namir's voice echoed through the ally abruptly breaking the tension that the creature had created. Halin tried to move away from the creature, but found that he was completely against the wooden fence and had nowhere to go.

The beast spun to face Namir and turned its attention away from Halin momentarily as it barked its reply. "I care nothing for your interference!" It growled threateningly as it turned its glowing red eyes onto Namir. "Be gone now... or die!"

Namir recoiled from the hideous thing as he saw it fully. "Get away from him!" He had somehow managed to shout while he tried to pull his knife free from its sheath.

The creature turned to Namir again; its red eyes glowed brighter. Their glow bathed the alley with its devilish light. "I told you to be gone! Do you not value your life?" It howled at Namir's defiance.

Namir noticed the steel clad feet as he traced the beast's figure from its armored chest down to the ground as he tried to take it all in. He realized that the feet inside the boots had to be dog's feet as the thing moved closer to him. Namir felt fear grip his mind, as the creature's gaze seemed to lock his limbs against his will. He felt himself back away from the thing, fearful and timid no matter how much he wanted to stand his ground.

'NO!' He tried to scream... but his throat clenched and would not let any sound out.

The thing moved closer and the fear drove deeper into Namir's soul. He smelled the beast's wet fur and rotting breath mingled with the smell of refuse in the alley and the combined stench was overwhelming. Namir fought as hard not to wretch as he did to stand his ground.

"So, you would protect this him?" It laughed. "You can't even protect yourself! Tell me… why should I let you live?" It waited a moment as if waiting for Namir to reply, but he could not find his voice. "Tell me child!" It growled impatiently.

"Because I'm not your prey," Namir said, almost whispering. He wanted to yell at the creature, but somehow he could not. Namir felt as if his mind were not his own to command anymore.

"Good! Now go!" The beast reached down and easily took Namir's knife from his limp hand.

With a quick flick, it flung the pathetic blade down the alley. It then grabbed the front of Namir's shirt and lifted him off the ground like a misused puppet. The thing carelessly flung Namir down the alley after his dagger as if he were weightless.

The loud hollow thud of Namir's body as it hit the cobbled stones of the alley was followed quickly by a sharp snapping sound of wood as it splintered and forced Namir's breath out of him. Namir lay slumped against a wall with pieces of wood splintered all around him in what used to be a shed of some kind. He did not move and to Halin, he looked dead.

The beast turned back to Halin again. "Now tell me, who will save you this time?" It sneered menacingly. "I have been waiting for this moment."

Halin stared at the beast unable to move. None of his muscles cooperated as it hovered over him once more. He felt its saliva trickle down from its hideous mouth and dribble down his cheek. Halin looked into up into the creature's maw as it gaped open, full of sharp teeth. Another gust of rotting air enveloped Halin's head in its putrid scent and he almost fainted. The creature grabbed Halin's shoulder and he heard himself scream as the beast's claws tore easily through his flesh.

"ENOUGH!" Halin's world shattered as the new sound engulfed him.

.His reality splintered and the shards seemed to fly every

direction. He desperately tried to find the source of these words. Halin felt the beast turn abruptly to face whoever had spoken. Pain erupted anew in his left shoulder as the beast released its grip on his right one and let most of his body fall towards the ground.

Blood pooled under Halin's dangling body. He felt it trickle from his shoulder, across his body, and drip to the ground. Even though he was losing consciousness, Halin could still feel the creature's claws imbedded in his left shoulder like hot irons that were barely holding him above the ground. It was only a matter of time before either the thing killed him or his shoulder snapped and Halin knew it.

"Another nuisance. You must be the luckiest prey that I've ever hunted." The beast growled at Halin angrily. Turning to face its new opponent it spat, "Go away. I am too busy to bother with you, elf!"

"I said enough and I meant it. Let the boy go and I just might spare your life." The elf replied in a harmonic voice. The elf's clothes seemed to blend into the alley and the debris around him. Even the pain that Halin was feeling did not seem to make the elf any clearer to Halin. Instead, his vision swam with the rippling that his rescuer's clothes writhed with as he moved closer and drew a silvery sword out from under his cloak.

"Ahhh… a guardian." The beast's eyes narrowed. "What business do you have here in Hornshir, eh?" It menaced.

"That is none of your concern. Now let the boy be!" The elf's voice pulsed with power and the beast felt it.

"If I leave, I will come for him again when he's outside of your protection." It challenged almost hissing at the guardian.

"Please do, then I can end your life with no fear for those around us, Morcant." The elf replied as he stepped ever closer.

The beast's eyes narrowed more. "How is it you know my name?"

"That is my secret, vermin. Now be gone!" The elf shot back.

"For now guardian… only for now." Looking down at

Halin, Morcant pulled his claws free. "I will be back… and I will kill you." It licked the blood from its claws as it leapt to the roof of the nearest building in a single bound easily. Within moments, it had completely vanished.

Halin's vision swam again as he felt himself hit the ground roughly. The sound of his body squishing into the pool of his own blood and the rank scent of the refuse from the alley were the last things he clearly remembered as darkness closed him off from the rest of the world.

Morcant sat on the roof glumly looking at his feet as his mistress coiled a whip and berated him for his stupidity. "But I didn't know there was a guardian involved." Morcant replied, as his mistress grew more impatient.

"Look at me." Her voice stung him more than her lash had. "I don't care who is protecting him. I wanted him delivered to me or killed. I cannot wait any longer. Do you understand?" Morcant withered under her glare.

"Aye mistress," Morcant's voice filled with remorse as he looked at her face.

"Good." She lifted Morcant's head until his red eyes stared into her deep brown ones. He could smell her subtle jasmine fragrance as it filled his senses. "Do not fail me," she whispered, "or next time I'll take more from you than a small piece of your ear."

Morcant shook with hatred as she walked over to the ladder and descended from the rooftop. 'One day I'll be allowed to fight back against you.' Morcant thought bitterly as his rage began to rise. 'Not today, but soon.' He suppressed these thoughts as he cleared his nose of her scent. Slowly he paced the roof as he sifted through the scents of the city. Wherever his prey had hid, it would not stay hidden from him for long.

'Where am I?' Halin thought groggily as he tried to open

his eyes. After a few moments, he realized that his eyes were open. It was the darkness in the room that prevented him from seeing anything. His head ached and throbbed with his every move, so Halin tried to lie as still as possible as he attempted to determine his location with the rest of his senses. 'How come I always wind up hurt and unconscious?' His rueful thoughts danced through his head as he gave up on his futile attempts at seeing anything in the darkness.

The noises that drifted into the room him helped him realize that he was in an inn or a tavern of some sort. Halin did not recognize any of the scents that wafted through the timbers of the room. Halin muttered quietly to himself. He winced in pain as his words, soft though they were, rang in his head as if he had screamed them.

Halin almost missed the soft creak of the floorboards as something shifted quietly.   The noise was so subtle that in the following moments of silence, he started to think it was his imagination playing tricks on him.   Then he heard it again. The sound was faint, but real. Halin held his breath as he heard the soft whisper of cloth as it brushed against the hard wood floor as the thing moved somewhere in front of him.

The movements were slow and calculated at first, but as he listened harder, he could tell that the thing moved a bit faster than he had thought. Aside from the soft fluttering of cloth, Halin could only tell that it came from across the room. It moved deftly in the blackness that enveloped. He could feel his heart leap from his chest as the soft scuffling noise came closer. Halin's eyes would not adjust to the darkness nearly as fast as he would like them to.

"I see you are awake." A voice floated to his ears like the soft melody of the wind in tall grasslands. It seemed as if the man sang to him instead of speaking. The man's accent was like nothing that Halin had ever heard. "Well, are you going to talk to me… or were you struck dumb as well as unconscious by Morcant's attack?" There was something familiar about the dark stranger's voice although Halin could not place until he heard Morcant's name.

"Why did you save me?" Halin's whisper was barely audible, yet the stranger seemed to hear it easily.

"That's a little better." The stranger replied. "I always prefer to have my guests in a light mood when I have a conversation with them." Halin's vision had cleared enough to perceive the light blue glow emanate from his host's eyes and even in the dim blue light, the man's smile was easily visible.

"That's not an answer," Halin noted. "Please tell me why you have saved me. I am no one important… "

"No one important you say." The elf said mockingly. "That may be true, but you were someone in need. Were you not?" The voice asked mirthfully.

"Well… aye… but… Hey! Don't change the subject." Halin grew less impressed with his benefactor the longer they spoke.

"I am sorry, I was just a little surprised by your question." The stranger replied, trying to sooth Halin's growing temper.

"Were you surprised, or are you just trying to come up with a good lie?" Halin asked boldly. He felt his fear lessen the more his eyes grew accustomed to his dark surroundings. He could now make out the fine slivers of light that came in through the slits of the door. The one thing that bothered him was that he could not make out any of the man's features other than the soft glowing blue eyes and the light smile that graced the bottom of his face.

"I needn't lie," the voice gained a steel-like edge to it as he answered Halin's last question. Its keenness made Halin wince as he heard it. "I just normally hear questions like, 'Who are you?' and 'Where am I?' It's a little refreshing, if not a little startling, to hear such a wise question from someone in your situation." All of the man's previous humor had left his voice and Halin fought the urge to interrupt his host to ask him those questions as well. "So, to answer your question, I did as I must. You were in need, so I helped you."

Sensing that there was more to it, Halin could not stop from interrupting the man with another question, "What do you mean, you did as you must? No one forced you to save me."

"Would you rather that I hadn't?" The question hung between them for a few moments as Halin gathered his wits to reply.

"No." Halin started to say, but was cut off.

"You really don't sound too grateful." The edge in the man's voice bordered on anger and Halin sensed the man's muscles tighten a little although he still could not make out any of his features.

"That's because I'm trying to determine the 'why' of it." Halin tried to sound more aloof than he really was. He was certain that if Namir had been in his situation it is what he would do. "If I was saved to be sold into slavery, for example, then I wouldn't be all that ready to thank you as my savior and rejoice in my fate."

"True enough." The man agreed with a chuckle as he admired Halin's presence of mind.

"So, what did you mean by your comment?" Halin asked again, this time a little more docilely.

"That I will answer later, for now all that you need to know is that I am a guardian and that I did what I must."

Halin realized that this was the only reply that this guardian would give him and he was none too pleased by it. "What exactly is a guardian?" Halin asked timidly. He felt like there was a lot more going on that concerned him than he was aware of.

"You have never heard of us?" The guardian asked. Without waiting for a reply, he continued, "No, you wouldn't have. Never mind. We guardians protect the races of the world from the creatures that would prey upon them. Usually we are assigned to a person or a task, but not always, as you found out today." Confused, Halin was about to interrupt the guardian again but stopped as the room was abruptly bathed in light.

"This is better for you isn't it?" The guardian asked as he shielded his own eyes from the light cast by the oil lamp on the table next to him.

Halin squinted at the abrupt light and shielded his eyes

from the bright light as well. After a few moments, his vision cleared and he saw the guardian again. He was surprised to find the guardian had very pale skin and wore strange cloths that seemed to shift to match his surroundings as they drifted on what little breeze was in the room. The only parts of his body was not affected by this phenomenon were his hands and his head.

The guardian's long brown hair was neatly tied in a tight queue behind his head and his glowing ice blue eyes were slitted like a cat's as the elf peered at Halin past the lamp's glow. Although Halin was not used to seeing people with cat-slitted eyes, the thing that caught his attention the most was the guardian's ears. Although they were almost completely hidden by his brown hair, the tips darted out through the sides and ended elegantly in graceful points.

As Halin stared at him in awe, the guardian smiled slowly. "It's just as I thought you don't remember seeing my kind before, do you?" This was more of a statement than a question and its meaning was lost to Halin as he gazed at the guardian's ears.

Halin struggled with the guardian's question and his own thoughts about what race he may be for a few moments before he replied in awe, "No... I've never seen any of your kind before."

The guardian's smile lingered for a few moments after Halin answered him and it was obvious he was amused by it as he commented, "you have, but you were... "

This sentence was cut short by the thunderous crash of the door giving way in large chunks as wood and debris splintered towards them. He threw himself on top of Halin as he pulled the edges of his cloak to cover them completely. Halin was amazed by the cloak's transparency and the way it withstood the force of the debris as it landed on them.

As soon as the guardian was certain nothing else flew at them, he stood to face their attackers. His movements were graceful and catlike as he instinctively pulled his sword from its scabbard and assumed a defensive stance. In less than a heartbeat, he went from a crouched defensive pose to an aggressive. It was apparent to Halin that the guardian was poised and ready to strike.

Chapter Fourteen: Confrontations

Namir stood behind Nurn in the hallway. His head throbbed painfully from the attack in the alleyway earlier. 'What was that thing and why was it after Halin?' Namir wondered as he replayed the events quickly through his mind.

He remembered nothing before a guard had revived him. It took quite some time for Namir to convince the guard that something had attacked Halin and himself. His main problem had been that there was no sign of the fight, somehow all of the debris and damage this creature caused had been returned to some semblance of order. Although it took a while, Namir finally managed to convince the guard to report the issue to his superior

Namir was relieved to find that this guard's superior was Faris, the guard he had met at the gate a week earlier. After listening to Namir's report Faris seemed concerned, but only about the beast. Namir asked Faris if he could spare a few guards to help him find Halin, but was summarily dismissed to find Halin without any help from the city guard. Namir hated to admit that he could understand Faris's concern about the thing that had attacked him; he just thought that the guards should also help him find Halin as well.

Once he made his way out of the guard tower, Namir ran as fast as he could back to the Flying Muses. He hoped he could alert the others as well as rally some help to find Halin amongst the inn's patrons. Nurn was the first one he came across and Namir wasted no time in telling him what happened. Nurn immediately went in search of his brother, and left Namir to rally any other support he could find alone.

Namir had just finished telling the rest of the group, and anyone else within earshot in the main hall, when Jaconis stood up and walked towards the stairs. It was not until Hessa demanded that he told them where he was going that Jaconis offered any help whatsoever, unfortunately the only help Jaconis offered was to stay at the inn in case Halin returned. With a sneer, Jaconis turned and headed up to his room.

Bitterness rose unbidden as he recalled Jaconis's uncaring attitude. 'Jaconis only cared how this attack affected further negotiations.' This thought boiled Namir's anger to further heights as his attention snapped back to the present by the sound of splintering wood.

The force of the door splintering almost drove Namir to his knees and the sound nearly crippled him as it rumbled in his throbbing head. Namir managed to turn just in time to see Nurn throw his weight into the remnants of the door and step into the darkened room beyond.

"I don't know who you are, but I will break you if I must." Nurn's voice grated like cold metal on stone as he stepped through the doorway.

"I hope it needn't to come to that," a lilting voice replied lightly in the darkness. Namir could make out a glint of light as it played along a silvery steel edge as the man replied.

"Nurn, he has a sword." Namir said quietly. He hoped only Nurn heard him as he uttered it. Namir was relieved when he saw Nurn nod almost imperceptibly. "Let the man explain himself." Namir said loud enough for anyone in the room to hear, "I'd rather not talk to the city guards a second time tonight."

"I am glad your friend understands reason." The voice came again from the darkness of the room as Namir's heart sank. He had hoped Nurn's nod would have gone unnoticed.

"Who are you and why do you hold my brother prisoner?" Nurn demanded as his voice peeled off the walls surrounding them.

The faint sounds of metal sliding across leather followed by soft laughter were the next sounds to emanate from the room. "If my prisoner, as you call him, is your brother then it appears I have made a grave error indeed. Please come in so we can discuss this matter, although the loss of the door will make this discussion a little less than private."

"If you'd come with us, I know of a more private place we can talk." Namir offered hastily. "Besides, I think my friend here," Namir said as he patted Nurn on the back, "would be in better humor if we were in a more familiar location." Namir held his breath as he waited for the man's reply.

"And how will the boy get there?" The man asked, still well hid within the shadows of the room.

"I'll carry him if needed." Nurn rumbled menacingly.

"I can walk," Halin's crisp tenor voice rang out from the dark room. Nurn visibly relaxed as he heard Halin's voice. "At least I think I can."

At that, Nurn briskly walked into the darkness and returned with one arm around Halin. It was obvious to Namir that Nurn supported most of Halin's weight as the two walked past. Namir motioned them towards the stairs and whispered to Nurn that he should lead them back to the inn via the back roads instead of the main ones. Again, Nurn nodded almost imperceptivity and Namir somehow knew the man in the room managed to hear what the two of them shared.

Namir stood silently as he watched them descend. It was hard for him to wait for the man to step out of the darkness of the room and when he did, Namir's eyes widened at the sight of him. Something about him was familiar to Namir, but he could not place what. As the man stepped from the shadows, it seemed as if the shadows accompanied him. It took a few moments for the shadows to fade. When they did the shades and images of the hallway blended into the man's clothes to take the shadows' place.

The man's hood was up, but it did not conceal his elegant features much and a few wisps of chestnut brown hair emerged from under his hood to lie neatly against his porcelain skin. The thing Namir found most familiar about the man were his ice blue eyes. Namir shivered as he felt the man's piercing gaze pass over him and take in Namir's every aspect.

"I'm ready to go, please lead me to this place you've mentioned." The man said quietly with a musical quality to his voice. Namir found this quality familiar and almost hypnotic.

Namir felt the man's eyes bore into him again as he turned toward the stairs. It felt as if his entire lifetime was stripped away as Namir strode down the hallway by the man's scrutiny. This eerie feeling left as quickly as it had come and it was hard for Namir to stay at a steady speed. Although the man was not openly threatening, Namir sensed that he was immensely dangerous.

To check his fear, Namir set a steady and purposeful pace as he led the stranger from the Dragon's Tale Inn out into the main market place. As they walked, Namir attempted to steal another look at his strange companion. Try as he might, Namir failed to see anything more. Each time he tried to catch a glimpse, the uncanny ability of the man's clothing foiled his best attempts. All Namir managed were a few brief glimpses of the man before they arrived at the Flying Muses.

Jaconis had just lain down to sleep when he heard footsteps approaching his door. He rolled quietly out of his bed and crawled along the floor to the nearby chair where he had left his belt. There he silently reached up and pulled his dagger free from its sheath. 'Whatever is out there will have a fight if it comes after me.' He thought quickly as he waited on the floor in the darkness.

Relief stole over him as the footsteps moved farther down the hall and away from his door. Jaconis's hands were still shaking as he climbed back into his bed. 'Whatever that thing was I saw earlier tonight on the roof isn't here,' Jaconis though happily as he relaxed under his covers.

"I should tell the others about it," Jaconis whispered to himself, still a little afraid the beast might hear him.

"Why?" A soft voice asked lightly. It came from the direction of the open window across the room. "Do you think that they could help you if they knew?"

Jaconis rolled out of his bed again. This time he gripped his dagger tightly in his hand. He directed his roll towards the window for more momentum as he lunged toward where he heard the voice. To his surprise, his dagger hit something hard and metallic. With a quick jerk, his dagger was wrenched out of his hand before he could finish his attack.

"Don't ever do something that foolish again," the soft voice laughed as it chided. "Next time I may do worse to you than taking away your pathetic little dagger."

The voice seemed oddly familiar to Jaconis. Try as he might, he could not piece together where he had heard it before. Jaconis slowly raised his eyes to the window and squinted against the pale moonlight that silhouetted his attacker. He hoped that he might discern who the voice belonged to.

To his amazement, a woman's form filled his window. She wore a loose fitting outfit, covering some sort of leather garment. In one hand, she held a short black blade and in the other, she held his dagger. The shadows cast by the moon behind her obscured her face, but there was something not right about her features although he could not see them clearly, Jaconis could feel it.

"Who are you?" Jaconis tried to sound brave as he squinted against the moon light framing her as he tried to get a better look.

"Stay where you are and don't move." She answered quietly as the moonlight glinted from her wet lips as she spoke. "I am here for a reason." Her voice seemed to roll out of her mouth with a strange cat-like sound to the way her consonants trilled. "As for my name, well, that is a matter of interest to many people and you do not need to worry yourself with it.

Just know I'm not here to hurt you, just to silence you."

She shifted to one side a little and easily brought her legs up into a sitting position on the ledge of the window.

"All of this should be over soon. We can't have you messing any of this up. If you cooperate and do as you're told, we will help you finish your job here. Do we have a deal?" Her eyebrow raised in an amused anticipation of Jaconis's reply as she finished her proposal.

Jaconis's heart raced to the brink of bursting out of his chest as his fear stole his breath. Once his heart no longer hammered in his chest, he considered the implications of her question. "What if I say no?" Jaconis asked her after he built up enough courage speak.

"Then I will silence you permanently." Jaconis watched her twirl his dagger in her dainty hand with ease as she purred her response to his question.

"So do I really have a choice?" Jaconis shot back almost immediately before his courage fled him.

"No, not really," she said as she shook her head lightly. Then, as if something caught her attention, she raised her eyebrow and cocked her head to one side as she stated, "Well, aye. You do have a choice, one choice. A very simple one at that," her eyes glowed green in the darkness and seemed to tear their way into Jaconis's soul as she continued. "You can choose to live or you can choose to die, that is the choice I offer you. It's a choice you need to make right now."

She raised Jaconis's dagger level with his eyes slowly as she let the impact of her words sink in. She held his poorly balanced blade with its hilt facing him and although the dagger was almost useless as a weapon, it did little to hinder her graceful movements.

Jaconis's eyes widened as he watched her raise his dagger. He noticed ruefully that her motions were that of a well-trained knife thrower and somehow Jaconis felt she would not miss her mark even in the inky darkness surrounding them. Jaconis also sensed she would not hesitate to kill him, so his decision came easily.

"Aye, I'll do as you say. I have just one question. How am I supposed to get your help if I don't know your name?" Jaconis flinched as his dagger left her hand silently.

His heart raced to the point of exploding as the blade passed within inches of his right ear. Even the sound of it sinking into his headboard with a quiet thud did little to ease his fear of the lady in front of him. Jaconis sat silently as he waited to feel blood trickle down his neck from where she had punctured him. When this vile sensation did not come, he opened his eyes to meet her amused gaze.

"Ah, another easy question to answer. You don't." Her smile was evident in her voice as she told him this. "You see, we have a friend in common and our friend will be in touch with you." She pivoted enough to dangle her legs out of the window a she turned her back to him. "And don't worry, I will keep my word. If you leave this room for any reason before morning, you will die." She said over her right shoulder in a matter of fact tone that caught Jaconis off guard. Before he could react, she pushed herself out of the window.

Jaconis fell to his knees and quivered for a few moments as he fought to regain some modicum of self-control. Once he was in control of himself, he rose to his feet and walked over to the window to gaze after his assailant. He was four stories up. There was no building close enough for her to jump to.

'I don't even want to know how she got up here.' He lied to himself and shook his head in confusion.

He made sure to pull both the shutters and the window closed before he walked over to the headboard of his bed. Several minutes passed as he worked his dagger out of the wood. He decided to keep a hold of it as he crawled back into bed. Hours slipped by as he tried to get his mind to rest long enough to drift off to sleep. His mind made its way back to her silhouette and replayed the scene repeatedly.

Each time he relived it, his hand wandered up to the newly formed hole in his headboard. Several more hours passed before he was finally able to succumb to the merciful grasp of dreams. Then he awoke abruptly to the sound of a woman's scream as it tore through the stillness of his room and the heavy scent of smoke filled his nostrils.

"So tell us, why did you take Halin hostage?" Namir asked, a little irritated by the man's carefree demeanor.

"Because I thought he was someone else, as did Morcant." The stranger replied nonchalantly. His hood was down now and he seemed at ease sitting on Namir's bed.

Although the room was big, it was not large by any means, so after the four of them crowded into the room, both sitting places and elbowroom was sparse. Nurn sat on the floor with his back against the door, while Halin lay on Nurn's bed and Namir sat under the only window, which they had closed and bared shut.

"So what's your name anyway?" Halin asked as he rolled over onto his side slowly.

"Jerine," the stranger replied.

"Who did you think Halin was?" Nurn demanded. "And why would you have the right to take him if he was the person you were looking for?"

"One question at a time Nurn," Namir cut in. "Please go ahead. Answer Nurn's first question." Something about Jerine bothered Namir… something familiar.

"I can't tell you exactly who I thought he was… "

"Why not?" This time Halin interrupted Jerine and Namir shot him a warning glance that quieted him down immediately.

"Even if I knew the person's name, I would not be at liberty to divulge it. I am sorry that I can't be more helpful in this." Jerine replied coolly.

'Nothing seems to bother him.' Namir thought bitterly. "Fine, then who or what is Morcant?" Namir struggled to keep the bitterness out of his voice. 'What is Jerine hiding?' Namir thought darkly to himself as he asked his question.

"Morcant is a nassarid, more specifically a lupine nassarid." Reading the confusion in the faces of the boys around him, Jerine elaborated, "A nassarid is a hybrid, mystically created to perform a set task. Lupine nassarid's are exceptional hunters and assassins, although not all of them are intelligent enough to kill quietly. Morcant is an exception. He is well known for his cunning and his speed. There are not many that cross his path that live to tell about it." Jerine leaned against the wall as he made himself more comfortable.

"Why would he have come after me? Can just anyone hire these things?" Halin asked, his voice became shallow and his complexion paled as he heard Jerine's description.

Jerine chuckled silently as he replied, "No. Not just anyone can hire them. For the most part, they are not for hire. As I said, they are created. Therefore, they are owned by the mages, or the group of mages, that created them. These mages usually have a vested interest in having their will done by their creations." A look of concern crossed Jerine's features briefly before he continued. "As for why he attacked you… he must have thought you were someone else as well. Perhaps he's hunting for the same person I am."

"That isn't really possible is it?" Namir asked. "I mean, from what you said. If Morcant is so good at his job, wouldn't he know Halin wasn't his target?"

"Not necessarily." Jerine replied. "He may have been given a description instead of a name."

"Like you were?" Nurn's question was more of a growl than words.

"Aye, just like I was." Jerine hung his head as he admitted this.

"So you think your target and Morcant's target could be one and the same?" Namir asked hesitantly.

"Aye, it is a possibility." Jerine answered quietly. "I hope not, but there is a chance of it. Either way, Halin is not safe."

"Why?" Nurn demanded.

"Because until Morcant realizes he has made a mistake, he will continue to hunt Halin. Even if Morcant acknowledges this mistake, he may not spare Halin's life. Morcant is cruel and hates to be robbed of his prey, even if the prey is not his intended target. Another possibility is that he was sent to kill his target, which means Morcant will not rest until Halin is dead."

"I won't let that happen." Nurn growled as he started to stand.

"Where do you think you're going?" Namir asked Nurn as his friend towered above him.

"Hunting," Nurn said fiercely. The anger in Nurn's voice was as palpable as the embers of anger in his eyes.

"With what, your knife and dagger?" Jerine shot at him with a derisive laugh.

"Aye, if I needed." Nurn replied angrily.

"I've seen this thing Nurn. I know you're very strong and well skilled in hunting, but this thing… this… Morcant. He truly is a beast. You won't be able to stop him on your own." Namir pleaded with his gigantic friend.

"Someone has to try!" Nurn retorted. "It's my brother this thing is hunting. I can't let it continue, I just can't. How do you expect me to turn my back and pretend that it'll end?"

Jerine laughed. "Let him go, he seems eager to die."

"Quiet!" Namir shouted at Jerine as he deftly stepped into Nurn's way to stop him from lunging at the guardian.

"Let me by!" Nurn growled.

"No. I have a plan to remedy this situation. Please sit down and listen." Namir continued his sentence in a scant whisper, "the best thing we can do is wait until morning. We can then buy some weapons and talk to the guards again." Namir realized his attempt to soothe Nurn was not working.

"What is your plan?" Nurn spat at Namir as he glared at Jerine for another minute before he moved back to the door and leaned against it. The timbers creaked audibly as he angrily pressed his weight against it.

"By getting Jerine to help us." Namir whispered to Nurn. He hoped Jerine would not hear him, but deep down Namir knew he would.

"Fine," Nurn said. It was obvious by his voice and his attitude that his anger still burned below the surface.

Morcant stood on the roof across from the Flying Muses. He could smell his prey's fear from here. He took in another deep breath, then Morcant spun around quickly and lifted the woman that had crept up behind him off the roof by her throat.

"Why are you here?" Morcant growled.

"Mistress sent me." The woman choked out her reply.

"Why would out mistress send you?" Morcant barked. His eyes narrowed as he allowed the faint glow cast by his eyes to envelope her body.

"I… I don't know." The woman lied. She coughed as she tried to force enough air through her throat to talk. "But if you keep squeezing my neck, it will break. Then you will never know why I am here."

Morcant took in another deep breath and then released her. "You smell of the inn below. Were you in there recently?" Morcant's eyes never left her as they cast an eerie glow directly onto her face.

She rubbed her neck lightly as she took a step backwards and looked into his glowing eyes. From the pale light that cascaded around him, she could barely discern his features.

'I wish he'd look away.' She thought, eager to be far away from him.

"Aye, I was in there on a mission for Mistress." She thought she saw the corners of his mouth fall into a scowl and she smiled at his chagrin.

"Tell me about the mission, Skara." As Morcant said her name, he felt bile rise in his throat. 'Why would the Mistress send a feline witch to oversee my activities?' Morcant was uneasy by this turn of events. 'It only bodes ill.' He decided as he waited for her response.

"Morcant, it warms my heart to hear you remember me so well." Skara said, the sarcasm dripped from her lips like a river and pooled around Morcant's ears. "But you, of all people, should know better. I can't reveal my deeds to anyone save our Mistress." Skara smoothed the wrinkles from her silk shirt as she scolded him.

The reproof in Skara's words cut Morcant like a lash. "That much I know, but if you cannot tell me of the deed, tell me what you can of your actions and to which room you went." Morcant could not stop his lips from peeling away from his teeth to reveal their glistening white surface in the soft light of the moon.

"I can see no harm in that. I went to the room facing the market, on the far corner. Mine was the task of delivery, which I have done. Now my second task is before me. I am to make sure you capture the boy… alive." Skara pulled her long grey hair into a loose queue before she made sure her soft blackened breeches did not pinch her tail.

She smoothed the pleated ruffles on the sleeves of her loose fitting slate colored shirt before she looked at Morcant again. 'Damn lupine is going to give me fleas… I just know it.' She thought momentarily as she felt the vestiges of an itch start just behind her right ear. Morcant growled as he heard Skara recite her mission. Skara allowed a playful smile to crest her lips at the sign of his discomfort.

"So, where is your prey? Don't tell me that the mighty tracker has lost the trail?" She toyed. She enjoyed the look of disgust that consumed Morcant's features.

The bitter taste of iron filled Morcant's maw as he felt his blood pressure rise. "He is in the inn, near where you were." Morcant took a few steps back from Skara as he smiled maliciously. "I have an idea. Why don't you just go in and get him?"

Skara stopped grooming herself and looked up at Morcant in surprise. "You mean it? You would let me gain more of Mistress' favor by allowing me to complete your task as well?"

Morcant laughed bitterly. "Of course I would my dear kitten." The malice of his words hung between them so thick that Skara felt her hackles rise. "That is if you think that you can."

"And why wouldn't I be able to?" Skara asked as her mind raced in a vain attempt to solve the riddle of Morcant's offer.

"Because he is being protected by a guardian or didn't our Mistress tell you?" Morcant answered her with a vicious and mocking look in his eyes. "You mean you didn't feel its presence when you were in there?" Morcant feigned surprise as he saw Skara cringe. "My… you must not be as good as I thought." Morcant laughed quietly as Skara fidgeted with her hair in agitation.

"A guardian here?!? Are you sure?" Skara felt her fear rip free from her control. 'A guardian… dear Jia no.' Skara's thoughts flew back to her youth. It was her sixteenth birthday and four men came and took her family away from her.

"Aye, a guardian. Hmmm… didn't I hear you had a problem with guardians when you were younger?" Morcant enjoyed every moment of Skara's discomfort.

'Finally a way to pay this feline witch back for her interference.' He seethed.

"Well, what are you waiting for… or should I assume you'll be letting me take care of the task after all?" His voice was harsh and full of hatred. Skara cringed away instinctively, still locked within her memories.

"How do you plan on getting him free from the guardian?" Skara asked after many long moments had passed. Her voice was quiet and she could feel a cold sweat form on her brow.

"I was hoping you could help me," Morcant glanced back at Skara as she pulled her cloak tightly around her. He enjoyed watching her try to hide within its folds, "indirectly of course."

"What do you mean?" Skara nervously tugged some of her grey hair loose from her queue and braided it absentmindedly.

"I need to have a fire lit… in the stables." Morcant explained as he turned and sniffed the breezes that danced around them.

"That I can do," Skara sounded a little more confident now. Her nerves slowly locked back in check.

"Good." Morcant grinned evilly as he saw her slip off the roof and move toward the stable of the Flying Muses.

'Hopefully she's able to do what is needed.' Morcant thought ruefully.

He paced the rooftop and anxiously waited to see if his plan would work. He knew guardians were fond of their steeds, but would he leave his charge alone to save his mount?

'We shall see.' Morcant thought viciously. When he smelled the first traces of the fire that Skara had set in the stables, Morcant's smile broadened. 'Soon,' he thought. Morcant slowly stalked to edge of the roof and hunched down so that only his eyes were above the outer ledge.

"So Jerine," Namir said as he turned to the man who sat on his bed. "How is it that you managed to get away from Morcant? You said so yourself, no one that crosses his path survives."

"That's easy, I am a guardian." A slight chuckle escaped Jerine's lips as he said this. "Morcant isn't dumb enough to challenge me openly."

"Ummm… what, exactly, is a guardian again?" Halin asked innocently from Nurn's bed.

"We are elves that have sworn our lives to protect those deemed worthy of our services. Those like my people's royalty as well as those chosen to gain our friendship." Jerine explained.

"Elves! Really?" Halin exclaimed as he struggled to sit up.

"Aye, elves, now lay back down and rest or you'll not heal as fast as we'd like." Jerine instructed in an attempt to calm Halin down. After Halin lay back down, Jerine turned and rebound Halin's wounds.

"Na'i nak tuch, hebasii Jerine." Namir uttered completely unaware of his companions' puzzled stares.

"Na'a quorun hebasii, mut aa garadin. Hab'e sa'oot miun kielten?" Jerine replied as he turned to face Namir slowly.

"I learned it as a boy from our Healer, Saril." Namir admitted abashedly.

"I see, Saril indeed." Jerine nodded, a knowing grin spread across his face as he leaned back against the wall.

"What did you two just say?" Nurn asked as his confusion got the better of him.

"I said that he has a good touch and I called him a healer." Namir said plainly, his gaze never left Jerine's face.

"And I replied to your friend that I am a guardian, not a healer. Then I asked him where he had learned my tongue." Jerine offered without prompting. Jerine's ice blue eyes penetrated deeply through Namir's steel blue ones and into his soul.

"Do you know Saril?" This time it was Halin's tenor voice that chimed in to ask the question that both Namir and Nurn were both thinking.

"Aye, Saril is known to me. And it doesn't surprise me that all of you know him." Jerine said with laughter in his voice.

"I believe Halin asked if you know Saril… not if you know of him." Namir said calmly, his eyes still locked with Jerine's slitted ones.

"Ahhh… aye he did didn't he. Well. I believe I have had the chance once, a long time ago, to meet Saril. Assuming he associates with a talented fighter by the name of Carness." Jerine said, amused by the look of surprise in Namir's eyes. 'Aye, he is the one I seek. Landolin will be proud of me.' Jerine thought happily. He was glad to have finally found the boy that he had been searching for.

"You know Carness too?" Halin asked in awe.

"Aye. I taught him several of my personal sword strokes." Jerine replied, still appearing amused.

"Hah. Now I know you're lying. Carness doesn't use a sword." Halin said obviously content with his victory.

"That's too bad." Jerine said a little sad. "He was one of my better students."

"Enough of this!" Nurn exclaimed. "Jerine, are you going to help us deal with Morcant or not?" Nurn demanded as he turned to face the elf fully.

As Jerine was about to answer, the conversation was brought to an end by the sharp pungent smell of smoke and a loud bang on the door. Namir stood and peered out the window through the cracks in the shutters. He turned abruptly and ran toward the door as he yelled over his shoulder.

"Get Halin out of here, the stable is on fire! I'll make sure the girls and Jaconis get out safely. Nurn, check on the horses! Jerine, protect Halin with your life!"

Chapter Fifteen: Fire

Jaconis was jolted awake by the woman's scream as it tore through the remnants of his dreams. He lay silent and still as her voice was joined by many others. "The stables are on fire!" The words stirred him from his fitful slumber for more reasons than the obvious message they conveyed. He knew the voice he heard. It was familiar and belonged in the nightmare that haunted his restless sleep.

He wondered if he should risk leaving his room, as he lay there inhaling more and more smoke. Her orders were clear. He was not to leave the room until sunrise. If he did, his life was forfeit. However if he did not leave, he might burn to death. Somehow, his choices became more limited faster than he was able think.

Jaconis slowly stood up from his bed, his lungs burned from this simple effort as he made his way to the window. He flung the panes outward as quickly as he could manage and the shutters with them. He ignored the pounding on his door as he breathed in the crisp clean air that flooded into his room on the cold night's breeze. It was not until his door was almost battered down that he decided to respond.

By the time Skara returned, people were milling all over

the market. First, they flooded out of the Flying Muses in a disorderly array when Skara burst through the doors and screamed the stables were on fire and then they flowed from all of the surrounding buildings. Panic was paramount. Skara was easily able to slip away in the confusion without being seen.

"It is done." Skara purred to Morcant. "They should be coming out anytime now, unless they have already fled." Skara said proudly as she walked over to where Morcant crouched.

"Get down, unless you are eager to taste the steel of the guardian's blade." Morcant growled. He was annoyed by Skara's arrogance. "They have yet to come out… but they will soon. If they see you I'll be forced to cut my losses and abandon you to them." He informed her as he directed her gaze to the inn's main entrance.

Namir raced as fast as he could through the crowded hallway. He fought his way through the throng of fleeing as he made his way toward his remaining companions' rooms. Every step was a battle as he fought for headway. He mentally appraised his position in the building and compared it to where he believed the fire was. Bitter thoughts burned at the edges of his mind as he berated himself for not getting rooms close to one another.

It seemed as if he had been struggling against the flow of people forever when he made it to Jaconis's door. 'Unfortunately Jaconis's room was closer than Aves and Hessa's,' but Namir did not linger on the thought.

He banged loudly on Jaconis's door and cursed at the time he had lost in his trek here. Namir waited impatiently as he strained to hear if there were any noises inside the room. His fist pounded a second barrage of rapid knocks and then he pressed his ear to the door again.

"Why doesn't he answer… can't he smell the smoke or hear the commotion?" Namir muttered bitterly. He tried the latch and found it locked. "Damn him!" Namir thought hotly as thick black smoke filled the hallway.

Namir pounded a third time on the door impatiently. This time he used all his strength and heard the wooden door begin to crack under the force of his fists. At odds with himself, he waited a few more moments before he turned to leave.

The door flung open and Jaconis stood silhouetted by the pale moon light that flooded through his open window. "What do you want?" Jaconis snapped at Namir's incredulous look.

"What do I want?" Namir asked as sarcasm filled his voice.

"Yes," a sneer played along Jaconis's lips, "I believe that's what I asked."

"Can't you see this place is on fire? Don't you hear the commotion caused by people fleeing the building?" Namir yelled over the din of the mass evacuation.

"Oh, that's what is going on." Jaconis said acting uninterested and uniformed. "I thought I heard someone say the stables were on fire, but I figured I was just hearing things. Oh well." Jaconis shrugged as he started to close his door.

With a grunt of disgust, Namir forced the door open again. "Oh well? What do you mean, oh well!" Namir screamed. "There is a fire! You can't just go back into your room! Even if it is just the stables, that's where our horses, our carriage and all of our supplies… or have you forgotten!"

"If the supplies are gone, our trip here is finished. We would be free to return to Ellsted all the sooner, even if we have to return on foot. Either way, it is none of my affair." Jaconis sneered. "You are the one in charge of our little expedition, aren't you? Isn't it your responsibility to safeguard our trade goods and safety? Put the fire out yourself if you're so worried about it!" As he said this, Jaconis slammed the door and made his way nervously back to his window. He hoped with each step that he had not just sealed his fate.

"He seems used to giving orders," Jerine commented as he moved deftly to the door. "I hope he has the courage needed to enforce his commands." He spoke more to himself than to anyone present as he closed the door and turned to face Nurn.

"What are you doing?" Nurn asked amazed as much at Jerine's comments as he was by his actions. "Namir instructed us to get Halin out of here while he makes sure the others get out safely."

"I know." Jerine replied offhandedly. "But there is something I need to know first." Jerine stated as he made his way to the window.

"What could be more important than getting to safety?" Nurn asked somewhat surprised by Jerine's actions.

"Knowing what we are getting into, of course." This time answered his brother's question instead of Jerine. Before Nurn could rebuke him, Halin continued, "Doesn't it seem odd that a fire would start in our inn the very night I was attacked?"

"You could be reading too much into this, little brother." Nurn soothed.

"Aye, he could. But sometimes it is best to overreact than to be slaughtered like sheep." Jerine rebuked Nurn as he turned back from the window and strode over to the door.

"What is that supposed to mean?" Nurn rumbled as he became more agitated the longer they stayed in the room.

"It means the fire was planned." Jerine stated simply as he opened the door. He turned slightly to face Nurn and said, "Coming?" He quickly vanished into the smoke filled hallway.

"Nurn," Halin called to his brother. "Can you carry me out? I don't want to slow us down by trying to run."

"Of course," Nurn moved over and lifted Halin easily. "I just hope Jerine is wrong and that Namir gets the girls to safety."

"No one cares about Jaconis?" Halin mused as Nurn lifted him.

"None, for all I care he can burn with the inn. Besides, that worm may have lit this fire for all we know." Nurn grumbled as he carried Halin through the door and into the smoke filled hallway.

"Do you think we should stay here?" Aves asked Hessa incredulously as the two lay on the floor trying to breathe.

"I don't know." Hessa replied as she choked back a coughing fit long enough to reply. It was difficult to get her bearings. Hessa felt the temperature rise in the room as they lay in the middle of the floor with their blanket pulled over their heads.

"I remember Sari say that if you're in a fire and don't know where the fire is, stay where you are and try to stay away from anything hot." Aves remembered aloud. "He also said to take shallow breaths."

"Well," Hessa started to say, but then coughed hard for a few moments before she could continue. When she regained control of her voice long enough to speak, she continued. "We know that leaving through the door isn't going to work." She remembered her ordeal as she had attempted to open the door, a thick black cloud of smoke that came rolling in to meet her followed closely by a searing blast of hot air. "And the window is just as useless since we are above the stables and it seems the fire has already consumed most of them."

"Now would be a good time for your lover to save you." Aves joked; half hoping her words would prove prophetic.

"Although he isn't my lover," Hessa gasped fitfully, "I wouldn't mind his appearance either." Hessa tried to hide her smile as she thought of her dark savior, but she failed as badly as Aves did in her pitiful attempt at humor.

"Aves! Hessa!" Namir's voice made both girls jump. They were both too surprised to move. "Aves!" They heard Namir cough. His voice sounded close, but not close enough for them to see him. "Hessa! Where are you two?!"

Nurn had just made it down the stairs and headed for the door when he finally caught up with Jerine. Jerine stood just past the foot of the stairs and turned to face them by time Nurn realized who it was. It took him a few more moments to realize who it was because Jerine did not blend in with his surroundings, which was not what Nurn had come to think of as normal.

"How well can you defend yourself with a sword?" Jerine asked as Nurn walked over to him.

"I can hold my own in a fight, Carnes trained me after all." Nurn replied not even struggling with Halin's weight. "But he never taught me to use a sword, only clubs, daggers and axes."

"A sword can be used like an axe, if needed." Jerine reached down and took the sword from his belt. He carefully handed the sword and his cloak to Nurn as he continued his thought. "Take these. I hope you won't need them, but you might. Try to avoid fighting at all costs. With your brother this weak he'll need the protection of both your brawn and your brains."

"Where are you going?" Nurn asked quickly as he freed up a hand to grasp the bundle Jerine had thrust at him."

"I have to ensure the safety of my steed. Once that is… " Jerine started to say as Nurn cut him off.

"You are choosing your horse's safety over my brother's life?" Nurn demanded.

"My steed is more than a horse, dear Nurn. And I always choose her over strangers, no matter how important they are." With that, Jerine turned and dashed back into the smoke before Nurn could say anything else.

To Namir it seemed like he was moving through molasses as he pawed his way through the billowing black smoke. It only took Namir moments to decide to rescue the girls and leave Jaconis to his own fate after his brief and bitter encounter with him.

Namir sprinted down the hall toward the ominous cloud of smoke that covered half of the inn and he was thankful there were less people in his way as he did so. This enabled Namir to move a lot faster mere moments before. As soon as he heard Aves's voice he ran in the direction they called from, unfortunately the smoke had become increasingly oppressive the closer he came to their room. The biggest problem was not the smoke, it was the intolerable heat.

Namir worried that the room was already consumed by the burning stables below them. Relief filled his mind as he found a way into their room and found it still intact, just mostly filled with smoke and soot.   Time moved agonizingly slow as he fumbled through their room before he realized they had taken shelter under a blanket on the floor. This realization came as he literally fell on them.

"How did you get to us?" Aves coughed as Namir crawled under the damp blanket.

"I ran." Namir said a little surprised by the question.

"What Aves meant is, how did you get through the fire?" Hessa explained.

"The fire isn't in the hallway. It is extremely hot, but the hallway is passable." Namir explained. "However I don't think the opening will last much longer, my shirt almost caught fire as I entered your room and I think some of the ceiling was smoldering as well."

"How are we going to get out?" Aves asked. The panic in her voice was obvious and unrestrained.

"I have an idea," Namir replied.

"What's your idea?" Hessa blurted on the verge of panic.

"It depends on what kind of bath they gave you." Namir said quickly as he waited for their answer anxiously.

"They brought in two tubs, but they removed them after we finished." Hessa admitted. She felt Namir's hopes fall as she said this.

"The only thing we can do, then, is try to run through the hallway." Namir slowly backed out from under the blanket as he said this and started to rise to his feet.

Hessa followed, insisting the whole time that Aves keep the blanket on her shoulders to keep the fire off her. While the two argued about who should wear the blanket as protection,

Namir surveyed the room as best he could. All he could see was thick black smoke. It filled the entire room.

A faint glow came from where he thought the window was. Namir moved in the opposite direction of the glow to where he assumed the door was. He bumped into the wall and felt the heat seep through it. Namir locked back his desperation as he traced his way up the wall and found the open window filled with smoke and flames. He stared into the smoke as he struggled with his anger. He almost though he was hallucinating as he saw a soft blue light ball move toward them in the smoke.

"I think we have a problem!" Namir yelled as dove to shield the girls from whatever it that flew toward them.

Skara's gaze followed Morcant's finger to the front of the Flying Muses. She crouched abruptly as she saw the guardian emerge carrying a boy in his left arm and his sword out and ready in his right. Her voice was almost a whisper, she muttered, "It looks as if your ploy didn't work too well. He seems to have chosen the boy over his steed."

"Shhhh… " Morcant commanded quietly. "Elves have great ears, don't forget that." His eyes narrowed as he saw Skara quivering behind the main beam of the roof. Morcant fought the urge to push her out into the open as a distraction to the guardian, it was a hard battle but he eventually overcame his desire to humiliate her. "When they get a little farther from the others, I'll finish him off." Morcant boasted as his lips curled away from his fangs in anticipation.

"Do you think the guardian will let the boy die so easily? Besides the Mistress said alive… remember?" Skara chided quietly.

"Who said anything about the boy? I was talking about the guardian. He robbed me of my fun earlier… now I am going to take something of equal value from him." Morcant's eyes gleamed at the thought of revenge, bathing the rooftop in an eerie red sheen.

"Are you mad?" Skara asked in disbelief, almost forgetting to whisper. "Do you really think to take a guardian on alone and survive?"

"Just stay here and watch." Morcant barked softly as he backed slowly away from the gathering crowd below.

Skara turned from the scene below to watch as Morcant crawled to the far edge of the roof and dropped down into the alley behind the building. She moved silently to the edge of the roof, father away from the guardian just in time to see Morcant dash across the road as quickly and silently as the shadows that he leapt from. She smiled when she realized his ploy as he stole towards the burning stables and the volunteers that assembled in their futile attempt to control the flames as they tried to save what was left of the Flying Muses.

Nurn set Halin down momentarily on the bar as he threw the cloak over his shoulders. "This won't take long, little brother." Nurn marveled at the fact that his clothing took on the cloak's blending effect. In fact, it seemed as if Nurn was no longer himself, but changed into something else completely different.

"How did you do that?" Halin asked as his eyes watered from the smoke.

"Do what?" Nurn answered confused.

"Blend in so well with the smoke. Halin answer as Nurn lifted him again.

"I didn't, it's the cloak I think, either that or some enchantment Jerine cast upon us." Nurn replied amazed at how well the effect looked.

Nurn made his way quickly to the door as he tested the balance of the blade in his hand. The blade moved easily through the air, almost as if it guided Nurn's arm instead of the other way around. The blade glowed as the light from the fire played off its highly reflective surface. This flickering light drifted to its edge as if the sword drank it in and its delicate curves seemed to invite movement while attracting the eye to its smooth surface.

After he took a few more practice swings of Jerine's sword, Nurn moved back to Halin. Nurn lifted his brother effortlessly with his left arm and carried him into the street. He paused momentarily to make sure that no one was lying in wait.

Nurn turned and slowly made his way toward the market. Every time Halin tried to talk, Nurn loosened his grip and allowed him to slip a little. That kept him silent long enough for them to get to the deserted booths of the market. After Nurn situated Halin in one of the harder to find booths, he bade him speak.

"Why did we come here?" Halin asked quietly.

"We're just resting," Nurn answered tentatively.

"Then where are we going to go?" Halin asked immediately after Nurn finished speaking.

"Hornshir's town hall." Nurn growled. "Now be silent and wait here, I'll be back in a moment." At that, Nurn stood and deftly moved back into the shadows and vanished from Halin's view.

As the soft blue light bathed them in its radiance, the first thing Namir noticed was the lack of heat. The second thing was the feeling of comfort and peace that spread slowly throughout his body. Namir opened his eyes and turned. He kept his back to the girls the whole time.

Before him floated a beautiful woman clad in a diaphones gown that floated around her like liquid cloth. It shone a brittle white against the soft blue glow that surrounded her. Her hair and skin all appeared to be the same shade of stark white. She hovered a few feet in front of him and she extended her arms toward him as if she wished to embrace him. Entwined in her fingers was a necklace made of the purest silver and Namir was tempted to reach out to take it from her. He stood there breathless and stunned. Slowly he leaned forward and reached for her.

"Namir!" Aves shouted as her hand connected solidly with the back of his head.

"Ow!" Namir yelled as he spun to look at Aves. He abruptly noticed the blue light had completely vanished. A pained look stole across his face as if he was mortally wounded and Aves noticed it.

"Namir, what's wrong?" Aves demanded for the third time.

"Didn't you see her?" Namir asked still confused.

"There was no one there Namir." Hessa said anxiously.

"There was a lady bathed in a blue light floating right there!" Namir demanded as he pointed to where the lady had been. Namir's senses reeled as he looked at where the woman had been. Only the smoke filled window and a perilous drop into flames met his gaze.

"Fine, you saw someone that neither of us could. Can we get out of here now?" Aves snapped as she tried to drag Namir away from the window and toward the door.

Namir pulled himself free and muttered to himself. "The problem is that the fire has spread to the door and the wall has caught fire. We have to go out the window if we want to leave this room without getting burned." Namir explained forcefully, his patience completely spent.

"Have you gone mad?" Hessa blurted out before she could restrain herself. "We are above the burning stables! There is no way we would survive the fall!"

"What other choice do we have?" Namir snapped as he regained the rest of his bearings. He noticed how the smoke had completely filled the room. He felt his heart drop a little as he noticed the panicked look in Aves's and Hessa's eyes.

"Why don't we try the door?" Aves chimed in trying to ease the tension between Hessa and Namir. "Even if there are flames immediately outside, couldn't we run through them fast enough to avoid getting burned?"

After a few moments of awkward silence followed by short bursts of overlapping sentences, both Hessa and Namir seemed to agree that Namir should speak first. "We would surely die if we did. If the fire has engulfed the doorway, then it has filled the hallway as well. Our only chance is to pray that we can come up with an idea or that the gods decide to help us to survive!" Namir exclaimed sarcastically.

Morcant lay quietly in the shadows as people streamed all around his hiding place with buckets of water. 'Something is wrong. They responded too quickly to the fire.'

He fumed as the smell of burning wood and steam filled the air. The scent of ash and burnt manure was heavy, as was the sweet smell of sweat entwined with fear and adrenaline. Morcant allowed himself to be carried off in the pleasant aroma for a moment before he located his prey.

His mind reeled as he sorted out the different scents. He slowly traced where the horses had been taken. Morcant felt his anger build as he picked his way through the darkened streets. It bothered him that he moved increasingly farther from the smoke that he had intended to use as cover with every step.

Soon the muddled scents of the inn and its burning stables faded and he was able to pick out the scents easier. He silently flowed from one shadow to the next as he moved closer to his intended targets. Something in the back of his head held onto one of the prevalent scents and would not let go. He worked on it over and over again as he tried frantically to place it.

He let the familiar scent fill his nostrils hoping to determine why it seemed so familiar to him. Morcant filled his mouth with it in an attempt to jog his memory with its taste. The realization of the scent's source finally washed over him and he trembled silently. He stood outside the entryway of Hornshir's town hall and knew that he had not only lost the horses' scent, but that he was in trouble.

"Guardian." Morcant growled to himself.

"Very good. Accurate if not quick." Jerine said haughtily as Morcant spun to face him. "It seems that your years are gaining on you Morcant." Jerine sneered as he saw Morcant's rage flicker in his glowing red eyes.

Morcant narrowed his eyes trying to hold his anger in check. "So you led me here," Morcant said as he motioned to their surroundings. "Did you think that you could trap me... or better yet kill me?" His eyes danced over Jerine looking for any weakness or advantage that he could exploit. "Tell me guardian, exactly how did you plan on fighting me without your much vaunted blade?" Morcant finally said after he finished assessing Jerine's belongings.

"Do you really think that I need my sword to fight a cur like you? Morcant, you really are dumber than people give you credit for." As Jerine said this Morcant threw himself at Jerine's chest.

Jerine sidestepped Morcant's lunge quickly. In one fluid motion, Jerine yanked a pair of knives from his boots and braced himself for Morcant's second attack. He knew Morcant would not be as hasty with his second attack and the first one had come a little too close than he cared to admit.

Skara watched silently from her rooftop perch as the guardian and Morcant's prey fled down the street toward the market. Her expert eyes followed them, easily taking in the way they moved and the fit of their clothing. Something bothered her about the guardian and it was not until he faded from view that she fully realized what it was. It was his sword. More importantly, it was the way he carried his sword. To Skara it seemed as if the blade was meant to be used on wood instead of men. Skara closed her eyes and mentally reviewed the scene again.

"His cloak was a little too small for him as well... interesting." She mused. Skara laughed quietly as she thought about Morcant's haste and his carelessness. "Too bad that mangy cur didn't look closer."

Skara opened her eyes and looked over to Jaconis's window. She knew her mistress would not be pleased if she let the human die. Sometimes Skara wondered what her mistress saw in them. Humans were frail and prone to stupidity, not to mention their fowl stench. The only redeeming quality Skara could see was their adaptability to unpleasant situations. Even that was a stretch for some of them.

Skara scanned Jaconis's room for any sign of life and she could not help but smile when she saw him huddled against the window of his room in fear. She sighed deeply then she slowly crept from her hiding place and walked briskly to the edge of the building. Her slate grey shirt caught the light breeze and she felt the cool wind filter through her skintight molded leather armor enticingly.

"If I wasn't on assignment I would love to just lay here and bask in this wonderful breeze," Skara lamented quietly as she gauged the distance between the buildings carefully before she leapt to Jaconis's windowsill.

Skara smiled as adrenaline pumped through her veins. The rush she felt as she landed silently on the edge of the sill brought a surge of ecstasy with it. She closed her eyes and allowed herself to enjoy this simple pleasure. Then she opened her eyes slowly and looked down at Jaconis's huddled body curled up against the wall just below her, his head rested between her feet and it was apparent that he was completely unaware of her presence.

She stood there a few more moments before she reached down and lifted his head gently with her hands. She peered into his fear filled eyes as she helped him to his feet. Before Jaconis could say anything, she motioned for silence. Jaconis stood before her bewildered and afraid and she liked it. Skara quickly scanned his smoke filled room for his scant possessions. She breathed a sigh of relief as she spotted them close by.

Skara looked back at him, her catlike eyes glowed green in the darkness, as she gathered his things and thrust them into the backpack that lay at the foot of his bead. She smiled as she saw the fear in his eyes and his tears make trails down his cheeks leaving dirty lines of soot in their wake. He was shaking with silent sobs as she watched him and she knew that he was in her complete control.

Namir's vision swam as he lowered himself down to the floor; the hot boards creaked as his weight pressed harder onto their warped surface. The room was unbearably hot. Even the surrounding smoke was superheated. Namir was unsure how much longer he could stay conscious. He had already lost verbal contact with both Hessa and Aves.

The worst part was that he had no idea if they were still alive, all he could do was try to breathe and even that proved to be a challenge. Namir knew he could not last much longer and was sad that he had led his friends to Hornshir and to their deaths. His last thoughts were about Halin and Nurn as the darkness claimed him in its satiny embrace.

Namir felt the unbearable heat ebb away from his body slowly and felt as if he floated in the cool darkness. While he drifted pleasantly in this unconscious bliss, finally free from the burning pain in his lungs and the hot blistering smoke of the warping wood floor, he heard soft music.

The light tenor voice seemed far away at first, but as a light crisp breeze blew across his face. The voice seemed to get closer with each passing moment and the lyrics sounded strangely familiar, like a song from his childhood. The familiar song beckoned to him, pleading him to stay in his gentle slumber for a little while longer.

After an eternity of senseless moments, Namir's head cleared enough to open his eyes. It was still dark, but he could breathe. The cool evening air was a blessing to his scalded skin. He lay quietly as he tried to discern where he was. In the distance, he heard the muted cries of a commotion of some sort. The ebb and flow of the hurried voices and clanging sounds added a hunted tone to the lyrics that provided him a solace of sorts.

Above him a bird cried, a nighthawk from the sound of it. From somewhere closer came a soft humming noise and the gentle splash of water. Namir tried to turn his head to face these nearby noises. But when he did, his vision swam and distorted everything around him.

"Easy does it. We wouldn't want you to hurt yourself any more than you already are, would we?" Halin's voice softly flitted.

Namir shook his head in an attempt to clear it, but a throbbing pain stopped his feeble attempt. He heard Halin's muffled laugh and, filled with dismay, he drew enough strength to ask, "Where am I?"

"Safe for now. Nurn has gone to find Jerine, but Hessa and Aves are here with us." Halin answer quietly, his voice no more than a whisper on the light breeze. "Now please be quiet. I don't want Morcant to find us."

Namir coughed lightly and acquiesced to Halin's wishes. His mind tried to piece together how he had made his way from the burning room and into Halin's care as he drifted back off to sleep.

Chapter Sixteen: Small Victories

Jerine dove to his right as Morcant's claws cleft the air beside him. Hurriedly he brought an elven dagger up in time to slice at Morcant's exposed forearm, but misjudged the beast's reflexes.

Morcant glared at Jerine, his teeth bared and a thick string of saliva fell from his curled lips. He lunged again before the elf could completely regain his footing.

"This fight has gone on for long enough." Morcant seethed. His hatred for the guardian welled up within him of its own accord.

This time he managed to catch hold of Jerine's shirt as the elf attempted to sidestep him. Morcant yanked the cloth sharply and drove his clawed hand towards Jerine's chest. Jerine spun as Morcant pulled him closer. Jerine's daggers flashed in the dim light and managed to cut his own shirt in half so he could roll to Morcant's left side, leaving the beast with only his shirt and not his chest impaled on his greedy paw.

"You're getting old Morcant." Jerine called out mockingly as best he could. Jerine thankfully sent a prayer to his god that he was immune to Morcant's stare as he felt the beast's burning gaze fall on him again.

"Guardian, I tire of this. As of yet you have nothing to save yourself with. I have only been toying with you. I have managed to draw your blood thrice now," Morcant sneered as he turned his glowing red eyes towards Jerine, "and you are calling me old."

Jerine spun raggedly towards Morcant to face him head on. He felt the throbbing pain in his left arm as he did so. The slow realization settled into the back of his mind that if he did not end the fight soon Morcant would. As he prepared for another of Morcant's lunges he spat vehemently in an attempt to get Morcant off guard, "I hardly think that you are worth the reply."

Jerine saw the light stream from Morcant's eyes as it reflected off his glistening claws. A stream of drool arced from Morcant's frothing mouth. Jerine had only a few seconds left until Morcant's claws tore at his body again. Jerine had to think of something.

He ducked under Morcant's left arm and brought his right dagger up into Morcant's exposed stomach. Even as Jerine felt the thrill of landing a solid blow, he realized how futile it was when he felt Morcant's claws catch the back of his neck in an iron like grip.

"What have I here?" Morcant bellowed as he lifted Jerine's writhing body up from off the flagstones. "It looks like I have a helpless guardian. Where is your steed or your blade now?" Morcant spat blood onto Jerine's face as he boasted. "Just as I had always thought, your kind is useless without your much vaunted magic's... aren't you!"

Jerine attempted to answer, but as Morcant shook him from side to side, he felt his neck crack in two different places and completely numbed his body. Jerine could only ponder what Morcant was going to do to him as darkness started to close around his senses.

"No answer, eh Guardian?" Morcant jeered as he saw the poison that he coated his claws with starting to claim his prey. "Too bad, I would have preferred more of a fight." Morcant dropped Jerine to the flagstones and took a deep breath. "Oh well, this way I still have enough strength left to hunt down my real prey." He licked his lips before he continued. "Hopefully

I can track your steed down as well; it has been a long time since I have had horse flesh to fill my belly with." Morcant stood over Jerine's limp body and rubbed his stomach while he sneered down at his helpless opponent.

"And it will be even longer still!" A deep voice boomed from behind them. As Morcant turned, a large fist connected with his jaw and knocked him against the wall. Before Morcant could react, another fist hammered into his temples and was quickly followed by a sword's hilt.

Morcant struggled to stand against the ceaseless blows of his invisible assailant, but failed miserably. Every time he moved, his unseen attacker hammered at him from a different direction. Morcant crawled against the wall as he tried to avoid another round of from the air around him. He tried in vain to catch the scent of his assailant, but the blood that flowed freely from his nose and eyes ruined each attempt. In one last desperate attempt, Morcant curled his powerful legs under him and launched himself as high as he could to break free from this dreadful assault.

Jerine struggled to turn and see what was happening. By the time he was finally able to prop himself up enough to see, Morcant had already made his desperate leap to freedom. However, Morcant's attacker did not want to let him have his freedom so easily. Jerine saw one of the smaller flagstones free itself from the road and sail into the air.

It hit Morcant's legs as he pulled himself onto the top of the closest building. Jerine scowled as he noticed Morcant pull himself out of sight in spite of his wounds. Gloomily, Jerine turned to see if he could find his rescuer.

"Well that should slow him down a bit." Nurn muttered as he drew Jerine's cloak off his broad shoulders and handed it back to the guardian.

"Thank you." Jerine croaked after a few moments, both surprised and relieved to see Nurn. "How did you find me?"

"I thought you might be with the horses… and since no one had come after Halin I thought you might need some help. Besides I had your cloak and sword." With this, Nurn handed the silvery blade back to Jerine.

Jerine took the sword graciously from Nurn. As soon as he felt its familiar weight in his hand, he felt strength pour into his muscles from the magic of the blade. The familiar burning in his veins and the warm pulse of life that beat in his hand from the touch of the hilt against his skin eased away his pain and discomfort. Jerine looked at the silver globe set into the pommel of the sword and saw a light tinge of tarnish developing there. He scoffed as he noted Morcant's ploy and use of poison as his gaze fixed on the growing tarnished section.

"It seems that Morcant likes to dabble in poison." Jerine confided, "I will have to find the antidote for the rest of you if Morcant persists in tormenting us.'

"Agreed." Nurn rumbled. "So what is her name?" Nurn asked deftly changing the topic as Jerine slowly started to walk towards the center of Hornshir.

"Whose name?" Jerine responded as he snapped out of his thoughts and back to the task at hand. His body was instantly wracked with pain as he refocused his attention on the world around him.

"Your sword's. You cradle her like a lover so I figured that she has to have a name. What is it?" Nurn asked again, this time helping Jerine by guiding him through the alley and back to the main street.

"Ahhh… ." Jerine nodded in understanding and slowly looked around. Aside from the pain, Jerine did not notice anything else wrong. No one lurked nearby that might overhear their conversation. "Her name is Nienna Nénharma. It means winter's first tear in my tongue."

"It has a nice ring to it… and it is aptly named." Nurn replied as they made their way to the market.

Skara stood on the building across from the Flying Muses and watched as the commotion died away. Morcant still had not returned and Jaconis had proved too bothersome to leave awake during his rescue. She turned to look at Jaconis's unconscious form and smiled.

She mused to herself about how peaceful humans looked while they slept as she felt the night's wind turn a little chilled. Skara sat down as she started the arduous process of cleaning her fur and clothing. The soot left behind from the smoke was atrocious and clung to everything.

"Next time I'll have to find another way to get him out." Skara muttered quietly to herself.

"And next time I'll have to send someone else to my dirty work." Morcant growled from the shadows directly behind Skara.

Skara jumped. The hatred in his voice was almost overwhelming. She spun around to face him. Morcant was propped up against the wall with blood flowing freely from his swollen face and battered legs. "How long have you been there cur?" Skara demanded feeling indignant by both his intrusion and her failure to notice him.

"Long enough to know that you have saved one of my prey's companions from the blaze you set," Morcant sneered back. A bloody trail wound its way along his blackened cheek and matted his hair dull black.

"My actions are none of your concern!" Skara chided, her voice became hostile as she turned away from him. She slowly made her way over to Jaconis and hovered over him as Morcant approached them.

"Have you gotten soft on the humans now, witch? Or are you merely performing our Mistress' commands?" Morcant leered as he drew closer.

The smell of ozone that immediately followed the blinding flash, which had silhouetted Morcant's body briefly, was the only answer he received. The air trembled in anticipation of thunder as the bolt stuck Morcant's back and brought the monstrous beast to his knees.

Skara craned her neck as she rubbed her eyes vigorously in a futile attempt to see past Morcant's hunched over form to make out the source of his misery. It was not until Skara heard the light laughter that rode on the cold breeze that she knew their Mistress had arrived. As this realization dawned on her, Skara fell to her knees and threw herself over Jaconis as if to shield him from her Mistress.

"You have no need to fear, Skara. You have done nothing wrong." Her deep satiny voice soothed away Skara's fear of reprisal. "The cur will awaken soon," ensure that he does so somewhere else… somewhere that he won't be easily noticed." She instructed as she made her way over to Jaconis.

She lightly traced his cheek with the back of her gloved hand. She lowered her moist lips down to hover just above his as she inhaled his fragrance. Then she lightly placed her lips on his and tasted the bittersweet spice of his flesh. Then the mistress slowly raised her head. She locked her deep brown eyes on Jaconis's lips as she did so.

"Mistress, is there anything else I can do for You?" Skara asked, her lithe body still pulled taught across Jaconis's. From her vantage point, Skara was able to tell that her mistress wore very little beneath her tattered cloak. Her Mistress' jasmine perfume mingled well with her own to create a musky scent that filled Skara's nose and sent a thrill of desire along her spine.

She leaning closer to Skara and lightly caressed the outside of Skara's chest. "Aye," she said as she licked her lips lightly, "there is something more you can do for me." The moonlight played along the threesome as the Mistress removed her cloak.

Skara looked up at her mistress as the moonlight played through her long brown hair and turned it an inky black. "How may I aid You?" Skara's voice was little more than a whisper.

"You can start by getting up and gather some soot from below." She smiled as Skara's features fell. "Once you have done that come back up here. I need to look like I survived the fire and may have been attacked." She instructed before messing up her hair and discarding her gloves. "We need to have the effect finished before he awakes. I'll not have anything go wrong." Skara nodded and fled to gather the soot as her mistress instructed, eager to do anything that her mistress commanded.

The cold water eased some of Namir's aches and pains as he poured it over his face. The sun was well up by time Namir managed to wake up and get moving. He was still stiff and sore from the night before and his lungs burned. His throat still ached from breathing too much smoke the night before.

Namir vaguely recalled being moved from the chilled flagstones of the market and into a bed of warm hay. Halin's half-finished story about the night before and their mad flight to the Mayor's stables did very little to clear up Namir's misgivings about their situation. 'Fortunately Jerine was a skilled enough healer to keep us alive through the night.' Namir mused as he drank some water from the pail in his hand.

"The healer is here Namir." Nurn bellowed from outside the stable door.

"I'll be out in a minute. Have you seen Jaconis and his lady friend yet? I think they should go first, if only to get them out of our hair." Namir called back to his muscular friend.

"No I haven't, but I agree." Nurn replied. "Until they get back I'll have the healer see to Halin's wounds. Hopefully she knows at least half of Saril's old tricks." Nurn replied as he walked back toward the courtyard beyond.

"Me too old friend, me too," Namir answered. He knew full well that Nurn could no longer hear him.

Namir finished washing his face and arms quickly and hastily donned his tunic and boots. His lungs burned even worse as blood pumped through them at a faster pace, but Namir did not let that hinder him. Namir's numb left leg barely slowed him as he hurried through the stables. 'Hopefully we can get patched up and out of here soon.' Namir though darkly. He tried to keep the stench of manure out of his nostrils by covering his nose tightly with his left hand as he pressed on. It was not until Namir saw the healer that he stopped abruptly.

Before him lay a scene straight out of stories Namir heard

from travelers when he was younger. Halin lay propped against the well and Nurn knelt beside him, as if in prayer. Halin's right arm reached toward a lady who sat above him, just out of reach. He stretched as if he were trying to touch heaven itself.

The woman, who must have been some sort of angel, of that Namir was positive, was clad in snowy white robes with a simple gold trim that collected the light from around and sent it dancing across the flagstones in a myriad of sparkling lights. Her garments were the cleanest things Namir had ever seen. Their cleanliness only added to the porcelain like quality of her skin. Her face was milky white and her pink lips drew his attention away from her small pert breasts and toward the deep blue pools of her eyes.

Namir felt his heart stir as she looked from Halin and Nurn and met his gaze. Her eyes briefly played over him as he stood transfixed by her beauty. He tangibly felt when her eyes lingered in spots. Namir took a deep breath and disregarding the pain it caused, as the wondrous lady rose to her feet. Her long golden locks cascaded from off of her shoulders and down to her slender waist as she stood.

She gracefully floated towards him. Her small lithe feet barely touched the ground as she traversed the small distance. Namir drank in every aspect of this marvelous woman by time she crossed over to him. He realized that he had not noticed her pointed ears or her almond shaped eyes until she was next to him. Her appearance and gait betrayed her elven heritage more than her appearance could ever hope to.

"Jerine said you were in need of a healer." Her voice had a light lilt to it and made her tone smoother than honey to his ears. In these few words she managed to melt away Namir's doubts about her skills. "Am I to assume that you are in charge of these two?"

"Ay... Aye." Namir said dumbstruck.

"So then you are Namir?" The beautiful woman asked somewhat amused by Namir's response.

"Aye... " Namir nodded absently. He felt lost in the

depths of her eyes and completely oblivious to the stress she added in reference to him.

The healer slowly and delicately held out her hand almost as if afraid that Namir might bite her, as she introduced herself. "My name is Alequa. I am here to do your bidding, at least until Jerine has deemed it safe for you and your little band to leave Hornshir."

Namir stood completely entranced by Alequa's voice and beauty. It was only when Nurn cleared his throat that Namir snapped out of his trance. Even then, it took Namir a few more moments to gather his wits enough to respond.

"Fine. Please see to Halin's wounds first. After that, I hope a couple of our errant companions will have returned. If they haven't, I would like you to tend the wounds of my friends in the stable. If the missing two aren't back by then, I'd like you to stay here until you have had a chance to see to their wounds as well." Namir tried to sound stately and official in his response, but he knew that his awe of her beauty betrayed his attempt.

"I have two questions for you then, if I may ask." The sarcasm in Alequa's voice brought a smile to Namir's lips unbidden.

"Then ask." Namir grinned even more when he noticed the slight gleam in Alequa's blue eyes.

"The first is about your wounds, milord. When would you have me see to them?" Her curtsy caught Namir off guard as she posed her question.

"I would like to be treated last. What is the other question?" Namir replied.

"I hate to challenge your decisions, no matter how sound they seem to be, but wouldn't it be better and more comfortable for you and your companions to stay somewhere other than in the mayor's stables?" Alequa bit back a smile as she said this.

"That is already being looked into. The Mayor has assured me that by this time tomorrow he will have found us better accommodations. The Mayor knows of a few inns that he might be able to get us rooms in, but it could take some time to do this." Namir replied surely.

"If I may make a suggestion, I know of a place that might prove easier to find and be a bit more suited than any the mayor might offer." Alequa added humbly. There was something about her manner when she spoke to him that caught Namir off guard.

"Please tell me more." Namir felt his voice soften as he noticed she had not risen. Her head was still bowed slightly as well.

"There is a manor, of sorts, down near the river. It isn't too far from here and it can be defended easily, should the need arise." Alequa offered.

"Does Jerine know about this house… and would we be welcome there?" Namir asked absently, as if he had asked himself instead of Alequa.

"Aye to both, milord." Alequa replied. She did not miss a beat in her response.

"In that case I agree. What must we do to gain access?" Namir was so completely lost in the moment that he failed to notice that Alequa still held her curtsy.

"I can make the arrangements for you milord." Alequa responded demurely. I can have it done within the hour." She straightened swiftly and made her way back to Halin. She immediately started to tend to his wounds, but she made sure to keep Namir within her view the whole time.

"We need to stay here until everyone returns, but the sooner we leave the better. After the others have come back, I would like you to make whatever arrangements are needed." Namir called after Alequa as he turned to Nurn. "Nurn, go get the girls and bring them out here. I think they're in the back near Jerine's steed. I'd like to get us all healed as quickly as possible."

Morcant awoke to the sound of flies buzzing in his ears and his senses reeled. 'Where am I?' He thought as he struggled into a crouching position. He slowly cleared his head enough to discern a few of the scents that wafted around him and he did not like what he smelled. The strong scent of methane mingled with the subtle, yet pervading, scent of damp soil told him that he was in a pasture of some sort.

"How did I get here?" Morcant muttered as he realized that he was completely covered in manure. His memory of the night before was vague, but bits and pieces returned sporadically.

"Skara!" Morcant screamed. "I know she had something to do with this." Morcant seethed as peals of his scream faded in the distance. He slowly rose from a pile of dung and made his way down to the river.

'The witch will have a lot of explaining to do when next we meet!' Morcant thought bitterly as he pried off his mail shirt and dove into the bitterly cold water.

"So tell me how you got onto the roof with me one more time?" Jaconis asked Tali as they walked through the crowed market.

Tali sighed deeply. She made sure that her cleavage pressed out of her tattered shirt even more as she did so. When she noticed that her actions made the impact she had tried for, she answered his question, "Fine, but I'll only tell you once more. We really should be getting me new clothes instead of sharing stories about last night's fire."

She enjoyed seeing Jaconis's face wince at her tone as if she struck him. Tali allowed herself a brief moment to savor his discomfort before she gave him what he wanted.

"All I remember clearly is my room suddenly erupting in flames. When I tried to run to the door, I found it blocked by a wall of fire. That's when I decided to go back into my bed and pulled my blankets over me. Unfortunately, the floor gave way and I fell. After that, everything went dark.

"The next thing I knew, I was in an alley being dragged across the cobbles by three burly looking men. One of them had just commented about their luck in finding some good flesh and he yanked me hard by my left ankle.

"I prayed for my safety and my prayers were answered in the form of two guards. While the five of them fought, I fled. I found a ladder propped up against the building and I climbed as high as I could. I guess I found my way to the roof, but I really don't remember that part. Everything else is muddled by exhaustion." Tali lied brilliantly.

Tali was a little amazed at how easily she could anticipate what Jaconis needed to hear in order to believe her. She felt the familiar welling of need in her as his thoughts flooded into her mind like the currents of a river. She actually had to focus in order to shield herself against the torrent of his thoughts or else her mind would be drowned by them. After she managed to shield herself, it was easy to sense what information Jaconis wanted to know and give it to him.

"Now can we please get me some clothing?" She asked with just enough of an edge in her voice to make Jaconis wince again.

"Aye… immediately." Jaconis replied unaware of the darkening shadows behind him. "I think there is a good clothier this way." Jaconis motioned towards a series of stalls down a shaded street.

"Finally." Tali sighed mockingly as they started walking arm in arm down the street completely oblivious to the ominous way the shadows thickened as she passed.

A soft blue glow spilled into the stable through the cracks in the door and was the first thing that Nurn, Aves and Hessa noticed as they made their way into the courtyard. The three of them covered their eyes so they could see anything else as Nurn opened the door.

Once through the door, they found themselves completely enveloped in the light. As the light faded, they were able to discern Namir as he stood next to the well and held Halin up as best he could with the healer's hands on Halin's exposed chest. Halin was unconscious and covered in a light sheen of sweat.

"What's going on here?" Nurn demanded as he ran to his brother's side.

Namir responded first, although he did so through gritted teeth. "Alequa is doing her job, that's what. Now please come here I need help holding Halin still."

Taken somewhat aback by the harshness in Namir's voice Nurn hastened to his side and scooped Halin easily into one of his muscular arms. Aves and Hessa followed slowly in Nurn's wake as they approached Alequa in awe.

"Your brother is lucky that he has someone who cares so much for him." Alequa said as she watched Nurn lift Halin off the ground carefully. "I'm finished with him now, Nurn. You may take him somewhere that he might rest more comfortably." She motioned towards either the stables or the sparse clumps of grass that grew nearby.

"How did you do that?" Hessa asked so completely enthralled by Alequa's magic that she forgot about introductions entirely.

Alequa smiled at Hessa's forwardness. "It is called Tayant's Light and is a gift from my goddess. Now that we have cleared up that topic, my name is Alequa... yours?" Alequa added more as a demand than an introduction.

"Hessa," Hessa replied a little embarrassed at her own rudeness. "That was amazing what did it do exactly?" Hessa could not help but let her curiosity run loose.

"It is a form of healing that my goddess grants to all her acolytes." Alequa answered curtly. "You'll be able to witness it in full soon enough. I'm going to guess that you are Aves?" Alequa turned to Aves as she said this completely cutting off Hessa's next question before she could ask it.

"I am. You must be the healer." Aves responded as if she were speaking to an errant servant.

"Aye," Alequa answered. She felt the sting of Aves's remark and deciding to ignore it as she turned to face Namir. "Who would you like me to treat next, my lord?" Alequa said with a deep curtsy.

"Treat Aves first and then Hessa, if the other two aren't

back by then you have my leave to treat me.” Namir instructed. He wondered why Alequa was so subservient toward him. “But one question first.” Seeing Alequa nod her acquiescence Namir continued, “Will all of us be affected the same way that Halin was?”

“No.” Alequa answered easily. “His reaction was severe due to the amount of poison that flowed through his veins. As long as the rest of you haven't been poisoned, your reactions will be easier.”

“Poisoned?” Nurn asked as he returned from laying Halin on the sparse grass nearby. “How could he have been poisoned?”

“I would guess from a nassarid… but that is just a guess.” Alequa realized that neither Hessa nor Aves understood what a nassarid was, so she quickly added, “A creature created through the dark arts. A minion of evil, some of them coat their weapons with poison on occasion.” Seeing both of the girls' eyes widen, Alequa shook her head in exasperation.

“From Morcant,” Namir said. This clarified the issue for the girls immediately. “Nurn, can you be ready to catch any of us, just in case?”

“Aye,” Nurn replied. He quickly walked up to Alequa at the same time Aves did. He easily made it to Aves's side before Alequa started the healing.

“Let's be done with this.” Namir said. He allowed just enough agitation through to lend an edge to his words in order to get his point across. “I want all of us to be ready for tonight. Tomorrow will be busy enough without the added complications of healing and rest.”

Chapter Seventeen: Aftermath

It was late afternoon by time Jaconis and Tali made their way back to the Mayor's courtyard and the sight that met their eyes utterly amazed them. Namir wrestled with Halin while Nurn, Hessa and Aves cheered them on. Amidst them sat a very lovely elf clad in snowy white robes.

Tali quickly tugged Jaconis into the shadows of a nearby building before they could step completely into the courtyard. She desperately hoped that the elf had not seen them yet.

"What's wrong?" Jaconis asked Tali. He tried to mask his surprise at her actions, but failed.

"I can't… I can't go in there." Tali replied.

"Why?" Jaconis pressed as he tried to figure out her strange behavior.

"The lady in there," Tali motioned towards the elf, "the one with your cousin and his friends… she knows me." She offered as an explanation. "If we hope to succeed with your plans I need to be unknown by the group as a whole."

"But you're from Ellsted. Namir and the others have already seen you with me. Surely they've already recognized you." Jaconis blurted out before Tali could cover his mouth with her hand.

"No they haven't." Tali motioned for silence as she continued speaking, though she still left her hand on his mouth as if unsure he would heed her wishes. "I can't explain why they haven't recognized me, the best I can say is that I kept to myself a lot and I only went to the Gathering Place on occasion and nowhere else. Now please, just go in alone… if they ask about me, tell them I had other matters to attend to and leave it at that." Tali pressed her lips onto Jaconis's tightly as she removed her hand from his mouth. "Now go. I will see you tomorrow beside what's left of the Flying Muses."

"Very well," Jaconis's whisper caught in his throat. "Tomorrow then," Jaconis said a little louder, more for the benefit of those in the courtyard than for Tali. He stepped out of the shadows and strode purposely toward the open courtyard.

Tali sighed deeply as she watched him stumble into the courtyard. She waited until everyone focused on him before she left her position and hurried off down the dark alley that opened to her right.

'How could I have let so many of my plans become pinned to that poor wretch?' Tali thought, her pace quickened with every step. She tried to put as much distance between her and Alequa as possible.

"I HAVE WAITED… AND I HAVE BEEN MORE THAN PATIENT." The voice boomed from all around Tali and brought her to a dead stop. "NOW WE SHALL SETTLE THIS… YOU AND ME."

The shadows coalesced in front of her and he threw them off him as he appeared in them. His bleach white skin reflected the dying rays of the sun just right to create a slight glow around him. This glow, eerie and unnatural, bathed everything around them in an otherworldly pallor. His long ebon hair caught the light breeze and playfully danced around his head as his black eyes created shadows wherever his gaze passed.

Tali took a hesitant step away from him. 'I hope I am far enough away from Jaconis and his cousin.' Tali thought hurriedly as she decided how best to react to him.

"FLEEING IS NOT AN OPTION!" His statement was nothing less than a command and Tali responded unwillingly by stopping completely. "THAT IS BETTER... CHILD. WHERE ARE THEY?" He wheeled his hands around as he gauged the location of his quarry by her reactions to the position of his hands.

"They're not here." Tali muttered as she hung her head.

"BUT THEY WERE HERE, WERE THEY NOT?" His right hand floated weightlessly to the hilt of his dagger as he waited for her response.

"Aye." Tali nodded. Although she feared his reaction to her words, she stood her ground without fidgeting. She desperately wished she could hear his thoughts like almost everyone else she had met. She hated how her powers fled her in this man's presence.

"WHY HAVE THEY FLED? DID YOU WARN THEM OF MY COMING?" His eyes narrowed and Tali felt as if he looked directly into her soul.

"Aye," Tali shook as she met his gaze, tears streamed down her face. Her composure was totally lost and she knew it. "What did you do to Skara?" She demanded. She put as much force in her voice as she could by channeling her fear into anger.

"SHE IS ASLEEP. I HAVE NO NEED TO HARM THOSE THAT YOU ENSLAVE. MY QUARREL IS WITH YOU AND YOUR MASTERS, NOT YOUR SLAVES." Disgust etched his porcelain skin as he spoke. His lips curled in disgust as he continued. "HOWEVER, YOUR DISOBEDIENCE SHALL BE PUNISHED." His voice was calm and gave away none of his intentions.

"How are you going to do that? Are you planning on killing me?" Tali tried miserably to refocus her anger onto a different topic as she felt relief spread over her at the knowledge of Skara's safety.

His smirk made Tali's skin writhe. "YOUR PUNISHMENT SHALL BE SWIFT, BUT NOT DEATH. DEATH IS TOO GRACIOUS FOR ONE SUCH AS YOU. JUST BE THANKFUL THAT YOU MAY STILL PROVE USEFUL TO ME." He said this as his right hand flew toward her.

Before she could react his dagger gracefully parted the

flesh of her cheek and left a gash from the left side of her mouth to her ear in its wake as it buried itself in the stonewall behind her.

Tali staggered backward from both the searing pain of the blow and the shock of his speed. Before she could utter a cry, her assailant was upon her again. This time he pressed his fingers into the wound on her cheek. He easily forced his fingers through the separated flesh and into her mouth. Tali struggled against him, but he was too strong.

She winced as he closed his fingers around her jawbone. Tali bit down as hard as she could in an attempt to hurt him in some way. The searing pain as her teeth shattered against his skin almost forced her to black out. Darkness spilled over her in waves and pulled her down into blissful unconsciousness as she felt him lift her off the ground by her dislocated jaw.

"I AM DISAPPOINTED THAT YOU CHOSE TO SUCCUMB SO EASILY," he said as he watched her slip into oblivion's warm embrace.

Jerine wound his way through the unlit alleys of Hornshir. His path traced a slow circle through the city's underbelly as he made his back to the mayor's house. Although the light waned, he could see easily due to his elven heritage. Jerine's ice blue eyes dilated to allow more light to flood into them as the daylight faded.

He watched the various shapes around him silently distort to lose both their color and shading. Twilight was his least favorite time of day due to the lack luster look to everything. Jerine sighed as he quickened his pace.

"Hopefully Alequa has been able to heal Namir and his crew." Jerine said to himself as he easily vaulted over a cart abruptly shoved into his way.

Jerine had been uneasy all day and he could not figure out why. He knew Nurn had bested Morcant the night before, albeit with Jerine's cloak and sword to aide him. He decided that Morcant might think twice about attacking Halin and the others, but more importantly, Jerine knew that as long as

Alequa was with Namir his mission had a chance of success.

Jaconis staggered up to the others and stumbled as he did so. Although he tried to draw their attention to himself, not all of his clumsiness was an act. Jaconis expended a lot of energy today and he would have been very happy to just pass out right then and there, unfortunately Tali wanted him to cover for her for some unknown reason.

He was certain he would find out why later, but for now he was just going to make sure that the odd assortment of people gathered in the courtyard paid attention only to him.

"Go and help him get over to Alequa." Namir instructed Halin as they stopped wrestling.

Halin stood up and stretched his sore muscles. He took time to catch his breath before he bounded over to Jaconis. He slowly escorted Jaconis over to the well where Alequa sat blissfully. On their way Halin inquired, "Where's your lady friend?"

"She was detained in town… something about wanting to find clothes that went well together." Jaconis lied easily. He readily accepted Halin's help to the healer, although he was a little leery of the healer. "So what is she?" Jaconis asked quietly as they crossed the courtyard.

"An elf," Halin replied quickly. "Although if I didn't know any better I'd swear that she was an angel."

The jest in Halin's voice did little to calm Jaconis dread. There was something about this elf that Tali was afraid of, something she saw as a threat and Jaconis wanted to know why. As they drew closer to Alequa, Jaconis studied the beauty as best he could without trying to seem unusually interested.

"Are you ready to be healed?" Alequa asked with a soft and beguiling lilt in her voice.

"Aye, he is." Namir answered for his cousin. "And I don't care if he isn't." Namir interrupted. "He has slowed us down far too long as it is. Just heal him so we can leave."

"Leave?" Jaconis asked confused.

"Aye, leave. As in, we're not staying here any longer." Halin chimed in. He mocked Jaconis's surprise flawlessly and he hoped the others would support him in his sport.

"Or would you rather stay here in the stables with the asses and mules, young master?" Hessa chimed in with perfect timing. Her sarcasm worked wonderfully with Halin's mocking tones.

"Well no." Jaconis started to answer.

His words stopped short as Alequa placed a cool hand on his chest. The shockwave that went through his body was not unpleasant, but it was a surprise. The world seemed to explode into a mixture of color and light as Jaconis felt a warm tingle pulse through his entire body.

The sensation started in his chest and moved outwards in waves until it eventually consumed him entirely. Although it had only lasted for a few moments, to Jaconis it felt like hours. When the effect finally ended, Jaconis felt lost, as if something had been stripped away from him, something vital, and he was not sure what it was. Whatever it was, its absence left Jaconis numb and completely unaware of his surroundings.

"Nurn, bring him with us." Namir instructed as he noticed Jaconis's lost look. "I know you said it would affect each of us differently, but I need to know what ailed my cousin." Namir asked to Alequa's surprise as he turned to face her.

Alequa curtsied, "I'm not sure, my lord. All I can say is that he has been afflicted for some time. As such, it will take him longer to recover from the healing process than it did for the rest of you."

"Be that as it may," Namir confided, "we'll need to help him if we wish to arrive at the manor before night fall." He turned to the rest of the group and continued, "Halin, get Jerine's horse. You seem to be able to handle it without incident. Aves, I need you and Hessa to get our belongings into the carriage. Thankfully, it was spared in last night's fire. I'll ready our horses and get them hitched up. Nurn, please get Jaconis into the carriage, then come back and escort Alequa to it as well."

Jerine had just returned from his errands as he saw the unlikely party make its way to the manor house. He was easily able to catch up to the group unnoticed before they actually approached the awe-inspiring sight.

Located near the harbor district, the house was one of the few in the city with walls built around its courtyard and grounds. The grey stonewall was chiseled and hewn smooth to ensure there were no natural hand holds to aid any that would try to vault the twelve foot tall obstacle. The gateway was a grand archway with two guards stationed at the top.

The gate itself was composed of two distinct parts, a cold wrought iron portcullis and two twelve foot solid oak doors. Both of these monstrous units could only be opened by the levers and switches manned by the guards above it atop the impressive fifteen foot tall arch.

The manor itself was just as impressive. The house stood four floors high, about two floors taller than its immediate neighbors. Like the wall that surrounded it, the manor was built from gray stone blocks. Each fitted together just right to make scaling it an impossible task, even by the most skilled climbers.

Each of the leaded glass windows had been set into a cold wrought iron frame. Not only was the windowsill and the shutters cold wrought iron, but there was a latticework of cold wrought iron covering each pane of glass. The overall effect was stunning.

"Impressive isn't it." Jerine stated as he effortlessly vaulted up beside Namir at the back of the carriage. Surprised by both Jerine's presence and the silence with which he made his appearance, Namir agreed wordlessly.

"Did you know about this place before last night?" Namir whispered quietly.

"Aye, but I was asked not to use it unless in dire need." Jerine informed him quickly, "and, in case you were unaware of it, we are in such a need now." His playful tone eased Namir's dread about their situation a little.

As they neared the gate, Jerine withdrew a small polished metal disk from one of his pouches. He used it to angle the waning light at the guards in sporadic flashes. The guards responded fluidly and as the small group neared the gates, they opened smoothly.

The effect of the unveiling courtyard was breathtaking. The courtyard inside the wall contained a wide variety of shrubs and three large trees, two oaks and one beech. Their spreading branches helped the shrubs form a beautiful pathway from the gate to the stables and to the manor house itself.

There was no noise, save for the clangor of chains and the sound that escaped the carriage's wheels as they ground against the cobbled road. The group was silent as they entered the grounds of their new sanctuary.

It was well past dark when Jaconis finally started to feel like himself. The sounds of voices made their way to him from somewhere far below as Jaconis's mind slowly took in his surroundings. He lay in a darkened room, with a slight fragrant breeze blowing in through an open window somewhere to his right.

Beneath him was the luxurious softness of a down mattress and feather pillows. A soft light spilled in through the doorframe across the room from him allowing just enough light in for his eyes to adjust slowly. With this light, he made a visual inspection of his cell.

To Jaconis's surprise he was dressed in evening clothes, his own had been folded neatly in a plush chair not far from him. All of his belongings were present and tidily placed on a small table just to the side of his clothes as well.

Some of the voices became more distinct as he scanned the room, Nurn's low rumble and Halin's whiny tones were the easiest to discern and were amongst the first he heard. Try as he might, however, Jaconis could not make out what their discussion was about.

He lay there a few moments longer before he decided to make his way to the window. 'Hopefully I can figure out where we are.' Jaconis thought as he crossed the room.

He slowly opened the shutters and drew a sharp breath. The view that spread out in front of him was breathtaking. From his window, Jaconis saw all the way across the harbor and straight to the river beyond. The smell of hyacinth and lavender filled the air as it wafted across the hanging plants just outside his window.

Jaconis's thoughts crept to Tali unbidden. For some reason he had a hard time remembering how and when they had met. Although his memories of her, what little there seemed to be, were filled with tantalizing images and activities, a fair share of horrors were there as well.

"Who are you?" Jaconis said to himself as he thought of his lover, "and where are you at right now?"

"So explain it to me again." Namir demanded as he sat next to the fire in the great hall. Beside him, to his right, sat Jerine and Alequa sat on a plush stool just to his left. Since Nurn, Halin, Aves and Hessa had retired for the evening, Namir was relieved to finally get the two elves alone.

"It's simple." Jerine said. "I spoke with my commander, Landolin of Esterheim. He was the one that sent me to find you." Jerine reiterated as he faced Namir.

Jerine allowed these words to sink in before he continued. While he waited, he pulled his pipe out from a pouch at his side and tamped it full of tobacco.

"My instructions were very specific. Find Kalta's heir and bring him safely to our main encampment ten leagues south of Hornshir. If for some reason I failed in that task I was supposed to get you, Kalta's heir, to a safe place and send word to the main camp." Jerine took a long drag from his pipe before he continued.

He found that these pauses helped people follow his

reasoning better. They also allowed Jerine a brief respite to gather his thoughts and cool his fierce temper. The longer Jerine lived, the more this simple dwarven custom seemed to make sense.

"Unfortunately there was an issue in finding you, not just Morcant either. It seems the information we were given was a little inaccurate. In this case I don't mind too much, since it seems Morcant was given similar information."

"But that doesn't explain anything." Namir cut in, interrupting Jerine's accounting of his task. "Why were you sent to find me? Why me?"

"That is much harder to answer," this time Alequa was the one who interceded. "When Landolin received Jerine's message that you had been found, he had asked that I find Jerine and aide him in whatever manner possible. He also instructed that we were not to say anything that might make your situation more precarious."

"How can you telling me why finding me is so important make my situation more precarious?" Namir demanded hotly. He felt his patience slip and he tried his best to keep it in check.

"It just would." Jerine added. "If the wrong people discovered what our reasons were, you wouldn't be safe anywhere." Jerine took another drag from his pipe, this one much shorter than before. "Besides, my commander wouldn't tell me too much about the reasons. So if it makes it any easier for you, let's just say that we don't know."

"Fine," Namir responded abruptly. "Just to humor me though, is it the same reason that Alequa curtsies when I address her?" Namir turned to face Jerine as he asked this, keeping Alequa in his view as he did so.

"Aye," Alequa responded. As she did, she bowed her head just as Namir expected her to. "Let these questions rest for now. Tomorrow we will travel to Landolin's camp and he will answer your questions better than the two of us can. I promise." She cooed, successfully calming Namir's rising anger.

"Namir slowly rubbed his eyes, more wearied from this conversation than from tiredness. "I guess I have no choice." Namir said as he rose from his seat. "On the morrow then," with that he walked off toward the stairs and his room.

When Jerine was sure Namir was well out of earshot he chuckled to himself as he drew deeply on his pipe once more. "Alequa, your magic will fail you one day. You know this, right?" Jerine said in Elven to his gorgeous companion.

"Aye milord, I know." Alequa responded in Elven coyly as she followed Namir's receding form with her keen elven sight. "And when it does I'll have to rely on my other charms and talents." She graced Jerine with a quick glance before she let her gaze fall back towards Namir. "Let's just hope that my magic's hold up for another few days." She said through her perfect ruby lips as she smiled broadly at Jerine now that Namir was completely lost to the recesses of the manor.

"Good morrow Namir, our journey awaits." Jerine's voice cut through the darkness that penetrated Namir's cloudy head.

Still half-asleep, Namir struggled to wake up. "Is it light already?"

"No. But we cannot afford to wait for first light," Jerine replied quieter. "If I were Morcant I'd be watching the gates of Hornshir for any sign of our departure."

"That makes sense," Namir replied. Still groggy, he tried to regain his senses. "Have you roused the others yet?" Namir asked.

"No. Are you sure you want all of them to come with us?" Jerine asked in response.

"What's the alternative, leave them for Morcant to find when he comes looking for us?" The sarcasm in Namir's voice was evident as he replied to Jerine. "No, I think it best that we all go. No matter how poorly that may sit with either of us."

"As you wish," Jerine replied, a little more humble than Namir had expected. "We ride within the hour. Alequa is preparing a light meal for the road. I assume that you can ride?" Jerine added the last part as more of an afterthought than a real question.

"I can, however not everyone else has been trained to. While you are waking the others, I'll get the carriage ready." Namir hastened to dress as he said this, but Jerine placed a hand on his shoulder and brought him to a fast halt.

"We can't take the carriage. The path is too rough for it." Jerine instructed as if he informed Namir that a loved one had just perished.

"But we must. Didn't you hear me when I said not everyone knows how to ride?" Namir demanded.

"I heard you, but there is no alternative except leaving those unable to ride behind." Jerine replied coolly. He hoped Namir would see his logic.

"That isn't an option and you know it!" Namir snapped and his voice became firmer with each syllable. "There must be another way."

Jerine cut off this statement with a gentle squeeze of Namir's shoulder. "There is, but you won't like it."

"Out with it!" Namir snapped again. This time the edge in his own voice took even himself by surprise. As Jerine started to speak, Namir forced himself to take deep breaths in an attempt to regain his lost composure.

"The only other option is to have those that cannot ride accompany us on foot, but it would slow us down greatly. It would also leave us very prone to an attack or ambush by Morcant." Jerine's voice developed an edge to match Namir's. "You must decide how important the answers you seek are to you." Jerine continued before Namir could interrupt him. "I'll be downstairs readying what steeds we have. Think about what I've said and speak to me when you are ready."

"Will we have enough steeds?" Namir inquired as Jerine opened the door.

"No." Jerine's answer was short and formal.

"How many do we have?" Namir asked.

"Just the three." Jerine sighed not wanting to pursue the conversation further.

"That isn't nearly enough." Namir hung his head. He felt defeat settle in as he lowered himself into his bed again, the soft feathers of the mattress parted soothingly. "Even if we were to ride two on each horse we would end up with two people on foot. How far are we heading again?"

"Ten leagues." Jerine replied tersely. He closed the door quietly and turned to face Namir. "It will take us most of the day if we ride hard and untroubled. If we have to slow our pace it will take longer."

"What choice do we really have?" Namir asked again not knowing if Jerine would actually help him find an answer. "Please help me reason through this."

"I know this is hard for you," Jerine started, "but the solution may not be one that you are not ready to accept."

"Such as?" Namir hung his head and braced for Jerine's suggestion.

"You came here with two tasks in mind, did you not?" Jerine decided that changing his rationale might help him persuade Namir to see the merits of his initial suggestion.

"Aye," Namir conceded.

"Well then, I'll say this as easily as I can. We take however many we can fit on the horses without over burdening them and leave the others to accomplish the second task." Jerine stated. He allowed the simplicity of his words to persuade Namir.

"What about Morcant? I know he has a scent for you and Halin. He may also know Nurn's and my own as well." Namir worked through the list as he picked his words carefully. "Do we leave Halin and Nurn to Morcant's mercy?"

"We could double up one of the horses. That way all four of us can go and leave the others here to complete their tasks in Hornshir." Jerine replied easily.

"What of Alequa? Isn't she traveling with us?" Namir asked surprised.

"No," Jerine smiled lightly. "She has other means of transportation. If I am right she will have more than enough time to alert them of our arrival before midday."

"Then so be it." Namir shook his head wearily. He was unsure if it was just the early hour or the knowledge that he would not be able to look after Aves and Hessa that left him feeling drained. "I will tell Nurn and Halin to be prepared to leave. I'll also leave a note for the others letting them know where we have gone."

"It might be best if the note was a cryptic one." Jerine interjected as Namir rose from his bed for the second time.

"A cryptic one?" Namir asked slightly confused. "Why?"

"I'm not too sure about the safety of leaving a detailed note. And from what you told me, it's miraculous that all six of you made it through both the trip here and the burning of the Flying Muses." Jerine pointed out. "I would even wager that someone in your group has a connection to the causes of both. I'm not positive about this. It just seems too much of a coincidence for me to accept. Either way, it would not be good for a note depicting where we went to be left lying around. You never know who might find it."

Jerine made sure that he held Namir's gaze in his as he added the last part to ensure that Namir followed his logic. Once he was sure of this, he continued.

"Instead I'd have it read 'Jerine, Nurn, Halin and I have left to see to some of Jerine's business. We will be back late tomorrow.' or something like that," Jerine took a slight pause before adding. "That is if it were me writing the note instead of you."

"And would it still be in my script?" Namir added more musing than asking as he sought out paper, ink and quill.

"Oh invariably, complete with the little shakiness you have at the end of your 'r's." Jerine added as he opened the door again and exited swiftly. He left Namir to muse about his last sentence in silence.

Thankfully, Namir found several sheets of paper. After only his fourth try, he managed to write a legible note to Aves and Hessa. Namir slowly made his way through the drafty halls of the manor and went up to the third floor where the girls' chambers were. A slight sigh of relief escaped his lips when he discovered that Aves and Hessa's room was still dark.

He swiftly pulled a horseshoe nail from his pouch that he had smuggled with him from Tipin's smithy before they left Ellsted. He deftly pushed the nail into the soft cherry wood of the door. With the note firmly attached to the door, Namir made his way back downstairs to Nurn and Halin's room. Namir knocked lightly on the door trying not to wake Jaconis in the room next door.

"I'm coming." Halin said tersely as Namir knocked for the fourth time. Composing himself somewhat, Halin opened the door. "Do you know what time it is?" Halin asked as the door opened and revealed Namir fully dressed and brooding.

"Aye, it's time to go." Namir responded dourly as he stepped swiftly past Halin into the room. "Halin, get your things packed and ready. Make sure to wear comfortable riding clothes because I don't know how often we are going to rest."

"What do you mean?" Halin asked as he watched Namir cross the room over to Nurn and touch his shoulder lightly."

"What is it?" Nurn awoke instantly and whispered his question to Namir.

"We leave soon, my friend. How quickly can you be ready?" Namir answered, temporarily ignoring Halin's questions and befuddled looks. When he was sure Nurn understood what he meant, Namir rose to face Halin. "I mean that we are leaving within the hour. We will be traveling by horseback and it will just be the three of us and Jerine. So, if you are hoping to eat before we leave, I suggest you hurry and ready your things." Namir whispered to Halin with an obvious edge in his voice. "Do both of you understand?"

"Aye." Nurn and Halin responded in unison, although Nurn's voice was the firmer of the two in its resolve.

"Good. Pack your things as quickly and quietly as you can. Then meet me in the stables when you have finished." Namir instructed as he slipped out of their room and quietly made his way down the stairs to the kitchen.

Chapter Eighteen: Departures

"If he didn't want the note read why didn't he seal it with wax or something? I mean he could have at least folded it more than once." Jaconis shot back at both Aves and Hessa. "Besides, what did he mean by 'I might not be back in time to aide you with your negotiations'?"

"I guess Namir wasn't planning on you coming up to our quarters and helping yourself to our messages." Hessa scolded Jaconis as she took a bite of bread slathered with butter and tartberry jam.

"This is exactly what my father was afraid would happen!" Jaconis exclaimed as he stuffed another pastry into his mouth. He was completely unabashed by Hessa's glare as he did so.

Aves moved closer to Hessa and whispered, "I don't understand why he left us behind. We were supposed to do this together."

The pained look on Aves's face hurt Hessa as much as her own dread. "Some things just can't be helped." She responded quietly. She wished there was more that she could do for her mistress. Hessa turned and looked at Jaconis as her voice assumed loud enough tone to command his attention as she asked, "What were you doing outside of our door this morning anyway?" Her disgust at him was evident as she watched him stuff his face full of pastries and buns,

"I was going to make sure the two of you didn't oversleep and forget our appointment with the mayor. A job that Namir should have done," Jaconis added.   He showed his obvious displeasure for Namir's actions with a slight sneer, "but since he chose to go gallivanting with someone he met while drinking, I had no choice. Someone had to follow up on his duties.   Duties that he sloughed off again, I might add." Jaconis purposefully let his tone change as if he spoke about a wayward dog instead of a person.

"So it makes no difference to you that this 'someone' saved our lives?" Aves shot back. Jaconis disinterest in her words just made her angrier. "I know for a fact that Jerine is solely responsible for ensuring that our trade items didn't go up in flames with the stable."   Aves's hatred for Jaconis was getting the better of her and she hated it.

"You are correct," Jaconis quipped, "on both points and I intend to let the council know of Namir's short comings, as well as all the problems we've had on this trip. Let's face it; Namir has failed as a leader."   Jaconis eyed Aves as he said this. He noticed her hatred build and he enjoyed it.

"What do you mean?" Aves demanded. "How has Namir failed us as a leader?"

"How about we start by discussing our trip to Hornshir and the lack of safety or would you rather talk about a poorly suited inn for us to room in after we arrived? You know that the inn that almost burned to the ground with us and our belongings in it."   Jaconis held up his hand and raised his voice so that neither Aves nor Hessa could interrupt him. "You're the one that pointed out that Jerine is responsible for our wellbeing, not Namir. Jerine also rescued our belongings, another job Namir should have done."

Jaconis glared at the ladies as his words struck them like daggers. Every time they winced, Jaconis's smile broadened as he forced them to hear him out.

"Not to mention that Namir has not attended a single trade negotiation. Nor, it would seem, does he intend to. Instead, he goes off with this 'savior' of yours and completely disregards his responsibility to Ellsted's needs. Do you think his failures end there? No, his errs in judgment are compounded by the fact that he took not one, but both, of the blacksmith's representative's with him. Do I need to bring up the fact that his attitude and domineering ways have proven detrimental as well?" Jaconis was almost yelling now, but the look in his eyes dared either of them to rise to his challenge.

"If it helps any," Hessa answered once Jaconis finally quieted down long enough for her to speak. "Nurn appointed me as Tipin's emissary in the event something important should occur that demanded his attention." She carefully took in Jaconis's reaction to her words as she continued. "So you see, Jaconis, we are not short anyone in these negotiations."

Jaconis's features softened a little as she spoke. Now instead of raw anger and hatred, she saw only loathing as she added.

"And you are right; Namir never intended to join in on the negotiations. Because of your father's refusal to accept him as the merchant's emissary, he was no longer obligated to attend the negotiations.   Instead, he felt that he could best serve Ellsted by spreading the word of Belanui's Feast and the festival that Ellsted is currently preparing for."

"Which is what, I'm sure, they are doing right now." Aves added, finally in control of her emotions. "Now if you please, Jaconis, I think we should all get ready for our tasks. The negotiations with the mayor are scheduled to start in just over an hour. So, before we lose even more time bickering, I suggest you mentally prepare for them." As she said this, Aves rose to her feet and led Hessa to the door.

"Very well ladies, I will meet you at the gate before the hour has fled." Jaconis replied to their backs as they walked away.

The ride to Landolin's encampment was a long and weary one. Jerine initially decided it would be best for Halin to ride on Valon with him, this would allow the three best horsemen to each have their own steed to ride. Jerine explained to his three charges that the other two would have a horse of their own in case Morcant decided to attack them.

Since Morcant may still believe Halin was his target, Jerine could defend Halin easier if they shared a horse. Halin seemed to believe him, although he seemed extremely moody throughout the ride. At one of the three rest stops they took, Halin approached Namir.

"Do you think the others are alright?" Halin asked. His concern for Aves and Hessa was as apparent as his shirt.

"Aye," Namir replied.   "Hopefully they have almost finished negotiating with Hornshir's elders and started to ensure that all of Hornshir is aware of Ellsted's fair." Namir added.

A slight smile played across his lips as Namir thought of Jaconis in the same room with Aves and Hessa as he tried to get his way.

"I'm just worried that Morcant will attack them while we aren't there." Halin added. His voice betrayed his fears better than his words could.

"I'm sure they're fine. Now go and get some rations from Jerine before we have to go." Namir shook his head as he watched Halin walk away.

"We are a third of the way there." Jerine called out as Namir walked over to Nurn. "The horses look almost rested, so we can leave soon."

Namir nodded in agreement and he was relieved as he saw Nurn nod as well. He waited a few moments for Jerine to help Halin get his belongings situated better on Valon, Jerine's horse, before he made his way over to Nurn.

"I'm worried about Halin." He said softly, as if he feared Halin or Jerine might hear.

"Why?"   Nurn asked.   His tone matched Namir's conspiratorial tone perfectly.

"Ever since Morcant attacked he hasn't been himself," Namir shared.

"I've noticed it too. It's almost as if he knows more than

he's been willing to say." Nurn's voice rumbled with unease as if in answer to Namir's fears.

"When we get to Landolin's camp, we need to find out what is troubling him so." Namir instructed.

He noticed that Jerine and Halin were almost finished resituated, so he motioned to Nurn that their conversation was finished. Nurn nodded imperceptibly as he made his way over to his steed and finished readying his belongings for the upcoming ride.

"They come, do they not?" His voice broke the silence around him like the crackle of a fire.

"Aye, they do." Alequa soothed as she brushed away the loose strands of white hair from the old man's pale and weathered face.

"Good, the movements in the heavens have worried me of late my love." The look in his dull grey eyes tore at her as she looked upon him lovingly. "I am sorry that I have failed… " A ragged cough ripped the strength from his voice as he tried in vain to continue.

"They will get here swiftly, my love. Landolin has seen to it." Her comforting words soothed him and distracted him from his thoughts. "Their path has been made clear and held secure since last night. I doubt that Jerine would allow them to stray from it." Her lips pressed gently upon his as she finished speaking. "Fear not, my dear Aras, they shall arrive soon."

"I know. The very ground trembles at their approach, yet these tremors also strike a chord within me that gives me pause." His voice, though harsh, held a certain softness as he smiled at the comely elf. "I just fear that I won't be able to hold out until I see the boy again."

"Shhhh… do not speak that way." Dread creased her delicate features as she continued, "Just rest, you'll have time to speak with him. Your time, though it draws neigh, has not come just yet."

The dusty ride to the camp ended anticlimactically. Namir pictured a large contingent of soldiers all bustling about a large war encampment. Instead, there were only a small handful of tents in a well-hidden clearing. These tents would be able to shelter only twenty people at best.

"I thought you said that Landolin was in charge of a large contingent? If this is so, where are they?" Namir asked as they rode down the slight hill towards the encampment.

"He is. In fact he is a general." Jerine replied coolly. "As far as their location, you just need to look harder." There was a hint of merriment in Jerine's voice that took his three companions a little off guard.

"Where?" Halin asked as he leaned past Jerine and squinted. He tried feebly to see where an army might be hiding and failed miserably.

"Stop squirming." Nurn replied before Jerine could chide Halin for his uneasy movement. "If you keep it up you'll fall off of Valon." Halin looked towards his brother in time to see his scowl and decided to stop his vain attempt.

Jerine chuckled as he replied, "how many soldiers do you think make up a large contingent, young Namir? A thousand… perhaps two? Do you think that elves need more than a couple hundred to travel with, let alone to face another army in battle?"

"A couple hundred?" Namir's tone betrayed his doubt in Jerine's words. "The number of tents that I can see will only house twenty men at best. Surely there can't be more than that here." As if to make his point more encompassing, Namir gestured towards the encampment and woods beyond it.

"There are more tents than you see… look again after we arrive." Jerine smiled as he finally understood the looks of confusion on the boys' faces.

Aves and Hessa relaxed as they ate their sandwiches in

silence. It had been a long and grueling day trying to maintain control over the negotiations without Nurn's quiet presence. Between Jaconis vying for complete control over the supplies Hornshir might grant and the mayor making advances on both of the girls, it was the best they could do to keep their composure. Several moments passed as each of them brooded over the recent turn of events.

"Do you think they're alright?" Hessa broke the silence first.

"Aye, at least I hope so." Worry spread across Aves's face as she spoke.

"They are." Hessa's tone surprised Aves. It betrayed a deeper need than Aves had ever heard Hessa use in the past. It seemed as though Hessa tried to bend reality to her will. "They will be back before the night has passed. Trust me milady." Hessa added as she bowed, taking on her old habits briefly.

Aves sat and stared at Hessa for a few moments dumbfounded. She scarcely noticed Hessa's slip up in how she addressed her. 'She's right,' Aves thought to herself softly. 'I'm not sure how I know, but she is right. They are safe... tired, but safe.' A smile played across her lips as Aves raised a cup of sunned tea to them as a toast and drank deeply.

"Are you two about ready?" Jaconis boomed as he stepped into the dining room. The thick oak floorboards did not betray his step and allowed him to take both ladies by surprise.

"Yes... " Hessa answered swiftly as she noticed that Aves was lost in thought.

"Good, we are almost finished with negotiations and I hope to get these discussions over well before nightfall. I can only hope that you two are more help in loading and organizing our provisions for our journey home than you have been throughout these negotiations!" Jaconis stabbed vehemently. He knew the impact that his words would have and he anticipated the girls' reactions.

"What do you mean by that?" Aves demanded. Jaconis's words brought her back to her senses abruptly. "You know that without us the negotiations would've ended before they ever began! Your failed attempts to hustle Hornshir's elders were appalling!" Aves glared at Jaconis as she flung her words at him. She hoped that he would get close enough so she could kick him.

"Think what you will," Jaconis retorted as he shrunk a little from Aves's withering gaze. "I will meet you at the manor gates when you are ready to leave for the final round of negotiations." Jaconis said over his shoulder as he stalked off. He hoped neither of them saw him flinch at Aves's words.

"How dare he!" Aves ranted after Jaconis had fled from the room. "He knows that we have been more of a help than he has been!"

"This is what he wants, milady." Hessa replied, relieved that Jaconis had left. "I'm sure that he hoped to get you angry, possibly angry enough to force your hand during the negotiations to side with one of his choices." Hessa soothed.

Aves took a deep breath and forced herself to calm down. "We have been successful thus far. I just hope we can continue to thwart his schemes." Aves put a hand on Hessa shoulder as she continued. "Thank you. If you didn't have such a level head I fear Jaconis would have succeeded in this little scheme of his."

As the small group rounded the last bend in the path, they saw what Jerine meant. The tents they initially saw were small and tied into the tree line. Their canvas shells were stained to match the color of the ground and brush around them, while their height was designed to blend in with their surroundings better. However, it was not this small handful of tents that caught the groups' attention as they rode into the encampment, it was the number of tents hidden within the forest.

Namir was stunned by how well hidden the entire camp had been. It was not until they were amid the bustling contingent that he was even able to see all of the tents. It was as if they had magically appeared around them. He looked across to Nurn and Halin and saw his own amazement reflected back in their faces.

The most amazing part was the people. All of them seemed to be at peace with their surroundings. The elves moved gracefully, each intent on whatever task they performed, yet somehow aware of everything going on around them. This was perfectly illustrated by the way they moved and helped each other without saying a word. To Namir's surprise, the first words he heard were directed at him.

"Please dismount and come with me." The tall elf said as he silently reached up and took a hold of Namir's horse by its halter. He was dressed like the others in a simple green jerkin with light leather breeches and boots. His long chestnut hair was pulled back into a queue and his topaz-like eyes stared into Namir's patiently.

Namir returned the elf's gaze completely dumbfounded, more by the man's musical voice than anything else. If Jerine would not have cleared his throat, Namir may have stared at the elf longer. Being prompted by Jerine's cue, Namir slid off his horse and asked, "Who is going to take care of my steed?"

The elf smiled and responded with a quick backward glance behind him, "Haradine will. Please, come with me. Landolin is expecting you, as is Aras and we shouldn't keep the elder waiting."

As Namir started following the elf that had hailed him, he saw Haradine step deftly past him. She was gorgeous. Although her long honeydew hair was pulled back into a queue like the others, her eyes hinted at an innocence Namir had only seen in children. He tried not to stare, but he could not help looking back at her lithe form as he hurried to keep up with his guide.

"What are the rest of us to do?" Nurn asked Jerine impatiently as he dismounted.

"What would you like to do?" Jerine replied as he helped Halin down off of Valon.

"I would like to learn to fight… if I may." Halin chimed in before Nurn could reply.

"And you?" Jerine directed to Nurn. "Would you like to learn the ways of the sword?"

"Aye, if that's an option. I fear that we may need to know more if we are to pursue Namir's dreams." Nurn conceded as he started to lead his horse in the direction Haradine lead Namir's steed.

"Very well then," Jerine agreed. "Let's leave our steeds to those that know better what to do with them. We need to find Karous and see what he can teach us." Jerine said as he motioned towards two other elves standing where Haradine had been previously.

Nurn nodded hesitantly as he handed the reins of his steed to one of the elves and stepped over to Jerine's side. "Are all of these elves mute?" Nurn asked, obviously unnerved by the silence that surrounded them.

"No." Jerine chuckled. "Elves have little need for talking. That is, unless we are amongst other races. Instead, we use motions and gestures to get our desires across for small things."

The tone in Jerine's voice bothered Nurn. It was as if he explained the way of the elves to children. Nurn pushed his concerns aside as he followed Jerine through the camp. Halin tugged on Nurn's sleeve as they made their way to a trail that led out of the main circle of tents and into a clearing beyond. "Where are we going again?" Nurn asked somewhat concerned.

"To Landolin's man-at-arms so we can begin our training." Jerine replied matter-of-factly. "I fear that Namir will be a while with Landolin and Aras, so we may as well do something useful with our time."

"Who is Aras anyway?" Halin asked as the three of them walked deeper into the forest.

"He is an old friend of Kalta's, Namir's father. For anything more you will need to ask Namir when he returns." Jerine offered as they picked their way through the gathering bushes.

"Namir's father?" This time Nurn voiced the question that

both of the brothers had been thinking. "He still lives?"

"No. Kalta died a long time ago, when you were both still children. Aras is, or was, his servant and friend." Jerine replied quieter than he had before. Jerine took a deep breath then stopped and turned to face the brothers before he continued. "I suggest that you hold any more questions you may have about Aras, Kalta, and Namir's past close to you until you can talk with Namir again. Elven ears are keen enough to hear thoughts… and this topic is one that we hold dear to us. Please bear that in mind as we continue on our way."

Nurn and Halin nodded in unison. It was obvious that they stifled the rest of their questions as Jerine led them further into the forest. A few moments later, the three of them stepped into a clearing. The scent of freshly cut grass filled their senses as they looked around.

On the other side of it stood an elf about Jerine's height and build, yet even at this distance he somehow seemed older. Although they could not make out his features, they could tell that he had an air of authority that settled around his shoulders like a cloak.

Like the other elves, he was dressed in a simple green jerkins and brown leather trousers and boots. The only difference was the simple metal band that was braided into his silvery white hair. This circlet not only held his hair back in a queue, it kept it off his neck neatly.

The old elf turned as the three approached and bowed slightly without uttering a word. Jerine stopped a few yards away and motioned for the brothers to do the same. He waited until he was certain that they obeyed before he bowed deeply to the other elf.

"So, you would like me to teach these seradin the use of weapons?" Karous asked Jerine after a few moments passed.

"Aye, but these are not seradin, ho'ulyn Karous. They are companions to sa'ouvant Namir. So please, humor me and accept them into your tutelage for the remainder of the day."

"Only out of respect for such an esteemed garadin and, of

course, to fulfill my pledge to Landolin," Karous nodded in ascension, seemingly satisfied by Jerine's reasons. He then shifted his gaze from Jerine to the boys that stood behind him. "So what do I have to work with," more to Jerine than to the brothers, "humans?"

Nurn responded with a deep rumble before Jerine had a chance, "No. We are of Calanari descent." Nurn bowed, mimicking Jerine's perfectly, "although our mother is of human stock."

"I see." Karous smiled slightly watching Nurn's actions. "Well then, I think these two may be more than worthy to be granted instruction. Not only are they sa'trandon, but Calanari as well." He chuckled quietly to himself as he turned from them and asked over his shoulder for the sake of the boys. "It has been quite a long time since I have had the honor of training sa'trandon. I don't recall the last time I trained a Calanari warrior either." With that said Karous stepped over to the tree line and reached deep into the surrounding brush. When he turned to face them, he held forth two wooden blades. "Now, please come and show me what you know so I can gauge your skills."

Nurn and Halin walked over to Karous unceremoniously leaving Jerine at the head of the clearing. Halin's step seemed more lively than Nurn's, but Nurn's was more determined. Each took a blade and stepped away from Karous to give themselves some room.

"What would you like us to do?" Halin asked nervously as he held the wooden blade clumsily.

Karous nodded to himself and then looked at Jerine. "It seems we have much work to do, garadin. I had hoped that you would have taken some time to teach them on your way here."

"I had not the time, ho'ulyn. Please forgive me." Jerine replied as he pulled out his pipe and smiled playfully.

"There is nothing for it then." Karous said solemnly. He turned once again to the brothers, "I was hoping that each of you would have some rudimentary skill, but it seems that I am going to have to teach you that as well. Let us begin."

Namir stepped into the tent that the elf had pointed to and ducked under the mostly closed flap of canvas. He stood for a moment to wait for his eyes to adjust to the enveloping darkness before trying to move. He was afraid to move for fear of knocking some unseen object over.

"You must be Namir," the voice floated to his ears melodically.

"Aye and I am to assume that you are Landolin." Namir replied to the voice in the darkness.

"You are correct. Please come and have a seat." The voice belied no indication of its owner's location.

"I'd hate to inconvenience you, milord, but I cannot see well enough yet to find a seat, let alone to sit in one." Namir offered. He hoped his host would understand.

"Ah, please forgive my ignorance." As he answered, he heard the soft sound of glass being slid against wood. As soon as he heard the sound, a soft light sprang forth from the center of the tent. "Is that better?"

"Aye." Namir said as his eyes adjusted to the soft glow.

Before him sat a tall well-built elf, with loose flowing hair that reminded Namir of a fire due to its deep crimson color and the way that it danced in the soft breeze that somehow managed to make it into the tent. The elf's garnet eyes tracked Namir's motions and seemed to pulse with a hidden passion.

The elf was dressed in a simple white loose fitting shirt that accented his silvery skin and black leather breeches. To the elf's right was an armor stand with silver scale armor complete with a silvery helm that somehow managed to glisten in the darkened tent. Slung across it were a sword belt and a magnificent alder wood bow.

"Please, we haven't much time sa'ouvant." Landolin offered as he motioned towards a chair to his left.

"Why?" The reference to time surprised Namir, "surely it matters little when I return to Hornshir." Namir responded as he made his way to the chair.

He was just as fascinated by the size of the tent as he was of its contents. From the outside, the tent seemed to be of a modest size almost as if it might be big enough for eight men at the most, instead it was much larger. There were at least ten good-sized chests, an elegant looking bed, four hand crafted chairs as well as rugs and other sundries. Against the far wall there was even a large table covered with maps and documents.

"And, if I may ask, why did you refer to me as sa'ouvant?"

A slight smile crept across Landolin's argent features as Namir asked his question. "That is one of the reasons we are pressed for time, sa'ouvant." He reached behind him and retrieved a wineskin that he offered to Namir with both hands. He bowed his head as he did so. "Please drink a little wine and I will explain as best I can. Sa'ouvant means honored one, and you are such... "

Namir cut him off as he finished his first sip of the sweet wine, "No. Sa'ouvant means liege, and I am not one." His initial thoughts of Landolin slipped a little as he caught the elf in this lie.

"Ah, I see you have an understanding of our language. That is good," Landolin recovered deftly, "but you are correct and not, sa'ouvant. You see. You have the meaning right... just not the last part of what you said." He cut off Namir's reply with a quick gesture as he continued. "But it is not for me to explain. Aras has traveled far to revel this and other things to you. It would be an insult, and very brash of me, to deny him this opportunity. Please have another drink and I will take you to him."

"Who is this Aras?" Namir asked before he took a second draught from the wineskin.

"He was your father's servant. Now please, drink." Landolin's request came out as more of a command than a suggestion.

"Very well," Namir replied as he took his second draw from the wineskin. "Is he close by, my father?"

"No. He died many years ago while protecting your

location with his life. Kalta was a good man and a trusted one. I am just sorry that I could not have been there to defend him when he needed me the most." Landolin answered solemnly. "But again, we can discuss this after your meeting with Aras. Now that you have had a chance to recover, though briefly, from your ride, we must go see him before he too passes."

Namir nodded as he swallowed another draught of the sweet wine and then stood to follow Landolin through the canvas opening in the back of the tent.

The tent beyond was smaller than the one they left, but not by much. It too held a bed and several trunks, but it was well lit in comparison. There were stacks of books and scrolls littering the floor and any surface they could be laid upon, and there were almost as many candles and lanterns as there were books.

In the bed lay an old man being tended by a female in white robes. The bed was positioned in the center of the tent and three chairs neatly ringed it. In the chair closest to the bed, Namir recognized Alequa as she tended to the old man's needs.

"Is that Namir?" Aras asked as he noticed the movement in the canvas.

"It is." Landolin replied before Alequa had the chance. "I brought him straightaway from his journey here. Please forgive our tardiness sa'ulyn Aras." He continued as he bowed deeply.

"There is nothing to forgive, dear Landolin. In fact I should be the one to thank you for your grace in all that has come to pass." Aras' words crackled forth from his frail frame. Although his words were directed at Landolin, his dull grey eyes never left Namir's features as he spoke. "I would be lying to you if I said you bore your father's features, young master, though I can tell of his impact on you by your manners and attitude." Aras raised a hand to silence Namir as he continued. "Please tell me what you know of Kalta."

"I know that he was my father, and that he and his wife lived in Hornshir until they died." Namir recounted. "Which is why I went there, I hoped to find some trace of him. I wish I knew him better, that way I might be able to understand who he was and who I should be."

Aras nodded as Namir spoke. "Do you know anything else?"

"I know he wasn't from there and that he had spent some time as a soldier, but I don't know much more than that. Other than a description of him and a vague recollection of what he was like when I was young." Namir confided a little embarrassed about his lack of knowledge.

Aras smiled to himself as Namir spoke and nodded feebly. "I know you have been told that Kalta is your father… and in many ways he was… "

A violent cough stole his words from him as Aras's frame shook. Several moments passed before he could muster enough strength to continue. Everyone sat in silence as the old man cleared his throat and brought a wine skin from its hiding place beside him to his lips.

"You see, I was there the day Kalta found you. He and Cerona, his wife, had longed for a babe of their own, yet Kalta found himself unable to sire one. I was the one that convinced him to take you from the rushes near Watch Keep. He wanted nothing to do with you… he kept saying things about the gods and not meddling in their affairs… " Aras got a faraway look on his face as he relived the incident in his mind.

Silence filled the room again before Namir got impatient and brought the old man back to his senses. "You asked to meet me so you could bring unfounded tales about my father to my ears." Although his tone was harsh, Namir could not bring himself to feel malice for this pitiful old man.

"No. I did not. I am sorry." Aras lifted his sleeve to his mouth and dabbed at it as he continued. "I brought you hear to tell you of your true heritage, which is far from unfounded. I have proof, "Aras glanced at a table across from them briefly, "But before I reveal it, let me tell you what I know of Kalta and Cerona."

Namir settled into his chair a little more firmly as Aras launched into what he knew of Namir's parents.

Chapter Nineteen: Arrivals

Tali lay motionless in her bed. The pain from her jaw, just a phantom of what had happened, reminded her of why she must complete her task. She wondered how they had managed to get a shadow walker as protection.

Tali wanted to scream, 'Just tell me which one of you is my target!'

She let out a muffled groan as she thought about it. She was tired of trying to decide which of them posed the largest threat to her cause. It would be easier to just kill all of them.

"Mistress, are you awake?" Skara's voice purred into the room, through the closed and barred door. Try as she might, Skara could not hide the worry from her voice. "I have soup and fresh bandages for you."

"Aye, I am." Tali said painfully as she gestured at the door from her bed.

She lowered her hand and the wooden beam baring the door slid in response to her gesture. She managed to slide it just enough to allow the door to open. A thin trickle of sweat rewarded her efforts. Tali took a few moments to recover before she continued with her thought, "Come in."

Skara heard the beam slide open and hurried into the room carrying a tray of provisions for her mistress before the door fully opened. Once inside, she placed the soup in front of her

Mistress and set to work changing her bandages and linens.

'At least I have someone here I can trust,' Tali thought to herself as she sipped some of the steaming broth.

"Again!" Karous yelled as the two brothers attempted the maneuver for the sixteenth time.

He could see that even Nurn's vast reserves of strength were being taxed as the two struggled to heft their wooden swords one more time. Each of the sixteen times was the same. The boys would rush Jerine as best they could and the guardian would gracefully maneuver out of the way either disarming both of them or tossing them into the mud of their sparing arena. Although Karous could tell they were improving, mostly through the level of exertion that Jerine put forth, he was not happy with their pace.

"This man will be the death of us, brother." Halin whined to Nurn as he lifted himself off of the ground.

"Quiet… and concentrate. Jerine is but one man, and we nearly had him on that last pass. I think we can do it if you focus more." Nurn instructed. He hoped Halin would focus more on the task at hand and less on his waning energy.

Jerine simply smiled as the brothers started to circle him again. He deeply enjoyed accurately predicting their every move with ease, although, in the back of his mind, he was a little disappointed. Jerine wished that Karous would let him at least give the boys some pointers instead of them having to learn its subtle arts the hard way.

The brothers slowly developed a crude system of communication through eye movement and body language. They tested it in a flash as they leapt at Jerine from opposite sides. This time, unlike their other failed attempts, Nurn struck first and allowed Halin to strike at Jerine's unprotected flank.

Jerine winced as he saw Nurn swing his practice sword. 'He's using it too much like an axe.' Jerine deftly placed his own blade closer to Nurn's hilt to use the force of Nurn's swing to spin himself into position to counter Halin's thrust.

'These boys are learning, but not at the speed I'd like.' Jerine's thoughts spun in his head as he fought. Although he admonished Nurn's usage of the sword, he admired Halin's natural talent for its finer motions.

"Enough!" Karous announced just as Jerine was about to disarm Halin. "I have seen enough of your sword play. Now let's see how well you can use distance weapons." He motioned towards two different racks of weapons. "Nurn, please retrieve some throwing axes. Halin you get to use the bow."

The brothers, still weary from the previous exercise, responded sluggishly as they walked over to the racks of weapons. Halin marveled at the racks as they approached them. "Nurn, you didn't see them there before, right? The racks I mean." Halin asked quietly as he regained his breath.

"No." Nurn panted.

Halin shook his head as they approached the racks. "These elven tricks amaze me. I have no idea what to expect next."

"Leave your wonderment for later, little brother. We can ask Jerine about them after Namir returns." Nurn instructed. He still tried to keep Halin focused on what they still needed to learn.

As the brothers retrieved their weapons, Karous moved to stand in between them. "Ahead of each of you is a copse of trees." He said as he motioned in two different directions. "I want each of you to stand facing away from each other, but beside one another. Each of you will target the trees and release one volley. Once this is done, I want each of you to try and get the rest of your shots as close to that spot as you can." Karous paused to ensure that the brothers understood his directions before he continued. "Once you are able to get all of your shots in a one foot radius, come and see me."

"A one foot radius?" Halin asked somewhat confused.

"Aye." Jerine said. "That means all of your arrows need to be within a half of a foot from where your first shot hits."

"It also means that you need to hit a tree." Karous said

nonchalantly as he shot a scolding look at Jerine.

"When we complete this," Nurn asked, "what are you going to have us do then?"

"Nothing, save speak with me." Karous smiled as he looked over the brothers. "I will merely council you on the weapon that I think you should start with and give you some exercises to practice on your own."

"No more instruction then?" Nurn asked incredulously.

"If we had more time, then yes I would have you practicing more with me. But, alas, we do not." Karous rebuked over his shoulder as he strode away from them and toward the edge of the glade. Once he reached the opening he said, "Now... commence and find me when you have finished."

Jaconis paced the temple's courtyard nervously. 'I hope she's alright,' he thought to himself. The feeling of dread roused by the message he received at the council hall and started to ebb as he made another round along the temple's inner sanctum.

The lush flowers and trees brought an air of peace to the place and he found it easy to let go of his anxiety here. As he paced, he could here faint footfalls approach him. Jaconis took a deep breath and leaned over to smell one of the plethora of roses as the sound stopped just behind him.

"She will see you now, milord." The voice belonged to a middle-aged man. Jaconis assumed that he was one of the deacons that resided here. The timbre was low, but the voice seemed to exude an air of peace.

"Was she bad off when you found her?" Jaconis asked. He was eager to find out as much as he could about what had happened to Tali.

"Aye. From what I was told, she was half-dead. Her jaw had been broken in several places and the poor child looked as if she had been brutally tortured." The man replied nonchalantly.

"Who would have done this?" Jaconis asked, more to himself than to the man behind him.

"I cannot say. There has been an upsurge in violence of late, but I have witnessed nothing like this. It was as if the person that did this to her wanted her to live and inflicted as much pain as they possibly could without killing her."

The man's voice remained calm as he spoke. To Jaconis it seemed as if the deacon spoke of the weather instead of something that had happened to someone that he held dear. Jaconis felt the familiar surge of anger build in his neck as he responded.

"Thank you," he replied a little more curtly than he had intended to, "I would like to see her now. Can you show me to her room?" He asked as he turned to face the man.

The deacon was a little shorter than Jaconis was and he wore a simple white robe tied shut with a blood red cord. He was almost completely bald, the only hint that this was not a normal state for him was the deep brown topknot that was elaborately braided and tied with another blood red cord.

The man's face was completely devoid of emotion. As Jaconis looked the deacon over, he saw him nod toward one of the many passages that led from the courtyard and then started to walk away slowly. Jaconis took the hint and followed him.

As they walked, Jaconis marveled at the elaborate maze that made up this temple. The smooth granite walls were straight and evenly lit in such a way that they gave the impression that the hallways stretched on forever. Each hallway ended in a hub that branched off to three other hallways just like it. Jaconis's head spun just trying to think of how anyone could navigate it from memory.

"Is it much farther?" Jaconis asked as the moments seemed to stretch into days.

"No. We are almost there," the robed man answered over his shoulder with obvious disdain in his voice.

"Are you sure? I think that we might be lost." Jaconis added sarcastically as he tried to bait the man into a discussion. To Jaconis's disappointment, all that he got back from his guide was the deep echoes of footsteps followed by utter silence.

"At least answer me this much. What faith is your brethren of and why was Tali brought here?" Jaconis asked with a small amount of humility in his voice. He was desperate for something to break the silence.

"If it means that we can continue to your friend's room, then I shall." His voice betrayed neither ire nor any trace of impatience as he responded smoothly. "Our order is called the Disciples of the White Rod." The man stopped and faced Jaconis as he spoke. "We bring peace to those in need. As for why she was "brought" here, that is simple. We were the ones that found her. She was not far from our abbey, halfway between our gates and the inner city below. Now please, we are almost there." Jaconis barely had a chance to nod before the man turned and started to walk farther down the hallway.

"Well, I guess that answers my questions for now." Jaconis muttered to himself as he hurried to catch up to the disappearing deacon.

"Now, I have a gift for you." Aras motioned to Alequa to bring him the small chest near the scrolls on the far table. After she handed it to him, he positioned the box so that if it opened, only he could see its contents. "This is not a gift from Kalta or Cerona; instead it's a link to your true heritage."

"Fine, but please understand that I find all of this a little hard to believe. I have lived in my uncle's house since my parents' deaths. I know that Daffer would not have harbored me if Kalta, his brother, were not my father." Namir rebuked as if he thought these words could somehow change Aras's mind.

"Be that as it may, Kalta is not your sire. While it is true that he and his wife raised you as their own, they were no more your kin than Landolin or Jerine." Aras raised a hand to stay Namir's objections as he continued. "I know Daffer and I know that he would have nothing to do with you if he believed otherwise, yet please understand that this was a secret that only a very few knew. If it weren't for Tipin and Allair, Daffer still would have refused to take care of you. They knew your secret, as did Carness. However, aside from them, your parents and I, no one else knew your true lineage. It was safer for you that way." Aras took another sip of his wineskin before he continued again. "You see, we found a note and an heirloom that marked your true heritage. Kalta and I took council with the others since they were fast friends and brothers in arms."

"Brothers in arms? Tipin?" Namir asked in disbelief. "You must be mistaken. He hates violence and shuns it in all forms."

"That may be true now, but it does not change what once was," Aras conceded. "When Kalta was in service to the crown, he served with the others at Watch Keep. Kalta already knew Carness, Allair and Cerona from his own youth in the northern plains of Jarstil."

"I understand that." Namir interrupted, "I also understand that he and Cerona were meant for each other since birth, bound by their traditions." Namir interjected impatiently.

"Good." Aras added a little frustrated by Namir's impatience. "Then I need not go back over it again." He cast Namir a stern look as he gathered his thoughts. "I know this is difficult for you to accept, but I am telling you the truth. Kalta was not your sire, and I am afraid that I cannot tell you who your father is for certain. However, I do know your lineage."

Aras glanced at the box in his lap longingly as he spoke. It seemed to Namir as if some presence within the box lent Aras strength.

With a frustrated sigh, Namir interrupted Aras again. "How can you know my lineage if you don't know who both of my parents are?" A look of disgust played across his face as he said this.

"Namir," Landolin started, as if to lecture him, but he was cut off by a stern look from Aras. "Never mind, I need to take my leave and check on my soldiers." Landolin grunted as he rose and stalked out of the tent briskly.

"As I said, we found a note and an heirloom. Which brings me to the proof I mentioned earlier," Aras took a small mouthful of liquid from his wineskin as he raised the box that he cradled throughout their discussion. "Before I give this to you," he said caressing the lid lovingly, "you must tell me if you will accept it. Know this, it shall prove my tale true and by accepting it you will have started a journey of redemption." Aras's voice held an air of malice as he stated this. The air in the tent became heavier as the small group waited for Namir's response.

Namir thought about it briefly and then nodded. After a few more moments of awkward silence, Namir realized that he needed to vocalize his acceptance. "I accept the gift, such that it is, as my birthright, if that is what it proves itself to be."

Aras let out a sigh of relief as Namir voiced his acceptance. "Good. Before I hand you the box, please read this. It was wrapped around you when Kalta and I found you a week before Belanui's festival." Aras took a small folded piece of linen from a pouch inside his sleeve and leaned toward Namir. Instinctively Alequa tried to assist him, but was stayed by Aras's fierce glare.

Namir could tell the linen was old by the discoloration along its folded surfaces. Aside from that, it looked like a small piece of linen. He took it from Aras's outstretched hand and opened it slowly. In faded letters, Namir could barely make out the original message.

Although it was a short one, it was well penned and succinct. As Namir scanned the well-written lines, he felt his face drain of color. He refolded the note carefully and closed his eyes. With shaking hands, he placed the note into his pouch and carefully caressed the wooden box that lay in his lap.

The small monkey wood box was surprisingly warm to the touch and felt impossibly smooth. Namir sat for a few moments and did his best to hold back the despair he felt building within him.

'My whole life has been a lie.' He thought miserably. He

felt everyone's eyes on him and it started to unnerve him.

He knew what they expected and he hated the feeling it gave him. Namir slowly lifted the lid and peered into it, not sure what he expected to find in the small box.

After an hour of constant attempts, Nurn was finally able to complete the task. He was relieved as he trudged the ten yards to his target and retrieved the twelve hand axes he had been given. He paused before he pulled the axes from the tree stump to see how Halin was doing. To his dismay, his brother was still performing poorly. He had managed to get three or four arrows into the target area, but the rest were way off. Nurn sighed heavily as he set to retrieving the weapons.

'I hope he manages to get the hang of this soon.' Nurn thought to himself as he slowly walked back to where they had been standing.

He noticed Jerine walk towards them as he walked back. "I have finished." Nurn said as Jerine approached him.

"Good." Jerine glanced toward Halin as he retrieved his arrows, "and how is your brother faring?"

"Not as good." Nurn grunted. "He has never done this sort of thing before. Maybe you can help him understand it better." Nurn replied, trying to disguise the hopefulness in his voice.

"Perhaps," Jerine nodded. "Either way it's time for a rest. I brought some food and water for you two." Jerine stated as he pulled two wineskins and two wrapped parcels from underneath his cloak.

Nurn smiled as the sweet scent of mutton wafted over to him. He set his axes down and stretched before he retrieved three logs so that they had seats. As he arranged the logs, Halin walked up with a frustrated look on his face. "Jerine brought us food." Nurn commented. He hoped that the prospect of eating would improve Halin's mood.

"Wonderful," Halin said genuinely relieved by the thought of eating. "I almost have it... I think." He added as if trying to convince Nurn that he was doing better than he really was.

"I see that." Nurn nodded. A part of him hoped that Halin really was catching on.

"Enough talk about target practice, let's eat." Jerine said with a laugh. "You need to build up your strength if you want to succeed." Jerine directed these last few words at Halin as encouragement.

Halin met Jerine's gaze and simply nodded. There was something about Halin's determined look that gave Jerine pause. He had seen that look on many of his friends' faces throughout his lifetime and it had always bothered him.

'He is driven by something. I just hope it doesn't consume him.' Jerine thought to himself as the boys started to eat.

Hessa and Aves made their way back to the manor through the winding streets of Hornshir as the day moved toward dusk. The shadows gathered in the corners of the alleys as they finished nailing the last notice that proclaimed Ellsted's upcoming festival. Both of them were sullen, sore from their long day of negotiations, and walking.

"Do you think they're back yet?" Aves asked with a hint of eagerness in her voice.

"I hope they are. I have been worried about them." Hessa replied. She tried her best to hide her doubts. "But the ride is a long one, so they may have decided to stay the night where they are safe."

A slight edge of foreboding slipped into Hessa's voice and Aves could not help but hear it. "They are safe… right?" Aves asked. She needed assurance from someone and Hessa knew it. 'I'm not sure what I will do if they aren't.' Aves thought ruefully.

"Aye, they should be, as long as they are with Jerine and the elves. Hopefully they chose to stay there instead of making the trip at this hour." Hessa's attempt at comforting Aves was a far cry from helping, especially since she had a growing feeling that something sinister had happened. "But let's hurry and see if they've arrived." Hessa added as she quickened her pace.

Aves nodded and matched Hessa's pace as she felt a pit start to form in her stomach. "Thankfully the council elder was brief and the rest of Hornshir's council had already decided yesterday about our proposition. Now all we have left to do is make arrangements to receive the new supplies from Hornshir and to ready our belongings for the trek home." Aves recounted as she tried to rid herself of the awful feeling that had started to creep up on her. "So how long do you think it will take us to prepare for our journey home?"

"A couple of days I would think. Definitely no longer than a week." Hessa replied as they turned the last corner on their way to the manor. "The thing that is bothering me is where Jaconis went in such a hurry after our meeting with the council finished."

"I don't know, but I think a messenger approached him as we were leaving, just before he got that frantic look on his face." Aves replied. She allowed her curiosity to pull her into the new topic readily.

"I just wish I knew where he went. I know that he's up to no good, I'm just not sure what." Hessa declared as they approached the gate.

Out of the corner of her eye, she thought that something moved across the darkening rooftops. She took a deep breath, paused a few moments, and then turned to see if she could get a better look. Nothing untoward met her eye as she scanned the buildings.

"Let's go inside. I will feel much better when we are inside safely with some cider in our mugs and food in our hands." She did her best to not sound frightened, but there was an obvious tremor in her voice as she heard Aves hail the guards.

Nurn walked away from the clearing and left Halin to Jerine's instruction. He thought about the trials they had to face and the look on Halin's face. He had been too serious all day. It broke Nurn's heart. What bothered him the most was his failure to understand what bothered Halin so much.

He was supposed to take care of Halin and ensure that no harm befell him. Nurn muttered a prayer under his breath to Tumere as he walked. He prayed for guidance and for the strength that both Halin and he needed to cope with what lay ahead.

As he walked and prayed, Nurn felt a presence about him. This presence was peaceful and unsettling at the same time. Nurn could only recall feeling this sensation one other time and that was when he was first taught the wisdom of Tumere by his father.

Nurn thought back to the day his father had taken him to an old forest, much like this one, and spoke to him of Tumere. He could still hear his father's voice telling him about Tumere's teachings and this comforted him.

"Remember," Nurn recalled Tipin saying in his deep rumbling voice, "Tumere is the mother of the forests and was born out of need. She was given the task of their defense and doing harm unto the forest does harm unto her." This memory gave Nurn pause.

He swiftly dropped to one knee in the middle of the path he was on, Nurn prayed for forgiveness. Not just for himself, but for everyone in these encampments because of their desecration to the natural beauty of the forest in which he found himself.

Nurn disregarded all of the noises around him as he prayed for Tumere's favor and he felt the sensation deepen into more of a presence than a feeling. The presence became more palpable the longer he prayed and Nurn was all but lost to it.

Morcant stalked along the rooftops of the buildings adjacent to the manor that the girls had taken sanctuary in. He patiently took account of the guards and the paths into and out of the manor.

He growled softly to himself in frustration as he realized the extent in which the manor was fortified. He sniffed the air deeply as he allowed the prevailing scents of the manor's grounds to fill his nostrils. What he found unsettled Morcant more than the imposing fortifications had.

"Elves," he muttered to himself darkly. "They have elves as guards instead of humans. This makes it a little harder."

He sniffed one more time before he vanished into the shadows and headed back toward the Disciples of the White Rod's abbey to report his findings to his mistress.

Jaconis opened the door to Tali's room slowly, not sure of what he would find. To his surprise she sat by the fire with her back to him. The tall chair in which she sat blocked most of his view of her so he could not see how bad she really was.

"Please find a seat near the door." Tali's voice was strained and Jaconis could tell that each word only added to her pain.

"I thought I would see just how bad off you were. I... I mean that I hoped what the deacons had told me was wrong." Jaconis still hovered in the open doorway. He was torn between approaching her and doing her bidding.

"No, I need time." Tali struggled with each word and it hurt Jaconis to hear her. "The monks here are good healers and they assured me that in a few months all vestiges of my attack will be gone." Tali hoped Jaconis would understand, but part of her knew he would not.

She waited with baited breath as she heard his feet shuffle across the floor toward the seat she had Skara place beside her bed.

She waited until he settled into the wooden chair before she continued. "Thank you for coming. I do appreciate it, really." She heard Jaconis's chair squeak as she forced each word out of her bruised lips. If she was not in so much pain, she might have enjoyed Jaconis's inner torment more.

"I'm just glad that you are still alive." Jaconis interjected.

He tried to spare Tali any more discomfort. "I just wish I knew what had happened and why." Jaconis said. He hoped Tali would answer, but he did not want her to at the same time.

"I was attacked… " Tali started to answer but Jaconis cut her off.

"Please don't answer my question. I was talking to myself more than anything." Jaconis blurted out abruptly. "I don't want to cause you more discomfort than needed." He added as he realized how rude he must have sounded to her.

Tali giggled a little as she heard Jaconis stumble over himself in an attempt not to offend her. "I want to tell you," she said after an awkward silent had set in. "Besides, I need to tell you something else and this way I might find it easier to say it."

"If you feel up to it," Jaconis replied sullenly. "So, what happened?"

Tali took a pain-filled breath as she launched into her story. She made sure to gloss over the parts that would reveal her connections to both the abbey and to her nassarid. She could not let Jaconis know too much, at least not yet.

Chapter Twenty: Lots

"I knew that my training would be hard on you, but I hadn't expected you to pass out while looking for me." Karous said as he placed his hand on Nurn's broad shoulder.

Nurn's eyes flew open at Karous's touch and Karous could see the tears that had formed within them. Taken aback, Karous was at a loss for words as Nurn slowly rose to his feet and regained his composure.

"Aye it was, but that is not why I was kneeling." Nurn said quietly as he bowed to Karous respectfully.

"My apologies, several people brought me news that one of the sa'trandon had collapsed near the edge of the encampment." Karous said as he motioned for Nurn to follow him. "It seems that their reports were slightly exaggerated. Mind if I ask why you knelt there for so long?"

"I was praying to my goddess," Nurn replied calmly. "I felt the need to pray for guidance. Now, may I ask you a question?" Nurn asked as he caught up to his instructor.

"Please do. I will answer any question you have to the best of my ability." Karous replied as they approached his tent.

"Why did you refer to my brother and me as 'saw trandon'? I am unfamiliar with the term." Nurn asked as he stopped and waited for Karous to untie the flap to his tent.

Karous did not respond immediately. Instead, he finished

unfastening the flap and then went inside the dark tent before he motioned for Nurn to follow. Once Nurn was inside, he refastened the flap from the inside and plunged the tent into total darkness.

The only sound Nurn could discern was a faint scraping of metal against wood, like something being removed from a chest. As soon as Nurn had recognized the sound, the tent was lit by a single flame that danced within the glass chamber of the lamp Karous set on the table.

"That is a difficult question to answer and one I feel that I should not provide." Karous said careful not to upset the large boy. "All I can say is that it is a title of respect and honor. The rest you need to ask Jerine or Namir. Either of them should be able to tell you."

"And the original term you called us? Sara-din, what does that mean?" Nurn asked civilly so as not to allow Karous to know how frustrated he was.

"Ah, that is not so nice, nor honorable, of a term. It means outlander or vagrant in your tongue." Karous admitted a little ashamed of his own actions. "Please understand that I did not know who you were. I have trained many fighters, but my teachings are usually reserved for only the best of elven decent and not just anyone may learn from me." He explained gingerly.

"I can accept that and no harm is done." Nurn acquiesced. "I have brought the axes you let me throw, with me. I am sorry that I didn't leave them there, but I did not see the rack from which I had retrieved them."

"That is fine. In fact, you may keep them. We have plenty and I believe you will need them more than I shall." Karous smiled at Nurn's thoughtfulness. "Now I would like to tell you what I have learned today about you and the weapons in which I believe you would do the best with. That is, if you have no further questions for me."

"I have none." Nurn replied as he bowed his head to Karous.

"Very well," Karous smiled as he motioned for Nurn to

follow him. In the back room I have something I would like to give you, as well as show you." Karous picked up the lamp as if an afterthought as he turned and walked deeper into his tent.

Nurn was surprised by both the size of the tent and its contents. The tent was almost the size of two tavern rooms and that was just the main area. As they walked to the other section of the tent Nurn saw a wide variety of weapons and chests. It seemed as if they walked through an armory instead of a domicile.

As they stepped through the flap and into the other section of the tent, Nurn saw Karous' other possessions. Although this room was sparsely decorated when compared to the many racks of weapons in the previous section, it seemed full of energy and ambiance. It was as if this particular area held a sacred stillness.

The only physical items in this room were four chests, a bed and a table. One chest was against each of the walls with the entrance in a corner of the tent. In the very center sat a large table littered with scrolls and maps. In the opposite corner of the entrance was a bed that looked softer than any Nurn had ever seen.

As they walked over to the table, Karous motioned for Nurn to sit in a chair that Nurn must have overlooked upon entering the tent. It was a simple wood and leather chair, and to Nurn it looked as if it had been made for someone of his build instead of for elves.

"Please make yourself comfortable. I need to get something." Karous instructed as he turned to the chest on their right.

Nurn walked over to the chair and sat down. It was more comfortable than it looked, and as he was testing its comfort, Karous had retrieved an item from the chest and returned.

"I would like you to accept this as a gift." Karous said quietly as he extended something wrapped in leather. He had his eyes cast down to Nurn's feet and his head was tilted in a gesture of respect.

Karous' actions confused Nurn, but he accepted the bundle

nonetheless. "What is it?" Nurn asked, a little afraid to open it.

"Please unwrap it," Karous said as he settled into a seat across the table from Nurn.

Nurn did so obediently. He carefully set the bundle on the table and cautiously unwrapped the soft oiled leather. Nurn's breath caught as he looked upon its contents. Within the soft leather wrapping, he found a footman's axe. It was beautiful.

The haft and head were both made of steel and had been polished to a mirror-like finish. The bottom of the haft was wrapped in black leather and padded to absorb some of the impact using the weapon would cause.

The head was just as beautiful. One side of it was shaped into a spiral spike, while the other side was a well-honed and elongated blade. The very ornate symbols and intricate designs etched into the steel of the axe blade and down the haft lent an otherworldly look to them and imbued it with a feeling of awe as the soft light from the lantern played along them. Underneath the axe was a hard leather cover and baldric that looked to be of his size.

A million questions swirled around inside Nurn's head as he looked from the axe to Karous and back to the axe. He took a few moments to organize his thoughts before he slowly held his gaze steady on Karous.

"Thank you, but why give such a fine weapon to me?" Nurn asked hesitantly.

"I give it to you for two reasons, the main being that you need a weapon to defend yourself with. You also need a weapon befitting your station as sa'trandon." Karous smiled as he saw the look of wonder spread across Nurn's face. "This weapon does both. Besides, I have a tradition of giving my students a weapon when my tutelage of them is done and, though your training is far from completed, I will not be able to aid you in your studies from here on out so now is when I must give you my gift of parting."

"Thank you again. Know that I shall take good care of this gift. Does this axe carry a name?" Nurn asked and felt immediately stupid for carrying on in this manner.

Nurn's aptitude to ask the right questions amazed Karous. "Aye, he does. His name is Séregon or Deep Bite in your tongue."

"A fitting name," Nurn murmured as he gazed upon the axe once more.

"Now, let's go over the exercises you need to work on in order to wield him proficiently." Karous said as he slowly stood and walked around the table towards Nurn.

Morcant sat on the cliff facing the abbey and stared through Tali's closed window at Jaconis. He watched intently as he monitored Jaconis's every move. Morcant knew that Tali did not like people to see her with either Skara or himself, but he did not like the thought of Jaconis being in the same room with her alone in her condition.

Morcant's muscles tensed as he saw Jaconis carefully pull his dagger from its sheath as Jaconis rose to his feet. Morcant readied himself, this might turn ugly and Morcant half hoped that Jaconis would do something stupid. Morcant got his wish. As he looked from Jaconis to Tali, Morcant saw Jaconis roll his dagger into an attack position, point down, and he took a few steps toward Tali. That was all the provocation Morcant needed. He was too wound up and this would help him work out some of his recent frustrations.

In one leap, Morcant sailed from his perch through the window and pinned Jaconis to the floor where he stood.

"That is far enough human!" Morcant growled as he pressed his full weight against Jaconis's chest. He could feel Jaconis's muscles spasm as Morcant's red eyes locked with Jaconis's terrified stare.

"What in the name of Lotevilar are you doing?" Tali gasped as she struggled to her feet. She was just as startled by the splinting wood and the shattering glass as she was by Morcant's voice. "Skara to me!" This command was little more than a guttural grunt of pain as Tali leaned against the chair she was sitting in mere moments before.

Skara rolled to her feet from the shadows near the window and hurried to her mistress' side as pieces of broken glass fell from her clothing. Morcant rose to his feet while he dangled Jaconis's now limp body from one clawed hand easily. He slowly pressed Jaconis against the wall before Skara could make her way to Tali's side.

"Your human was about to attack you, Mistress." Morcant sneered as he threw a glare over his shoulder at Skara, "and, as usual, that witless feline witch was going to do nothing about it!"

Tali shook her head in pain and frustration. "Put him down, Morcant." She commanded wearily. "Skara, please search the room for any signs to prove Morcant's story."

She held Morcant's gaze as Skara started her search. Her stomach churned when she saw Skara pick Jaconis's unsheathed dagger up from underneath the little table beside the door where it had skittered to in Morcant's attack.

"This is all I found, Mistress." Skara said as she fell to her knees in front of Tali and held out the dagger in her upturned palms.

Morcant sneered deeper as he witnessed this and lowered Jaconis enough to let his feet brush the floor. "I only broke your command to protect you, Mistress." He said as he did so.

"Very well," Tali nodded. "Lay him on my bed. When he regains his senses, I will question him about this." She motioned feebly towards her bed as she continued. "I want you," she directed at Morcant, "to go tell the brethren that my window needs fixed immediately. Skara and I can handle him from here."

"Are you sure?" Morcant barked. "The witch failed to protect you this time, why do you think she will be of use now?"

"Are you questioning my orders?" Tali mustered as much anger as she could. She slowly released her grip on the chair to add an air of menace to her unspoken threat. "I hope not, for your sake." To her relief the promised violence in her voice proved to be enough to quell Morcant's rebellion, because she saw Morcant cringe as he hurried to do her bidding.

Jerine watched as Halin loosed yet another arrow into the brush surrounding his target. "You are holding the bow too tight. Try relaxing your grip as you shoot."

He knew that Halin was getting frustrated. Unless Halin started to understand what he needed to learn in order to operate the bow proficiently, he would be at it all night. Jerine also knew that Halin was not going to quit until he could finish the task, which meant that his trial might never end.

"What do you mean?" The strain in Halin's voice was palpable.

"Hand me the bow and I'll show you." Jerine said patiently.

He watched Halin's body language as Halin handed him the bow and an arrow. Jerine looked over his shoulder at Halin as he knocked the arrow. Jerine took a moment to familiarize himself with the weight and draw of the bow as Halin retrieved an arrow for him.

Jerine was pleasantly surprised by the craftsmanship of the bow. It was lighter than he expected, yet it had more power in its release than it required to pull it.

As he took the arrow from Halin he instructed, "Stand to my right and watch me." He waited until Halin was in place before he knocked the arrow, drew the string back, sighted his target and released the arrow all in one fluid motion.

"So you want me to let the tension of the string hold the bow in my hand?" Halin asked as he replayed Jerine's perfect shot in his mind as he spoke.

"Aye, if you can." Jerine nodded, obviously impressed by Halin's observation. "If you can't get it perfect, hold it as loosely as you can. Remember to relax while firing. Don't anticipate the release of the arrow or the snap of the string. Instead, just focus on your target and allow your arrow to find its own way there. Now you try." Jerine said as he handed

Halin the bow.

Halin took the bow from Jerine and nocked an arrow. He held the bow as lightly as he could as he drew the string back and released. To his amazement the arrow did not skitter into the brush like so many of his others had, it did not hit the target either. Instead, it shot about a foot to the left of the target, but it was at the right level.

"Good." Jerine nodded his approval although he could see that Halin was still very frustrated.

"What do you mean good? I missed!" Halin snapped. His irritation at his shortcomings carried its message through the tone of his voice.

"But you missed differently. That is progress." Jerine smiled as he said the line that he had heard so many times from Karous. "Learning to shoot a bow is not something that can be fully accomplished in one day. Karous knows this. Instead this is a test of your determination, not your skill." Jerine put a hand on Halin's shoulder to help reassure him that he was doing all right.

Jerine smiled as Halin stalked off to retrieve his arrows. 'That boy is headstrong.' He thought to himself as he watched Halin disappear into the brush only to return a few moments later with his lost arrows.

When Halin made it back to him, Jerine added, "I need to check on Valon and the others. But before I go, I was wondering, has Tipin ever told you about your namesake?" Jerine worked through how he was going to reveal his next bit of information to Halin as he waited for the youth's response.

"Aye, Halin was a great Calanari warrior. He had no rival with either sword or bow." The disgruntled tone of Halin's voice drove his loathing for stories about his namesake into the open.

"Then it would be no surprise to you to discover that Halin had taught his skills to others," Jerine posited in an attempt to bait Halin's interest.

"Nope," Halin replied. "It would only be logical for people to want to learn from him."

"Good." Jerine nodded. "Then it may not be too much of a surprise to learn that he also chose to teach a very few, those he determined to have enough merit to learn his skills." Jerine waited to see if Halin would respond favorably. When Halin refused to rise to his challenge he continued, "One of his few students, the only one to obtain any of your namesake's mastery was Karous, his old friend and adventuring companion." Jerine reveled at the look of astonishment that swept across Halin's face.

"But that means that Karous is over a hundred years old." The incredulity in Halin's voice was apparent and his wonder only increased as Jerine nodded in agreement. "My father named my brother and I after him and his brother."

"I know, as does Karous," Jerine conceded.

"Is this why he was so tough on us?" Halin asked a little afraid of the answer he was going to get.

"It is a possibility. Maybe he just hopes to help you live up to your potential." Jerine smiled as Halin's wonder forged itself into determination.

Halin took a deep breath and released it slowly. "Fine, I will keep at it though. I'm not going to quit. Not unless Karous tells me himself that I have completed the task he gave me." Halin said obstinately.

"I have to go now, but I will be back by later if I don't see you in the encampment." Jerine waited until he was sure that Halin understood him and was ok with the idea of being left alone, before he left the clearing as the shadows of early evening started to deepen.

A soft blue light filled the room as Namir gazed upon the amulet inside the box. Although the amulet looked simple, it was beautifully made. In the center was a sapphire a little smaller than Namir's palm. A finely braided silver wire completely encircled this gem and held it securely in place. The braided silver wire created a barbed effect to it and artfully wove itself into the petite chain in a way that made it impossible to separate them. The gem was so perfectly cut that the light in the room seemed to be pulled into its depths and then spill back out as if the gem itself glowed with a brilliance all its own.

To Namir it seemed as if the amulet was the only source of light in the room, as if all of the other lights had been extinguished. He glanced around the room quickly and saw the faces of those around him frozen in a look of awe.

Namir licked his lips nervously as his eyes drew his attention back to the gem of their own volition. "It's beautiful." Namir exclaimed softly as he started to close the box slowly.

"Please, put it on." Aras instructed. His voice, though old, had lost some of its frailness and sounded almost commanding in its insistence.

"Why?" Namir inquired, still staring at the gem. "I usually don't wear necklaces." Namir continued as he tried to figure out why the box's contents looked so familiar and captivating.

"If you wear it, you will understand more of what I am about to say." Aras said a little quieter.

"Please, Namir. Please put it on, if for no other reason than to humor him." Alequa added gently. "He has been through so much and isn't going to live much longer."

"Very well, but I don't intend to wear it out of here." Namir said as he reached into the box.

Everyone in the room seemed to hold their breath as Namir delicately reached into the box. The moment seemed to stretch into infinity as he gently touched the finely crafted wire. He was amazed to find it warm to the touch as he traced the workmanship with his index finger.

He pulled the amulet and chain from its container ever so carefully. Then, making sure he did not drop either the box or the amulet, he lowered the box to his lap and rested the amulet within it as he separated the loop of the chain. Even the chain was warm. As he slowly lifted it up over his head, he carefully tested the weight of the amulet against the strength of the chain. Namir was a little surprised that the chain was able to support it.

Although the amulet was not heavy, the chain looked too frail to hold it. Namir leaned back to rest against the back of the chair. The amulet felt good as it rested against his chest, a warm sensation spread from where it touched his skin.

Namir had not realized he had closed his eyes until he heard it, the soft sound of a woman's voice singing to him softly. It was both familiar yet strange. Namir's eyes flew open abruptly as he lurched to his feet, the contents of his lap spilled onto the rug at his feet.

A beautiful woman stood a few feet in front of Namir. She wore white flowing gowns and smiled at him lovingly as she brushed a stand of long platinum hair away from her face. Her eyes shone like sapphires as she looked at him and he found it impossible to look away from her beauty. Her pale skin reminded him of something, yet he could not place it. She stood silently as she teased her silver necklace and looked at him patiently as she waited for Namir to find his voice.

"Who are you?" Namir's voice caught in his throat as he asked the only question that his mind could grasp. His voice seemed raspy and alien to his own ears as he asked it. His heart sank as his answer was met with silence. She simply stood and smiled at him, as if her silence was all the answer that he needed. "Please, tell me why you have shown yourself to me." Namir added self-consciously.

"I AM ZELIOS, KEEPER OF PASSION AND THE BEARER OF SORROWS." Her voice was satiny and Namir felt his very being yearn for as she spoke, "AND I AM HERE TO ENSURE THAT YOUR DESTINY IS REALIZED."

The room spun as Jaconis sat up slowly. He was a little unsure of where he was until he saw Skara lean over him and offer to help him stand. He tried to pull his arm away from her, but she was too quick. Since she already held his arm firmly, he leaned against her as he stood slowly from the bed.

As he rose from the bed, Tali started the conversation. "I am sorry that things had to happen this way." Tali was thankful that Jaconis had remained unconscious long enough for Skara to place fresh bandages on her face to cover her wounds completely. "Please understand that Morcant was just defending me." She narrowed her eyes as she recalled Morcant's entrance. "I still wonder why he felt that he needed to defend me though."

Jaconis felt a chill run up his spine as Tali spoke her last few words. He could feel her gaze harden as looked him over. It was as if she had never seen him and it hurt.

He licked his lips nervously as he answered her unspoken question hesitantly, "he probably thought I was going to attack you." Jaconis realized that she would not understand his reasoning, but he could not think of a better answer.

"Why would he think that?" A deadly edge slid into voice as she tried to mask the knowledge that she already possessed.

"Because I had carefully unsheathed my dagger after I sat down." Jaconis replied before impulsively. Before Tali could comment on it, he continued. "I saw this creature by the window," he nodded at Skara as he said this, "and I thought she meant you harm." Fear was evident in his voice and he yelped unconsciously as he felt Skara's claws sink into his arm that she still held.

"I see." Tali motioned for Skara to release him and to return to her side. "I am sorry to say that I have not been completely honest with you." She watched Skara pace across the room to her reluctantly as she waited for the question she knew Jaconis was about to ask.

Tali's tone sounded sincere to Jaconis, but he remained leery since he could not see her face. He looked into her eyes as he tried to discern the veracity of her words. He cast his gaze from Skara to Tali slowly as he mulled over her words.

"So you are the friend I have in common with her?" Jaconis's words sounded more like a statement than a question and had an acrid air of bitterness to them.

Tali nodded her head and forced the words from her lips through the bandages, "Aye."

"Why didn't you tell me sooner?" Jaconis said. He cut Tali's response off before she could finish it with another question without hesitation. "How many of the other tales you've told me were lies?" The hurt look on Jaconis's face stung Tali more than she cared to admit herself.

"Not much, although the lies I did tell were necessary. I didn't want you to get too involved in my life without good cause. If you did, you would never be able to leave it." Tali said with cold certainty. Although her words were forced, they held the ring of truth in them. "Please understand. I need you even now more than I did before. Thanks to what happened, I am not going to be able to follow your cousin and his friends. More importantly I can't help get you what you deserve."

She lowered her head. The sound of tears was thick in her voice from her pain and she used them to convince Jaconis of her sincerity. She knew that he would succumb to her plans, she just needed to play him a little more than she would have liked to.

"How can I believe you?" Jaconis asked incredulously. He felt his strength returning in droves the longer he stood and faced Tali. "Better yet, why?"

Skara growled menacingly at Jaconis as he said this. Tali motioned for her silence and answered his question bluntly.

"The why is easier to answer than the how, but I will try to answer both." Tali motioned to Skara to help her to her chair, which Skara leapt to instantly.

When Skara had turned the chair so Tali could sit and face Jaconis, Tali continued. "You should believe me because I will have Morcant or Skara kill you if you don't." Her tone was level and her gaze was unfaltering, both of these things bothered Jaconis deeply. "But I would prefer if you agreed to help me out of your own free will. You still mean much to me and I would hate to have to kill you and loose someone that has grown so dear to me. There is more going on than you know, but you can rest assured that by helping me you shall be helping yourself as well."

Jaconis gulped as Tali spoke. He felt a little weak in the knees as he processed her words, so he sought out the chair he had occupied earlier and sat down awkwardly.

"I will grant that either of your beasts could kill me." His words elicited another growl from Skara before she could stifle herself. Jaconis looked worriedly at her as he continued, "but you still haven't told me how I can believe anything you say."

"If you agree to help me, I will agree to tell you as much of the truth as possible." Tali said. She watched Jaconis closely to see if his body language would betray his words.

"I will under these conditions. You tell me who you really are, what your goal is, and what has really happened since I met you." Jaconis face was stern, but Tali could tell that he was nervous by the twitch in his eyes and fingers.

"Agreed," Tali smiled as she saw Jaconis relax a little. "Would you like me to start now or in the morning?"

The sound of the monks as they gathered outside helped Jaconis to realize that it would be best to find out as much as he could as soon as possible.

"Now please. If we run out of time this evening, you can proceed in the morning. Agreed?" Jaconis did his best to sound completely calm, although he knew some of his fear crept into his voice.

"Aye," Tali acquiesced. "To begin with I am a Darque Traveler, meaning that I am a follower of the goddess Lotevilar and am a member of The Way of Transcendence." Tali started as the sounds of construction started to drown out her voice.

Halin brushed the sweat from his brow as he steadied another arrow. His arms and back ached as he aimed carefully in an attempt to find the right position to loose the arrow from. The string cut into his fingers and blood trickled down the string from where his skin started to crack. Darkness settled in hours ago and Halin was acutely aware of his hunger.

Although Jerine had left only a few hours ago, to Halin it

seemed as if had been left alone in the clearing for an eternity. At first, his thoughts turned towards waiting out the period that Jerine had said would pass instead of actually attempting to meet the expectation Karous had placed upon him. Then he remembered Morcant and how helpless he had felt. These thoughts gave him the determination and drive he needed to press on.

The soft thwack of the arrow as he loosed it from the bow gave Halin almost as much satisfaction as hearing the dull thunk as the arrow hit the tree trunk. He managed to get six of his last volley of arrows into the target area.

'Only six more to go,' Halin thought sarcastically to himself as he walked to his target to retrieve his arrows.

The twigs and rocks under his feet shifted familiarly as he walked the now familiar path in the dark. The white feathers and tan shafts of his arrows shone in the soft light provided by the moon and stars. Halin paused and hung the bow across a couple branches, close enough to his target and at the right height so he need not travel too far from his target, in order to free up his hands.

Then, grasping the shaft of the arrow firmly, he tugged the arrow free from his target with a slight twist. Halin grinned as he saw how close to each other they were, well within the one foot radius that he needed.

'I may be finished in the next volley,' he thought proudly to himself. 'Now all I need to do is find my wayward arrows in the dark.' This thought brought his spirits down a little as he set to his task.

After he freed his arrows from the target, he grabbed his bow and plunged through the thick brush and into the black forest beyond the glade to retrieve the rest of his arrows.

"Are you alright Namir?" Alequa's musical voice drifted into Namir's senses as if she spoke to him from afar. "Please let me help you." She cooed as she cradled his head in her hands.

Namir blinked a few times and was instantly confused. He was lying on the rugs of the tent with his head in Alequa's lap. He was sprawled out on the floor and the amulet was grasped tightly in his hand. "What happened?" Namir asked completely bewildered.

"You fell." Landolin interjected from across the tent as he replaced the flap on his way back in. "One moment you were putting the chain around your next... then you leapt to your feet and fell over."

Aras smiled from his bed as he heard Landolin's recounting. "You saw Her, didn't you lad?" He asked as a sly smile spread across his face.

"Who?" Landolin asked, but was cut off from further inquiry by Alequa, as Namir tried to rise.

"You should lie still for a moment." She advised, as she ran her fingers through Namir's thick hair. "Your strength will return shortly."

"How long was I unconscious?" Namir asked. He was still trying to piece together what had happened.

"Several hours," Alequa replied as if the time were of no consequence.

"Please answer me." Aras requested, his patience worn thin. "You saw Her, right?"

"Aye and she is beautiful. Who is she?" Namir answered somewhat lackadaisically.

"She is the guardian of both the amulet that you hold and your bloodline." Aras answered cryptically.

"She looked so familiar." Namir continued as if he had not heard Aras's comment.

"She should." Aras sighed deeply. Then, he tossed a small wooden disk at Namir to ensure that he had his attention before he asked, "Do you remember when you first saw her?"

"About three nights back." Namir's voice was filled with awe as he made this realization. "I saw her when we were trapped in the fire." His gaze fell from Aras to the amulet that he still clutched with a look that fluctuated between astonishment and disbelief.

"I thought so." Aras simply nodded and then looked at Alequa with a wry grin. "My love, can you please get me my journal?"

Alequa nodded and walked across the room to collect it as Aras had asked. As she walked, she noted Aras's reaction and gazed back to Namir often. She remembered her first encounter with the ancient magic, the dazzling power embedded in these deep pockets of mystery.

She recalled her amazement and wondered if she had looked so pathetic to those that had gazed upon her and decided against it as she picked up Aras's thin leather bound journal and walked back. She gingerly handed it to Aras as she sat down in one fluid motion.

"You thought what?" Landolin's irritation at being left out was evident in each word he spoke.

"If you will be patient enough for me to find it in my notes, you will be more than informed," Aras said as he started to thumb through his journal feebly. A gleam of eagerness played in his eyes as he scanned every page thoroughly.

Nurn tested the weight of Séregon as he walked through the encampment. He looked for either Jerine or Halin as he made his way from the clearing that he left Halin in. Nurn rolled the well-balanced axe from one hand to the other as his eyes scanned the darkness. Nurn felt secure in the fact that had taken the precaution of securing the stout leather covering over the blade itself, yet remarkably the axe's balance was not altered. As he neared the horses, he saw Jerine glide up to him.

"Have you seen Halin?" Nurn asked as he tried to keep the concern and disappointment from his voice. He had hoped that Halin would be with Jerine.

"Aye, just before dark," Jerine replied as he scanned Nurn's face for a hint of trouble. "I left him in the clearing after I showed him how best to handle the bow. I needed to check on Valon and your steeds, as well as secure some dinner for all of us. Speaking of which, you need to come with me if you would like to eat."

"I can't, at least not yet." Nurn shook his head as he continued. "Karous asked me to find Halin and see if he had completed his task. If not, I was to bring him to Karous anyway." Worry crept into Nurn's deep voice as he thought about Halin.

"Have you checked the clearing yet?" Jerine asked. He felt worry creep into his mind and he did his best to shut it out.

"Aye, I just came from there." Nurn remarked. "I had hoped he was with you getting food or on some other task."

"No, as I said I left him there." Jerine's voice grew softer as he thought about where Halin could have disappeared. "Go back to Karous and I will check the clearing again, mayhap my elven eyes can see some trace that you missed."

"Very well," Nurn replied. The look of dread etched into his features as he turned to leave tore at Jerine's heart. "Tumere watch over him," Nurn muttered under his breath as he sped off for Karous's tent.

As Jerine heard Nurn's prayer, his thoughts whirled from where Halin may have gone to the fact that Nurn was a follower of the old Gods. 'At least they are in good hands,' Jerine thought to himself as he offered a silent prayer to Tumere as well before he turned and made his way meticulously to the practice clearing.

Chapter Twenty One: Revelations

Jaconis sat in the chair lost in thought as Tali finished her tale. "Let me see if I understand this." Jaconis said slowly. "You are after an heirloom that you believe someone from Ellsted brought with them to Hornshir." Jaconis waited until he saw Tali nod before he continued, "which is why you offered to help me, why you stole the carriage and then returned it, and why you had these things attack Halin and the others."

"Aye," Tali croaked, her voice having finally failed due to her injuries. "But not quite. Halin being attacked was a mistake." Tali replied after much effort. She shot Morcant a warning glance as she saw that he was about to respond to her explanation.

"And you believe that this 'shadow walker' is helping them keep possession of it for some unknown reason. And you think that his willingness to help them is why he keeps attacking you." Jaconis continued incredulously. He just could not bring himself to believe her story.

Tali simply nodded acquiescence as she heard him mull over the scant details she had provided him. She was still upset at Morcant for barging in and ruining her previous plans, but she acknowledged that his actions might have made it easier in a way. Either way, after she had time to recover, she would punish him for his carelessness.

"Either this shadow stalker is smarter than you and a better tracker than your creatures or he is just extremely lucky." Jaconis thought aloud. He realized that the two beasts in the room were scowling at him as he said this.

"All of those assumptions are possible." Tali nodded. She hated the situation that she was in. "So, knowing this, are you willing to devote yourself to my cause?"

"You said that in my aiding you, I would aide myself as well. Aside from being the only survivor of the excursion, I cannot see how." Jaconis stated grimly. "So unless you allow me to help with the planning, I cannot."

"You know that means death!" Morcant spat as he leaned forward ready to spring.

"Morcant, settle down." Tali said as loud as she was able. The look in her eyes was lethal and Morcant caught their intention perfectly. "I agree to your stipulation," Tali nodded at Jaconis, "if it means that much to you. There is just one more thing that you need to do."

"Which is?" Jaconis asked. His curiosity peaked as Tali succumbed to his bluff.

"You must join the brethren." Tali said as sternly as she could.

"You want me to become a member of The Way of Transcendence?" Jaconis asked a little doubting.

"No, but you must become one of the Disciples of the White Rod." The finality in her voice set Jaconis's hairs on edge and the look in her eyes ensured him that he had no say in this if he wanted to live.

"Agreed," Jaconis nodded hoping that he knew what he was getting himself into. "What do I need to do?"

"… and the Goddess Patiun granted a gift unto the line. A protector to ensure that the stability of this world and she was called Zelios. She could be called upon whenever the need was great by those of the blood of the land." Aras concluded as he closed his journal. He surveyed the faces of his companions before he continued. "Three nights ago the case I stored Zelios in fell from the table. Remember that, Alequa?" Alequa nodded as Aras picked up his recounting. "The jewel glowed a deep blue and the image of flames danced across the face of the gem. I didn't know what it meant then, but I do now. She went to you Namir. In your time of need, she sought you out to defend you." Aras turned his eyes to take in Namir's reaction. It was subtle, but he could see the acceptance in Namir's steel blue eyes.

"So I am bound then." Namir's voice broke the silence that had settled around them after Aras's last words. "What can you tell me of my blood line?"

"They were great people," Landolin answered. He hoped to spare Aras from any more exertion than was needed, "the last rulers of Cennicus."

"Rulers?" Namir's voice betrayed his disbelief more than the look of shock that shaded his features.

"Aye," Alequa added, "miun ta' kunin." She added with a deep courtesy.

Namir blushed as he recalled the preferential treatment Alequa had paid him ever since he first met her. "So… I am to be king?" Namir repeated softly, more to himself than to the others. "You knew this whole time?" He felt betrayed and could not fathom why they had kept his heritage a secret from him.

Alequa nodded and was about to say something, but Landolin cut her off, "as did Jerine and myself. I hope you understand that we needed to be sure." Landolin studied Namir and could see the anger rise in him.

"Sure of what?" Namir replied curtly, unable to keep the bite of anger from his words.

"Sure that we were right." Aras replied feebly. "All of the signs and books seemed to hint that you were the heir, but we needed proof. We needed to see how Zelios reacted to you."

The end of his sentence was swallowed as another cough rocked his body and brought flecks of blood to his lips. Aras waved a hand at Alequa to tell her to stay where she was.

"You cannot understand all of this and I am sorry that we have forced it upon you without any warning, but there was no other way. Already someone has dispatched the nassarid against you." Aras saw the look of surprise on Namir's face and continued. "Aye, I know of the attack. I also know why they thought Halin was their target instead of you," Aras looked away from Namir as he continued. "I forgot how old you would be and I told Jerine to look for someone younger than yourself. I also misunderstood Tipin's letter. It has been quite some time since I had read Calanari script," Aras offered apologetically as he used his sleeve to wipe the blood from his lips.

"Tipin knows of this as well?" Namir's emotions kept leaping from shocked disbelief to anger faster than he could think.

"No," Aras chuckled raspingly, "not entirely at least. I had sent him a message in Calanari asking if he knew what had become of you and in his response, he told me of Nurn and Halin as well as yourself. I mixed up the descriptions he sent me."

He took a deep breath and surveyed Namir's complexion as he attempted to read his emotions. "It seems whoever intercepted the message drew the same conclusion I did. After Alequa told me of the attack, I reread the letter and I found that Tipin had purposely used old Calanari when he described you boys. I think he understood my need to keep your whereabouts a secret more than I had anticipated."

"And now people want Halin dead instead of me because of my lineage." Namir concluded as Aras succumbed to another coughing fit. His words bore his inner regret and as he said each of them and he felt his spirits sink deeper as each one left his lips.

"Aye," Landolin agreed woefully.

"But if my ancestors were such good rulers, why do people want me dead?" Namir asked not sure if they would give him a straight answer.

"These lands have been without a real ruler since before you were born," Landolin explained. "There are those that wish to keep it that way." The look of pain on his face was evident as he continued, "many are the minions of strife and corruption. These are the ones that caused the rift between the races before the old queen was killed and these are the ones that would do anything for your death."

The small commotion outside intruded on Namir's thoughts as he was about to ask about what this meant to him and his future. He looked up to the others and then towards the outer walls of the tent. There was something familiar about the sounds he heard. It was not until he saw Jerine that he recognized Nurn's voice raised in discussion with one of the elves outside.

Jerine ducked through the opening quietly as all eyes turned from Namir to him. His face was flushed and he had a worried look in his eyes. "Miun porva, mut nehiru nataa ha Halin etuva."

With his utterance, the tent was instantly a buzz with activity. Landolin instantly rose to his feet and started questioning Jerine. They were conversing so fast in elven that Namir was unable to follow them. When Aras heard Jerine's words, he started coughing uncontrollably and Alequa leapt to his side to do whatever she could to ease him. This left Namir alone to worry about Jerine's words.

'What does he mean that Halin is gone?' Namir thought to himself as he wrestled with the possible meanings. After several long minutes, he could not stand it anymore.

"Will someone please tell me what is going on?" His voice was stern, but not overly loud, yet everyone around him started as if he had shouted.

"I am sorry, sa'ouvant," Landolin responded before the others could. "It seems that Halin is missing. They have already performed a cursory check of the perimeter and inside the camp and have not found him anywhere."

As Namir heard this, his jaw dropped and he felt the color drain from his cheeks. He slowly turned to Jerine. It felt to him as if he moved through molasses. Namir struggled to form his questions, "Is it Morcant? Could he have taken him?"

"I don't believe so, sa'ouvant.   But there is a chance." Jerine replied as he dropped to a knee in front of Namir.   A courtesy that made Namir smile and feel awkward at the same time.   "Halin was left unattended in the practice clearing to work on his archery skills when I last saw him."

"Have you checked the clearing since?" Namir asked. He noticed that an air of authority had snaked its way into his voice unbidden.

"Aye," Jerine replied as if Namir were the only one in the room. "I even checked for signs of struggle and found none." Namir nodded as Jerine reported this, obviously disturbed by the news. "I plan on going back to the clearing again to see if there are any signs of someone entering the encampment via the surrounding forest." Jerine continued kneeling, "that is if I have your leave to, sa'ouvant."

"Of course, go." Namir instructed, "And do your best to bring him back safely."

As he watched Jerine rise and leave the tent, Namir grew weary. He knew that Jerine did not need to be told to bring Halin back safely, just as he knew that Jerine would do his best to find him. Jerine took Halin's absence as a personal mistake, one grave enough to completely drain all semblance of cheer from his elven eyes.

Namir shook his head and turned to Landolin. "What can we do to help?"

Landolin smiled inwardly as he saw Namir's reactions to Jerine. The ease in which he assumed authority and his skill at saying what was needed. He was impressed. This boy was obviously born to lead. Landolin just hoped that he could help Namir live long enough to get the chance. As Landolin saw Jerine leave and heard Namir's question he was already formulating a plan of his own.

"You need to stay here and speak to Aras more. Learn of what needs to be done in order to regain your birthright and unify the continent once again." Landolin looked at Namir with a supportive look as he continued, "My soldiers and I, with the help of Nurn and Jerine, will search for your missing sa'trandon."

Namir nodded as he received Landolin's advice and recognized the wisdom in it. "Please keep me informed and let me know the moment he is found."

Landolin nodded to Namir as he turned to leave the tent and left Namir alone with Aras and Alequa once again. Alequa glided over to Namir as he finished with Landolin and waited patiently for him to acknowledge her.

"Aye," Namir asked as he noticed Alequa standing beside him. Her head was bowed in respect and other than her breath, she made no sound. Namir rubbed his forehead, a little weary of everything that had happened, as he waited for her response.

"As I said before, Aras is not going to last much longer." She said quietly, almost whispering. "It would be best if you asked him few questions and did not interrupt him."

"What do you mean he's not going to last much longer?" Namir asked halfway wishing that he understood as much as the elves seemed to think he did.

"I mean that his time is almost nigh." Alequa responded, raising her eyes to gauge Namir's understanding. Seeing that he still seemed a little puzzled she added. "His death approaches. This is nothing new to him. He is glad that he could live long enough to see the moment that Zelios was returned to you." She bowed her head once again and waited for Namir's instructions.

Namir sighed deeply and looked at the frail old man laying a few paces away. "Then we can't wait any longer. You heard Landolin. I need to find out what I need to do to regain my birthright and the throne. Hopefully I can glean enough from him to plan what needs to be done next."

Alequa nodded and quietly led Namir back over to Aras. She gently touched his shoulder to rouse him from the light sleep that he had fallen into after his last attack. "My love, the sa'ouvant needs a little more from you."

Nurn stepped into the tent nervously. Ever since Jerine left, a sinking feeling had formed in his gut. Jerine had left him with Karous to search the camp while he went and informed Landolin in an attempt to elicit aid in finding his brother.

Karous immediately sent someone to check with hebasii Doriana, the camp's healer, to see if Halin may have turned up there. While they waited for a response, Karous decided that they should thoroughly search every tent and the areas around them.

"Ios take you," Nurn cursed under his breath as he moved a chest so they could better see under a bed.

He was distraught at the thought of Halin's disappearance more than he wished to let on. Although he was sure that he was not fooling anyone.

'If it wasn't for bad luck, you would have no luck at all, brother,' Nurn thought as he leaned over to peer under the bed. 'Maybe father had been right to keep you sequestered with mother all these years.'

The thought ticked in his head as his heart fell at the sight of the emptiness that loomed before him. Nurn could not help it. Every time he looked under a bed or in the lee of an awning he expected to see Halin. He knew it was foolish, but he could not stop the desire to find his brother that burned so strongly within him.

"Nothing here either," Karous called to him from the other side of the tent. "Hopefully we have better luck in the next tent." He clapped a reassuring hand on Nurn's shoulder as he added, "we will find him. I know it seems hopeless right now, but we have at our disposal some of the finest troops in Cennicus."

Nurn looked back at Karous and nodded as if he believed him. As the two left the tent, Nurn saw a beautiful young lady stride up to them. She wore close fitting soft leather breeches and a matching tanned leather tunic. Her short-cropped black hair framed her face and her emerald eyes seemed to glow as they darted from Karous to Nurn and back. She barely waited for them to exit the tent before she addressed them.

"Miun porva, mut sa'trandon Halin va net onastrasi gevont." Her musical voice was laden with fear and sorrow as she spoke to Karous.

"Please, I am sorry. I do not speak your tongue. Can you repeat what you said about my brother?" Nurn asked as his voice grew deeper out of concern for his brother.

She blinked at him as if she had not noticed him, then, slowly, she repeated herself so that Nurn could understand her. "I am sorry. I was unaware that you would not be able to understand me." Her accent was thick, but Nurn found it enchanting. "I simply apologized for interrupting your search and informed Karous that sa'trandon Halin had not been brought to my tent."

'These elves and their titles,' Nurn thought ruefully as he gazed into her beautiful green eyes. 'Why can't they just call each other by name instead?' His thoughts turned vicious and he realized it a little too late as a look of disdain washed across his face.

Trying to avert Doriana's attention from Nurn's gaze, Karous nodded to her and said, "thank you Doriana. We will continue our search then. If you have time, could you please assist us by checking the tents near yours?"

"Aye," Doriana replied as she nodded in agreement and then hurried back whence she came.

Jerine knelt in the center of the clearing. He had just finished dispatching men to search the road back to Hornshir as well as sending others to search the forest around the encampment. He was relieved that Landolin agreed to give as many men as needed for the search and was astonished when the great general decided to assist himself. He was more than thankful since Landolin was one of the best strategists and trackers he had ever met, not to mention his unwavering loyalty to those around him.

Jerine's heart fell as he investigated the area. He had been moving his hand though the grass where Halin and Nurn stood while practicing. He hoped to find a clue of Halin's whereabouts. He raised his fingers to his nose to smell the liquid he had found, not wanting it to be what he knew it was. The familiar scent of iron mixed with sweat came to his nose and he knew it was blood, more specifically Halin's blood.

As Jerine looked up, he saw Landolin kneeling near Halin's target. Landolin slowly raised his head and peered over at him. "I have found something," Jerine's voice was not much louder than a whisper, but it carried to Landolin's ears as if he were beside him.

"As have I," Landolin nodded sagely as he glanced at his bloodied fingers nervously. "It seems as if the boy wounded something."

"Or was wounded," Jerine replied as he walked over to Landolin. "I think the blood belongs to Halin." The message was grave and as Jerine said the words aloud, a knot formed in his stomach. "I found more where he had been standing while practicing."

Landolin nodded as he looked from the target area toward where Jerine had just been and back. There were no signs of a struggle or of anyone entering the clearing. Only the practice area and the paths to the targets were trampled. Whatever happened, it was either remarkably fast or it had been welcomed.

Landolin crouched near the target again and allowed his eyes to adjust to the darkness. He took everything in, from the direction of the breeze as it blew through the grass to the minute sounds of the insects as they prepared for their nighttime activities.

"Any sign of where he went from here?" Jerine asked quietly so as not to break Landolin's concentration completely.

"He had the presence of mind to take his bow and quiver with him at least." Landolin offered in a vain attempt to diffuse the dreadful feeling that spread itself through his mind.

Landolin's voice was weary as he looked into Jerine's hopeful face. "I know which way he went, but I don't understand why."

Landolin knew that Jerine could sense the foreboding that had risen up in him unbidden. As if to answer Jerine's unasked question, Landolin raised an arm and pointed deeper into the forest.

"I hope he only went to retrieve his arrows. Whatever his reasons were, we need to find him quickly. There are things that lurk within the forest that might challenge even my small contingent."

Landolin's words cut into Jerine's heart as he heard them. He had made it his personal quest to ensure Halin's safety since his brush with Morcant. "I will do what is needed." Jerine lowered his head as he addressed Landolin. "All I ask is that your men aid me in this. As you said we need to find him swiftly."

"Aye old friend, you can count on me and mine." Landolin replied as he clapped Jerine on the back warmly.

"Good. I shall go while you muster your men." Jerine stated as he started for the woods, only to be brought short by Landolin's hand as he gripped Jerine's cloak firmly.

"No. You need to spread the word amongst my men, as well as to the boy's brother and Namir." Landolin's eyes pierced Jerine's like hot brands. "My men will listen to you and follow your lead." Landolin weighed Jerine's expression carefully as he continued, "we both know that I am the better tracker between us. It will be faster if I go. I will mark my path so it will be easy to follow. Now go."

Landolin's tone brooked no resistance and Jerine found himself agree as Landolin turned to enter the forest. Jerine took a deep breath and then set off to rally the men and to tell both Nurn and Namir of what they had found.

Chapter Twenty Two: Pain

Namir awoke and tried frantically to collect his thoughts. He had slept far too little for his liking and his dreams were plagued with dark thoughts and visions of nassarid hunting him. He slowly walked over to where Aras had lain the night before and his thoughts turned unbidden to the old man's passing. He stared at the bed for a few moments before he retrieved Aras's journal from the table beside the bed.

"Rest in peace, my friend." Namir said as he left the room.

Somehow the whole thing felt wrong to him. Halin was still missing and he was collecting things that belonged to a stranger from his past to take with him back to Ellsted, a place he never expected to return to.

"Are you ready to leave, sa'ouvant?" The voice that called out to Namir was musical, like all of the elven voices he had heard, as well as humble.

Namir smirked to himself before he answered. "In one night my whole life changed," he said to himself as he grabbed his pack and exited Aras' tent.

"I beg your pardon sa'ouvant, I did not hear you." The female elf lied as Namir approached her.

"It was nothing important." Namir replied awkwardly as he realized for the first time that elves had better hearing than he thought. The fact that he did not know the name of the lady that attended to him also brought him a moment of grief. "Now it is my turn to apologize, I have forgotten your name." Namir knew this was not a lie. He distinctly remembered Landolin telling him the name of the soldier being sent back to Ellsted with him to serve as both guide and guard, but he could not recall what it was.

She giggled as she saw the awkward look cross Namir's features. She tucked a loose strand of honeydew hair behind her ear as she glanced up at him with deep azure colored eyes and answered as demurely as she could.

"I am called Haradine, sa'ouvant, and I will serve you in any way you command." She bowed deeply, bending nearly in half and somehow managed to almost touch her head to the ground while she retained her footing with one foot delicately placed in front of the other. She held this pose as if waiting to be told to rise.

Namir gazed upon her dexterous feat in awe as images of her from the day before flitted in front of his eyes. He stared at her embarrassed that he did not recognize her from yesterday. Namir attributed it to the fact that today she wore the well-made elven armor instead of the form-fitting jerkin she wore yesterday, but he knew that it was not the only reason he did not recognize her.

Quite a bit had changed in his life since he had last laid eyes upon her. The strain of his ordeals bit into his psyche a little harder as they hammered their way into his consciousness. Namir regained his composure as best he could while he chided himself for not being more observant.

"Please, we do not have time to stand on protocol." Namir said coolly as he reached down to touch her shoulder. "You need not bow to me, or call me sa'ouvant. I fear those that want me dead may see your actions and know who I am." He added as Haradine rose from her bow.

"What would you have me call you then, sa'ouvant?" Haradine asked innocently, as if she believed Namir had only his title as a means of reference.

"Just call me Namir," he said as he wondered what she was thinking about.

"It would be wrong of me to be so familiar with you, sa'ouvant." She blinked genuinely confused.

"I don't care." Namir said as he pieced together why Landolin decided to send her with him. "You need to get comfortable with doing improper things on occasion if you are to be an efficient soldier." His tone was even and calm, the sort of tone he remembered Carness use with him when he taught Namir the use of club and dagger.

Namir's veiled reprimand stung a little as Haradine nodded in agreement. She knew he meant well and, although she was a little surprised that he knew she had problems adapting to the life of a soldier, she did her best to conceal it from him. "Our horses are ready," she covered her concern at being reprimanded with this statement as she let her soldier's training take over her thoughts. "We can leave as soon as you are ready."

Namir smiled as he saw her dedication. "I need to speak with Landolin and Nurn before we leave. If you could have my things packed on my horse, we will leave within the hour." Namir watched as she fought the urge to bow again. Instead, she bit her lip and nodded to him as she grabbed his pack and walked toward the horses with determination in her stride.

"What do you mean you're not coming back to Ellsted with us?" Aves demanded as she glared at Jaconis. "You are a member of this party. You know that if you are not numbered amongst us it will reflect poorly upon Namir."

"Be that as it may, I am not returning." Jaconis said smoothly. He loved how Aves looked when she got upset, the way color flowed into her cheeks to rival the beauty of her hair not to mention the fire that burned in her eyes. Either of the two alone would be captivating, but combined they were completely enthralling.

"He wants Namir to fail." Hessa interjected snidely. "His

problem is that he was unable to make it happen any other way." Hessa stood in the doorway to the manor as she watched Aves confront Jaconis in the cobbled yard of the compound. "He probably stayed up all night concocting this excuse."

A wry smiled played at Hessa's lips as she thought about Jaconis's claim. 'Jaconis devoting himself to any religion is absurd.'

"You are right." Aves agreed with Hessa as she saw Jaconis's face drop. "I mean you were out all night." She said as she confronted Jaconis with her statement as if she accused him of conspiracy.

"Aye, I was," Jaconis confessed, "mainly because I thought to enjoy Hornshir now that our duties here are done. However, that does not change the fact that I have decided to join the Disciples of the White Rod and devote myself to the service of Lotevilar." His glare made Aves take a step back. "I don't care what you two decide to tell Namir or the council in Ellsted when you return. I only ask that you deliver this letter to my father for me." With that said, he waved the letter in front of Aves impatiently as he waited for her to hold out her hand.

Aves snatched the letter from Jaconis's hand as if he was going to bite her and stepped away from him. "I will deliver it." Her voice fit her mood and perfectly expressed her annoyance and anger at him. "Just know that your plan will not work to discredit Namir. I will do everything I can to ensure that the whole town knows about all of your attempts to undermine our endeavor."

Aves bit back tears as she turned away from Jaconis and fumed back into the manor. Hessa followed close behind her and the two of them left Jaconis in the courtyard alone.

"And know that I care not for your wishes or your plots!" Jaconis fired back at her retreating form. He did not want to let Aves get the last word.

Namir rode behind Haradine as they followed the trail

toward Hornshir. The trip was uneventful and painfully dull. His senses strained as their steeds traversed the distance at a comfortable pace as he tried to ensure that nothing slipped past Haradine's notice. Although Namir wanted to ride the horses at a gallop, he knew it was unwise to tire the horses needlessly, especially since they had already decided not to stop for a brief lunch.

They were about two hours away from Hornshir when Haradine slowed down and came alongside Namir. "When we get to Hornshir, let me talk to the gate guards." There was an edge to her voice that shocked Namir a little. She gazed into Namir's steel blue eyes and understood his concern.

"We have an arrangement with them." She said coolly. "So just follow my lead and we should be able to get into the city without having to wait."

"Very well so long as you do not mention my new status to them," Namir cautioned. "I think that it might make things harder instead of easier."

"Fear not, sa'… I mean Namir." Haradine corrected herself with a playful look in her azure eyes.

Namir shook his head wearily at her. He could not stop himself from liking her, her playful nature mixed ideally with her elven looks.

'Whatever her reasons for joining Landolin's army are, I am glad that she was selected as my escort.' Namir thought to himself as he reached for Zelios.

The unfamiliar weight of the amulet hung around his neck, yet there was something comforting about it. Namir initially tried not to touch it overly much believing that it was best left hidden beneath his shirt, but he found the idea as impossible as he had found staying detached from Haradine. He glanced over at Haradine again. The playful look was still in her eyes as the wind swept the hair from her ponytail across her face momentarily. She looked stunning.

"Why did you sign on with Landolin?" This question had plagued Namir ever since he first saw Haradine and it came back to haunt him every time he looked at her. "I mean, you don't seem like the soldier type," he stammered as he tried to sound more curious than interested.

Haradine giggled as she answered him. She obviously found him or his question as a source of great mirth. "I didn't have much choice… " Her comment was cut short as a crossbow bolt lodged itself up to its fletching into the armor of her left shoulder. Its impact almost threw her from her saddle. She yanked her horse's reins hard as she spun about to see who had fired upon them.

Namir also spun to find their assailant, although he was in more shock than he cared to admit. Zelios' weight pulled at his neck and he noticed a soft blue light emanate from it as he spotted their attacker at the same time Haradine did.

The man stood in the road not more than a hundred paces ahead of them. His black banded armor glinted in the sun as he reloaded his crossbow. From what Namir saw, the man was about Namir's own height and was bristled with weapons. Their attacker had at least two swords across his back and his belt was full of daggers, all of which were as black as his armor. The most striking aspect was his helm. It looked as if someone had wrapped a decaying head with leather and attached a mane of platinum hair onto it.

Haradine wasted no time. She spurred her steed toward the man as she yelled back at Namir over her shoulder, "Run, I will slow him down if I can!"

Namir watched as Haradine pulled her sword from its scabbard hidden in her saddle as she let out a cry that was lost to him in the wind. He wanted to shout at her. To tell her to stop, but his words caught in his throat. To Namir's horror, he saw the man level his crossbow at Haradine's chest and fire again. This time the bolt scored a hit dead in the center of Haradine's chest plate.

Namir sat helplessly as she flew from her saddle and onto the hard packed dirt. He spurred his horse to assist her instead of running as she had told him to. Namir grasped the hilt of his sword fervently as he urged his horse into a gallop. In one fluid motion, he drew his sword from its hidden scabbard and tugged on his horse's reigns to bear down upon their assailant.

"Zelios defend her!" He cried as loud as he could as he galloped towards the assassin.

Namir was not sure if Haradine was dead or not, but the fall combined with the two bolts she that were lodged in her armor left him little room for doubt. Namir felt a warm glow surround his body as he bore down upon the man in the road. Like Namir, the man had drawn one of his swords as he quickly discarded his crossbow.

The man swung at Namir's steed as they approached and to Namir's dismay his steed reared and tossed him to the ground before it bolted away. Namir cursed his poor horsemanship as he hurtled toward the ground. His whole body went numb as he felt the ground rush up to meet him.

With a loud thump, Namir felt all of the air in his chest forced out by the force of his landing. He lay there trying to catch his breath as he realized that his sword had slipped out of his hand. Namir frantically tried to locate it as he attempted to scramble to his feet.

He finally managed to get into a crouching position when the man's boot hit him in the chest and drove him onto his back with enough force to rob him of what little breath he had managed to catch. A wave of panic flowed through Namir's veins as the realization of his situation fully dawned on him.

He was lying on the ground, pinned beneath his attacker's boot weaponless and his only ally lay dying a few feet away. He yearned for Nurn's intimidating presence or Jerine's fast blade as his assailant leaned down and put more pressure onto his chest.

"What a pleasant surprise." The man leered.

Namir was surprised as he realized that what he had though was a helmet was actually the man's face. Somehow this thing's face was made of leather and the rotten smell that emanated from it was nauseating.

"I came looking for a meal and found something better."

The man's crooked smile etched into Namir's mind as he struggled to get the man's boot from off his chest. The warm glow he felt moments before fled him as fast as it had come and was replaced by the numbing feeling of terror as Namir looked up at the man that towered over him.

"Looks like I've caught you speechless," the creature's voice sounded as if it belonged in the grave instead of speaking to him and Namir winced as much at the sound of it as he did from the pain of its heal pressing into his chest as it twisted slowly from side to side.

Namir tried to compose himself enough to respond. He forced himself to look into the man's pitch black eyes as he responded, "I have very little money, but it's yours if you will just let me tend to my friend." His words were forced, but Namir did not care how he sounded to this wretch.

"I can already have all that you own." The man leered down at Namir. As if to make his point, he leaned forward and brought more of his weight down on Namir's chest as he reached down to grab for the glowing pendant partially concealed by Namir's shirt.

Namir struggled when he realized the man's intention. He grabbed the man's foot and attempted to lift it as he twisted his own body in an attempt to make it harder for the man to reach Zelios. No matter what Namir tried, the man did not deviate from his goal. A cold sweat broke along his whole body as the man tugged Zelios's chain as he tried to dislodge it from underneath Namir's shirt.

"I think this will be the first thing I remove from your corpse." The brigand's words carried a nauseating gust of his breath and Namir almost choked on the bile that rose in his own throat from the stench.

The man locked gazes with Namir as he pulled on the chain and pulled Namir's face a little closer to his own. His hand slid closer to the pendant and he smiled. The sharp yellow teeth that poked out of the man's lips spread a feeling of dread across Namir's body.

Namir watched as the man's hand moved closer to Zelios. He wished he had Nurn's strength so he could just throw the man off him instead of being forced to witness the man steal the only link to his past that he owned. Namir tried to look away as he felt Zelios's weight lift from off his chest, but found himself unable to.

"I know just who I can sell this to." The man said as his fingers brushed the smooth silver wire wrapped around the sapphire at the pendant's center. "I have heard tell of a lady who is asking for a piece that looks just like this one."

Namir grit his teeth as he felt the man slip Zelios into his hand. A feeling of pressure developed in the back of Namir's head and then faded as he focused on the man's actions. Abruptly the man's leathery face went slack and Namir felt a pulse of energy free itself from the amulet. The shockwave that followed threw the man off of him and left Namir somewhat dazed and blinded.

Although he was not able to see, he scrambled to his feet and braced himself for another attack. Several moments passed as Namir stood braced and ready before his eyesight returned. Even then, Namir could only see blotches as globules of green lights floated across his field of vision. A renewed sense of urgency spread through Namir as he noticed the man laying twenty yards away.

Namir ran over to the man swiftly and he picked up one of the man's swords as he closed the distance. Without any hesitation, Namir drove the sword through the man's chest and threw all of his weight onto it as he did.

A spray of black ichorous fluid covered Namir's face, hands and chest as the blade punched through the man's armored body and lodged itself into the ground below him. Namir pulled himself away from the corpse as he fought off another wave of nausea. He slowly turned to where Haradine had fallen and staggered over to her.

As Namir neared Haradine's unmoving body, his eyesight returned more pronounced than he remembered it being. Everything was bright, as if light poured out from everything instead of onto it. Every edge was crisp and vibrant colors met his eyes everywhere he looked. As he peered down at Haradine, he noticed the black sticky liquid that covered his shirt and hands.

Namir quickly removed his shirt and wiped off his hands and face with it as he lowered himself to Haradine's side. Namir frantically felt for a pulse and was instantly relieved when he found a weak one as he allowed the training take over his thoughts and lost himself in the task of assessing the damage that had been done to her.

After Namir did a cursory review of her injuries, he took a deep breath. He was afraid to remove either bolt since he had nothing to clean and bandage it with. Out of the two injuries, the second one concerned him the most.

Although the first bolt was lodged deep in her shoulder, the second was embedded directly in the center of her breastplate. Even though the second wound was shallower by far, Namir feared that removing it would end her life. Namir cursed himself for getting his shirt covered by the man's blood as he pulled Haradine's boots off.

He carefully folded one of them and placed it under her feet to elevate them as he scanned the barren hills for their horses. He folded the other boot and placed under her head carefully so as not to block her airflow. Namir carefully loosened her belt and untied the draw sting on her breaches as a precaution against any circulatory issues she might develop as he worked with her wounds.

His eyes lingered for a few moments on the small amount of exposed flesh near her waist as he loosened her armored breeches. He cursed himself for even momentarily entertaining that kind of thought as he unfastened the buckles of her armor so he could better assess the damage.

Namir slowly released a stream of air through his teeth as he carefully lifted the soft leather edge of the breastplate and peered under it. Blood trickled from the center of her chest and pooled slightly between her pert breasts. He cursed himself again for acting like a hormone-crazed child as impure thoughts of her danced through his mind.

The sound of hoof beats drew Namir back from his whirling fantasies about Haradine to focus once more on the task at hand. He gently lowered her breastplate and turned slowly with his hand on Haradine's sword.

He did his best to act as if he was merely searching the ground for something instead of scanning for threats. A sigh of relief escaped his lips as he realized that the hoof beats belonged to their own horses as they trotted back toward them.

"Now I might be able to get something to bandage her with." Namir said to himself as he rose to approach the horses.

"Good." Haradine's breathy response startled Namir and he quickly looked down in time to see a slight smile play across her soft lips. To ease Namir's fears, she assured him, "Aye, I still live. I can only trust that we are in no immediate danger."

"I dispatched our assailant," Namir replied as the memory of the man's rancid blood covering him played back through his mind.

"Good." She said again, this time she said it as she lowered her head back onto her boot and closed her eyes. A look of relief spread across her face lending it an angelic quality that Namir found difficult to pull his eyes away.

Namir walked over to the horses quickly and grabbed their reins. He swiftly led them over to Haradine and used them to create a makeshift shaded spot over Haradine. Namir then drove the blade of the sword into the ground and tied the horses to it. Deftly he reached into his saddlebags and removed two linen shirts. He knew that Alequa would understand the need for their sacrifice, although she did express that these were hard to come by due to their quality.

Namir made his way back to Haradine's side while he turned the shirts inside out and freed his dagger from its sheath. As he sat, he quickly sliced the first shirt into ribbons. The second one he cut into long strips and laid them carefully beside them.

"I have a wineskin in my saddlebags." Haradine mentioned as she saw Namir return with the shirts.

"I hope it contains something other than water." Namir said softly with a slight hint humor in his voice.

"Aye," she replied weakly. Haradine still keeping her eyes closed although the light no longer shone directly into them.

Namir stood and walked back over to the horses. After a few minutes of sifting through her saddlebags, he returned with her wineskin. He carefully removed the cork as he knelt beside her and lowered it to her lips. After she managed a few mouthfuls, he raised it and replaced the cork.

"This may hurt a little." Namir said in as even a tone as he could. The only reply she offered was a quick nod to signify that she understood what he meant to do.

He took a deep breath before he reached down and grasped the bolt with both hands. He steadied himself and then pulled on it as hard as he could.

Haradine's scream echoed off the hillside as he freed the barbed tip from her body. Namir quickly tossed the bolt aside and carefully removed her breastplate in a way that did not jostle her pauldron too much so as not to irritate the other wound.

He quickly reached over and wadded up several of the smaller strips. He pressed these into the wound as he picked up two of the longer strips with his other hand.

He worked deftly. First, he cleaned the wound with the ruby colored liquid in her wineskin then replaced the wadding with new ones, which he placed directly on the wound. Namir was relieved when he saw that the bolt had hit her breastbone instead of by passing it and puncturing something vital.

"Press against this and sit up," Namir instructed as he guided her right hand to the wadding. As she sat up slowly, Namir tied the remaining strips together to form a longer bandage. He kept an eye on her the whole time to ensure that she complied.

After she was in a sitting position, Namir said, "I hope you don't mind, but I will have to touch you to dress your wound." Namir forced the words out as he tamped down his carnal desires.

"It is fine, hebasii Namir." Haradine acquiesced as she stared into his steel blue eyes.

Namir felt his passion for her surge as he met her gaze. 'No… this is not the time.' Namir chided himself as he leaned forward and started to wrap the bandage diagonally over the wound.

He made sure it laid flat and that each the knot binding the strips together was directly over the wound to add more pressure to the dressing. After he had made a few wraps, he added a few more strips to the makeshift bandage and then altered the pattern to wrap around her waist and then back across the wound from the other side.

When he had finished the final wrap, he looked her. Her face was only inches away from his and, as his gaze met her deep azure eyes, he felt his desire surge within him anew. Namir made a furtive glance from her captivating eyes to her lush lips and then leaned closer and placed his lips upon hers.

Jaconis walked down the hallway to his cell as he prepared mentally for his first day of instruction in the faith. He had just spent several hours having his measurements taken for his robes and travel clothing, as well as donating his every earthly possession to the church. In the back of his mind he felt uneasy about his choice, but he had given his word to Tali that he would help her and this seemed to be his only option to do so.

He mulled over the choices he made as he opened the door and walked into his new room. He had barely made it to his cot before he realized that the room was not empty. He glanced up at Skara as she sat on the ledge of the small window, the only window in his cell. She quickly leapt from the sill and landed on his cot forcefully.

"You are set on this then?" Skara asked. It was obvious that she was unable to contain her curiosity any longer.

"Aye," Jaconis nodded. He refused to give her the satisfaction of meeting her gaze.

"You know that the initiation will occur after you have completed your passage into the faith three months from now."

There was a note of concern in her voice that struck Jaconis as odd.

He wondered about this and her role in Tali's plans. "I know and I have given a letter to Aves with instructions to deliver it to my father stating as much." Jaconis felt tired. In a few hours he would be summoned to the main library and his first steps in his path as a Disciple of the White Rod would begin. "You know that I have little choice in this if I wish to aid Tali."

Skara nodded and peered more intently at Jaconis. "Aye, I just wonder what it is that makes you wish to assist my mistress." Skara's eyes narrowed as she stated this. Her tail twitched nervously as she waited for Jaconis's reply.

Jaconis smiled and chuckled quietly. "I have been wondering the same thing myself." He shook his head as he rose to his feet. He slowly paced away from the nassarid down the length of his room and back as he continued, "at first I thought that she was the one who was helping me, but as I replay everything that has come to pass I realize that I have been quite the fool. Tali has been the real person in charge of thwarting Namir's plans and not me." He rubbed his eyes wearily. "There is a part of me that is envious of her for her ability to wrap others into her schemes. I would like to blame that part of me for my desire to help her, but I cannot." Jaconis took another deep breath as he finally met Skara's gaze. He stared deeply into her green catlike eyes as he uttered his final statement. "I realize now that my desire to help your mistress stems from my love for her."

Skara smiled and nodded her approval, "Very well. I would like you to know something. Think of it as an exchange of knowledge." She stared into Jaconis's pale green eyes as she licked her lips with her rough tongue. "I love my mistress as well and I will do anything to protect her, even if it means disobeying her wishes. If anything you do causes her harm, I will hunt you down. Do you understand?"

Skara had leaned so close to Jaconis that he felt her breath on his face as she whispered the last words of her threat.

Jaconis swallowed hard as she all but touched her face to his. He could almost feel her claws sink into the soft skin around his throat as he struggled to break her gaze.

Tired and sore, Namir climbed the steps to the manor slowly. Night had settled quickly around him after he managed to get Haradine into Hornshir and to its healer. The trip back from the elven encampment had almost been too much for him.

He mustered his strength to confront Jaconis's demands and Aves's barrage of questions that he was sure awaited him as he opened the door and crossed through the entryway. To his surprise, no one lay in wait. Namir sighed deeply in relief as he slowly walked to the main sitting room and succumbed to the allure of the fireplace therein.

Namir cringed inwardly as he saw Aves and Hessa sitting near the fire with their backs to him. He steeled himself mentally as he stepped into the room and made his presence known. "So is everything ready for our departure?"

Both Aves and Hessa jumped at the sound of Namir's voice and turned to face him. It was obvious that they were both visibly startled by his unexpected appearance. Namir took in their every move and noticed both relief and fear mingled in their faces. He sorely wished that he had not been forced to leave them behind.

'Where is Jaconis?' The questioned loomed in his mind. He quickly brushed it aside as he waited for a response from either of his friends.

"Aye," Hessa answered as Aves started to reply.

"He isn't returning with us." Aves blurted out.

"One at a time please," Namir said wearily. A sudden headache developed as he lowered himself into a chair near the fire and the girls took turns recounting the events that had transpired.

Haradine winced as she leaned over the table and looked

over Hornshir's troop reports.   She read the disbursement notices as well as the troop allocation papers carefully before she met Faris's gaze.

"I understand that your troops are thinned due to sizeable cuts and losses due to attacks," Haradine started diplomatically, "but I also know that old alliances run deep. General Landolin and his guard have helped your men keep the lands to the south of Hornshir well protected from all threats. All that he has asked in return for our services is that you assist us when we have a need."

Faris nodded sullenly, his shoulder length peppered brown hair fell across his face as an errant wind blew through the open door of his office. He narrowed his chestnut colored eyes as he took in the elf's features.

"I understand how much your kind has helped us, but I do not have enough guards to cover your request. We barely have twenty guards to man the walls, which is hardly enough. I'm not even going to mention the inadequate numbers that I have to run patrols within the city's walls." The lanterns in his meager office cast dark shadows over his rough features. "Even if I did have enough men, how would you expect me to pay them? With our desertion rates at an all-time high due to the pathetic funds that we are currently allocated from the council? I'm sorry, but I have to deny your request." The tone in Faris's voice was final as he scowled at the young elven lady that sat across from him.

Haradine shook her head in disgust at the man that sat across from her. 'Landolin spoke so highly of this man,' she thought bitterly.

"If your promise is broken so lightly Captain, then perhaps I need to bring this matter to your precious council's attention." Haradine did not even try to mask her disappointment in both the man and his race. "I think that they might be interested in the fact that you have just agreed to let your southern borders go undefended."

Faris threw his hands up in disgust as he raised his voice letting his anger show.   "What do you expect me to do, materialize men and arms from thin air!" He pushed himself out of his chair with such force that it skidded into the wall behind him with a loud thunk. "We have no funds to support this venture of yours! How can I make it any clearer?"

"Is it gold or soldiers that you lack?" Her statement cut through his argument with the accuracy of a marksman.

"Both!" Faris snapped. His patience with her was finally at an end.

"I can solve the funding issue, if you can get me seasoned soldiers. I am not asking for an unreasonable amount, ten of your finest. Is that really too much to ask?" She stood slowly and leaning against the table on her knuckles. She ignored the pain that shot through her recent injuries as she leaned menacingly forward.

"What do you mean that you can solve the funding issue?" Faris snapped as he leveled another glare at Haradine.

Without blinking Haradine reached down and removed three small pouches from her belt. Before Faris could blink, she flung them onto the desk in front of him.

"In those bags there is enough coin to pay all of your troops for the next four months. All I am asking for is ten of them to accompany me for one trip to Ellsted and then they can return here." She held his gaze as she reiterated her request.

Faris looked from the three pouches up to Haradine and then back a few times before he responded. He hated the feeling that crept into his gut. For the last few years he had constantly fought against politicians and their ceaseless greed and now he felt as if he was turning into one of them. The feeling did not sit well with him. Faris ran his fingers through his hair as he took a deep breath.

"I'm sorry for lashing out." His words faltered and stuck in his throat as he spoke.

"I understand the problems that you face, captain." Haradine said as she took her seat. "We are not your enemies, although I fear you have more than you know of." She read the look of disdain in his face and realized his discomfort. "We elves do not want to add to your problems, which is why I have been sent with more than enough coin to help you out of your dilemma."

Faris looked up at Haradine and let out a derisive snort. "I suppose that you thought you could come and throw a few coins at me and I would just go along with your plans. Unfortunately, you may be right." A wry smile played along his lips as he added, "the real issue is that if I give you your ten men, I will be shorthanded and I'll have no guarantee that the ten I send will even return."

"Which is why I trust you to pick those most loyal to you," Haradine interjected. "As well as those you can trust. I do not presume to be the one to pay them or to pick them. That task is all yours."

"How much coin are we talking?" Faris asked as he reevaluated her proposal.

"Enough. The task that I have been sent on was not undertaken lightly. General Landolin will not be able to stay in your lands much longer for our duties call us elsewhere. To honor our agreements, he has authorized me to help you recruit enough men to fill the gap that will be left behind when we depart."

"How long will I have to recruit and train the men I need?" His question held more despair in it than he wished to show.

"No more than three months, though it may be less." Haradine said. She knew that her message would be ill received.

"By Ea, that short?" The look of shock seemed to add ten years to Faris's face.

"Aye," Haradine nodded, "Which is why I wanted to look over your records. It pains me to see this fine city so ill equipped. Believe me when I say that we mean no disrespect to you or your men, but soldiers do not come cheap."

"You're right, they don't. I will need at least three times the amount shown for the annual allotment." Faris braced his head in his hands with his elbows placed firmly on his desk as he said this.

"Done," Haradine responded before Faris could

reconsider. "We will also help with weapons and armor for your troops. The training you will have to provide yourself."

"Agreed," Faris said as he raised his head to look at Haradine once more. "I would expect it no other way. How soon can I get the coin and arms?"

"The arms will be delivered after your troops are trained and before we take our leave from our current encampment." Haradine said as she kept his gaze locked in her own. "The coin will be given to you after I inspect the soldiers that you are going to send with me. I need those ready by tomorrow morning, so I suggest that you get them ready immediately." She tilted her head to one side as she continued, "I am sorry to give you such short notice, but we have had little time to make our preparations as well." She motioned to the three bags sitting on the desk between them. "The coin in those bags are yours for your help in the past and are not part of this arrangement."

"Very well," Faris nodded and then extended his hand. After they clasped hands he said, "If you would like, I can escort you to your manor."

"Thank you, but that is not necessary." Haradine replied trying not to sound rude. "I have a few arrangements that I need to see to before I go to the manor." She slowly turned toward the door and then stopped as she was about to walk through it. Haradine called back over her shoulder to him almost as an afterthought, "thank you again and I am relieved that you are as honorable of a man as I had been told you were."

"What do you mean Halin is missing?" Hessa asked aghast.

"I wish I had more details, but I don't." Namir replied suddenly feeling much older than he was.

"What happened?" Aves asked. She tried to remove some of the tension that had developed in the room as Namir had informed them of their situation from his perspective.

"I'm not real sure. I was escorted to a tent where an old man, my father's servant, was." Namir shook his head. "No, I mean where Kalta's servant was."

"But isn't Kalta your father?" Aves asked confused by Namir's explanation.

"I thought he was, but it seems that everything that I knew to be true was really a lie." His heart sank as he said the words that he had been fighting against believing.

"If Kalta and Cerona are not your parents, who are?" Hessa asked as she tried to understand what Namir had just said.

"I can't say," Namir shook his head in frustration. "I want to, but I can't, at least not here. Once we get safely back to Ellsted I'll go into more depth, but until then just know that I don't even understand everything that I've learned."

Aves looked nervously at Hessa as she fidgeted in her chair. "Namir, how can we help?"

"By making sure you're ready to leave at sunrise and by helping me figure out what to tell the council when we get home. It's going to be hard enough for me to come up with the words to say to Tipin and Allair that will not fill them with dread. Having to also worry about what to tell the council on top of that is almost impossible."

Both girls nodded acceptance at Namir's request. This brought him little joy as he looked from one to the other.

"I would also ask that you give me the letter Jaconis gave you," Namir directed this last comment to Aves. "I think its best that I break the news of Jaconis's new found dedication to a higher calling to his father. If for no other reason than I can take one of his blows better than either of you can."

Aves nodded. "Here it is," she said as she handed Namir Jaconis's letter. "And we will help you with the council, I promise."

Namir sighed once more and rose to his feet. As he walked to the door, he looked back at the girls and added, "We will be traveling with an elven soldier named Haradine. I will introduce you to her in the morning. Now I'm off to bed, I recommend that you two do so as well." With that said, he turned and made his way to his room. He muttered darkly about Jaconis's choice under his breath the whole way there.

Chapter Twenty Three:
Dawn

Morning came too early for Namir. His muscles still ached from the trials of the previous day and he was reminded of these ordeals painfully every time he moved. Namir slowly sat up in his bed and carefully raised his hands to his head and massaged his temples wearily. Harsh voices and the sound of wood against stone drifted to Namir's ears. He had a hard time deciding if they were real or just vestiges of the dream that plagued him all night. The sharp sound of a key as it turned in his lock startled Namir.

He quickly shook his head as he tried to clear the fog that consumed his thoughts from it as he pulled his breeches on hurriedly. He managed to finish fastening his belt as the door scraped open and the scent of fresh food met his eager senses. Namir pulled his shirt over his head as he heard the soft footfalls of someone entering his room.

"Are you alright?" Haradine's voice sounded worried as her eyes adjusted rapidly to the dim lighting of the room.

She saw Namir pull his shirt on and blushed as memories of their kiss flooded into her head unbidden. Although something seemed wrong about the kiss, a part of her yearned to repeat it.

"Aye," Namir barked and was immediately embarrassed by his rudeness.

"I heard a noise… " Haradine started to explain her actions to Namir. She was afraid that he would be angry with her for entering his room unbidden.

"It's fine." Namir replied as he was finally able to focus his eyes on her without the normal morning haze blurring them.

'She looks radiant,' Namir thought to himself as he drank in Haradine's features.

Her long hair flowed loosely about her shoulders like liquid honey and her azure eyes shone with a light of their own. The white shift she wore turned almost translucent in the backlit glow of the candles in the hallway.

"I'll take my leave then," her musical voice was almost a whisper as she caught her breath and turned to leave.

"Before you go, can you tell me what that racket is?" Namir asked. He was not ready for her to leave and he wanted to keep her there as long as he could.

"Preparations for our departure I think." Haradine cocked her head to one side as she listened to the noises wafting up from the courtyard below.

Namir swallowed hard again as he saw her honeydew colored hair spill off her shoulder. "Is it that late already?" Namir asked. He hoped to disguise the quaver in his voice with a brief stifled yawn.

Haradine looked at Namir as a smile playing at the edges of her lips. "Aye, sa'ouvant, it is." A wistful smile played along her soft lips as she curtsied. "If you have nothing more, I need to see to our escort."

Namir dreaded to let her go, but he realized the need and accepted it. "I see that you have healed well from our ordeal." He attempted to sound removed, but he knew she could sense his concern.

"I have." Haradine nodded. "Would you like to check the work of Hornshir's hebasii?" She added, not wanting to leave.

"I would, but not just yet." Namir conceded. "As you said, you need to ensure our escort is ready for the trip and I must ensure that the rest of our party is ready as well.

"As you wish," Haradine bowed deeply and turned to leave. She hesitated a moment before she left Namir's room and cast one more look at him to etch his emotions into her memory.

The awkward silence was almost more than Namir could bear as he watched Haradine pull the door to his room closed behind her as she left. He slowly walked over to the table on the far side of his room. He then lifted the metal basin up from the floor and set it onto the table. After he splashed a little water into it, swirled the water around the basin and then filled it before he fully dunked his face into it to clear his head.

The cold water sent enough of a shock through his system that it banished the remaining pull that sleep still had upon him. After he refreshed himself, Namir walked over to the dresser and packed the rest of his belongings.

Aves and Hessa awoke to the bustling noises of items being loaded on wagons and the wonderful smell of fresh baked bread. The two girls lay in their bed for a few long moments before they grudgingly rose and packed their remaining possessions.

"Do you think the trip will be easier than on our way here was?" Aves asked as she laid out the dress she had chosen for their trip home.

"I hope so." Hessa replied as she tried in vain to hide the fear in her voice. "It certainly can't go any worse."

Aves morbidly giggled at the thought of their return trip turning out worse than their trek to Hornshir. Her mind seized on the fact that Nurn would not be there to protect them with his brawny arms and his silent vigilance. She also felt a twinge of sorrow that Halin would not be able to raise their spirits with his songs since he too would not be returning with them. These thoughts brought a hint of tears to her eyes and made Aves falter as she pulled her chemise over her head.

Hessa mistook Aves's pause as trouble with the chemise and walked over to help her pull it on the rest of the way. As she tugged on the hem of the chemise, she heard Aves stifle a sob and instantly knew where her friend's mind had gone. "They will be alright you know." Hessa assured her as she fussed the chemise into place.

"I hope so." Aves sighed as she waved Hessa away from her. "Please don't. It is hard enough to go back to Ellsted without them, I don't need to be reminded that once we're home you will cease being a friend and return to being a servant."

It was Hessa's turn to falter as she stepped away from Aves. She enjoyed her role as confidant and diplomat too much to want to return to the life she had left in Ellsted. Although she still thought of Aves as her better, her mind rebelled at the thought of resuming her duties as a maid.

Aves saw the look in Hessa's eyes and silently nodded her approval. "I will ask my father to relieve you of your duties if you'd like." Aves offered with a hint of sorrow in her voice.

"What would there be for me in Ellsted then?" Bitterness clawed its way into Hessa's voice unbidden as she asked the question.

"We could find something." Aves assured her, even though she knew that in Ellsted the roles one's life played were mostly set at birth. "You proved you worth as a diplomat. Maybe we could convince Armani that there is a need for a constant position within the council for that."

"It would go to a public vote," Hessa said flatly, "which means that any number of people would be accepted before I would."

"Not true." Aves declared. "You have experience. That matters. Maybe not in the eyes of the townsfolk, but in the eyes of the council it means something."

Hessa merely shook her head at the notion as regret surged up in her. "Wild fantasies of youth have no place in the realm of adulthood. You know that. The townsfolk will credit you with my success. We both know this." She wished her words did not have such a ring of truth to them as she said them.

"We can face that problem when we get home, I guess."

Aves said as she tried to reassure both Hessa and herself. "Now let's get done here and go eat breakfast. There is no telling when we will be able to stop and eat lunch."

Haradine walked out into the brisk morning air as the sun rose above her and into the manor's bustling courtyard. She saw Faris and his men standing near the gates lined up and ready for her inspection. As Faris saw her, he broke rank and walked over to her with a purposeful stride.

"My men are present and ready for your inspection." His military training revealed itself in the crisp tone of his report.

Haradine smiled at his professionalism. "I see only nine men here. Could you not find a tenth that met with your approval?"

"I am the tenth." Faris' reply was as crisp as his report had been and held the same level of authority.

"Is that wise?" Haradine's question held no surprise in it. She expected Faris to accompany them since there was so much riding on the success of this escort. "Can the city spare your absence?"

"Aye on both counts," Faris replied quickly with no sign of emotion.

"Very well, take your place in line. We will discuss the convoy line-up and the security detail once I have finished the inspection." Haradine held Faris's gaze steadily and waited until he broke it before she blinked.

'He is good at what he does,' she thought to herself as she watched him march back to his place in the line.

Haradine walked past the line of soldiers three times. She mentally assessed their strengths from their stances and assessed their equipment physically with each pass. She held the calm demeanor that Landolin had taught her throughout her inspection. On her fourth pass, she decided to test their reflexes.

Without warning, and without breaking her stride, she palmed one of her daggers and threw it at the head of the fourth man in line. His reaction time astounded her. Not only did he move his head to the side, but he caught her dagger as he pulled his sword with his free hand.

The remaining soldiers all drew their blades as one in perfect timing with the fourth; even Faris had his sword ready as if on cue. Without a word, they moved to cut off her immediate routes of escape and surrounded her. Haradine was genuinely impressed by their efficiency. She raised her hand and signaled that the test was over.

Haradine turned to the forth soldier and smiled. "I am impressed with your response time," she confessed, "I just have one question." Her musical voice carried a twinge of curiosity with it as she spoke. "Why did you hesitate to throw my dagger back at me?"

The soldier smiled as he met her blue eyes with his black ones. "I wished to ensure that you had one less weapon with which to attack." His voice, though gruff, was smooth and confident.

"Would it have not been better to throw it back at me to wound, if not kill, me?" She stared into his eyes and bored into his soul with her own gaze.

"No." He maintained his composure as he replied, completely professional.

"Why not?" She already knew what she wanted to hear, she just hoped he was smart enough to understand and not just credit it to his training.

"From the skill you used, to not only throw the dagger but to brandish it, I judged there was a fair chance that you would catch it if I threw it back at you." The soldier held her gaze as if his life depended on it.

"I am pleased." Haradine nodded. She turned and addressed Faris. "Have your men assist with the preparation of the carriages. I want them to know what items are where and to able to judge the distance needed to clear obstacles for each." She waited until she saw Faris nod. "I would like you to come with me and discuss the security placement, but I would also like Namir to be included in this discussion."

Faris raised an eyebrow as he heard this. "Why?"

"He is in charge of the convoy so he deserves a say." Haradine did not let her true reasons show as she lied easily to Faris.

"Very well, I will be attending to my soldier's supplies and horses. Come get me when you are ready." With that, Faris turned and walked toward the stables.

Namir watched as Haradine inspected the guards. He was impressed with her skills, if not somewhat afraid for her as she tested their abilities. Namir marveled at how well she moved and enjoyed the thrill of anxiety that ran through his nerves when he saw her throw the dagger. He was unsure how she could have made the necessary arrangements for the guards or how she could afford them, but he was glad that she had managed it.

As Namir saw Haradine pull Faris aside, he turned from the window and focused his attention on his compatriots. Aves and Hessa wore very nice gowns, but not the finest he had ever seen them in. In fact, these looked more comfortable and better suited for the long trip home. Namir was still a little shocked at how similar the two of them looked and acted.

'They could be sisters,' he thought as the two ladies ate, each of them adding little tidbits to the conversation they engaged in about their ride home.

"You are both packed and ready then?" The question was unneeded, but Namir felt that it was his responsibility to ask it.

"Aye," Hessa said as Aves put a slice of apple into her mouth delicately, "and we have packed some of the food from here for the three of us, as a sort of mid-day meal, in case we don't have time to stop for lunch." She added as she motioned to a basket beside her.

"Is there enough room in the basket to add something for Haradine as well?" Namir did his best to say her name evenly to hide his growing affection for her.

"There is," Aves spoke as she raised an eyebrow at the

subtle twinge in Namir's voice as he said Haradine's name. "Will we be able to meet this lady before we leave or were you going to save the introductions for the trip home?"

A slight flush filled Namir's face as he smiled. He realized that Aves had caught a hint of his concern for Haradine from his voice. "Aye, you will get your chance to meet her as soon as she has finished with her inspection of our escort."

"Isn't that something you should be doing?" Hessa asked completely unaware of Namir's plight.

"No. Haradine is much better trained at it than I would be." Namir confided. His voice took on an air of conspiracy as he continued, "she is a soldier and was entrusted with my safety by her general. What little knowledge I have about sword play is nothing compared to her training."

"That is not true, sa'ouvant." Haradine's voice cut through the room and made all of them jump. The playful lilt to her voice also conveyed a wry sense of humor to it as well as an air of authority. "You did save my life from the moharii that attacked us. If anything, I am in your debt for saving my life." She smiled at the two girls as she reached between them and snatched a fresh roll from the plate on the table.

Haradine's words hung in the air as Hessa turned to Namir with a look of shock on her face and asked, "Sa'ouvant? Why is she calling you that?"

The color on Namir's face intensified as he heard Haradine respond before he had a chance. "Because that is who he is." The simplicity of her tone almost made any argument against her words seem futile.

"What does this word mean?" Aves asked completely at a loss in the conversation.

"Sa'ouvant means liege." Hessa and Namir said in unison and exchanged glances afterward. Namir shot Hessa a look indicating that he wanted to explain it and Hessa nodded in agreement.

"I didn't mention it last night, because it seems so impossible." Namir took a deep breath. "I also didn't think it was safe to mention here so I was going to wait until we were back in Ellsted or at least on the road there before I spoke of it."

Haradine felt the sting of his words and realized her error as Namir spoke. A look of silent remorse filled her face as she listened.

"That was one of the things I found out at Landolin's encampment." As proof to his words, Namir pulled the chain to Zelios and removed it from under his shirt delicately. "According to Aras, this belonged to the last rulers of Cennicus and was with me when he and Kalta found me as an infant." The pained look on Namir's face was evident as he finished his explanation. "I would appreciate it if none of this was mentioned outside of this room until we are on our way back to Ellsted." Namir waited to ensure that each of them nodded before he tucked Zelios back under his shirt.

"We need to speak with Captain Faris about the security placement." Haradine said quietly in an attempt to ease the tension in the room.

"Very well, but first there is something a little more important that needs to be done first." Namir hated how everything was happening so fast.

The more he tried to sort things out and deal with them individually, the more twisted and convoluted they became. He felt like he was being pulled under a dark tide with no way out. Namir took a deep breath to settle his mind, and then he set his jaw and did the inevitable.

"Haradine, these are Aves and Hessa. They are friends and companions of mine." Namir tried to sound detached. He motioned towards each as he said their name. "Aves… Hessa, this is Haradine. She was sent by Landolin as a personal protector for me."

"So she is to ensure your safety at all times?" The implication of Aves's question was clear as she raised her eyebrows expectantly.

"Aye, at all times." Haradine answered Aves's question instead of Namir and the hard tone of her voice made it clear that she took her job seriously.

Another awkward silence fell over the group as each looked at the other as if waiting for some sort of escape from the conversation. Namir provided it as he shrugged his shoulders and turned to Haradine.

"Let's get this meeting with Faris finished so we can leave. I would like to be well under way to Ellsted by noon."

Namir followed Haradine in silence as they left the manor and walked across the courtyard to the stables. Namir slowed his pace as they neared the workers loading the wagons and carriages for the journey back to Ellsted. He motioned to Haradine to stop several times as he regarded the supplies that were being loaded as well as which supplies were stored where. Namir wanted to make sure that there were few surprises on their trek.

Namir also insisted on taking the time to familiarize himself enough with the other drivers and their assistants so that he could recognize them by both name and face. Although this took time away from their trip, Namir decided that it was best for their safety.

As they headed from the bustle of the courtyard to the stables, Namir turned to ask Haradine over his shoulder. "I need to know what everyone's task is as we travel; can you find this out for me?"

"Aye," she nodded quickly as she fought her urge to curtsy.

"Good." Namir replied.

As he turned, he saw a lithe form leave the stable. He was able to tell that it belonged to a woman and that she wore some sort of leather armor, but more than that he could not say. Namir stopped and motioned to Haradine in the direction of the gate and the woman's rapidly disappearing form.

"Who was that?"

Haradine blinked at Namir in confusion. "Who?" She glanced in the direction Namir pointed and then back at him. "I saw no one." She caught herself before she added his title, but just barely and she knew Namir saw her chagrin.

"I saw someone leave the stable and exit the compound fairly quickly. A woman of some sort wearing leather armor, I thought it might have been one of our guards." Namir said as he shook his head in disbelief. "Did you see her?"

"No, I did not," Haradine admitted, "and all of the guards allotted for our trip are men."

"Are you sure?" Namir looked in the direction of the gate with a puzzled frown.

"Aye and I'm willing to stake my life on it." Haradine assured him. "It may have been a messenger, they do occasionally need to have their captain authorize forms or accept orders."

"You're probably right." Namir shook his head as he agreed. 'There was something amiss about her… something catlike,' he mused as he resumed walking to the stables.

As they entered the stables, Namir let Haradine take the lead. She deftly led them through the mostly empty stalls to where Faris sat at the back of the stable amid the guards' horses. Faris lowered a parchment he had been reading as he heard their footfalls on the straw covered floor.

"About time," Faris muttered. He stood and stretched as they neared him. "I was wondering if we were going to leave today, or if you had decided to keep us here until tomorrow." He threw the words at Namir venting both his frustration and his boredom at him. Faris's belligerent comment forced Haradine to step towards him. Only Namir's quick tug at her arm stopped her.

"I am sorry if we kept you from an important task that required your immediate attention." Haradine shot back. The anger that flared in her eyes was unmistakable.

Faris smiled at the attempted reprimand. "I can take care of whatever tasks that need my attention as easily from here as I could from my office. I was just under the impression that time was of the essence."

"And it is." Namir stepped between the two of them in hope of routing their argument. He reached into his pouch and pulled out a piece of parchment. "Here is what I came up with for the order of the wagons." He said as he handed it to Faris. "Where do you think would be the best placement of your soldiers?"

Faris snorted as he opened the paper and laid it out on the stool that he had just been sitting on. After he scanned it briefly he said, "I think we should have five soldiers at the front of the line, four riding alongside, with the remaining one in the rear." His tone brooked no argument as he said this.

Namir smiled and shook his head. This simple motion easily indicated his disagreement of Faris's assessment. "I think it would be best if we had the same number in front and back, in case there are any problems that follow us from Hornshir."

"What sort of problems are you anticipating?" Faris' question was more of a challenge than a question.

"I'm not sure." Namir replied honestly. "But with all of the issues that we had while in Hornshir, not to mention the ones we had on our way here, I think it would be best the best course."

"What about having three on each the forward and rear positions and the remaining four for defense along the middle?" Haradine asked as she eyed Namir's diagram of the wagons.

"Three will not be adequate defense if we come upon a band of brigands." Faris retorted.

"It might if we staggered the four patrolling the sides." Namir replied as he pictured the route in his mind. "If one of the four rode closer to the front and one rode closer to the back it should allow for adequate defense for both areas. The other two could be staggered as well to allow for ease of communication between the guards and the drivers."

"I don't like the idea." Faris answered a little perturbed.

"Do you not think your soldiers are capable enough?" Namir allowed an innocent look to shadow his face as he weighed Faris' response internally.

"They are more than capable." Faris growled.

"Then what is the issue?" Namir asked as he maintained

his innocent façade.

Faris looked over the diagram one more time and nodded reluctantly. "So be it. When are we to leave?"

"Within the hour," Namir replied as he turned and walked away. He stopped when he reached the door and looked back at Faris. "If you will have your men ready, I will spread the word to everyone we are leaving."

Faris seethed at Namir's tone of authority. He walked with them in silence as they left the stable and waited until both Haradine and Namir had entered the manor before he barked orders to his men to ready their steeds.

Chapter Twenty Four: Homecoming

Namir stood outside of Tipin's smithy nervously as he built up enough courage to face Halin's parents. The news of his disappearance would not be a welcomed one and Namir knew it. He would also have to explain that he had left Nurn with the elves in order to bring them this news, another thing that would not sit well with them. Namir reached an eager hand to Zelios as he raised his other hand and rapped on the door. He waited. After what seemed like an eternity had passed, he heard the tumblers of the lock move and the door opened slowly.

Allair's words greeted Namir before the door was even cracked. "Who is it?"

"Namir," he said softly. A bout of shame filled him for disturbing her rest with the news he bore. "May I come in?"

Allair pulled the door open the rest of the way and stared at Namir in what little light spilled upon him from around her. Her long chestnut brown hair spilled over the shoulders of her thick woolen shift and a look of surprise tugged at Namir's resolve.

"Are the others with you?" Although her voice was full of sleep, she managed to speak clearly.

"No, this is why I came to you now instead of waiting until morning." Namir cast his eyes at his feet uncomfortably as he waited for her to invite him in.

Allair refocused her eyes on Namir as she felt an undercurrent of dread tug at her soul. "What do you mean?"

"I think its best said within the walls of your home… and with Tipin present." Namir still could not meet her gaze. He knew too well that she could read his thoughts plainly in the pained look on his face.

"Very well, please come in and make yourself comfortable. I will go and wake him." Allair motioned for Namir to follow her into the house as she turned and walked inside.

The Gathering Place was alive with activity. For the past four days Alequa had found it almost impossible to sit near the fire, as she had liked to. She took a small sip of warmed spice cider from the wooden tankard that she gripped with both hands. She looked at Haradine and regarded the unease that had settled around her with a keen eye.

"Anything unusual happen other than the attack by the moharii assassin?" Alequa's voice was unusually quiet as she questioned Haradine again about their trip.

"No." Haradine confirmed.

"And the letter you carry, it was given to Aves and Hessa by Jaconis?" She tried to piece together a situation that would convince Jaconis to stay behind. Although she did not know the boy well, from what she had been told, it made no sense.

"Aye, Aves handed it to Namir and he asked me to carry it. He thought it would be safer in my care than in his own." Haradine twirled the letter in her hand again as they exchanged words. She knew that something was upsetting Alequa and she hoped that it was not something that she had done.

"Hand it to me." Alequa's tone made it clear that her statement was not a request.

Haradine looked from the sealed letter to her mother's demanding blue eyes and back. She slowly handed the letter over to Alequa. "What do you plan to do with it?"

"Read it of course," Alequa replied as if there was nothing

unusual about the idea.   She motioned for Haradine to stay seated as she looked at the seal closely. "It is marked by evil," she said quietly to Haradine in a conspiratorial tone.

"How so?" Haradine's attention perked, but she remained seated against her own will.

"It is sealed with the mark of Lotevilar, goddess of hurt and mistress of pain." Alequa lowered her voice to a whisper as she uttered the goddess's name.   To Haradine it seemed as if her mother was afraid to say the goddess's name in case she invoked her.   "I fear Jaconis has involved himself with something more sinister than he knows."

Alequa cupped her hand over the seal and mouthed a prayer to Tayant as she did so. There was a subtle shift in the mood of the room.   Everything seemed a little brighter and happier than it had been as Alequa removed her hand from the letter.

The seal was still attached to one-half of the letter, but it had grown darker in color and seemed altered somehow. Before Haradine could ask any more questions, Alequa opened the letter and read what Jaconis had to say about his plans.

Armani sat across from Aves and Hessa near the fire of their house and listened to their harrowing tale. His face filled with apprehension and joy as each girl took turns telling him about their journey to Hornshir and the adventure that followed. As they finished he breathed a sigh of relief to have both girls returned in one piece.

"So the trip home was smooth then?" Armani asked. He hoped that they had not just forgotten to mention any more problems.

"Aye it was."   Aves leaned deeper into the chair as she brushed a wayward strand of hair from her face. "Namir's planning made it even better. It's amazing how well things go when there isn't any bickering about who is in charge."

"Don't forget that we actually had an escort this time," Hessa added as she settled into the chair with a cup of tea a little uneasily.

Although Armani had invited her to sit with them, the role that she was accustomed to still weighed heavily upon her. She felt that it was somehow wrong as she struggled with the idea of why this was so inappropriate.

'This should be a time for a father and his daughter,' Hessa thought to herself as a sense of guilt descended upon her.

"Would you like to review the agreements that we arrived at with the elders of Hornshir?" Aves asked as she glanced at her father's worried face.

"Aye, but not just yet." Armani said. He was surprised about how much he enjoyed being in the girls' company.

"I'll go get them to have them ready for when you do, sir." Hessa commented as she set her cup down onto the small table gingerly.

"There is no need." Armani said as Hessa left the room. He shook his head at his reticence. "She is too good at her job." He muttered not expecting a response.

"Aye," Aves agreed as she shifted in her chair uncomfortably. "Father, I was wondering… " She cut her sentence short as she saw Hessa glide back into the room.

"You were saying?" Armani felt Aves's mood shift and was unable to fathom the reason for it. He hoped that she would continue, but he knew that she would choose not to.

"I was just wondering if you would like to look over the papers now instead of later." Aves lied as she feigned a yawn. "I'm getting tired and would like to be present in case you had any questions about our choices."

Armani nodded as he extended his hand toward Hessa. The gesture was an old one and he instantly felt awkward as he saw Hessa glance towards her feet and hand him the scroll case obedient to his silent command.

'Ea damn me for a fool,' he chided himself as he tamped down another feeling of loss.

Armani struggled with his emotions as he opened the scroll case and broke the wax seal of Hornshir's council with his thumb. He looked over the papers scarcely seeing the words as he fought against his inner turmoil of emotions that threatened to swallow him whole.

Aves and Hessa exchanged nervous glances as they both misread Armani's clouded emotions. Each of them imagined that his internal struggle was with a section that they had prepare or argued for so they sat in silent anticipation of his stern disapproval as he scanned the pages. An oppressive pall fell over the room when Armani scanned them for a second time.

"I knew that they were not coming back." Tipin's voice filled the room. The strain in his voice was apparent. "But I had not expected to see you either."

"I am sorry to bring you this news." It was all Namir could to hold back his tears. He had failed them and he knew it. As an uneasy silence filled the small room and Namir could not help but think about how he had sworn to Tipin that he would watch over both of his sons. Namir recalled their first discussion as they planned the trip to Hornshir. He though it odd that Tipin had recommend that both of his sons accompany him.

Allair broke the silence first. "Halin was alright though, before he went missing?" Her voice held a slight tremor as she asked.

"Aye," Namir wished he could do more to allay her fears.

"He is in good hands," Tipin assured her as he squeezed her hand gently. "We both knew Landolin when we served in Watch Keep. I can think of no better man to be charged of finding him."

Namir could sense the pain in Tipin's voice as he reassured his wife and longed to know more. "May I ask a few questions of you two, not concerning your sons?"

"Ask," Tipin's voice seemed to boom in Namir's ears. He could feel a sense of threat in them, but he was unsure about why.

"I always thought that Allair was from Ellsted," Namir

broached the subject delicately. "Yet I was told she knew Kalta, Carnes and Cerona from their youth in the plains of Jarstil. How is that possible?"

"My family was originally from this area, but the city was only a tight grouping of family owned farms back then." Allair answered. Her voice seemed distant, yet insistent. "When my father was young, he and my mother traveled to Jarstil to avoid the war that was brewing here in the Three Rivers Shire. There was talk of an invasion from the Burning Lands and my father, like many others, fled instead of staying to fight for the king's interests."

"Why?" Namir felt drawn by Allair's words as he uttered the question.

"Because if there had been an invasion from the Burning Lands they would have faced my people," Tipin's voice blended with Allair's and accented her story perfectly. "Although it wasn't true, not many relish the idea of fighting a Calanari war brigade."

"If there was no war brewing, why did the people flee?" Namir's mind raced with possibilities and fear. Aras had told him that his ancestors had been good rulers, yet he could not understand how a good ruler would have started a war with a peaceful race like the Calanari.

"That was the start of the turning." Tipin's voice carried a dark edge to it. "Many of the provincial governors started to create strife in the outlying regions to gain more power for themselves. Although the King was a fair and honest man, his advisors were not. The rumors of an impending war had even reached my people in the Burning Lands. It was this invasion, which my people had been told was from the Deep Marsh that forced me into service of the crown."

"It was still a threat then, even after you had grown?" Namir asked as he tried to get his head around what he was being told.

Tipin laughed quietly as he shook his head. "No. I was young when the rumors started, but not too young to carry an axe in service. I was given training and the blessings of

Tumere before I was sent off to help the King guard against the invasion from the Deep Marsh." Tipin saw the confusion as it etched Namir's face. "My race is longer lived than yours. When I joined under the King's banner he was not a young man, but he was not old by any means."

"But by the time war became a reality, he was." Allair chimed in. "That is when Kalta and I enlisted. By then the war had consumed the continent from the Bright Desert to the shores of the Estan Ocean. Only some of the southern isles remained free from it." Allair paused as she shook her head in sorrow. "The King's advisors had managed to cause enough strife and hatred amongst the races that even though he was a great ruler, the King was unable to stop it until he could fully unravel their plots."

"Shortly after Allair and the others were stationed to Watch Keep, the king died. There was talk of a conspiracy, but none could prove it. So the King's daughter, Cerius ascended the throne at a young age," Tipin interceded.

"There were rumors that, although she was young, she was with child." Allair interrupted. "The advisors did not like the thought of the line continuing without their input, so a new plot was hatched, one with dire circumstances."

"The queen was slain about four cycles into Kalta's service, which is about when they found you." Tipin explained. "At first the idea that the queen had given birth without anyone's knowledge seemed strange to me. However, when her lover finally revealed the truth to the kingdom, all of the ties that bound it together fell apart. That is when the reality of the situation became much more believable."

"Which leaves me where I am now," Namir muttered disheartened.

"Aye," Tipin said solemnly.

"How long have you known that I am the heir to the throne?" Namir was shocked at how easy the question was to ask.

"We were never sure." Tipin answered readily. "We had our belief and some of us hoped that it was true, but there was no certainty." Tipin shook his head as he recalled those troubled times. "We made a pact, those of us that were there when you were found, to do what was necessary to ensure your survival until we could get proof of your lineage. Aras was given the task of researching it, while the rest of us stayed close to Kalta and Cerona in case we were needed."

"Why did you send me to Hornshir to look for Kalta if you knew he wasn't my father?" Pain was etched in Namir's face as he asked the one question that he was unsure if he wanted answered.

"Because I knew that Aras would find you," Tipin stated plainly. "And I was afraid to let you stay here in Ellsted." The admission wore heavily upon Tipin's heart as he uttered the statement.

"Why?" Namir's mind spun in circles. Every question that he sought to answer seemed only to spark more questions. The cycle seemed endless and unbreakable and Namir did not like it.

Allair put a reassuring hand onto her husband's arm to encourage him. After a few moments of silence, Tipin looked into Namir's eyes as he answered. "I had a vision." Namir could sense Tipin's unease as he spoke. "Ellsted was in flames and this… thing… was bellowing your name."

"Morcant," Namir mutter as he recalled the fire at the Flying Muses.

Tipin's eyebrow raised and Allair leaned forward as Namir mentioned the nassarid's name. Namir could read their interest on their faces even before Tipin had replied.

"No… not Morcant. It was different. Like something out of a nightmare. It was larger than a house and was covered in scales of some sort. The only thing similar between Morcant and this thing was the aura of evil that emanated from it." Tipin shifted in his chair uneasily. "How do you know of Morcant?" The question was firm and Namir knew he could not dance around its edges like he had countless times before.

"He was sent after me, actually he was sent after Halin to be exact." Namir started to recount the journey and stopped at the look of shock that spread across Allair's face.

'She didn't know of Tipin's code,' Namir noted.

"For some reason," he continued refusing to elaborate on why, "Morcant thought Halin was the heir. From what Aras and I were able to discern, they expected me to be about Halin's age. That might explain the beast's mistake."

"And you think that Halin's recent disappearance is in some way related to Morcant." Tipin's voice sent shivers down Namir's spine. The dread and hatred that issued forth was worse than anything that Namir had experienced.

"Aye," Namir nodded. "Which is why I came back to bring the news myself."

"I see." Tipin lied as he looked from Namir to Allair. "Then I am to assume Aras is continuing his research alone?"

"No," Namir took a deep breath, "he died before I left him." Namir raised his eyes in time to see sorrowful looks pass between Tipin and Allair. "But he lived long enough to gain proof of my heritage."

As Namir finished his sentence, he lifted Zelios out from under his shirt. Namir felt a little pain as pressure built behind his eyes, and then suddenly a soft blue light spilled out of the sapphire's heart and bathed the room in energy.

Allair gasped as Zelios appeared, her hand fluttered to her mouth. Tipin slipped from his seat directly to his knees in front of the spectral image. Namir sat in awe as Zelios materialized and stepped away from him to address the two before her. A feeling of relief spread slowly from Namir's temples to encompass every facet of his being.

"Rise and know no fear. Though I am of the gods, I bring not their wrath." Zelios's incarnation waited patiently as Allair lowered her hand, although she still stared at her in awe. Tipin remained on his knees, but allowed his eyes to rise to meet the angelic form before him. "I present myself to you, devoted followers of Tumere, in thanks for what you have sacrificed in service, both unto the gods and your own liege. I ask that your faith not waiver in the dark times to come. Know that Tumere favors you and yours and that your struggles shall not be in vain."

She slowly faded as she spoke leaving only the hint of an image as she finished speaking to them. The three of them sat in wonder for a few moments before Namir tucked the amulet back into his shirt in silence.

Alequa lowered the letter and refolded it slowly. Her mind easily understood the simple plan that Jaconis outlined in it for Daffer. She wondered why it was not a more elaborate one, but as she glanced over at Daffer's hulking form behind the bar she understood that as well. He did not seem bright enough to follow anything more complex.

"Sometimes the simplest plans are the hardest to foil." She muttered as she delicately placed the wax seal back into its place and slid the letter under her steaming mug of cider. She made sure the seal was under the center of her tankard as she focused once more on Haradine.

"What plans are you referring to, the one in the letter?" Haradine inquired.

Alequa marveled that Haradine had managed to keep some sense of innocence about her despite the hard life she had lived thus far.

"Aye," Alequa nodded as she scanned the inn's occupants. She was relieved to see that many of them were still lost in their merrymaking and had not noticed her actions. "Where is Namir? Did he go to his room?"

"No, he went to the smithy." Haradine responded. Her agitation was evident, not only in her features but in her pose as well.

"You let him go alone?" Alequa closed her eyes and issued a prayer for Namir's safety. "You will not make a good guard if you allow your patron alone too often."

Haradine felt the sting of Alequa's words and nodded her understanding. "I did as I was told." She knew her excuse was a weak one, but she offered it anyway. "Namir was determined to speak with Tipin and his wife alone. He insisted that his words were for their ears alone."

Alequa did not take her eyes from Haradine's as she listened to her explanation. "Do you know where his room is?" She asked as Haradine finished.

"Aye," Haradine glanced at the stairs. "Namir gave me the directions to it before he left.

"Is yours close to it?"

"No. His room is not near those of the guests." Haradine closed her eyes to break Alequa's knowing look. She mentally pictured the layout of the inn so she could recall where all of the rooms were located. "In fact, I am not sure if it is accessible from the inn directly."

"I suggest you find out. You should also go to his room and ensure that it is safe." Alequa felt pity for Haradine.

She knew how hard Haradine tried to fulfill her role in Landolin's army and she knew how poorly she managed it. This was Haradine's last chance and she was sure that her daughter was aware of it.

"I will share your room with you. That way no unneeded attention is drawn if you decide not to stay in it." Alequa hoped Haradine would understand the underlying meaning of her suggestions.

Haradine stood slowly, as she took in the occupants of the room. She quickly gauged the amount if threat each of them posed to her liege. "Would you prefer if I took care of that arrangement as I leave?"

"No," Alequa said as she raised her tankard from the table and took a sip. "Let Namir know that I have taken it upon myself to deliver Jaconis's letter to Daffer for him." She held up her hand to ward off Haradine's unspoken protest. "Unless you are skilled at copying someone's handwriting, it is the best way to ensure that the plan he outlined for his father is thwarted. Hopefully Namir will understand this. If not, I will convince him of it in the morning. Now go and see to your duties."

"I will, but I may need your help since I must leave the inn in order to see to the security of Namir's room." Haradine leaned closer to Alequa to ensure that no one could overhear them. "I have an uneasy feeling about Faris' guard. They have rooms in the inn, I know that this is usual, but there is something not right about them. Namir noticed it as well on our journey from Hornshir. Although they are set to leave in the morning, I would appreciate it if you could watch them while I am seeing to my other tasks." Haradine waited until she saw Alequa nod in agreement before she left though the front door of the inn.

Armani slowly set the papers down and looked at the girls. A tear crept into his eyes as he thought about how close he had come to losing them. "I didn't see anything that I would not have suggested. It is also apparent that Namir succeeded in his part, judging by the amount of travelers that have arrived from Hornshir." His warm voice stilled the girls' fears although the sadness he wore leant an air of doubt to his words. "Tomorrow I will present your agreements to the council. Both of you will need to be there. Jaconis is needed as well, so prepare yourselves for any accusations he might try to level against you."

"Jaconis will not be in attendance, father." Aves voice bore an air of strength in it that Armani was unaccustomed to.

"Why is that? Are you suggesting that I try to exclude him from the meeting?" Armani scrutinized Aves's face as he waited for an answer. He could not believe that she would dream of stooping to Jaconis's tactics.

As Armani was about to scold Aves for the atrocities he imagined that she was suggesting, Hessa answered his question. "He chose to stay in Hornshir." Her words cut through his question perfectly. Hessa saw Armani's mouth fall open as he searched for the words that seemed to elude him. "He was not detained by any of our deeds," Hessa assured the aging man as he still groped for some semblance of composure. "He sent a letter with Namir stating that he decided to become a disciple of Lotevilar."

"That makes no sense." Armani shook his head as he tried to fathom the full scope of Jaconis's actions and how they might fit into whatever plot that he had dreamt up.

"That was our conclusion as well," Aves assured her father. "Namir, Hessa and I tried to piece together whatever treachery Jaconis was planning during the trip back from Hornshir. Nothing that we came up with seemed to make any sense and without opening the letter that Jaconis sent, we could not find any real reason for it."

"You didn't break the seal on his letter, did you?" Armani hoped that they had at least maintained enough decency to not succumb to temptation.

He felt relief spread through him when he saw Aves and Hessa both shake their heads in unison as a rebuttal to his question.

"Good, we don't need to have Daffer upset by that as well as his son's reticence." Armani rubbed his eyes wearily as he rose from his chair.

He slowly collected the papers from Hornshir's council and made his way to the door. As he walked out, he called out.

"You both need to rest. Forget about whatever chores are pending, your sleep is more important tonight."

Namir walked back to the Gathering Place as he replayed Zelios' message in his mind. He sifted through their discussions mentally and attempted to put what he had learned into perspective. The hammering from the festival grounds died down as Namir distanced himself from the heart of Ellsted. In a day or so, the whole center would be filled and the town would pulse with life in a final attempt to stave off the coming chill of winter.

The first sounds from the Gathering Place drifted to Namir on the light breeze as he reached the northern edge of town. Namir pulled his cloak tighter as he glanced at the inn. It was so full of life and he felt an odd urge well up in him to join their festivities.   The only fact that stopped him was the knowledge that Daffer would put him to work the instant he stepped through the front door and into the main hall.

Namir deviated from the path that lead up to the main doors of the inn and followed the less used one that lead toward the back of the inn. He kept to the shadows and scanned the building for anything that seemed unusual or out of place. Every little noise seemed amplified as he rounded the far corner of the woodshed and the inn's stables came into view.

Namir paused as he searched the darkness that surrounded both of the buildings with as many senses as he could. When he was satisfied that the stable hands were either asleep or inside the inn keeping warm, he continued to his room. Although it was crudely attached, to the back of the stables, it was completely separated from the stables and had only one entrance.

Namir grunted as he lifted the old door and pushed it open. It creaked and moaned as it slid against the granite floor of his room. Namir muttered to himself. He listed off the numerous things that he would not miss after he left Ellsted for good and this door was one of them. Once inside, he pressed his weight against the door to close it. He let out a sigh as it settled back into place loudly.   He did not pause to take off his cloak. Instead, Namir reached for the oil lamp on the desk and dragged it across to him.   After a few long moments of fumbling with the flint and steel, he coaxed a flame onto the wick and replaced the glass flu carefully.

"So this is the room of a sa'ouvant."   The silken voice drifted to Namir from the shadows across the room from him.

"Not for much longer if I can help it." Namir responded somewhat startled as he lifted the lamp above his head.   He relaxed when he saw Haradine standing near the window on the far side of his bed. "So, you decided to ensure my safety?"

"Aye," Haradine nodded as she stepped toward him, "and I would better be able to ensure your safety if you permit me to stay in your quarters with you. The fact that your room is so far removed from the rest of the inn does not sit well with me."

Namir lowered the lamp as she neared him and shrugged off his cloak. The room was a little chilled, but a fire would solve that problem. He smiled at her as he carried the lamp to the small fireplace and knelt in front of it.

As he arranged the logs in it, he commented, "If you insist, however my accommodations are scant. The only bed I can offer you is my own." Namir removed the flu from the lamp and touched its flame to the logs. As the fire crackled to life, Namir replaced the flu and set the lantern down on the hearthstones.

"I could not impose on you, sa'ouvant." Haradine replied coquettishly. "I can sleep in the chair or on the floor if need be." She tore her gaze from him as she saw him stretch near the fire. "Does the door have a lock? I noticed the windows had none, so I wedged some nails into them for security."

"No," Namir admitted somewhat abashed by the meagerness of his room.

Without another word, Haradine turned and walked over to the door. She pulled out several daggers from within her cloak and wedged them between the door and its frame. "That should bar anyone from entering unannounced." She said as she turned and faced Namir once more.

Alequa approached Daffer as she watched him empty another tankard. It was the fifth one she had witnessed him drink in the time it took her to cross the mostly empty room. Most of the patrons had either made their way to their beds or passed out where they were as the festivities ended. She was disgusted by more than Daffer's appearance and enjoyed his presence less the closer she came to him.

"I need a word with the owner of this establishment," she said demurely.

Daffer let out a belch as he replied. "You've found him, what sort of word do you need with me."

He raised his eyes from the empty tankard and almost soiled himself. He had never seen a woman more comely in his life. Alequa's beauty was more than stunning and her scent forced his knees to weaken. Daffer's mouth fell open as his eyes wandered across her shapely figure and finally came to rest on her face.

"First, I wish to inform you that I will be sharing the room with Lady Haradine." She forced the words out as best she could. She had to fight the rising urge to slap him for his rudeness, but she restrained herself. "I also come bearing a message from your son."

Daffer's eyes darted to meet Alequa's cool gaze as her words registered. In his drunken state he was a little slower than normal, but even now he could feel the embers of rage stir in his breast at the mention of his wayward son. "Where is the whelp and why isn't he here?" His words flew from his mouth in a drunken slur. Each syllable threatened to bath Alequa with a spray of spittle as he vented the anger for his son.

"Jaconis has chosen the path of faith, good sir." Alequa bobbed her head in false respect as she continued, "as such he will be unable to return for many years. It should be seen as a great honor for him and for your household."

"Honor?" The word flew from Daffer's lips filled with contempt. "Where's the honor in discovering your only child has abandoned you! Am I to assume that he has cast his lot in with your faith then?" The accusatory glance he gave Alequa forced her to step a few paces away from him, while the volume of his voice threatened to awaken even the soundest sleeper.

"No. I am but a simple messenger sent by the Disciples of the White Rod in Hornshir." She bobbed her head again as she took yet another step away from him. "I was loathe to deliver it for fear of your reaction, especially when his words are told to you."

"What had the whelp to say that made you fear me so?" Daffer's glare held the threat of pain as he leveled it on Alequa.

"He said that he was glad to be rid of you and your pitiful establishment." Alequa lied as she set the beginnings of her charm. "He went on to rail against the town and expound on how much he liked the confines of Hornshir better. He spelled it all out in this letter that he asked me to deliver for him, milord." Alequa handed Daffer Jaconis's letter as she bowed. He snatched it rudely as she continued, "Jaconis laughed when he mentioned how he had deceived both you and the council to do exactly as he had hoped by sending him to Hornshir."

Alequa stepped toward the hallway as she finished. Daffer was in a rage and she could tell. She smiled inwardly as she saw him throw the letter into the fire unopened. Alequa just hoped that she could make it to the stairs and into her room before he lost what little control over his anger he had. The sound of splintering wood chased Alequa all of the way to her room.

She barely had a chance to close the door when she heard the door across from her room open. The cries of Faris's men as they rushed down the hall and plummeted down the stairs were welcome ones as Alequa slid the latch into place and walked over to the bed.

Epilogue

The sound of metal on stone echoed through the darkened hall as he made his way to the throne room. Every soldier he passed melted into the shadows in his wake. The time was drawing nigh when the demonic hordes would overrun the palace and he knew it.

The flames from the torches forced dark shadows to cascade down the walls and cast everything in a hellish glow. He dropped to his knees in front of the throne in one fluid motion. Before him sat a demonic shape cloaked in darkness and exuded a fearsome aura.

"What news do you bring me?" The Darque Lord's voice echoed through the hall like broken glass.

"The pieces are in place and Zelios has awakened." His words carried to the Darque Lord easily as he whispered them.

"Perfect." The Darque Lord leaned back in the blackened throne and steepled his fingers in front of his glowing violet eyes. "And what of the others, have they been dealt with?

"I have sent them a message. They know that I am close by and that I will not rest until I know the whereabouts of the rings." His whispered words echoed across the room.

"Good. Then see to your tasks, shadow walker." The Darque Lord's cackle followed the shadow walker as he exited the throne room and into the shadows beyond.

ACKNOWLEDGEMENTS

I just feel the need to say thank you to a few people that really made this labor of love a little more of a reality than I ever imagined it was going to be.

For starters, I need to thank George Decker for betting me that I could never write a novel. Because of that, I have not only realized my desire to be an author but understood what pains that writing a novel really can bring. While I regret losing touch with you during the many months that it took to write the story… then the many years it took me to decide to publish it, I know that you are a man of your word. So, if you read this, I like my steak medium rare and a New York Strip Steak would be a nice way to concede that you lost the bet.

The next person that needs to be thanked is my friend, and fellow author, C. E. R. Ellwood. If not for her, this newer, more streamlined version would not have been possible.

I feel the need to thank my two artistic friends that helped in this book, though it was somewhat indirectly. John Williams, thank you for the wonderful map work. Without your blood sweat and tears, I would have had to use the map I created as a kid. It wouldn't have been anywhere as nice as yours, nor would it have been as cool looking. Helne, I need to thank you again for allowing me to use the wonderful image you created as my initial cover image. Although it has since been changed, the new design is in direct relation to the one you had created. Your work is amazing and I am still humbled that you loved my story so much that you created it for me.

The next group of people that I need to mention is my beta readers. Of these Derek Savage and David Camden-Britton were the most outstanding of those that I invited to read the story prior to its release. Derek, thank you for the many hours of discussion centered on the story in this book and the need to have it mapped across the four books to follow it. The long hours in your bonus room shooting pool and discussing the book paid off. David, or should I say Groovy, your need to have the grammar be as pristine as possible was a godsend to me and I am forever indebted to you for it.

Another few people are my close friends that have helped in their own unique ways. Trevor Hall, thank you for being a voice in the darkness. Your sales skills and willingness to point out where I may have missed things is always a godsend. A sincere thank you needs to be given to Paul Britton; if not for you, I would not be as ambitious in my writing.

One of the last groups that I want to thank is a rather large one. This group encompasses everyone that has ever played in any of the role-playing games that I hosted. This world would not be as filled out as it is if it were not for all of the many hours that you sent playing in my various campaigns.

The final round of thanks is to you, the person reading this. Without your desire to purchase this book and take the plunge into the Shadow Saga, this endeavor would amount to nothing. Like most authors, I feel this story needs to be told, but without my treasured readers, the telling of it would be pointless.

Thank you all.

About the Author

A Reiki Master and accomplished author, John Harrison lives in central California and enjoys spending time with his family when he is not trying his hand at literary endeavors.

His current projects include: *Shadow Guard* (the fourth novel in the Shadow Saga) and *Bella Rouge* (a standalone novel based on "Unholy Trinity"—a short story published in Michael Moorcock's New Worlds Magazine).

John has been writing since he was in elementary school. His family and friends all love his imagination and his ability to weave a good story in a very short time. His professional writing has ranged from business processes to short stories and now novels.

For more information about John, or to find other works by him, check him out on the web:

www.amazon.com/author/johnaharrison

http://jalbertharrison.wix.com/author-page

www.ingramcontent.com/pod-product-compliance
Lightning Source LLC
Chambersburg PA
CBHW051004180726

48291CB00006B/1963